On the Line

New Gay Fiction

Edited by Ian Young

THE CROSSING PRESS / Trumansburg, New York 14886

Acknowledgments:

"The Passionate Friends" is copyright Edmund White, 1978

"Some of These Days" is copyright James Purdy, 1977

"Under the Hollywood Sign" is copyright Tom Reamy, 1975

The excerpt from "Port of Saints" is copyright 1973, 1980 by William S. Burroughs, and is reprinted here by permission of Blue Wind Press, Box 7175 Berkeley, CA 94707. All rights reserved.

"Some of These Days" was published in *New Directions 31*. Some of the other stories were published in the following periodicals: "Christopher Street," "Gay Sunshine," "Gaysweek," "GPU News," "Paragraph."

The editor and publishers wish to thank these publications for permission to reprint.

Copyright © The Crossing Press, 1981

Cover design by Anne Trovinger
Cover photo by Harvey Ferdschneider
Book design by Mary A. Scott

Printed in the U.S.A.

Library of Congress Cataloging in Publication Data
Main entry under title:

On the line.

    1. Homosexuality--Fiction. 2. Short stories, American--Men authors. 3. American fiction--20th century. I. Young, Ian. II. Title. Gay fiction.
PS648.H57O5   813'.01'08353   81-640
ISBN 0-89594-048-5   AACR2
ISBN 0-89594-049-3 (pbk.)

Contents

  5 Introduction
 11 Peter Robins / *A Friend of the Family*
 21 Edmund White / *The Passionate Friends*
 35 John F. Gilgun / *Tragic Event*
 47 David Watmough / *Black Memory*
 58 Peter Robins / *Cheriton*
 69 Jerry Rosco / *Three Friends*
 83 Felice Picano / *Hunter*
100 Richard Hall / *The Servant Problem*
109 James Purdy / *Some of These Days*
117 Tom Reamy / *Under the Hollywood Sign*
137 Daniel Luckenbill / *Ask A Marine*
147 William S. Burroughs / *Meet Me in St. Louis Louie*
160 Graham Jackson / *Charm*
165 Peter Burton / *A Marriage of Convenience*
171 John Mitzel / *The Last Piece of Trade in America*
175 George Whitmore / *The Guermantes Way*
182 Daniel Curzon / *Virility*
201 Graham Jackson / *Another Time, Another Place*
207 Notes on Contributors

Introduction

Homosexuality as a subject of fiction is as old as *The Epic of Gilgamesh* or *The Satyricon*. But only in the past century—and especially in the past decade or so—has fiction begun to reflect the emerging feeling of homosexually-inclined men and women that we are a people, not like other peoples to be sure, but nevertheless with our own history, traditions, art and folkways. As part of this new self-identification, a "gay literature" has emerged, with important perspectives, concerns and insights of its own.

The spokesmen for convention have continually denounced, distorted, sneered at, sniffed at, and tried to dismiss this gay literature (from the rewriting by scholars of Michelangelo's sonnets or the London *Times'* shocked throat-clearing over Tennyson's *In Memoriam* for Arthur Hallam, to the refusal of the *New York Times* to run ads for Gore Vidal's *The City and the Pillar* or the sarcastic homophobia of *The Village Voice*'s review of James Baldwin's latest novel *Just Above My Head*). Yet the sheer quality, scope and amount of gay literature—and the eminence of some of its authors—make it increasingly hard to ignore.

Why has homosexuality been so intimately associated with the arts? Why are so many artists sexually unorthodox? These questions are often asked, and they seem to me interesting and important, though they embarrass some of my fellow activists who regard them as irrelevant or apologetic, or deny their premise. (One recent book—by a gay writer—denied that homosexuals have more than their share of writers, and even appended a list of great straight authors—including one or two unintentionally amusing entries!) There is a current strain of opinion that homosexuality is merely an accidental and meaningless attribute, either inborn or 'learned' willy-nilly, like red hair or a liking for strawberry ice cream. Though this is a view that has its political advantages for those who seek the assimilation of gays into society as it is ("We're just like you except for this one little thing") it does harm by trivializing deep and important perceptions and feelings.

Both the artist and the homosexual have avoided, for whatever reasons, the general conditioning that moulds children and adolescents and causes them to see the world through the eyes of others. Instead, their vision is their own, and that, inevitably, sets them apart. Whatever qualities contribute to the emergence of such an individual, and whatever forces help to shape him or her, they are much the same forces and qualities, whether the open-eyed child turns out to be an artist or a homosexual—or both.

Homosexuality, then, is by its nature both idealistic and subversive—which is not to say that it cannot be co-opted, sometimes with disheartening ease. Gays, unrestrained by the old harness of family/job/overtime/mortgage, are free to explore other ways of living that are more relaxed, less subservient to the work ethic, more oriented to personal relationships and creative leisure than to money-making and civic duty. Or instead, they may simply fall into a hyped-up consumerism of disposable and expensive commodities—clothes, gadgets, luxury vacations, drugs—a choice reflected in the "reader surveys" of "upwardly mobile" men undertaken by the glossy gay magazines in order to entice big business to advertise.

So the results of "gay liberation" may be very different from those intended by its standard-bearers. Ideology, after all, is not magic. Art, however, is. And since the movement for homosexual emancipation entered its more assertive phase (usually dated from the riot at the Stonewall tavern in New York City in 1969) gay fiction and poetry have come out too—reflecting both the advances and the ambiguities of gay life.

Though it is undeniable that the new gay fiction owes a great deal to the gay liberation movement (and in many cases, the fictioneers and the activists are the same people) the relationship between art and ideology has been an uneasy one. Reality, for good or ill, often lags behind ideology, while imagination often outruns it. In neither case are the ideologues pleased.

When I asked the writers represented here to contribute to this volume, I asked them to comment, if they wished, on a number of questions that have been raised in the gay press and among gay writers. "How do you feel about being referred to as a gay writer?" "Is there a gay sensibility?" "What do you think of the call for a gay literature that is 'positive,' reflecting positive aspects of gay life?"

On the question of the designation "gay writer," the feelings of most of the contributors were reflected by David Watmough: "I like being called a *gay* writer as much and as little as I enjoy being referred to as a *Canadian* writer. I accept the qualification and can even see its usefulness. But I soon fret if it is employed as a restriction to the catholicity I fervently seek. (This has nothing to do, of course, with my pride in being gay and my gratitude for the rich literary resources my gayness has brought me.)"

Daniel Curzon wrote that "I increasingly grow to dislike the term 'gay fiction' because it implies a narrowness that it doesn't possess. Who speaks of 'straight fiction'? In reality gay fictional themes are just as diverse as heterosexual ones... Does anyone consider John Updike limited because of his obsession with male-female relations? This attitude, of course, is just another as-

aspect of the anti-gay sentiments... My personal solution is to write fiction that humanizes gay people, no more, no less."

I think most out-of-the-closet gay writers do not object to being referred to as such, but do resent commentators overemphasizing the gayness at the expense of everything else—what might be described, remembering a telling Monty Python sketch, as the "Two Sheds" syndrome. This sketch had a television moderator interviewing a hapless composer, Arthur "Two Sheds" Jackson. The nickname, it was revealed, was a trivial joke among a few of the composer's intimate friends and had no bearing whatever on the issue at hand, the man's latest symphony. Nevertheless, the notorious "two sheds" comprised the one subject continually returned to, belabored, harped on, by the interviewer. Enormous slides of sheds were projected onto a backcloth, and so on. The exasperated artist, pleading to be allowed to discuss his work, was eventually kicked brutally from the stage by the interviewer and director with jibes of "We don't want your sort here, you pansy!"

No writer wants to come out of the closet only to have it replaced by a couple of sheds. One hopes that gay stories like the ones in this anthology will also find their way into other anthologies, collections and periodicals, not specifically gay.

On the question of the existence of a "gay sensibility," Edmund White wrote, "I don't think there is a single gay sensibility, but I do find that much gay writing tends to be more *elaborate* than straight fiction—not necessarily more elaborate in diction but in its density of fictional structures and in the complexity of the relationship with the reader. Sometimes the tone is elaborately ambiguous, shifting mercurially from seriousness to irony to affection to coolness to ceremonial politeness. I attribute this elaborateness to a delight among gays in their mastery of theatrical self-presentation; I think of all social life as theatrical (and addressing a reader is a social act), but gays are more *aware* of this theatricality, and manage it with more skill than other writers."

John Mitzel also supported the idea of a gay sensibility. "I know there are those like Mother Vidal who pooh-pooh, but my answer to them is as follows: queers are an oppressed group. There is a documented oppression against homosexuals since the beginnings of our history. Modern oppression has been particularly severe. I think any reasonable person would acknowledge that oppressed persons develop special defenses, ingenious ways of getting by and tricking those who would kill or hurt them. What makes the history of oppression of homosexuals different from, say, that against the Jews is that there is no continuity to the struggle against our oppression. Until now." To Mitzel, it is what he calls the "hard core homos" who fascinate him. "They have sociologies within sociologies; they absorb, throw off and recreate mythologies with each season. They need to be supported and admired as much as studied."

Yet when the time comes to outline this "gay sensibility," it can seem to resemble a desert mirage—convincing and enticing at a distance, utterly elusive up close. But if anyone is attempting to articulate a sensibility that includes (limiting the terms of reference to writers alone) Noel Coward and Stefan George, Ronald Firbank and A.E. Housman, Amy Lowell and Frank O'Hara— and Patrick White as well—I wish him luck!

The demand—often raised by gay liberationists—for a "positive" gay literature was strongly resisted by a number of contributors, who deplored what they feel is a simplistic and misguided attempt to judge art by political or sociological standards. (In 1979, the New York Gay Activists' Alliance's annual "dishonor roll"—a sort of enemies list—included along with gay-hating California Senator John Briggs, three gay writers—Quentin Crisp, Andrew Holleran and Larry Kramer.)

Ed White summed up several writers' feelings on the subject: "I think the most destructive and primitive attitude in current gay literary criticism is the call for 'positive' gay literature in which 'ordinary' and 'normal' gay figures are to be portrayed in 'happy' stories. Of course such fiction does exist (as in *The Front Runner,* say), but it is only a kind of pop entertainment, of no literary interest. Serious fiction can never be programmatic, propagandistic, journalistic; it never sets out to deliver a particular message. It is, rather, a pure act of freedom, never bound to polemics. Its value is that it provides a model of what freedom could be like, a priceless gift to an age in which the only 'freedom' is the choice of one product rather than another, very similar product. Our society has few images of freedom, but fiction provides one: the full, creative exercise of individual powers within a social relationship."

Felice Picano wrote, "I would like to have those who call for more depictions of 'normal' gays show me an example. Doubtless somewhere out there a genius exists who can write a brilliant novel about a retail clerk's recipe for tuna-noodle casserole, but . . . to provide something *new* is a novelist's responsibility."

George Whitmore, referring to John Gardner's call, in his book *On Moral Fiction,* for a fiction that "establishes models of human action" and "carefully judges our right and wrong directions," that "does not sneer or giggle in the face of death . . . " replies that gay fiction "should not approach life down such sacred aisles as Gardner's. Its trick, instead, is to concern itself with what moralists would traditionally decry as trivial, degenerate, or at the very least, ephemeral. If we do have any function as gay writers, surely this is it." What gay liberation has done for the gay writer, Whitmore adds, is to make it possible now to write without "doctoring the reality of gay life to fit the reality that the straight world has invented to comfort itself." He adds that we should have the right to sneer and giggle if we wish.

The "positive," after all, is not always what it seems. Are the wish-fulfillment novels of Gordon Merrick more positive, or less, than Christopher Isherwood's *A Single Man,* in which the value of a long-term gay love relationship is seen, indirectly, through the muted grief of its surviving partner? Perhaps, though, there is a place for wish-fulfillment. Daniel Luckenbill wrote that "magazines such as *Straight To Hell* (which prints readers' raunchy sexual incidents and fantasies) probably open new realms of what is printed and this is extremely healthy."

Peter Robins was not as dubious as some about the search for an affirmative gay fiction. "I find contemporary gay fiction as damply depressing as it mostly always was," he wrote. "Sure, when we come to the last chapter we no longer find the hero marrying/committing suicide/bravely facing a lonely sunset ... What the piece as a whole so often lacks is joy and comedy—a true gaiety ... I'm not an integrationist," he adds, "so, for me, the function of writers who are gay would seem to be to record the climate in which we live with a cool and slightly distanced irony. Satire and comedy are probably our best implements." And he cites "that great, mercurial dramatist Joe Orton who farted at the bourgeois."

There are few outlets for contemporary short fiction on gay themes. Outlets for short fiction of any sort are limited, and many of them are reluctant to print gay stories. Often stories have been censored by editors before publication. In 1974, for example, the stories of Edgar Pangborn's serial *The Company of Glory,* previously published in *Galaxy* magazine, were censored for book publication by an editor who found them "too faggotty." And of course gay books are still being censored—and even destroyed—by governments. Richard Amory's detective novel *Frost* and Edmund White's and Charles Silverstein's *The Joy of Gay Sex* are among the books that have been burned by the British Customs authorities.

Some gay magazines print erotic fiction, but feel anything too "serious" will turn their readers off. To their credit, such periodicals as *Gay Sunshine, Christopher Street* and *GPU News* consistently publish serious gay fiction, and among "glossies" popular for their erotica, *Blueboy* and the now defunct *Quorum* have offered gay fiction writers a chance to reach a far wider readership than a "little magazine" could offer. And there is now a magazine, *Paragraph,* devoted solely to gay short fiction.

The stories in *On the Line* deal with a wide variety of themes: the results of society's judgements on a young homosexual and his adult friend (in Peter Robins' "A Friend of the Family"); the contrast between older and younger gays and their lifestyles (in Graham Jackson's "Another Time, Another Place"); fashions in gay taste and influence (in John Mitzel's "The Last Piece of Trade in America"); contradictions between eroticism and ideology (in Daniel Curzon's "Virility"); the diverse kinds of affectionate gay relationships (such as those in Daniel Luckenbill's "Ask a Marine" and Graham Jackson's "Charm").

When collecting material for the anthology, I was intrigued that several of the best stories involved the supernatural, and that another, Peter Burton's "A Marriage of Convenience" was one of the most chilling stories I had ever read. This was something I had not thought to expect. Yet this feeling for the sinister behind the everyday, an apprehension of other worlds and other modes of being is, I think, a particular ability of gays, excommunicated as we are from so many of the bland normalities of life. It is a talent shared not only by fiction writers but by gay occultists like Aleister Crowley and Montague Summers, and by such film-makers as F. W. Murnau *(Nosferatu)*, James Whale *(Frankenstein)* and Jean Cocteau *(Orphee* and *Beauty and the Beast)*.

On the Line is the result of a long process of selection, involving the reading of a great deal of short fiction in many books and periodicals, as well as the pieces submitted in response to my general invitation. Anatole Broyard once wrote that short story anthologies devoted to the idea of illustrating a theme are very often more faithful to the thesis than to literature. He added that they remind him of such expressions as "elephant ballet" or "flea circus." His point was noted. In this collection, as in my previous anthology of gay poetry, *The Male Muse,* though all the contributions share a very broad subject matter, they have been chosen for their interest and artistic success—and secondarily for their illumination of some aspect of gay life. As for a theme, if there is one, or several, that will have to emerge from the stories themselves, and I shall not make it my business to pronounce one here. While I agree with Mr. Broyard that an elephant ballet or a flea circus might not have much claim on our interest, a male ballet—or an intergalactic circus—would. This collection, it seems to me, is its own justification.

There have been a number of previous anthologies of homosexual fiction. For the most part they have been historical anthologies, emphasising homosexual writing of the past. *On the Line* is the first collection of contemporary work, i.e. of gay fiction written since the Stonewall rebellion of 1969. It collects only work dealing primarily with gay men. A number of lesbian anthologies have been published, and they can be obtained through women's and gay bookshops.

The stories in *On the Line* are diverse in many ways, but united in the commitment of their authors to tell the truth about sexuality no less than about anything else. I consider all the authors represented, whatever the extent of their personal involvements, to be a valuable part of the movement for gay liberation. Their talent, honesty and independence are among that movement's greatest assets.

Ian Young
New York, March 1980

A Friend of the Family

by Peter Robins

LIFE AT MY grandmother's was more exotic than at home. Exotic, my latest word, was spattered through school essays and murmured privately to myself when thinking over a Saturday morning film I had seen. I'm talking about the summer when I was twelve, the June when my younger sister was born and I went to stay for some weeks in that narrow mid-Victorian house on the other side of town. For one thing, my grandmother didn't seem to observe rules that made so many experiences unsuitable for children. I could drink coffee for breakfast rather than weak tea and for supper there was a glass of beer with my bubble and squeak, always on the assumption that I'd not tell my parents. The house, too, was more roomy and unpredictable than our own terraced villa. In a deep cupboard under the stairs, home-made wines matured and from time to time exploded among abandoned chemistry sets, a model theatre and steam-engines still oiled and in trim.

The two upper floors in which my Aunt Sarah and her husband, my new uncle, had made a flat were equally exciting. They'd been given a wind-up gramophone as a wedding present and I could play Tea For Two and The Donkey's Serenade until the needle or my aunt's patience wore down. More relevant, as a couple they were so much younger than my own parents. I'd been a page-boy at their wedding in a holly-green velvet suit only six months before and they themselves would have been in their early twenties. They sped off to exotic (what else?) cocktail parties and people of their own age dropped in, treating me not as a child who should be given sixpence to lose himself for a few hours. One girl who'd been a bridesmaid taught me the Valeta but, better than that old rubbish, there was Donald—though I had to call him Uncle Donald in the house. He'd been best man and, although he was only twenty-two he already owned a motor-bike and sidecar. I soon learned that by not hinting too crudely when he popped in at the weekends, he'd offer me a spin along the raw arterial road that was pushing out towards Staines and Windsor.

That was as good a summer as any I have known since and the windows were pushed up every morning as I came down ready for breakfast and school. My grandmother would have been out and about and have already picked a large blue bowlful of raspberries from her bright untidy garden. She'd be singing

The Lily of Laguna in the kitchen and feeding Ganymede her cat or Caligula her Airedale, unaware of the kettle-lid dancing away behind her on the gas stove or my breakfast egg embroidering a brown edging round itself in the pan.

I really didn't care about the complications that were keeping my mother in hospital with the baby—neither of them was in any danger—and the weeks tumbled along. Until, one Friday, my grandmother was not singing. She seemed distant, occupied—so much so that she almost forgot to give me the milk money for school though I had reminded her twice. When I came back that evening she was waiting for me in the hall and asked me not to rush up the stairs to see my aunt and uncle. The reason was obvious enough. I mean I could hear a noisy row going on for myself. When I'd half-eaten my tea my grandmother asked me which way I'd come back from school. Seemed a curious question but I told her the usual route, what else?: over the iron bridge where the tubes tore by to Hounslow, then along the path by the stream, through the new housing estate and what was left of Willow Farm and round the back of the new tire factory. She said nothing for some while, just cut herself another piece of Leicester cheese and skewered two more pickled onions from the jar. Then she asked if it wouldn't be more direct for me to walk along the High street, across the Belisha crossing—we call them zebras now—and round by Station Parade. Well of course I agreed that it would but hadn't she herself said it was such a drab suburban route and I was only making the detour she herself made with the dog? No argument developed. Instead she asked what I'd been doing at school and whether I'd made the House Team for athletics. When the plates had been dried and put away we took coffee into the garden. She settled herself in a wicker chair and I recited to her all the Kings and Queens of England from William the Conqueror to George the Fifth with their dates. Honouring our bargain, since the list had been accurate enough (not forgetting Richard Cromwell) she produced a sixpenny supplement to my weekend pocket money. As I was finishing my coffee, Aunt Sarah came through the garden door. Her eyelids were raw as steak and she was very brisk and practical not giving anyone time to ask questions but talking for fully five minutes about food that would have to be bought for the weekend. When she did pause, my grandmother asked, innocently I thought, if Uncle Richard was coming down. My aunt burst out:

"There are times when I think I've married an idiot. Can't or won't see what would be plain enough to a blind man in a fog. And always has been as far as I can make out."

My grandmother's reply had little bearing on this. "Stephen," she was patting her blouse noisily, "I do declare that coffee's given me a touch of heartburn. Run in and fetch me a glass of cold water from the tap."

When I came back my aunt had taken the dog for his walk.

Next day, more oddities. Donald and his motorbike did not appear at noon. It was Saturday and he'd joined us for lunch each Saturday for eight weeks. When the grandfather clock was chiming a quarter to three and there had still been no reference, no explanation, I asked. Aunt Sarah allowed no one else a reply.

"Donald has gone abroad to work. It's not likely we'll be seeing him again for a very long time." She finished counting the stitches in her row of white knitting and added, "If ever."

It was not only very disturbing news but odd in that Donald had said nothing to me. I had believed he thought of me as someone special. It's how I thought of him. He was, after all, no more than eleven years older than I was. Hadn't he chosen me to go with him on Sunday mornings to cheer when he scored a goal for the local team? Hadn't he, a County swimmer, taken afternoons to teach me to do the Australian crawl? That night in bed with the thick warm air of August round me I was lonely without him and needed him near me, touching me carelessly as he often did. Better than the scent of the syringa outside the open window I could recall the slightly acrid smell under the arms of his shirts. More pleasurable than that as memories were the moments when we'd wrestled in Oxshott Woods after a picnic lunch. The family looked on and laughed but I was left breathless not only in a physical way but with a weird excitement that was connected with a need to lie on my stomach. I said it was easier to regain breath control that way. Did Donald or any of them guess I wanted to conceal what I feared might be as obvious to others as it felt to me?

It was certainly during one of our picnics that June when the suggestion of a trip to Brittany for my grandmother, aunt, uncle, Donald and me was discussed. Now it seemed the plan would have to be jettisoned if Donald had indeed emigrated for ever. And with the plan, our secret. There was no chance at all that we might actually share a room in Brittany.

The weekend was rounded off with the news that my mother would be leaving the hospital at long last with my baby sister—"the afterthought" as my grandmother called her, though not in front of my father who wasn't best pleased when I used it as what I thought was a witty phrase. Leaving my grandmother's was all right but it really was like going back to black and white films after the exotic technicolour triumphs that were beginning to unroll at our cinema in the High Street.

So it was home again for what remained of the summer holidays. It's difficult to be exact but I do know that the short marble season which precedes October conker matches was on when my father asked if I'd care to stay at my grandmother's again for a couple of weeks. Our own house was to be shut and my parents would be taking the baby away to Cornwall. The arrangement suited me so well that I'd packed my case and lashed it round with string within ten minutes though Saturday was three days off.

The weekend went well for the weather was still kind and I was out for hours with Roger the boy who lived opposite my grandmother. We took sandwiches for lunch and bottles of Tizer and made a raft that floated and then disintegrated in the stream which men from the Town Hall were canalising with concrete banks. I regretted this and told Roger it would be goodbye to the frogs and minute creatures that thrived in the rushes and hawthorns. He said the whole idea was to drive off dirty old men who hid there to take away children in sacks, or so his father had told him. True enough we did see the bearded tramp we called The Old Man but he only waved his bottle of stout at us when we jumped out and made monster faces at him. The only things he'd ever been seen to pop in his sack were torn handkerchieves or broken shoes. His sack would certainly have been too small for me.

The raft sank. We sank. Then swimming ashore in our clothes we raced through the Sunday afternoon sunlight to scrump for apples until Major Perkins chased us over his orchard wall threatening that he was off to the Police Station, that he knew quite well who we were and would prosecute.

The following afternoon, despising the straightforward route as always, I made my way from school to my grandmother's over the iron bridge. Pausing to check the horizon for any stray zeppelins, I waited for the next tube train to flash under me, aimed an apple core, mistimed and hit the roof of the second compartment rather than the driver's lookout window. It was then that I glanced across the park for the first time and in that instant knew who it must be on the farthest bench. I took those steps down the bridge three at a stride, nearly spilling my school things from my satchel. Away I went along the towpath past the ice-cream kiosk, the smelly public lavatory and the sight boards of the cricket pitch.

"Donald," I called, "you're back. I knew they were lying. They said you'd gone abroad forever."

He didn't look very sunburned. Not at all like the people my parents had known when they had been abroad: those veneered mahogany figures who called to have tea with us and discuss old times when they were back on what was called Home Leave.

"Hello Steve," he said. He'd altered. It wasn't the smile I remembered. This time it was brief and closed up and he glanced round endlessly as our cat did when it was in a corner with its back to the wall.

"You didn't get much sun abroad," I said. "How long have you been back?"

"Back? Oh, two or three days. It was mainly indoor work you know. If you're in a garage pit, doesn't make much difference if it's Venice or Vauxhall, does it now?"

"Donald," I was anxious for the answer was most important, "tell me the truth."

His hands were very wobbly as he lit a Woodbine. I began to fear the worst.

"What do you want me to tell you then?"

"You didn't go to Brittany without me?"

He looked at me and it was the old grin. Nearly Donald of the early summer. He leaned a little so that he could punch me on the shoulder lightly and then he turned away and seemed to choke on the cigarette smoke.

"Now would I have done that to you, Steve, after all those promises we made?"

I had to believe him since he was the only adult I'd ever known who hadn't said one thing and immediately done another.

"Steve," he was saying, "you didn't, well, you didn't tell your gran about our secret plans for Brittany by any chance?"

"What for? It's nothing to do with her. Torture chambers wouldn't drag it from me. Have you been round to see them all yet?"

"There's been a lot to do, you know, I just haven't been able to find that moment yet. I will be round though, pretty soon."

"What's wrong with now? Tea'll be ready."

"Can't manage it this evening. Got to see . . ."

"I know—a dog about a man. Soon eh?"

"Soon."

I was looking along the towpath towards the farm gate.

"Think I'd better vanish, Donald. There's a copper coming along on his bike. He could be looking for me. Roger and I went scrumping yesterday and we're wanted men. Major Perkins was screaming Borstal and blue murder."

Donald stood up and buttoned his gaberdine raincoat though it wasn't cold.

"Away you go then. See you soon. If he says anything pretend you're thick. If he asks me I'll say you wanted to know the time."

"Right," I whispered, "I'll tell them at home I saw you."

And I nipped away whistling tunelessly. The policeman hardly glanced so maybe the Major hadn't told or if he had, my name wasn't on the constable's list. He'd cycled on, when I looked back at the farm gate, beyond Donald and seemed pre-occupied with a problem: his corns perhaps or possibly his tea.

My aunt and uncle were entertaining my grandmother and me to supper that evening. I decided to detonate my big surprise after we'd finished the egg-custard and were on to the biscuits and cheese.

"Guess who I saw today and you've only got three tries. One each."

"Amy Johnson," suggested Uncle Richard who was bored with clerking for a Travel Agency and dreamed of being a pilot.

"The Princess Royal." Aunt Sarah didn't amaze me for she was obsessed with her royal contemporaries and wore frocks as near their originals as she could devise. My grandmother, who would have danced on the Music Halls if she could have persuaded her parents that theatres weren't Stage Managed by the Devil bid "Nellie Wallace."

"All wrong; all three of you. Knew you would be. I saw Uncle Donald. He's back and I talked to him and he'll be coming round. Doesn't look too good though. Not much of a sun tan after three whole months."

The effect was unbelievable. Not one of them seemed a bit pleased. My grandmother said nothing but started scrunching up the edge of the blue and white check tablecloth in her fingers; a sure sign, my mother would have diag-

15

nosed, that she was in a state. My aunt flushed and straightway jumped up to collect our pudding plates with such speed that she dropped one and smashed it. A pity since it broke a set which had been a valued wedding present.

My Uncle Richard fumbled with a box of matches. "Where did you see him, Stephen?"

"In the park by the stream," I said. "We sat on a bench and talked."

"Never mind what you did," said my aunt. "I thought you'd been told never to come that way from school? I want your solemn word (she was pointing the dustpan at me like some sacred relic on which poor King Harold was made to swear) and I want it here and now that you will never, never walk through that park again and talk to strangers."

"It was Donald. It wasn't a stranger."

"Uncle Donald," Uncle Richard corrected mechanically, still tumbling the matchbox from side to side.

"I did speak to you about coming back through the town." My grandmother appeared to be more concerned with clearing herself than rebuking me.

"I can assure you of one thing young man," Aunt Sarah, I noticed, though red in the face was by contrast quite white round the lips. She was very angry. "You will not be seeing Donald again in this house."

"Why won't he be coming? What's he done to annoy you? He's a friend of the family isn't he? That's what you always say when you introduce him."

By then I too was annoyed at their altered manner to Donald. Another stupid adult secret no doubt, quite unlike sharing a room in France or going camping together next year when I'd be thirteen.

Uncle Richard had also irritated my aunt. At least she grabbed the matchbox from him and hissed a couple of words in his ear. He ran his teeth up his lower lip and looked at me.

"Donald, Uncle Donald, hasn't been very well; that's why he had to go away. Your aunt's thinking about you. That's why she doesn't want you to see him just at present. Easy does it, Sarah. Hold on. You see, Steve, he suffers from these headaches and then he does some odd things that could, perhaps, if you were by yourself with him, well, put it this way, frighten you."

He flicked his plus-fours and then turned a fraction towards my grandmother so that I couldn't tell whether he was winking or not. What I did know was that what he had just told me wasn't the truth. Some story they'd agreed on more like.

"If he hasn't been well, I should have thought you'd have wanted to see him." I was talking to all of them. "After all you took it in turns to go to the hospital to see my mother and she hasn't been well. He was your friend, Uncle Richard. You played rugger in the same team and you went on holidays together before you were married. He told me. Anyway he was best man at the wedding. . ."

"Perhaps you ought to go and do your homework." My uncle was now turning his cigarette case over as rapidly as Gracie Fields did cartwheels.

"Now just look at that face in the coals: the image of old Gladstone." I knew my grandmother was causing a distraction. She always did at awkward moments. My father said so.

My aunt was still white-lipped as she poured our coffee.

"As long as we all understand that I don't want Donald Allerton mentioned in my flat ever again."

That, I thought, would be difficult when she was showing visitors those wedding photographs she was for ever dusting on the sideboard. I sneaked a look and realised that they'd been changed. The one of the two bridesmaids in girlie pink was there and the family group too. The happy couple with their best man and me had gone.

"You've changed it." It was an open accusation of disloyalty. "You've got rid of his photo. You're trying to make him disappear."

"Go and do your maths." My uncle was getting edgy.

My grandmother, ever the peacemaker, tried again.

"Sarah, I do think you're making a scene out of nothing at all. I'm sure nothing will have happened."

"I just hope we can be sure of that. How would we know if a certain person was telling the truth?"

In some way then I was involved. My grandmother smiled and put down her cup.

"We'll soon see. Stephen," she rested her chin in her hands and was looking at me with a twinkle that almost put me off-guard. It would do her no good if she wanted to find out about plans Donald and I had made but I listened. "Donald never did anything that frightened you, did he, Stephen? Never interfered with you in any way or put his hand on your things when you talked to him on your way back from school? You can tell me, you know. I'll not be angry."

What a relief I thought. Adult questions were often odd.

"Of course he never touched my stupid old things. They were in my satchel anyway. What would he want with a lot of school books and set squares...?"

My grandmother's laugh was bright as the rings on her fingers as they flashed in the firelight.

"You see. You see," she laughed more and more, "nothing to fret about."

"You may be right." My aunt was in no way as relaxed as my uncle and grandmother appeared to be. The apostle spoon from her coffe-cup became another improvised relic and was pointed at me. "Now Stephen, I want the truth. Scouts honour mind. Would you look me in the eye and swear that you had no secrets at all with Donald. Just remember God can hear as clearly as I can."

"No. I wouldn't." I didn't care who heard my answer. "We did have one secret and that was about Brittany but we're not going anyway. He's still my friend even if you don't want him so I'm not going to tell you and wild horses won't make me. Thanks for the supper, I'm going to do my maths."

17

That night I dreamed Donald and I were careering through Oxshott Woods on his motorbike and Aunt Sarah was standing up in the sidecar swinging my satchel about her head like a sling until, as we touched seventy, the sidecar detached itself as it often did in comedy films and away she went surfing along the stream by the tube line while Donald and I laughed and spread out a check tablecloth for a picnic of pickled onions and Tizer which we never finished because we started wrestling and I knew it was happening to me again but somehow with only Donald about it didn't matter and there was no need to roll over embarrassed onto my stomach because he was smiling and running the first finger of his hand round and round the top button of my shirt which was coming loose and then...

"Breakfast Stephen," my grandmother was calling.

When the weekend arrived, I went to a Saturday morning match with my uncle. After lunch we took my aunt to the cinema. In the evening friends came round. My grandmother insisted on going to church twice that particular Sunday and even in the afternoon I was bribed out into the garden to help my uncle who was suddenly enthusiastic for clearing up a couple of beds to sow vegetables. I began to think that it must have been agreed not to let me out of the house alone. Some changes from the freedom of those summer weekends. During the days that followed, there was always either my grandmother or my aunt at the shops near the Grammar School at half past four. By Friday no one could have convinced me it hadn't been some kind of a plan.

That evening I made a bid for freedom. It was Scout night and off I went with Roger, the boy from the house opposite. When the rough-house session was over we sprinted along together and had eaten our chips before the church clock had finished striking nine. The evenings were still warm and on the off-chance that I might meet Donald and ask him for the truth about this illness business, I suggested we make a detour over the iron bridge and through the park. Roger was terrified. Started carrying on again about a man with a sack who would take us away. You wouldn't have thought he was eleven. I told him he was worse than my girl cousins but he kept on whimpering that his Dad had read a case in the local paper and shown it to his Mum and then hidden the article because it was about Riverside Walk. He came with me in the end but I knew he was scared because every time we passed a stretch of road where a street lamp wasn't working he'd pretend he was cold and wanted to run. As far as the next lamp anyway.

As we hung over the parapet of the iron bridge I spotted it. Donald's motorbike was parked under a chestnut tree away from the lights above the path bordering the park. I didn't need to glance twice at the registration. He was nowhere to be seen but he was around. Although I told Roger nothing, I was checking the benches as we strolled along. No sign. Then I asked Roger to check the bankside itself for ducks or frogs. He did so right enough, mumbling all the while that he ought to be home. The ice-cream kiosk was bolted and dark so there really wasn't any place at all other than the sour smelling lavatory. I told Roger I wanted to nip in there.

"Can't you do it here, in the river, if it's that bad?" he shivered.

"Only peasants do it in public," I said.

"Well I'm not going in there, I'm going home," I saw him half screwing up his eyes as he ran hard for the farm gate.

There was no light in the lavatory but helped by the full moon I trod with extra care keeping to the grass and not breaking any twigs. It was applied scouting that would be useful if some old tramp rather than Donald was in there. At last I stepped onto the concrete base which supported the rusty peeling ironwork. I was still very wary because although there were no cubicles, tramps had been known to shit on the concrete itself. Scared that even my breathing might betray me, I inched into the doorframe. Donald was there. That one thick strand of black hair which would not conform despite oil and brush was recognisable immediately in the moonlight. He hadn't noticed me; nor had the other man who stood so close to him. They were much the same age. Standing very close; not talking or even appearing to whisper. It was pointless to interrupt so I edged out as stealthily as I'd gone in and prepared to wait until Donald had finished and we might talk.

I thought I'd been proficient on the silent field-craft technique but the policeman I'd seen ten days previously had been more so. He was standing in the shadow of the ice-cream kiosk with his bicycle lamp turned off. Major Perkins had won, I thought, I'd be up before my grandmother's friend the Mayor on that charge of scrumping after all. The copper was beckoning me over. As I was about to admit that I'd nicked the Major's apples he tapped his finger against his nose and breathed down at me "What did you see in there then?"

"Just two men," I realised I was also whispering.

"And what were they doing?"

I knew something must be amiss because he was sliding a black pocket book from his tunic. Something was going to happen. It was worse than scrumping and it could involve Donald.

"What do you think they were doing? Going to the lavatory. That's what it's there for."

"Boy Scouts tell the truth don't they?" He raised one eyebrow and unscrewed his fountain pen. "Could you describe them?"

"One of them." A mere description could hardly be incriminating.

"See him before perhaps? Talked to him? Been in there with him have you to earn a bit of extra pocket money maybe?"

"What for? We've got our own lavatory at home. Besides, he's a friend of the family."

"I see," and to help himself do so more clearly he shone the flashlight from his bike right in my face. "I suggest you nip off home to your people laddie and leave this to us."

Whatever this was, it was ugly. I was certainly not going to desert Donald. One course of action was open.

"Donald," I yelled, "Donald it's Stephen... run."

Within two seconds he did, sprinting out and along the asphalt like the sportsman he was, with his shirt tail flapping as I had seen him when flying off to make a touch down.

Then the second man ran out after him as though chasing a thief and calling back "O.K. Ted. We're home and dry. Got his registration number too."

"What's he done? What is it?" I shouted at the copper who was unhurriedly fixing his flashlamp back on its bracket.

"Bugger off home you," he grunted, hopping on his bike. "Watch who you make friends with in future. Nice one you had there. Worse than a bloody animal."

As I stood with my fists tight, half-weeping with impotence and anger I heard Roger whisper from behind the nearest tree. He'd doubled back after all. Afraid of crossing the fields no doubt.

"There you are," he said, "Told you. There was an old man in there."

"No there wasn't you bloody fool. There wasn't. It was Donald."

"Don't care who it was." He was confident now with the policeman on his side. "He'd have run away with you. He would."

"Roger, you're stupid. That's what you are. He wouldn't have needed to. I'd have run away with him anytime. Anywhere. Anywhere in the bloody world."

And although he screamed after me, I was the better runner and left Roger there as I raced through the farm and past the tyre factory to my grandmother's house. They'd gone to the cinema. I emptied my supper down the lavatory and then I was sick until there was nothing left in my stomach to come up. Careful as a master-thief not to disarrange a hairpin, I searched my aunt's flat until I found the photograph of Donald that she had removed and hidden under the bedroom carpet. I placed it under my mattress turned off the light and then for the last time as a boy, I wept.

The Passionate Friends

by Edmund White

WHEN DAN ENTERED the University of Chicago in 1953, he was sixteen, fat and slovenly. By this gross neglect of his person he was not trying to defy convention; he was simply unaware of how he looked. If asked to describe even one article of his wardrobe that wasn't in sight, Dan would have been at a loss. If asked how often he brushed his teeth or trimmed his nails, he would have had no answer. He had no sense of his body. He had a mind, and then there were legs and a trunk that moved the mind about from this book to that friend, from a film to a classroom, a library to a bed.

He had been a brilliant child, a prodigy, a non-stop talker and reader. He read everything. He talked about anything—as long as the subject allowed him to shine; he imagined people wanted nothing so much as for him to shine; he was the adored bar mitzvah boy. Curiously, his thoughts, his private thoughts, were neither vain nor brilliant. Before he was ten he had tacitly dismissed Judaism and embraced Buddhism in its oldest, most austere version because only the Theravada sutras confirmed his feeling that he was alone, he had always been alone, he would always be alone. Nirvana would be nothing but a return to original and enduring solitude, empty, finally, even of oneself.

Maria was sophisticated—or was she very simple? Her makeup, her cucumber soap, her toothbrush and a little washcloth that fitted over the hand like a mitten were lined up neatly on the top of a dresser in her dormitory room at the University of Chicago. She wavered between sobriety and luxury. The wavering was dramatized in every corner of the room, even on the dresser top, for the mitten was a homely mittel-European touch packed in her suitcase by her German-American mother, whereas the cucumber soap was a folly ordered through Caswell-Massey's excruciatingly affected catalogue. Her narrow bed seemed to Dan irreproachably virginal, a bright white pillow on a wrinkleless cotton spread, but above it hung one of her paintings, a sumptuous, scary abstraction. Maria's hands were rough from scrubbing her floor and the worn marble threshold, but her palette, a board resting on the windowsill, was an advanced disease, alizarine crimson a half-healed sore beside an ochre bruise. She read Aristotle, a lot of Aristotle, and discussed ideas aggressively, crisply, but she thrilled to Puccini. She was the first living human being whom Dan ever heard use the word charming in conversation.

Both she and Dan were true Midwestern intellectuals, that is, self-created beings who had read books but had no one whom they could talk to about literature, who could write and recognize on the page many words they couldn't pronounce (Maria said "respite" so that it rhymed with "delight" and Dan made three syllables out of "aegis") and who never suspected that other people might pretend to knowledge they didn't as yet possess. For Maria and Dan, being smart was something you did, not something you were or might want to be. When Maria returned to her Lutheran home in Iowa for Christmas, she was shown off to the relatives as the good student, but she was expected to behave as she always had, as everyone else did, and most of the time she obliged except when she argued with her father over politics. "There, there," her mother gently interposed, "don't get worked up over nothing. What you both need is a cup of hot chocolate. And Maria, have you called your Aunt?"

Dan might talk his head off to his mother as she did the dishes in Evanston, and she might nod as though giving her blessing in general, but she didn't listen very carefully. He was the good Jewish boy, bright to a fault, and she wished that fault were better disguised when his less clever friends dropped by. The psychologist had always known that his high aptitude and equally high performance had made him maladjusted to his peer group. She had informed him when he was still quite young of this problem; he himself had long considered his intelligence to be a threat to others less gifted.

Maria would have taken Dan in hand, only she was too fastidious to interfere in anyone's life. But he did annoy her, talking her night away, drinking away at her wine.

She had felt nervous about going into the liquor store to buy the wine. She was underage, though her casual, direct manner and possibly her green eyeshadow had made her appear years older. It must have, since the man had put the bottle in a paper bag seconds after the difficult French name was out of her mouth.

It was the first bottle of French wine she had ever purchased. Tasted good, but surely a whole bottle should last two people at least a week.

Dan poured out another glass for himself and as an afterthought jabbed the bottle in the general direction of her glass; Maria placed her hand over the glass. It was her toothbrush glass. Looking at it reminded her of her usual preparations for bed and she became angry all over again at this talking machine. When would he leave?

She snapped off the phonograph in the midst of Manon's "Tu, tu, amore, tu?" and the soprano's *tu* collapsed into an ugly bass *taw-w-w* . . . and on into silence, a bird shot out of the skies. As Dan continued to talk, she took mental potshots at him. It was an old game she had played during church back in

Iowa. By the end of every service she had killed off the entire choir and the minister was writhing, his white hands scarlet, over his Bible.

She had detested Lutheranism the moment she'd learned in catechism class that women couldn't become ministers. "Why?" she'd demanded. Up to then she had intended to become a minister herself.

Unpacified by the teacher's explanation that girls can grow up to be deaconesses and help out at Luther League meetings, Maria converted instantly to atheism. Her new belief, however, did not cool her ardor for Amana, the religious colony where her grandfather still lived. If anything, her admiration increased for Amana's communal economy and clear, logical laws and the spirit of fairness and compassion that pervaded every aspect of its life. Like many adolescents (something adults refuse to remember), she had the feeling that she was already too wise, already old, irremediably disillusioned by the world's vanities—and this precocious ennui made her feel more at home at Amana than in her parents' big suburban mansion. She agreed with the founders of the colony that romantic love is sinful and childbearing cruel; how sensible they'd been to separate for a year a man and a woman who wanted to marry in hopes that the separation would reconcile them to celibacy. And how sensible to divide the wealth, share the labor, assume community responsibility for the sick and the aged, love your neighbor ...

Zing! One of Dan's ears whizzed off his head and lay flattened out against the far wall like a bass clef: she added two bullet holes just to its right, marking the center line of the stave.

She switched off her rosy atmospheric lamp and turned on the horrible overhead light, but still he talked and drank.

While she had been wrestling with the corkscrew he had eaten all the pepperoni she'd sliced for snacks. They had never made it out to dinner; the wine must have killed his hunger or so entranced him with the sound of his voice he'd forgotten his belly for once. Of course he *had* eaten a whole stick of pepperoni.

When he left, no matter how late it might be, she'd scrub down the whole room. The ashtray was full of butts. He had smoked his way through two packs, she figured. The butts led her thoughts back to bullets.

She incised a shot neatly through his trachea, but his voice droned smoothly on.

She looked longingly at the open volume of *The Metaphysics* beside her bed; she'd have done the same if Aristotle himself had been her visitor. Tomorrow she'd play no music at all, or if any then Bach; yes, she'd have dear old Casals sawing his way through unaccompanied cello sonatas, as bracing as Lysol; at all costs, no more Puccini.

There. He'd polished off the bottle. A four-fifty bottle of French wine. As the green glass exploded it took off his hand.

She had perfect contempt now for what had at first seemed fascinating about him: his utter unawareness of his surroundings. It mattered very much to her which cup she drank from. To him not at all. In fact, she doubted he ever knew what—or even that—he was drinking. Certainly he was unconscious of his appearance. His fingernails were dirty and ragged, his shoes a scandal, and he had become terribly obese. He had put on at least thirty pounds in the last two months. She brought this calamity to his attention only after he'd complained there was something wrong with his new trousers, must be cheap wool, the fabric had deteriorated for some reason just below the crotch.

"That's because your legs are so fat they rub together; you've worn your way right through the cloth."

He looked down at his belly in disbelief—and unfamiliarity.

"Don't you ever weigh yourself?"

"No."

"Don't you watch what you eat? Of course you don't."

"This never happened to me before."

"You're getting older. Your body is slowing down."

Dan had looked troubled, perhaps realizing for the first time that his life was running out as rapidly as his body was filling up, that he was racing towards becoming an expressive three-hundred pound corpse.

Was he never going to shut up? His upper lip was so long you seldom saw his upper teeth, but every time Maria glimpsed one she shot it out of his mouth. She pressed her fingertips to her temples. The overhead light tortured *her*, not him as she had intended. She turned it off and they sat in darkness. He didn't notice. He ignored her altogether. She might as well be asleep. Which wasn't a bad idea. "Would you mind talking a little softer?"

"Am I keeping your neighbors awake?"

"No. Just me."

He shut up at that. She had been cruel. She hadn't meant to be cruel. What was he doing over there in the dark? Was he feeling—oh, that big talking machine didn't feel a thing.

But she knew he did. Perhaps he'd wounded her vanity; he could be talking to anyone! Fathead, she called out at him silently, while in the same instant she stood and would have stretched a hand towards him had she not swerved away and gone to the window.

Was that the sound of Dan crying? She looked around at him. His hands covered his face. A light from the courtyard was reflected in his high forehead.

He put on the Puccini very low and came over to her. His face was wet. He took her hand. "You may think this is preposterous."

She waited and finally asked him to go on.

"I love you," he said. "I know I'm fat and younger than you and an egotist, and you don't need to say anything, I'm surely not expecting you to say you love me, because I know you don't, but if it doesn't repel you, I'd like to come by, of course not too often, but I'd like to be near you, and when we leave school I'd like to live in the same city as you, whichever city you choose, if that wouldn't make you too nervous. I don't want to cramp your style; I'm all too aware that I must strike an absurd figure as the lover."

The dark signs of weariness under her eyes made her face more tender, as though she had been crying, too. She took his hand. Her hand was small and as rough as a cat's tongue—all her scrubbing and cleaning.

They were very happy. They found an apartment together, a big rangy one in what would eventually be called New Town but was then just another Chicago no-man's land. She was handy, in fact mannish and had a neat, practiced way of hauling in wood for the fireplace, of driving her old station wagon, of installing bookcases for him. She had almost no interest in food and seldom sat down to a proper meal; by opening a can of cold salmon, peeling a few carrots and boiling two eggs she imagined she had prepared dinner, which he found very Gentile and fascinating. He lost weight.

In the evening she'd paint and he'd write and they'd listen to music. She wore a white smock covered with paint stains. Her art entailed so much puttering about (building stretchers, sketching, buying supplies, sizing a canvas), whereas his demanded instant performance the moment he opened his notebook—how unfair! he thought.

Before he met her he had written easily and had hoped to finish a novel without much bother, publish it and become rich and famous. Now he was ashamed that he had ever entertained such shallow ambitions. Although she seldom spoke about making art and considered political debate much more worthwhile, nevertheless he was able to deduce from her occasional remarks that she envisioned the artist's life as a long one, to be led patiently. Your twenties were a period of apprenticeship, your thirties and forties of growing mastery, your fifties of success. The success was personal and very small. You could expect nothing more, but that was enough. Whenever he let slip that he hoped to change people's attitudes on such and such a subject through something he was writing, she mercilessly reminded him, "But people don't read novels." If he admitted to a hunger for fame, she'd look at him first in disbelief, then with pity.

He was writing very much under the spell of Dostoevsky in those days. The fat egotist abandoned himself to crazed orgies of gambling, feverish drinking and uncontrollable eating, but at unexpected moments he would burst into tears, repent of his ways (though not for long) and prostrate himself before a very pure, calm, virginal creature from Iowa who forgave him everything, though she sadly acknowledged that she knew he would never be redeemed. The book was tentatively entitled *Revulsion*, but Maria called it *The Overwrought Urn* and criticized it for not being "objective."

Through a long winter he lived with the smell of paint in the sheets, in his shirts—he smelled it two landings below their door as he came upstairs. She was sitting on a high stool, smoking, dressed in black pants, sneakers and her paint-stained smock, staring at a huge canvas placed against the opposite wall. She kissed him, took the packages from his arms, fluttered about, but in a few moments she was back on her perch, eying her canvas. She could take only short flights away from inspiration.

No doubt she would have been embarrassed by any mention of *inspiration,* would have considered it immoral to take art too seriously, but that's how she took it. He'd wake up in the middle of the night and through the half-open door see her still sitting on her perch, smoking, one leg dangling, the other bent, her sneaker pressed against an upper rung of the stool. She held her cigarette in her lap and the smoke drifted upwards. She raised a hand and blocked out of her view half of the canvas. As he fell back to sleep, she became Kuan-yin, Goddess of Mercy, haloed in incense, one foot folded under her, a hand raised to still fear, merciful, meditative—alone.

She was determined to preserve their solitude, or at least her own. When he took her out two nights in a row she burst into tears. The next night, after a full day of their being alone, they sat looking into the fire and she said, "Isn't this much better?"

He nodded enthusiastically but wasn't so sure. He now loved people as much as he had once craved an unsocial Nirvana, although his knack for making friends was probably as shallow as his now-abandoned hopes to be a famous novelist quick. He glowed in crowds; she smouldered. Her early goodnights were famous. "I've got to feed the cat," she would whisper, putting on her coat.

He copied her; whatever she did or thought must be right. Their solitude was so profound that it could be broken not even by his mother, whose visits Maria kept putting off, though Maria enjoyed hearing from Dan about even the minutest details of his mother's life. "Oh, tell her to take vitamin B for that," or "The new sofa sounds perfect; I'd love to see it someday"—but that day was never to come. Maria mailed friendly little thank you notes whenever Dan's mother sent them food. Maria worried over reports of the mother's cat's fleas and bought a flea collar for Dan to take along on his next visit to Evanston.

"Is she terribly ugly?"

"No, mother. Quite beautiful. We'll have you down one of these days. She wants to meet you, honest."

"So you say . . . Surely she doesn't think I disapprove of your living in— together?"

Dan shook his head. "You have no idea how few people we see."

"What's her family like?"

"All reclusive. Very strict Lutherans. Her parents grew up in Amana, the German religious colony. No, she's an atheist."

Dan stood at the window of their apartment and looked down on the surrounding streets, the snow the same gray as the sky. He knew Maria was happy and wondered why he wasn't. So mild and unvarying was his unhappiness that he would have stopped noticing it if he'd not gone out from time to time. At parties he kept his listeners spellbound with reports of his odd reading (Maria would have accused him of showing off); he drank too much and ate too much and agreed with silly or dangerous opinions advanced by handsome or beautiful people (Maria would have asked him how he could buy such crap); he was the last guest to leave (Maria would have been the first). When he returned home he was as bright as a beach towel. She pretended she was delighted that he had enjoyed himself, but he felt her shrink in his arms a millimeter from the liquor on his breath, the fire in his eyes, from the ease and easy affection his body radiated. Nor could she disguise the condescension in her voice when she asked, as a mother might ask a child too young to be interesting, what he had done, whom he had seen. When he went into detail she interrupted and said, "Good, good. Sounds like fun. Now where did I put the hammer? Have you seen the hammer anywhere?"

The odd thing was that their life together pleased him most when he was away from her describing it to other people. Their solitary evenings (his writing, her sitting on the high stool and squinting at the canvas) became romantic and enviable only after he had served them up to a noisy crowd.

And yet he had enough sense to recognize he was vulgarizing experiences that were precious, and he feared he was proving himself unworthy of her. His need for general admiration drew him away from her night after night. She never complained. She worked, cheerfully. But he sensed that every day he was slipping in her esteem, as he was in his own. When he was able to force himself to stay at her side, he knew for the hundredth time that she was the perfect companion, that she understood him better than anyone else, and that when he was with her he became a better person. Again and again he was haunted by the fear that he was muffing his one big chance.

One evening she agreed to go out with him. A young man observed Maria from a distance and on subsequent evenings the man always asked Dan for news of Maria. Maria intrigued him for some reason—he claimed he'd heard she was an "original." He wanted to know what Maria thought of Existentialism and this Jean-Paul Sartre. What about Martin Buber, the *Thou and I* guy? Who were her favorite composers? What did she make of Jackson Pollock— how did all that flung paint fit in with Aristotle's concept of art as imitation?

"Aristotle spoke of art as an imitation of an action, hence the very name, Action Painting," Dan reported saucily, bringing back Maria's answer, reworked, to the only question he'd bothered to remember. This conversation at one remove with an eager young man she didn't know failed to interest Maria; what did amuse her, however, was guessing how Dan would distort her deliberately bland remarks into witty retorts.

The young man persisted with his questions and Maria grew as reluctant as an oracle in her answers. What did Dan find so fascinating about Philip Diamondstein?

"Is he terribly handsome?" Maria asked Dan.

"Yes."
"I see."
"See what?"
"Why you see so much of him. Here, pull the canvas tight."
In a fresh white coat, wielding her staple gun, she stooped over the frame and secured the square linen to the wooden two-by-fours.

"Daniello, I wish you wouldn't write about us," Maria said one night after he'd read her a new chapter.
"Why?"
"Because you write as though everything were all over between us. It isn't, you know. Or is this novel the kiss-off?"
"Maria—did I portray you inaccurately?"
"No . . . but I didn't recognize myself. Oh, dumpling, don't look so crestfallen. All I meant to say is that you've made me too virginal, too cold, too much the great saint. It's not disdain for the world that makes me stay at home—you got that part wrong. I just prefer being alone."

She pulled the cigarette out of her ivory holder and crushed it in the ashtray. How she hated smoking—but Dan had glamorized even this filthy habit. He was slumped very far down in his chair, the firelight traveling across his face, his chin retracted. She'd turn on a light except she was wearing only a slip. The peeping Tom across the street might train his binoculars on their windows. Two weeks ago she'd first noticed those silver dollars glinting in the light of the street lamps. They'd have to buy window shades.

"Of course there's another reason I don't go out with you," she told him. "You're too friendly. You like everybody, or at least you like everyone to listen to you."

"If that offends you, of course I'll stop."

She didn't like this show of sullen gallantry. Apparently, she must never criticize his writing again. Praise is what he lived for. That she found very odd, since neither criticism nor praise affected her. Was she fooling herself? Was she really so indifferent to the opinion of others? Oh, yes, she was indifferent.

But not to him. She sat on the edge of his chair. He kissed her, but it was a cold kiss, a conjugal duty. "Would you rub my shoulders?" She snuggled up next to him on the floor, her back turned to him. "Ouch. Not so hard."

The passionate singing of Puccini's lovers swept over him, melting tormented, breathless, and infused his feelings for her like whiskey spreading through water. Under the influence of this music he could feel tenderness for her entering his entire body, warming him, flowing through his hands and out onto her shoulders. He imagined himself breaking the delicate bones, then weeping over them; he pictured the soft hair, shining in the firelight, going up in flames—and he was there to mourn.

These alternating flashes of violence and tenderness drove him a long way off, and from that great distance he looked back at her and himself, a man and a woman whose faces were glowing, whose eyes were looking into the source of light but not at each other. That man and that woman seemed much older than they, Dan and Maria, actually were.

Des Grieux and Manon were singing and the music came to Maria from a world where passion swept aside every hesitation and from which irony had been banished forever. Manon fascinated Maria. Maria pictured her wandering about Geronte's *hotel*, irritable and restless. She lifted her silk skirt, pursed her lips, examined her little foot, twisting it this way and that.

She laughed loudly, but her laugh only reminded her how tedious her days had become. Of course it was amusing to go to balls and inspire jealousy in other women.

And then Des Grieux emerges out of the shadows. His warm hands are on her cheeks. But what's wrong? He suffers! It was true. She had made her angel suffer unbearably. But she knows he can't resist her. He's already weakening. His eyes are reading her body like a familiar map—as a last, futile gesture towards freedom, he rushes to the window, flings it open and gulps in fresh air. He buries his face in his hands; she admires the cut of his jacket . . .

But that was another world, Maria thought. She got up and made a pot of coffee.

Dan and Philip Diamondstein saw each other every day. They ate, studied, walked, talked together. No matter how much ground their talking covered, it always came back to the story of Dan's life with Maria. As Dan fashioned that life for Philip, he knew he was betraying it, reducing the subtle planes and coloring to a crude icon, yet like all objects of worship the icon made worship itself seem more plausible, a more likely thing to do.

But one day Philip dropped Dan. The phone was mysteriously silent. Philip missed the regular meeting of their discussion group that was trying to relate Jung to T.S. Eliot. Dan was distraught. He wanted to say "Philip" to someone but dared not say it to Maria. Finally, he called Philip's girlfriend, whom he'd met only once, and asked her to join him in the student cafeteria.

Over coffee he told her his story and she told him hers. "At first," she said, "I knew nothing about you. Philip spoke only about Maria. He told me he was having an affair with her—"

"No!"

"—and I, yes, I believed him because he knew the minutest details—why, he even knew her favorite composers. He'd throw the composers up to me. "You might have admitted to Puccini," he said, "or pretended to Bach, but to say both names in one breath, *that* takes Maria's sort of style." He had once gotten me to agree that monogamy is unworkable, and so I couldn't really object to his affair with Maria, could I?"

"But there was no affair. He was never even introduced to Maria." Everything in Dan strained to know more about Philip, to castigate him, to fathom his bizarre psychology, to praise him, and in this girl he found an eager collaborator, for she was just as consumed as he with thoughts of Philip. She, too, wanted to free herself of him and at the same time sink deeper into his toils. Yet, obsessed as they were, determined to hear more, to hear everything about their monster, their Philip, they nonetheless found time to steal glances at each other.

In the high-ceilinged room, sitting at a long table, the girl's spoon poking at wobbling lucid squares of jello she couldn't eat, they were an island of intense conspiracy in a cafeteria half full of other students chatting or reading over cold cups of coffee. A dark oil portrait of a retired professor hung in dimmed gilt on a panelled wall. Below, a cashier sat behind a register, its chrome paw noisily sliding coins to people in line.

They compared notes and out of them pieced together Philip's movements on a particular Wednesday or a subsequent Monday. Hours she had been certain Philip was spending with Maria she now found had been devoted quite innocently to Dan; appointments Philip had told Dan he must keep with nameless professors were now reassigned to this girl.

"I've got to leave him," Philip's girlfriend said without conviction.

"Yes, you must," Dan replied, equally reluctant to have her lose touch with Philip. "Why has he dropped me?"

"There's only one more thing," the woman said, ignoring his question. "I'd love to meet Maria."

Philip's friend bought two paintings for five hundred dollars each. Maria was shocked at all that money and tried to talk her patron down, but the young woman kept writing and didn't look up from her checkbook; she had a surprisingly experienced way of settling and dismissing money matters. "Well, here, take this sketch, at least, as a present," Maria insisted, following her to the door. The woman was so beautiful; Maria felt like the citizen of an underprivileged country meeting her first American.

"Alexandra Jones," Maria said, reading the name on the check. "Where did you find her?" Dan made up an answer. "I think I like her—she knows a lot about painting. She makes me look at my work more seriously. I keep forgetting painting is something people buy, study, argue about, display in their houses, write books about. Of course they make the same fuss over cooking. There's nothing especially evil about selling a painting. That's two hundred and fifty dollars a month as a salary, which is reasonable. The paintings didn't hurt me; they won't hurt her. Harmless. But terribly wrong. With my parents' ill-gotten gains I had the time to stuff my head full of notions about "being creative." And I was able to pick up avant-garde tricks, and imitate the latest fads—and she, with precisely the same education, can decode the signs and recognize the fads."

Dan hated it when Maria despised her art, her sacred art. Art linked them. They were both artists. And she was a genius! He was certain of that. Besides this Marxist talk made him uneasy; maybe that peeping Tom was really a government agent.

She was pacing around in long strides, puffing her cigarette, both the engineer and the engine. "Of course what I hate about my art is that it's so damn difficult and elitist. But maybe"—she stopped still and smiled, as though wakened from a bad dream—"maybe I'm painting for the masses of a hundred years from now."

Dan couldn't grasp the theory, but he approved of anything that reconciled her to her sublime art. "Yes. Precisely. But aren't we being children?" He was using the polite *we* since in fact he was speaking only about her. "Scaring ourselves with bogeyman stories? There's a morbid thrill to be had from saying art is worthless, but you care about it, you know you care."

"I could be just as passionate about knitting."

Dan frowned. "I promise never to repeat what you just said. Someday you'll be ranked with Rothko."

"I won't," Maria said. "But take Rothko, for example. I'm no dummy, I can see he's the great painter of the day, but so what? If someone is hungry, or has a toothache, or is about to murder his wife, will a Rothko bring him any relief or pleasure or divert him from evil? No painting, for instance, can ever bring you as much pleasure as this kiss." And with that, she put her arms around him and kissed him deeply. He was delighted and shocked by her unexpected conclusion to the argument. He felt her body shaking under his hands with suppressed laughter; finally her mouth bubbled over with hilarity, but he didn't release her lips. They were toying with each other, toying with their affections, they were toys, yet animated ones, and even though it was broad daylight, even though his brain was still racing with points he wanted to make, even though they were laughing and tickling each other, rolling on the floor, he was sexually aroused, as was she. Their sobbing laughter changed to sobbing pleasure; he wasn't quite sure when the one became the other. Ordinarily their lovemaking was tender, exalted, poetic, but because it existed in such dim, romantic light he (and she, too, he suspected) would worry that the lights might not be adjusted properly for the next encounter. But now they were still half-dressed, they were not even in the bedroom, strong sunlight rendered every line and blemish, and they had come to sex not down the stained glass aisle of supper and soulful talk but rather through an argument about ideas in the middle of the day. Like all lovers they had worked up, without discussion, a repertory of sexual practices, limited by their inexperience, inspired by daring and sentiment, governed by a strong but unrecognized sense of propriety. Always every kiss or caress had been a metaphor for an emotion, and making love had been sign language between lovers. Now, however, love was at best an excuse for sex; sex itself expressed all the meanings they wanted to know about. They were speechless when they disentangled themselves and, still breathing hard, looked up and saw the peeping Tom across the street watching them.

Alex came back with a van and an expert mover of art objects; the mover was an Australian with rope-burned hands and hair the color of wet straw but the texture of dry. Dan wandered about and watched the women and the mover, a retired sailor, fit the paintings into solid wood cases. "This is house paint, Miss," the mover informed Alex, pointing to part of one canvas. "Doesn't stick for long and when it cracks, it cracks in circles. And this here's charcoal; it'll smudge unless we spray it."

Dan was offended by the man's remarks, but Maria wasn't; treating art as a craft, even if one she practised badly, fitted in perfectly with her disgust with estheticism. In fact, Maria asked him to look at another painting that she'd kept rolled up for more than a year but now wanted to stretch without damaging it. A long technical discussion ensued in which Alex took as active a part as the other two. It finally came out that Alex was a sculptor, studying at the Art Institute.

"Come by my studio if you get a chance," Alex told Maria. Dan waited for Maria politely to decline, but to his surprise she took down Alex's address and phone number.

"Cultivating a customer?" he asked when they were alone. Maria didn't answer him. She made much of being busy the rest of the day.

The two women spent long hours in Alex's studio working, talking, modeling for each other (drawing from life was something Maria had never been interested in doing before). Dan would catch her sitting on the floor surrounded by sketches of Alex—Alex as Olympia, Alex as an odalisque, Alex bathing, smoking, sprawling in a wicker chair, Alex *sur l'herbe* minus bearded men friends. The first and the second batch of sketches seemed to pick poses out of the air at random; the third, fourth, fifth batches kept returning to Alex's face, closer and closer, as though dollying in on it, and to a certain expression: a firm, masculine stare at the viewer and a smile, like Maria's, that was either very sophisticated or very simple. A complex smile, which both invited and held at an ironic distance whatever tribute you might care to offer her.

Philip Diamondstein stopped seeing Alex. He dropped her as capriciously as he'd dropped Dan. In New York later and even much later, they kept expecting Philip to turn up. Everyone comes to New York eventually and there all stories, no matter where they might have started, end or begin again. But they never heard so much as a word about him, and Maria at last concluded he was a god disguised as a cad whose only earthly mission had been to bring them together.

Alex built a big easel out of heavy oak and with the art mover's help they installed it in Maria's and Dan's apartment. Every night for a week the women attended a festival of post-war Italian films ("All the actors were amateurs!"

Maria exclaimed triumphantly. "And the director was obviously *engagé*"—using the vogue word of the early fifties). Maria began to wear eyeshadow again, green by day and blue by night, although her clothes were as simple as ever— sneakers, black jeans and a white blouse: the "nun of art," as she called herself, whooping with laughter. One morning as she was dressing and preparing to go to Alex's, she dispensed with the blouse and her bra and slipped into one of Dan's t-shirts. Tossing her bra into a drawer she laughed and said, "Who am I kidding? I'm about as busty as a nine-year-old boy."

If Dan had coffee with the women he felt he was an intruder and bravely hurried them on their way; they seemed grateful to be let off so easily. He reread the Lotus Sutra. Maria began to talk about their spending the summer together in an art colony in Michigan—"All three of us," she hastened to add.

Alex called him "Daniello;" she must have learned the nickname from Maria. Dan didn't really mind. He sensed they were superior to him, were his beautiful and wise sisters. They teased him about talking so much and about exaggerating, but the fun was affectionate and, taking turns, they assured him he was the most intelligent, generous and sensitive man alive.

After working late one night Maria fell asleep in her clothes on the cot in her studio outside the bedroom door; the second night she did the same; before the third night she'd put sheets on the cot.

And yet he was satisfied. He sometimes wondered how long his contentment would last, but he didn't want to question it too closely. Like a Byzantine ruler watching his empire shrink, he couldn't bestir himself as long as he held on to Constantinople, and for him enjoying Maria's even occasional companionship was what mattered and he could surrender her time to Alex, perhaps even her love. They didn't discuss love. They didn't discuss their feelings at all or the shift that was occurring in their friendship.

"Daniello," Maria said one morning as she was painting at home. "This thing isn't working with us. I want you to move out; Alex is going to move in."

Dan was shocked, but his shock was quickly absorbed in what seemed the more important issue: how to conduct himself. Not that he wanted to make a good impression. No, he simply was in search of a style for pain. It never occurred to him to argue his case with her, to attempt to win her back. "What went wrong?" he asked, touching his soiled shirt collar, as though that were what had gone wrong.

"It's very simple. You like men and I like women."

He started to laugh at the bald absurdity, but then he realized her few words described perfectly everything he had been seeing peripherally for so long through averted eyes: his involvement with Philip Diamondstein; his restlessness with her; her attachment to Alex; even his masturbation fantasies, in which a man made love to a woman (so far so good) but in which he kept watching the man (not so good). And so he did not resist her verdict; it was as though they'd flown for hours over a vast and varied ocean and she had named it all with the single word, *Pacific*. He asked, "Are you angry with me?"

"Yes. Because you left me alone so much. I accuse you of gross neglect."

They sat in silence for a while. He thought of a new episode for his novel, *Revulsion*. Then he began to agonize out loud and at length over their terrible illness, their homosexuality, but she indicated that for her it was a subject that could not be discussed. Talking about it was a deviation from her high standards of what grown-ups can say to one another. Her reserve had always been strong, selective and active, a force that imposed silence on topics not consonant with her elegant personal style. He wanted to lament their disease; she wanted to express her resentment.

But resentment is irrelevant, she thought, and smiled at him. "You couldn't help it," she said. "We like each other so much we imagined we were in love. We knew we weren't just friends so we assumed we must be lovers. If not A then B. But there is a C—call it passionate friends. That's what we are."

Tragic Event

by John F. Gilgun

I HAD BEEN BACK in town less than a week when Byron Lewis phoned me at my mother's place, where I was staying. "Hey, Wim! Wimlo!" he said, using a nickname I hadn't heard in seven years. "Good to have you back. Thought you'd moved to San Francisco for good. Say, old buddy, we're having a pig roast out here on the river bank next Sunday. Can you come?"

"I can come," I answered, excited by the idea.

My mother was in the room, drinking coffee. "That Byron!" she said, after I'd hung up. "He's living in a cabin out there on the river with another one of them young girls he finds. The girls get younger, but Byron gets older. How old is he now, thirty?"

"He's twenty-nine. Same age as myself. You know that."

"Well, he's a scandal. But then, he always was an odd one," she said.

"He's no odder than most," I answered. "And a lot less odd than some."

Myself for instance. What I mean is, I had just done an odd thing—given up a fairly good job in San Francisco after seven years to return to the town where I was born. It's a fact of life that gay males born in small Midwestern towns like this one get out in their teens and twenties or they die inside, and I had gotten out, found the city where I was really meant to live and settled down. But now I was back here! Why?

My mother was staring at me with a look that was hard to decipher. "It takes some people a long time to find themselves," she said. "And it looks like it's going to take Byron Lewis forever."

The following Sunday I drove out along the river to Byron's cabin. It wasn't much of a place, but it was perfect for what Byron did, that is, commit himself to the art of enjoying himself. I had forgotten about pig roasts, not having been to any in the seven years I'd lived in San Francisco, but there it all was, spread out along the river bank under the cottonwood trees, just as I remembered it—the suckling pig turning on the motorized spit, the kegs of beer, the scruffy guests (good old boys and their women) milling around. Byron Lewis, as the only son of K.W. Lewis, owner of the only factory in town, surrounded himself with the dregs of our town's society. It was his way of asserting himself, of rebelling. But he worked for his father, so the strings were always around him, holding him in. I parked my car behind a pickup truck and sat there watching. Byron was not in the crowd and I knew no one there. Also, I had to psyche myself up for the encounter. The distance in time was so great and I had gone through so many changes.

And, of course, the distance in time since I'd first met Byron was even greater. It was, in fact, my whole conscious life, since we'd met in grade school and been friends ever since. That kind of friendship is a matter of cells —brain cells, I mean. Byron was just always around, influencing me, even, in a sense, *creating* me, like the brother I never had. If that sounds sentimental, I don't mean it to be. It's just a fact. I never had a brother, or a father either (my father left my mother when I was six months old), so Byron became that brother and, by extension, his father, K.W., was a father surrogate for me. I've loved Byron all my life, but I have to point out that when we were growing up together we did not have sex. During all those years, through all those camping trips, overnight hikes, skinny-dipping swimming parties and beer busts, we never had sex. Byron was my roommate for a year and a half at State (after he had managed to flunk out of a big-name Eastern college), and I knew about myself by then, but it never happened. Byron has always had a girl, some appendage of himself, some shield. I've never known anyone who seems to need this protection more than Byron, which is a way of saying I have never known anyone more afraid of being called gay. And the girls are always available, for Byron is good looking. He's also rich. That's a cliche, but every town has a Byron—the son of a rich man who can be "a scandal" and get away with it simply because of his name. In our part of the world, the young prince still has his privileges.

As I got out of my car, I saw him, moving up from the boat landing, barefoot, shirtless and wearing cut-offs. A girl was walking beside him. "Wim," he shouted, when he saw me. And then there we were, facing each other again after seven years. In San Francisco we'd have hugged at that moment, perhaps even kissed, but here I settled for the smile and the light punch on the shoulder. That he was happy to see me was something he communicated with his eyes. Eye contact is allowed if it doesn't go on too long.

"Are you back for good now?" he asked.

"Yes," I said. "I'm taking over that weekly paper my uncle runs. He wants to retire."

"Well, good. Let's plan a fishing trip. You still like to fish? Hey, have you done white-water canoeing? I'm into that. We could go down the Osage. It's great."

The girl merely stood there, saying nothing, during this exchange. When I finally looked at her, I knew I'd seen her somewhere before. Of course, in seven years . . . Byron did not introduce her, however. Instead he said, "Wim, you got here just in time. The Snowbird and I were just about to go up the river in the boat. C'mon." So he called her "The Snowbird," but I'd be damned if I'd address her as that.

It was only later, when we were actually in the boat and on the river, that Byron shouted, over the roar of the motor (which he had open at full throttle), "You two know each other. Carla was in the choral group the year you taught music in the high school." I had taught in the local high school the year before I went to San Francisco. It had been the worst year of my life. But now I remembered her.

"Carla . . . Carla *Wray*. Right?" I said.

"Right. You remember."

"Sure. You were good." She had, in fact, won prizes in state competitions. "You were *very* good."

She didn't reply to this, but she gave me a vague smile. It was impossible to carry on a conversation over the noise of the motor, while bouncing along over the choppy water. With part of my mind I was calculating the distance to shore and wondering how cold the water was. I'm a good swimmer and I knew I could make it to shore if the boat capsized, but I wondered how long a man could stay alive in that water.

Then Byron shouted into her ear, "I want you to take the wheel, honey. I have to go back and adjust the motor.

"Oh, no," she answered. "I don't know how."

"There's nothing to it. Just hold it steady."

"Oh, no. Please. Let Mr. Simmons do it. I don't want to!"

"Baby, you've got to learn. You'll need to operate the boat this summer."

It was an odd feeling, being called "Mr. Simmons." If I'd stayed on at the high school that's what I'd have become—"Mr. Simmons," a fussy bachelor teaching Chorus and Band, whose nervous stomach jumped whenever he walked by the "boy's room."

She took the wheel and Byron crawled past me to the back of the boat, where he did something to the motor. We slowed down to a reasonable speed. It wasn't much of a boat, but that was part of Byron's pose, like the scruffy friends and the roast suckling pig. He could have owned a better one if he'd wanted that.

"Adjusted the throttle," he explained, as he crawled back. He brushed against me. The thought flashed across my mind, "Sunlight on a basket of peaches!" Yes, that's how I thought of his body in my younger, romantic days. And it was an accurate image for that blonde skin. And he *did* look sexy in those cut-offs. Carla moved over and he took the wheel. "Start looking for the channel marker," he told her. Then, turning to me, he said, "Wim, we found this fantastic place. It's a sand bar—a quarter of a mile of pure white sand. We're going to live there this summer, away from everything and everybody. You'll love it!"

And I did, from the moment I saw it, glistening there in the sunlight, like the island in the movie *Blue Lagoon*. Ducks went up as we neared it and I realized that they must be ready to hatch out their offspring. A few saplings had sprung

37

up and beavers had gnawed at some of them. It was untouched, unspoiled. I knew that only Byron could have found it and only Byron could have dreamed up the idea of living on it over a summer. As he was beaching the boat, I talked to Carla. "What did you do in California?" she asked.

"Worked for a newspaper," I answered. I did not tell her that it was a gay one.

"I thought you might have been a teacher out there."

"No. What are you doing now?"

"Nothing. I have a B.A. in Music Education. I applied for a job in the school system here, but they gave it to someone else. They're so narrow. They thought my hair was too long."

"Why didn't you cut it?" I asked.

She looked at me as though the answer was obvious, that is, that your individuality was more important than any silly little job. She was young and her vulnerability touched me, which doesn't mean that I liked her. As for her talent, her voice . . . I decided not to ask her about it. I was afraid she'd answer, "I didn't enter any more contests after high school." Or, "I let it slide." Or even, "Why bother?"

After Byron came up from the boat, he rolled a joint and passed it to me. It was like going back ten years in time—the clandestine, "Now we're getting away with something" feeling of it, I mean. I almost explained, "I'm not into grass now," but in the end I took it, drew on it and passed it to Carla. What I was experiencing was the time lapse factor in small towns. Things move so slowly in small towns that fads which surfaced and then died back years ago in urban centers are still going strong here. I felt a kind of temporal disorientation. I was twenty-nine. I was nineteen. It was 1978. It was 1968. Byron was a kid. Byron was a man pushing thirty. I realized that, until I adjusted to the place, I'd be living concurrently in three or four different time periods. And there, on the sand bar, we were back in the 19th Century, in the frontier era of George Caleb Bingham, who painted this river hundreds of times.

But there was a kind of simple-minded happiness in being there, sitting on that white sand under those saplings, watching the sunlight on the water. I say simple-minded because to maintain your happiness you had to cancel out most of the facts of human existence, like birth, death, pain, disease . . . "We're going to live up here over the summer," Byron said. "I've got a tent, a Coleman stove, even a chemical toilet. I want you to spend time up here too, Wim, as much time as you can. It's going to be great."

I glanced at Carla to see what she thought of this, but she was indifferent. It occurred to me that Byron had allied himself with a girl so spiritless she didn't care about anything. Suddenly I could write the whole script. It was all there in the act of passing the joint to me before he passed it to Carla. I saw Byron and myself fishing, drinking wine, smoking grass and being "good buddies" together while Carla sat by the tent staring into space. It was a situation I'd have fled instantly in San Francisco, but here it was likely to be the only game in town.

I did not have the strength at that moment to say no.

I came back home for so many reasons that it took me some time to sort them out and decide that none of them made sense. First, my mother was ill and I felt an obligation toward her. I knew though that her "heart condition" would respond to medication and that she could conceivably outlive me. Then, taking over my uncle's paper seemed to offer a chance to be independent at a moment when I had come to the conclusion that my job on the gay paper wasn't leading anywhere. I must have known, however, that I was not designed by nature to run a country weekly. What did I have in common with the people! And finally, I had broken up with my lover of five years, and suddenly San Francisco seemed impersonal—brutally indifferent to me, really—and complex. I developed a foolish nostalgia for what I remembered as the friendly, uncomplicated relationships in my home town. Once I was back I realized the mistake I'd made. Civilization began with man's impulse to construct cities like San Francisco as a defense against the intolerable, cramping complexities of small towns. You can take all the friendly, uncomplicated relationships in every small town in America, stuff them into a flea's navel and still have room for the Revised Standard Version of the Holy Bible. But once I was back, I found I couldn't get out. I was trapped.

When I wasn't trying to save the weekly, which was failing, or fulfilling what I still felt was an obligation to my mother, I was with Byron. And that was a "time lapse" thing too, of course—two men our age, both unmarried, drinking together, fishing on weekends, driving around together. And we drove around endlessly, because that's what "boys" do in small towns, consume gasoline and whiskey while driving around on country roads. When they graduate from being "boys" to being "men" they don't drive around together any more. They sit at home with their wives and watch television.

My friendship with Byron couldn't go unnoticed or uncommented upon. After I left my mother's place and took an apartment of my own, Byron was there three or four nights a week. It was the sort of situation that could become sticky. Byron could get away with anything as long as it involved women, but spending time with me was something else again. There was a lot of hatred in town against the Lewis family, since it appears to be human nature to hate the man who employs you, and I knew it had to surface. Our relationship was not sexual, but it was a dry season for gossip, and people were ready to seize on anything. Sometimes Carla was with us, but that made it a threesome, which was even worse. I lived on a working class street and many times I caught the looks on the faces of the people sitting on their porches as we three left for the movies or a bar. Yet Byron was able to ignore it. Perhaps he was unaware of it.

And Byron was living on that sandbar. He used to commute down the river to the landing and then drive to his father's plant, but he had more or less closed up his cabin in favor of his tent. I never spent the night up there, though Byron begged me to do it. I thought it prudent to refuse, because of the gossip in town. I suppose I'm alive today because I never took him up on his invitations. I don't remember if he asked me to stay with them on the night of the tragedy. But now I see that I have come to a place where I will have to write about that.

We had a period of clear, dry weather in June, after a severe winter (the worst in history, people claimed) and a spring that was late in coming. So when that good weather arrived, people let their guard down and began to enjoy it. The atmosphere in town became almost festive and I found myself reporting on a lot of strawberry socials and sunday school picnics for the paper. However, in our part of the world good weather almost always ends with torrential rains, tornadoes and floods. I think this has a lot to do with the religious outlook of the people, which is Calvinistic and focussed obsessively on Hell. Anyway, it ended just that way, with a cataclysmic storm roaring out of the southwest during which the wind gusted to seventy miles per hour, nine inches of rain fell and the river rose until it went over its banks in places.

Byron and Carla were swept off their sandbar. Byron, caught up in the branches of a fallen tree, was hurt, but he survived. Carla, carried down the river in the darkness (the storm struck at two in the morning), was killed. Her body wasn't found until two days later, on the bank near a little town on the Kansas side. The river had carried her twenty-five miles downstream before it deposited her there.

Terrible things happen to people and you hear about them and you think, "That's really tragic." And you get the tragic feeling, as if someone had brushed a cold knife over the back of your neck. But you know too that with billions of people on the earth, someone is dying somewhere every second. But that thought is no help. An individual human being you've known, a person whose life was tied up with your own in some way, is dead, and you're alive, alive and aware of the inevitability of death. So you tremble at the touch of that knife. The morning after the storm there was no electricity on our street and tree limbs were down everywhere. As I was leaving for the office, Mr. Roskey, my next door neighbor, leaned over the porch railing and said, "A girl was drowned last night on the river during the storm." And I did not connect this with Carla until my uncle gave me her name for the story we would have to print in the paper. I remember that I said, "My God, my God!" And my uncle said, "You knew her."

There was a hearing, of course, and the finding was that Carla, while camping out, had died by drowning during a cloudburst. Byron had done all he could to save her ("All that was humanly possible," the members of the committee decided), but, caught up in the branches of that tree, thrashing around in rampaging water in the pitch darkness . . . Well, you get the picture. There were people in town who grumbled, saying that no member of the Lewis family could ever be convicted of anything in that town. They wanted a charge of criminal negligence brought against him. But how could negligence have been proven? No storm had been predicted. And no precautions could have prevented what happened.

    I did not see Byron for several weeks after the accident. I heard that he had gone out of town. I doubted that and suspected that he was in seclusion in his father's house but, at any rate, he didn't come by to see me. On the morning of the day I heard about Carla's death, I went home during the lunch hour and wept. Men shouldn't weep. It's a sign of weakness. You learn that by the time you enter grade school. But I wept, as much for the living—that is, for Byron—as for the dead. My apartment had thin walls, so I'm sure the Roskey family heard me. I'm pretty sure it got back to my mother because, one night as we were sitting in her back yard drinking lemonade, she said, "William, whatever it is, it isn't worth this. I don't know what brought you back from California, but it isn't working out. You're unhappy here. This is no place for you. It never was and it never will be. If you came back because you thought I needed you, you can see now that I don't. Why don't you go back to San Francisco where you can be happy?"

    "Someone else might need me," I said.

    "Your uncle doesn't need you. He told me himself he thinks the paper has served its purpose. It's losing money. Why not just publish a final edition and forget about it?"

    "I'm not thinking about Uncle Jim," I answered. But I didn't go any further.

    A long silence followed. Then my mother said, "When I was a child I thought as a child, but now that I am a man I have put away childish things." Her tone was bitterly sarcastic. When she saw that I wasn't going to reply— what could I say?—she gathered up the pitcher of lemonade and the two glasses and went inside. I heard the hook lock snap on her side of the screen door. With that symbolic gesture she shut me out of her home and out of her life for good. It was ten days till my thirtieth birthday.

    One afternoon, after a difficult day at work, I stopped at the Muny Tavern for a cold beer. As I stepped out of that blinding summer heat into the air conditioned darkness of the bar, I saw Byron sitting in a booth by the pool table alone. What can I say? I was touched by pity for him, and by love, but I realized at the same time that he was a fool, perhaps the biggest fool I've ever known. Only fools defy time, trying to remain a thing of beauty and a boy forever. Only fools find romantic sand bars, ignoring the fact that death dwells in such places. But love was stronger than common sense, so I sat down across from him, touched the back of his hand and said what any man would say under the circumstances, "Byron, I'm sorry."

He took my hand and squeezed it very, very hard. He did not look at me. Nor did he say anything. When he finally took his hand away I could see the marks of his fingers on my skin. When the waitress came over, I ordered a beer, but Byron said, "Bring me a shot of bar whiskey. Then, when you see that I've finished it, bring me another. Keep bringing them until you can see that I don't need them any more. Then just bring me beer."

The waitress was an attractive young woman. I was watching her face as Byron gave his order and I felt that I could read her thoughts. They were, "Good looking man." Don't let anyone tell you that gay men don't understand women. They understand them too well.

After Byron had finished the first of the whiskeys he said, "You know, I haven't talked to anyone about it since it happened."

"You could have come to me."

"You have troubles of your own . . . Yes, you're right. I should have done that. That's what you do when something like this happens. You go to your best friend. My family doesn't understand. But why should I cry on your shoulder?"

"Because human beings weren't meant to suffer through these things on their own," I said. "I mean, what are friends for? And we've been friends for twenty years."

"More than that. More than twenty years. And you're right. What are friends for?"

There are some thoughts you should never admit into consciousness, because once they reveal themselves you can never view yourself in the same light again. At that moment, while expressing those noble sentiments about friendship, it came to me with exceptional clarity that with Carla gone Byron would have to come to me, and that I was glad she had died.

I knocked over my glass of beer. In the confusion that followed—with the waitress rushing over to mop it up with a bar rag and Byron standing to brush it off his trousers—I heard myself say, "Look, I'm sorry. I just remembered something. I have to go. Call me tomorrow."

But Byron's eyes said, "I'm lost. I have no one else. Don't go." It was a look like the one my lover in San Francisco had given me before he said, "I love you and I know I'm doing a terrible thing by leaving you, but I can't help myself." I believe that when we're driven by these forces—by these terrors really, these inner demons—we know the real meaning of being human. But what a damnable thing it is to be human. I sat down. Byron said, "Bring two more beers and another shot of whiskey, Mary, please." Then, after she had left, he said, in a low, husky voice, almost apologetically, "Wim, put up with me tonight for my sake. I have to get blind drunk. It's like I have a cyst inside myself and it has to be broken. I haven't been able to feel anything since they pulled me into the boat that morning. I'm just like a stone inside. And when I get so drunk I can't see straight, drive me home."

"To your father's place?"

"No. Not there. I can't let him see me drunk."

"Not out to the cabin?"

"No, oh God, no. Not out there. Take me back to your place. Let me sleep on the floor. I'm afraid of waking up alone. I don't know what I'll do if I wake up alone. Please."

The implication was that he would kill himself. That was communicated to me so vividly, I shuddered. "I'll do that. Sure," I said. Out of the corner of my eye I watched the bar filling up with men and I knew that death was at the center of each of their lives. It was there and they fled from it, as all human beings must, with trivialities. It's easy to despise people, particularly small town people, for their cramped and limited lives, but the gossip, the backbiting, the waste of human potential, what is it except a defense against the knowledge of death! And though I had just admitted to myself that I didn't give a damn for Carla, that I was in fact selfish and cold in an inhuman way, I didn't despise those men at that moment. I understood them. I was one of them, after all. And while I could not forgive myself for what I felt (or failed to feel), I forgave them.

"Thank you," Byron said.

I want to make this clear. When I woke from a deep sleep at five o'clock the next morning, conscious of the fact that someone was standing by my bed (the primitive part of the brain awake and wary, while every other element in the organism sleeps) and that it was Byron, I did not reach up and pull him down toward me. He reached down, placed his arms around me and drew me up toward him. I had wanted this all my life and now that it was happening I felt that I'd bought it at a price no human being should ever be asked to pay. Had I been fully awake, perhaps . . . No, I would never have turned him away. And he had had to overcome the deepest inhibitions of his life to reach down and touch me. That's why he was shaking all over. "Listen, Byron," I whispered. "This is right. What you feel is right. Forget about what other people have told you. I'm your friend and this is right."

"I know it's right," he answered. "I've always known that."

So I took him. Or rather, we took each other. And what can I say now except that it had been a long time coming and that it was satisfactory. How could it have been otherwise?

Afterwards he said, "We could have done this any time in the past fifteen years."

"Would it have changed anything?" I asked.

"You might not have gone to California," he said.

"Nothing could have kept me from that."

"Then what would have changed?"

"You might have come with me."

"Yes," he said. "I might have done that."

"It's not too late. We could do it now."

"Yes, we could," he answered, turning over. "We could do that."

"I mean, what does this town have to offer you, really? How do you see yourself in ten years if you stay here?"

He was thinking. "I'd have to get married. She'll have to have money, too. My father will cut me off if I don't get married. I can't play around for the rest of my life."

"But how do you see that marriage?"

"Terrible. Oh, terrible. Being tied to one woman for the rest of my life, to someone I don't love."

"A relationship based on property values," I said. "I . . . I can't let that happen to you. Come to San Francisco with me. It's beautiful there. We'll get a place on a hill with a view of the bay. If you've never seen it, you can't imagine how beautiful it is in San Francisco."

"Yes, I've heard it's beautiful there." He was drifting off to sleep. "I could get a job. I've had experience working with my father. Yes, I could. I could go there. Yes."

It was the last word he spoke before he fell asleep.

When I woke at midmorning, in a room full of summer sunlight, Byron was gone. He had not left a note. Nor did he phone in the next few days.

Suddenly I was thirty, too old to be suffering through what I had begun to suffer through. I could not forget that at my moment of climax with Byron a line of poetry had moved through my mind: "I desire my dust to be mingled with yours forever and forever and forever. Why should I climb the look out?" I was fifteen years too old for that kind of sentiment. But the emotion had been real. I couldn't deny it. What had always been a matter of brain cells—that is, of Byron's influence on my whole mental life—was now a matter of body cells. Mind, body and spirit, I seemed to belong to him. It was time to get out of town.

I told Uncle Jim that the paper had died years ago and that the only decent thing to do was to bury it. He seemed relieved. I had given him permission to do what he had wanted to do anyway. Now he could retire with a clear conscience. Then I went to my mother and we were reconciled. "I'll miss you," she said. "But I'd rather have you alive eighteen hundred miles away than six feet underground half a mile from here in Woodlawn Memorial Cemetery. Besides, I can come out there to visit you. I hear it's a beautiful city."

"There's no more beautiful city in the world," I told her, as I kissed her on the cheek. And that was our goodbye.

There was only one thing left to do and, though I hated myself for it, I did it. The day before I was to leave for California I drove out to Byron's cabin to offer one last plea. He had moved back to the cabin after a disagreement with his father. I knew this from town gossip, not from Byron himself. I had not heard from Byron since the night he shared my bed. His disagreement with his father had been a serious one and some people said that his father was going to disinherit him (though how they knew this I never determined).

I parked in the same place I had parked in three months earlier, though there were no pickup trucks there now, no roast suckling pig turning on a spit in the yard. The river was still the same, the glacial clay on the bank still as dark and terrible as ever. For the rest of my life the idea of that clay will be associated in my mind with death. I got out of the car and walked through the heat haze toward the cabin. The sunlight reflected off the river struck my eyes like a fist.

Byron was not in the yard, though one of those plastic and aluminum lawn chairs with a book open on it indicated that he wasn't far away. A glass of red wine with melting ice cubes in it was on the ground beside the chair. I can't pass by an open book without reading the title. The title of this one was *Self Direction: How to Change Your Life in Six Months Through Therapy*. I went to the door and knocked.

It was opened by a girl I'd never seen before, a dark haired girl wearing shorts and a halter. She had a small, cute mouth and perfect teeth. You could see that when she smiled, as she did immediately. "Byron's not here," she said. "He went into town for a few hours. But he'll be back soon. Do you want to come in and wait?" So the wine and the book belonged to the girl.

I could see cardboard boxes piled up behind her. They contained records, books and clothes. I had stepped into the middle of a moving day. So, I thought, Byron is moving out and this girl is moving in. Well, anyone could have predicted it. Hadn't he told me himself that he couldn't bear the thought of coming back here after what had happened to Carla? After the argument with his father, he had had nowhere else to go, but now he was moving, perhaps even taking the ultimate step and getting out of town for good. Perhaps the heat had sapped my reason, but I couldn't see the truth of the situation even as it stood there staring me in the face.

"Does Byron need help moving?" I asked.

"Moving?" she answered. Then she glanced around at the boxes. "Oh, moving! Well, it's just a matter of taking my things out of the boxes and arranging them on the shelves and in the closets. I can do that myself. But why don't you come in and wait. Byron's been gone since nine-thirty and he promised to be back for lunch."

"Oh, you're moving *in*," I said. I felt like a fool, and it was the right way to feel, since that's what I was.

"What? Oh, yes. I brought my things in Friday. I just haven't unpacked. You see, yesterday we had some people over and . . . I don't think I know you. You're not . . . You're not someone his father sent out, are you?"

Since I couldn't think of anything to say, I turned my back on her and walked away across the yard. She came out of the house and followed me.

"Who should I tell him was here?" she asked. She was beginning to plead. I really had her worried.

I opened my car door and slid inside. The plastic seat cover burned through my trousers into my skin. I had foolishly parked in the sun.

She was beside the car. "Look, mister, if you're going to make trouble!" Her hand was on the door. I felt suddenly sorry for her, as one can only feel sorry for the victim who's about to experience the same torture you've just managed to endure. "No, no trouble," I told her. "His father didn't send me. I'm on my way to San Francisco and I stopped by to say goodbye. Just tell him that. He'll know who it was. Tell him I can't cope with this small town life. It's too complex for me. Tell him I'm going to a place where human relationships are simple. 'Wham, bam! Thank you, man!' And that, sweetheart, is it!"

"How can I tell him that?" she cried. "I can't remember all that."

"Then just tell him I said, 'Kiss off, buddy! Kiss off!' "

And I drove away, spinning my tires over the hard baked clay . . . Three days later I was still driving. I had reached that point twenty miles from the Nevada-California border where the desert gives way to the first pines of the Sierras. I stopped my car, got out, scratched away the brown, resinous needles with the toe of my boot, knelt and kissed the warm, dry, infinitely pungent California earth. I was home, home at least, and this time, oh *this* time, for good.

Black Memory

by David Watmough

IT IS ONE OF THOSE days when Manhattan quartz gleams hard to the eye, when the wind wins a battle and dismisses the smog but the sun loses out against the February cold. A healthy day, though, with a champagne tingle under the skyscrapers' keen shadows—so that the shoes of women shoppers tap briskly along sidewalks and it looks, for once, as if all New York loves work, and is geared to high-pitched efficiency.

It's eleven o'clock, though, and I've walked about in it feeling good for a couple of hours. Now I'm sitting slouched in a Choc-Full-Of-Nuts sipping coffee, the euphoria slowly evaporating.

For one thing, whether I like work or not, I don't have any. I have money —two hundred bucks, freshly drawn from the Poughkeepsie Savings & Loan— but no job. Nor do I have a place to stay. Since riding the Greyhound down to the city I've been at the 'Y'. And I suppose I can stay on there for a while. But it isn't what I wanted.

The dreams, (if that's what you call a vague fantasy occurring every now and then over the past few months) were of a smart paying job—I didn't really care what—and a nice little bijou place down in the Village. Then, you see, I'm all of twenty-three and *very* naive . . .

How naive should be clear a few minutes from now. Coffee drunk, waitress indifferent, a rather smelly man at the counter next to me, I slip off the mushroom, pay, and stand out in the sunny cold again.

Where to go? What to do? Done the U.N., the Metropolitan, the Frick, and shivered in the shade of the Rockefeller Center—all in the space of two days. I'm bored with culture, tired of following up job ads in The Times that end in dingy offices and frostiness over my British accent. (This was pre-Beatle, by the way, when all the English were snobs and strictly irrelevant to the American scene.)

One place still on my list of places to be visited is the Bronx Zoo. That and the Empire State Building I had heard of, even on the farm, growing up in faraway Cornwall.

The skyscraper hadn't particularly impressed, but I was still hankering after visiting the zoo with its animals—as subconscious antidote, perhaps, to the animal-less 42nd Street I had just reached. If I walked towards Grand Central

47

Station, I told myself, I could take the subway directly to the zoo in the suburbs.

The aura of busy people, intent upon their activities in the steely resilience of this winter's day, petered out by the time I got to Times Square and turned east towards the great station.

Amid the gaudy dreck of eternally open cinemas, midnight cowboys screwed up their eyes in resentment of daylight: pasty faces above upturned collars hung about frosty doorways. I felt quick glances searching me out— then their owners tarrying . . .

If it weren't for the sprinkling of ashen-skinned, blond haired men amid the posses of foot-stamping (but dallying) Negroes, this sudden escape from the Protestant work-ethic ethos of Fifth Avenue and the Fifties I'd just left behind, I might've thought I was in somnolent South America, or even parts of the Mediterranean, in its motiveless indolence.

This street was new to me. Alien. Just a little scarey maybe. But even so, I felt a particle of my tension slacken as I walked the *louche* length of 42nd, amid throngs of my fellow-unemployed.

Someone in England had recently written a book about the outsider—but that had been head stuff: grand ideas requiring massive reading from Dante to Dostoyevsky, for comprehension. The kind of outsider I felt now, walking this gimcrack street with my fellows, was quite different. In fact, this style of outsidering involved the opposite of effort. All of us, I reflected, as I sauntered vaguely towards Grand Central Station, black men and white and the infinite variations of complexion that New York uniquely offers, all of us walking as slowly as I am, without concrete objective, (it was too early in the day for serious whores or prostitutes), are living outside the contoured existence of the millions. And I liked the notion as it took shape in me. 'Alleluia,' I told the inside of my head (though not without a certain self-consciousness) 'Alleluia, I'm a bum with the rest of them.'

True, as I walked past the New York Public Library, a different image crept suddenly under my skull and caused me to quicken step a trifle. It was of my mother sitting, peeling at the wooden table in our moist-warm farm kitchen, addressing my back as I stared gloomily out over the half-door at the hayrick which in winter took up much of our farmyard.

"The devil foinds work for idle hands, Davey. All this loungin' about . . . 'twill get 'ee into trouble afore you'm through—mark my words!"

But for her "thinking" was lounging, reading on top of that haystack, "idleness" and refusing to join the others upfield and help move the sheep from Bullen to above the railway line, signified only "sloth" and an ominous future for her sullen son.

Then I snorted that stinging little cameo outside of me again. Was it my fault I hadn't found a job yet? Was I to blame that I still wasn't famous, because an American publisher had found my one and only novel to date, too British for the U.S. market? Or that a British company had thought my tale of a Cornish transplant to Upper New York State, "excessive with Americanisms"?

"Fuck 'em" I told myself. "Fuck Heinemann in England and Doubleday here! Don't fit in anywhere, eh? So? What better than good old Forty-Second Street—the Champs Elysees for the world's outsiders?"

Beyond the library I crossed the street to the north side—narrowly being missed by a murderous yellow cab whose driver swore the nastiest things about me as I gave him the finger. (I might as well admit that at that point I wasn't exactly concentrating on externals.)

Nor was I as I entered Grand Central, wandered about the entrance hall of mainly unoccupied benches, stood for a moment in the even larger, cathedral-like expanse of the ticket wicket and information booth areas, watching the Kodak ad changing shape and color, before making my way down various corridors and tunnels towards the men's room: a pee vaguely in mind.

Standing there at the john though, things suddenly began to shape more firmly. And I'm not just describing the goings-on in my head.

Right next to me was a tall Negro and I hadn't got my zip right down before I grew acutely conscious he had an enormous erection.

Now I don't want to pretend I didn't understand all that stuff. In fact I'll even admit that in the back of my mind, I knew my presence there amid that long line of men, was not entirely to do with plain old peeing.

My neighbour continued to play with himself, and both by gestures towards myself and by a deliberate leaning over towards him, I made it perfectly clear that I was keenly interested in his activities.

He seemed to take that more as a right, though, than as a compliment. Indeed, his casual attitude embraced a looking right over my head, (I told you he was very tall), and down the line of men as if inviting their admiration and involvement too.

Then he suddenly looked slightly over one shoulder nudged me and spoke in a low voice.

"Cops. See you outside, Man."

I don't know how he managed to put that huge thing away so quickly or even so completely. But before I had time to make myself respectable for public scrutiny away from the urinal, he was walking towards the entrance.

I didn't catch up to him till he had actually climbed the exit slope and stood there on the sidewalk. He nodded curtly and I felt embarrassed. What the hell did one say? However, he took care of that.

"I know somewhere. Gotta take a bus."

He didn't speak again until we were sitting together towards the back of a stifling bus, bumping heavily along Forty-Second Street, this time westwards. I could see glimpses of the Hudson River every now and then. Not that I was doing much looking. At least in that quarter.

Having taken off my raincoat, I now draped it across both our laps. And as he made occasional grunts and mutterings I worked away at keeping the spell

49

of erotic desire alive in him by playing with his genitals under the concealment of the coat.

"Gee, that's all *right,* man. Hmmmmm-hahahahahah!"

I caught the glance of a man sitting just across the aisle from us. His face reminded me uncomfortably of my father's and I looked away. Too late. Father's image resurrected, now refused to return to the quiet grave in St. Kew churchyard. Or rather it bade my presence there.

So as I bowled along a noisy New York thoroughfare with my black man by my side, as twitchy fingers sought to sustain that initial erection that had caught me in its thrall, my head became a battleground between that big black prick and Dad in his thick Sunday clothes, unusual collar uncomfortable against that wind-reddened neck, standing in the rarely used front parlor after chapel, asking me awkwardly whether I still wanted to be a veterinary surgeon or stay at home and work the farm with him when I left school.

Incongruity wasn't in it!

"Oi'd loike to have on 'ee, Son, you know that. But I baint gin try and persuade on 'ee, one way or t'other."

'Oh huge penis, the largest I have ever seen, you melt my will.'

"Oi should loike 'ee to pray 'bout it, Son. Your mother's bravun worried 'bout what you'm gin do arter your matriculation."

'O blackman, O stranger, where are you taking me? Where are we going?'

"You've 'ad so many notions, Son. One toime 'twas the Ministry, wan' it? Another 'twere the Navy. We bide you'm bright enough wi' the book learnin' to put your hand to whatever 'ee do want."

'My hand lies between a stranger's legs in a crowded bus. I am breaking the law. And if you'd lived to see this, Dad, it would've broken your heart.'

"Get up. This is where we get off."

He almost bustled me off the bus, and once down the steps onto the sidewalk, he started to walk with enormous strides, so that I almost had to skip to keep up. Block after block we walked, and always westward though further and further north of Forty-Second Street.

I grew aware as we crossed Ninth Avenue, then Tenth, that the neighborhood was growing ever poorer, ever more bleak. Tenement houses with black children playing on crumbling front steps, a deserted corner store with its windows boarded up . . . garbage everywhere . . . In my hurry to keep up with my companion I nearly trod on a dead pigeon and looking down, noticed that a cat or something had been mauling its head.

Whether it was this specific incident or the quality of those slums, I'm not quite sure, but I found myself faltering: now no longer so keen to keep up with my tall black man. Whispery warnings formed inside me.

'You're in a really rough neighbourhood . . . better turn back . . . You haven't seen another white man in the last five minutes . . . Admit it, that group of Puerto Ricans in the previous block—they weren't whistling at that mongrel dog pissing against the brimming garbage can, they were whistling at *you*...

I stopped. So did the Negro. As he turned and faced me I felt the whole world suddenly hush with the weight of danger.
"Wait here. Gotta check it's okay over there."
He nodded at a tenement house opposite.
Before I could speak he had crossed the street. Standing uncomfortably on the curb I watched him bound up the steps and talk to a young black woman who stood by the front door, holding a wailing child in her see-sawing arms. Why didn't I turn heel and run? Flee the gritty hostility of that place where my white and alien skin loomed pallid in a sepia sea? I find it hard to answer. Lust was now just a skeleton. Fear was palpable: a cold and clammy moisture to my forehead. But not enough to inhibit movement. Indeed I shifted uneasily from foot to foot, walked a space across from the house where the man stood talking hurriedly, and then walked back to my original position.

True, that tall, lithe figure was still a fascination, and that as his hand went up to beckon me over, I felt a thrill of excitement. But it was some strange sense of passivity that set my feet obediently across the street. That giant Negro stranger was my doom, and whatever was to happen within the confines of that gloomy house, was a price I had already paid.

I have never felt such inevitability guiding my actions: in truth, my mind was blank and only vague things like apprehension and the sense of being victim stirred in me.

Our shoes clacked hollowly in the empty hall (the woman and child had disappeared) and again as we climbed three flights of uncarpeted stairs.
"Quite a ways," I said to his back.
He didn't answer. Then we entered the room. And it wasn't only my forlorn mood and sense of impending disaster that made me feel it was the ugliest, the most sordid room I had ever entered.

There was first darkness, which my friend partially redeemed by switching on a light in the center of the flaking ceiling. If there is a less than 25 watt bulb on the market then it hung there on the naked cord, casting a sickly light on two unmade beds, and shadowed walls huge with damp stains and peeling paint. Apart from the beds the room was empty of furniture.

With no further reference to me, my man crossed to the furthest bed which was pushed against the wall under a sheet which did service for a curtain, and began to undress.

Cold to the point of shivering, I crossed the bare floorboards too and began to take off my clothes as well.

In seconds we both lay under the sheet and thin, flannelette blanket which he pulled up over him from the bottom of the bed. I wanted no more than to huddle there alongside him, seeking his warmth for physical ease as well as emotional comfort. But he wasn't having much of that.

"Get on with it."

He had left his jockey shorts on and I began to tug timidly at the elastic tops, hoping he would ease up and relieve his weight.

"No need for that, Man." Tetchiness edged his voice.

I may have shrugged in the darkness under the bedclothes, as I now sought instead to extract his penis from the slit of his underpants. Certainly the last thing I felt was anything remotely like sexual passion. I didn't have to touch myself to know I was lifeless between my legs. The knot of foreboding lodged deep in my stomach saw to that.

With difficulty I finally got his thing out; held it nervously: unsure of what to do.

"Leave your hands out of it, Man. Blow me."

But my lips never made contact with any part of him.

"That you, Hank?"

My fingers clenched tight, my nails dug into my palms in the realization there was a third person with us in that room.

"Yeah. It's me."

"You got the fairy there?"

"Yeah. He ain't much good, though."

"When you're through, let's have him over here."

As I hunched foetally, now as far from that hostile black body as the cover of the sheets would allow me, I heard the springs of the other bed creak. Third man was sitting down . . . waiting . . . waiting for what?

Did I say I felt sexual passion was remote a moment ago? Jesus! By the advent of this new man I could've done nothing for Adonis himself. Prayers, not hard-ons, were what occupied me now.

"C'mon kid," my bed-partner ordered. "Get on with it."

"I–I can't." I whispered. "I don't feel like it."

"Okay, Joe. See what you can make out of him. Maybe you can relax him, huh?"

An ugly laugh from somewhere above my head. A bare leg kicked roughly against one of mine.

"Go on! Get your ass out of here. Take care of him."

I hated emerging from the darkness under the bedclothes, to feel the dirt and grit of the floorboards on the soles of my feet, then to turn and shiveringly face a total stranger: my hands cupped miserably (what a time for modesty!) over my sex.

Smaller, more compact than my recent bed partner, this one lay lengthwise and fully dressed on the other mattress, his hands joined behind his head and pressed back on a dirty pillow.

His face, even in that poor light, was obviously much pockmarked, and his skin seemed lighter. My friend from Grand Central seemed to take words out of my head, so that I jerked abruptly.

"Joe's what we call a yalla Niggra. They's meaner than the rest of us."

"Come on here, fairy, you ain't got much time."

"Time?" I echoed, quavery-voiced.

"Forget it. Don't like the looks of you. Git your clothes on. We got business to do."

Desperately I searched the floor. My own garments were all mixed up with those of the man in the bed behind me. I grabbed a shirt—the wrong one—dropped it: pulled on my pants, only to find I had them the wrong way round.

"Kinda in a hurry, huh? Goin' someplace?"

The drawl was lazy, relaxed. But there was nothing relaxed about those eyes watching me. And I sensed the eyes of the other, behind me, watching my progressively panicky movements too.

"Relax, Whitey. You ain't goin' *no* place. No place at all." The one called Joe sat himself up on the bed, his eyes never leaving me for a moment.

"You ain't gotta bother too much about dem clothes, either, Man."

"I—I don't want to take Hank's by mistake."

"You done already *made* your mistake—back at Grand Central."

So he knew about that, too. If it were possible, I felt even worse. So it was all a put up job then? I bit my lip as my mind raced in reconstruction of the past hour or so. I put on my shirt but couldn't do up the buttons.

"Put your coat on," commands Joe.

With difficulty I struggle, pushing arms jerkily through sleeves. It's a heavily-lined English sports coat of Harris tweed: my last purchase in Southampton (or rather, my mother's) the night before I boarded the Queen Mary. I begin to sweat the moment I've got it on.

With a bound, Joe's up, standing at my back. Deftly he feels my back pockets.

"All right," he says softly. "Where is it? Where's your money?"

I suppose I should've guessed that was what it was all leading up to, but even so it comes as something of a shock. And the switch from fear of physical hurt to being robbed, gives me breathing space which I use to tell a lie.

"I'm sorry. I haven't any."

"You're lyin', Man. You're lying through your fuckin' teeth."

"I'm not. I'm supposed to be looking for a job. All I've got—"

"Yeah?—*What* you got?"

"A bit of change."

I'm sullen: this ugly man's taunts getting through in spite of my fear.

Then the big one, Hank, gets up, starts to frisk my upper portions. Without a word he retrieves my wallet from where I carry it, British style, in the inside pocket of my jacket.

"This is what we was lookin' for, lil' fairy. Now how come you didn' own up? You wi'd dat fancy accent an' all, huh?"

But he isn't smiling. Instead, without waiting for an answer from me, he takes the stuffed packet of twenty dollar bills from the back section of the wallet where, the day before, I had so proudly inserted them. He holds them

53

all, fanwise, in his huge hand. Two hundred dollars in stiff, fresh denominations of twenties and tens.

Joe watches all this, his face expressionless, but the sides of his temples twitching—a danger sign, I knew, in some people of brimming anger.

Hank hands him five twenties.

"Here, Joe. For your trouble."

Joe takes them, folds them carefully, sticks them in his billfold which he then replaces in his hip pocket. I sag with some kind of relief. At least the suspense is over.

"I'm sorry. I shouldn't have lied."

But they both ignore me.

"What we goin' to do with him?" says Hank.

Joe's response not only takes my breath away but all the moisture in my mouth. A black gun has suddenly materialized between Joe's pale fingers.

"He can go out there. So soon as it's dark we can throw him in the river."

The words are nonchalant, but the gun holds firm, steady, in the direction of my stomach. And I know that death is not so very far away.

And in the simplicity of that a star of desperation rises from deep in my stomach and explodes in my head. They don't know it but a transformation takes place before them. From a stupid little queen, prepared to flirt with life for a few seconds or minutes of sex, I turn into an animal aware of impending death—only an animal devoid of teeth or claws, whose hairless skin covers no vigorous muscle, no physical strength. The only armor this animal has is a racing mind and a tongue adept in keeping up with it. I begin to talk . . .

"Kill me. Kill me if you have to. But why take risks? Look, I don't blame you. If I were in your place I'd probably do the same. I can see you're poor. I've seen how—how people like you are treated. You probably need money more than I do. Honestly, you have it with no ill-feelings from me. I—I took a risk. And I deserve to pay. What do they call it? Chalking things up to experience. I'm sorry if—"

"Where you from, Man, with dat accent of yours. De West Indies?" (That's Hank talking.)

"I says hold him till dark. Then get rid of him. The safe way." Joe's pockmarked face is alive now. The hate runs across it like fast-moving shadows. I can't look at him: turn to Hank.

"Cornwall—well, England. I haven't been here long. I'm not responsible for what's happened to the Negro people. I sympathize with—"

"Sure sounds like a fuckin' book, don' he?"

"The British Embassy knows I'm here, of course. If I were missing they'd start to look, to check into—"

"Shut your mouth, white boy," says Joe to the back of my scalp, which prickles in response to the venom.

"No, Joe. I wanna hear what the kid's saying. Gotta admit he talks real nice, Man."

I have no way of knowing whether giant Hank is kidding because he isn't looking at me but carefully counting his share of the dollar bills—for the second time I think it is. Anyway, I decide to risk that with him, and pour out words for the life of me.

"There's another thing. I think I've got a job, starting tomorrow. It's with The New York Times. I was with a paper in England. They want me in their crime department."

I falter as imagination takes fresh breath.

"Of course I'll be fairly junior. But I shall be working with Ted Thompson—the chap who exposed the Albany Racket last year?"

"You play cricket?" asks Hank. "Wi'd a voice like that you gotta play cricket."

"You seen this Thompson guy?" Joe asks, his voice still soft, menacing—so that I cannot tell whether it holds disbelief or not.

"Yesterday. I'm due back there this afternoon. He wants to show me around New York I think."

"That man's gonna have one helluva wait. Fact he ain't never goin' to see you."

"Yes he can, Joe."

"How come?"

" 'Cos we is goin' let him go, Man."

"You kiddin? Let the little fruit go when he seen us both and done know our names? You're crazy, Man!"

I distinctly see the hand of Joe tighten around the gun.

"What could I say to anyone?" I ask Hank. "That I've been hanging round Grand Central Station trying to pick someone up? You know what the cops 'ud say to that."

"They wouldn't say no more when they fished you out the Hudson and found you was a goddamn homo. They got more to do than check out every fuckin' fruit what's washed up."

Joe spat his contempt, the gob of spit falling on my still unstockinged foot.

"C'mon Joe. Put that away, huh? You got your share, man. Why don' you split. I'll take care of things here."

I saw Joe hesitate, look me up and down with a contempt so fierce that I looked down towards the ground.

"Sheeeet, Man. This punk ain't worth fightin' over."

And the yellowish, scarred face came close to mine, the gun going back inside the clothing.

"You're lucky, fairy. Jesus man, you're lucky." And the slim, panther form turned and sauntered towards the door at the far end of the room.

There was silence until Hank and I both heard the gentle click and knew we were alone again.

The pent up air came out of me in a desperate hiss.

"He's right, Man. You is real lucky. I told you yella Niggras was mean. An' he's the meanest around. He'd have killed you, you know that?"

"Yes I do. And I'm grateful. To you I mean."

"How old is you?"

"Twenty-two."

"My boy's fifteen. An' if I see'd him doin' what you was up to down there at Gran' Central I'd take my belt and beat the fuckin' daylights outta him."

I didn't speak.

"What you wanna be a fruit for, eh?"

That I *couldn't* answer.

There was a longer pause and I eventually sat down on one of the beds and put my shoes and socks on.

"Giss you'd better go, Son. 'Fore Joe gits back."

Inside I was struggling with myself. If this man had a son of fifteen, (my brother Michael's age) he could be as old as my own father. And I had thought him less than thirty . . .

"You—you live here?"

"Nope. We jest use it. Joe and me. Like today."

I stood up and looked at him. My head just reached his shoulder. Then I swallowed hard.

"I'm—I'm not sure of my way back to Grand Central Station. And I haven't any money now."

He stared back at me. But I couldn't read much there.

"Yep. If you was my son, I'd beat the daylights out of you."

And with that he suddenly thrust his hand into soiled khaki pants and brought out the dollar wad he'd stuffed in his pocket.

"Here's ten. You don' deserve *nuttin'* mind. Fallin' for the oldest game in the world. Come on, I'll show you the way myself."

It was all unreal that bit. When he spoke I couldn't believe what I was hearing. Anymore than I could believe that a ten dollar bill now lay in my own trouser pocket. Until we got out on the cold street once more, and walked briskly for a block or more.

"You take the subway—it's quicker. Here, take this token."

He handed it to me by the subway steps and, not caring, I thrust my hand into his and shook it.

"Thanks. I won't forget, you're a nice man."

"Bullshit. I jest like that stoopid way you speak. It's, well, kinda different."

"You didn't *have* to give me any of the money back. I—I think you're the only really generous person I've ever met."

"I'm going thataways. You take that subway, though. It's only three stops. Change at Times Square, understand?"

I nodded.

"Sounds funny, but I wish I wasn't saying goodbye. Goodbye, Hank."

"Now you jest git right back to England, huh? New York aint no place for you Kid, talkin' like that. You git back and play that there cricket with the fuckin' King, you hear me?

"Know what I won't forget, Boy?"

I shook my head.

"Them fingers o' your'n . . . in the bus . . . when you was playin' with me? You got magic in them fingers, Boy. Jeeze—that was veeerrry nice . . . verrreee nice, Man."

And he turned, long legs vanishing him soon into the milling sidewalk throng . . .

Cheriton

by Peter Robins

I WAS GLAD when the guide announced briskly that we'd only glance at the Morning Room and then have tea in the gardens. Stairs have become increasingly tiresome at my age and though I'd no wish to join those, ten years my junior, who were content to gossip in the coach until it was time for sandwiches and buns, I'd found the tour a little exhausting. I was happy then to lean unobtrusively against the lintel and admire the dove-grey paintwork, the lilac damask panelling and the early Laura Knights which gave the north facing room a mood of airy cheerfulness.

There was no restraint at the tea-tables in the walled garden beyond the conservatory. For most of the old biddies it seemed a re-enactment of school treats or the street parties with which they'd celebrated George and May Teck's Coronation (and that's going back sixty-five years). Most of them would have been pinafored tots. I would have been fifteen, though only just, because I'd used the cut-throat razor dad bought on my birthday for the first time.

". . . and now, boys and girls, yes of course you're still boys and girls Mrs. Moss, you've all had a chance to admire this lovely wee garden. Do you know there are two dozen varieties of clematis here alone and those Russell lupins are still looking perfect against the French marigolds, aren't they? Now can anyone guess the special name the Colonel and Countess gave to their favourite retreat?"

Few paused in their munching or in the surreptitious palming of chocolate cakes that would be smuggled back to dank bedsitters. One old dear did hazard 'The Morning Garden' but that was not quite right. I was certainly not going to volunteer. Yet again, I felt one pace apart from this group. Not snobbishly. I hadn't fallen on hard times; merely different times that compelled me to take what outings I could manage with folk who prattled endlessly about grandchildren or the way their milkman was switching the gold tops for silver.

Being what people today call gay and what we referred to as 'different,' I felt alien to their interests and was content, at the lunch-club hops in Clapham, to let them suppose I had been jilted in the Great War and so, never married. Attempts to liberalise septuagenarians seemed a daunting prospect for too slim a reward.

58

"... now, what about you Mr ... I'm sorry, I don't know your name ...?"

"That's Mr. Hodges, he'll know, he was a country lad," Annie Moss clacked between slack dentures and a rock bun.

"Mr. Hodges then. Can you think of a name for such a glorious place all planted in yellow and purple? Now there's a clue if you know your ... "

"It's called the Regency Garden," I found myself saying, "Is there a drop more hot water for the tea, otherwise I'll not sleep tonight?"

"Excellent. Are you sure you weren't cheating? You didn't read up Cheriton Hall in the library yesterday?"

"No," I said, "no cheating. Call it a good guess. Aren't yellow and purple Regency colours?"

"I think you've been here on an outing before."

The helper brought hot water at that moment and I'd no need to reply. The restless guide hadn't really a second to listen anyway for she was already organising a stroll through the park itself for those who felt energetic enough. I did not. At eighty-one, with an unimpaired intelligence and a shrewd use of pretense, I could avoid most activities that bored me.

The woman had been right, of course. This was my second visit to Cheriton. I can't rightly recall when I first heard the name but it must have been connected with one of the quarterly visits of my mother's eldest sister, Aunt Finlayson. If I had, as a five year old, any image of the place where my aunt worked as Housekeeper, it would have been of a house wrapped in trees: all of them in bloom like the cherry trees in Bushey, the south Hertfordshire village — of course it's still a village to me — where my father was gardener to Professor Herkomer. In practical terms, Aunt Finlayson's visits meant half a sovereign, so it was worth cultivating the stately lady and offering artlessly to go and play on the slopes overlooking Watford while she and my mother chatted. Sometimes I would return early; maybe it was my Father's half-day and I'd meet him by the great copper door of the Professor's Folly, carrying a basket of apricots that tasted of fruit in those days not cotton wool as they do today. Then, as I pushed open the parlour door, I'd heard the tail end of the women's conversation, sealed with a not-in-front-of-the-child sniff.

"Just look at these brave beech leaves Bessie has brought from Cheriton," my mother would be saying but not before I'd overheard, "... so naturally, neither the boy nor the girl will ever marry."

Slowly I matched the outlines of the jigsaw. There was a park round Cheriton House and there must be beech trees rather than cherries. It was evidently a picture in all seasons. And there were children too. Obviously they were older than I, else how could the idea of marriage be important? And why couldn't they, with all the money to support a mansion and twelve servants supervised by Aunt Finlayson, get married? That was a question I'd not resolved by my fourteenth year. In those days it was not a question to put to one's parents. And yet, later that summer, I stumbled on a reason why the Cheriton boy at least might not wish to marry. Maybe, like me, he'd little interest in girls and it was always possible that, again like me, he'd known a hot and bewildering romp in the August fields with a young butcher's boy. It's a laugh to think back in times like these when there are clubs and holiday groups and gay dances, to that twilight before the Great War when any lad wondered if he was the only such person in the world, rather as we speculate today that somewhere out there intelligences such as our own roam the galaxies.

I've read books written for schoolrooms nowadays explaining that the 1914-1918 War marked the break-up of a way of life in England. Our family lived it. In August 1914 my father died; finished by tuberculosis contracted years before in the appalling between-decks conditions of Victoria's Navy. As a sixteen year old telegraph boy I was hardly able to provide for a widowed mother and on New Year's day 1915, she married again—a clerk in the wine trade near Waterloo. One of the early commuters, he was also a lay preacher in the local Baptist Chapel. In a household such as his: no books other than the Bible on Sundays, no smoking and—strange paradox—no drinking, I had no place. Had he suspected that my bicycle did not really break down so regularly on Stanmore Common and that Vic—the butcher's boy—and I were, in fact, exploring one another well away from the pony-traps and occasional passing motor, I should have been cast out pronto among the wailing and gnashing of teeth. But there was the War and, like many another, I put up my age and volunteered. Apart from my mother, there was only Aunt Finlayson to whom I wished to say goodbye before leaving with the South Hertfordshires for France.

It was an early February morning with snow already beginning to settle between the rails as the train left Waterloo for Twickenham. Cheriton, like many business houses and family places was by then on the telephone and the Watford operator, on the strength of a couple of pleasant Saturday afternoons when Vic had been unwell and Stanmore Common handy, had not charged for the call to Aunt Finlayson. The Family, as she always called the Colonel and Countess, were away, Miss Victoria having gone with her mother. Only the boy (who had to be more than twenty I reasoned) and the staff were at Cheriton. I would be welcome for lunch and might stay for tea in my aunt's room before returning on the up-train.

Aunt Finlayson's directions were clear and economical, as I might have expected. Fifteen minutes' walk through streets hushed with heavy snow brought me to the eight-foot walls surrounding the estate. These were surmounted by iron spikes as if an invasion by Kaiser Bill was expected daily. Eventually I found the gatehouse and was let in. It must by then have been about noon for I can recall the winter sun hanging ripe as a peach in a rough sky as I strode under naked trees to the house itself which was sited nearer the Thames than the Richmond Road.

I saw no-one until I had skirted the rhododendrons which almost concealed a small summer-house. Perhaps because the sunlight reflected from packed snow dazzled me, I could not see more than an outline until I was close to him. Sitting rather awkwardly I thought, on an oak bench, as though some injury to the base of his spine made the position uncomfortable, was the most handsome twenty-two year old I'd ever seen. And he'd been watching, maybe appraising me for fully five minutes. Those eyes, matching in bronze the beech leaves Aunt Finlayson had so often brought, had noticed me right enough. His looks had far more to them than the obviousness of touring actors or the withered prettiness of a curate. The bone structure was firm and the set of those eyes faunlike; a characteristic of the German race I was going to fight. That, I thought, would be from the Countess who was Bavarian born. His skin was creamy white against silky black hair cropped short and lying uneasily. The eyebrows were delicate and the chin slightly pointed. Though he was clean shaven, I was certain that, with such a colouring, he would already be having to shave a couple of times a day' What a magnificent figure he was against the snow: something untamed, impatient with the fixed patterns and corset of society life. The black coat he wore was tailored to him like a glove. He'd turned up the fur collar against a light east wind and his coat contrasted becomingly (and he knew it) with the white lambswool scarf knotted in a V at his neck.

"Good morning," I called, almost certain that this must be the son and heir.
"Who are you?" He didn't take his hands from his coat pockets, hardly moved his lips but his eyes showed an even keener attention.
"I'm Miss Finlayson's nephew. Come to say goodbye. You're Master Herne?"
"Just so. Are you staying long?"
"I'm only here for an hour or so. Lunch and a cup of tea. My train's just after six."
"A pity that. We have very few visitors. I have none."
"You'd find me very dull, Master Herne. A simple country boy."
"Not too simple, I think. I'm sure I'd find it, what's the word—sympathetic?"
"I'm not certain that I know what you mean."

I had expected that when he stood up he might limp or be ungainly as a cripple. No such thing, so I wondered if he had affected that cramped pose on the bench to show off his slim build or the firm muscularity of his legs. There was certainly no physical impediment to marriage and I began to think I understood well enough what Master Herne meant by sympathetic company. At seventeen I was romantic as the next lad, and in those few seconds was over-eager to imagine the beginnings of a companionship more meaningful than the careless encounters on Stanmore Common. It was then that we heard a voice shouting from the house.

"Come along, Master Herne, It's most vexing of you to hide, sir. Now come along please, luncheon is ready."

A man of thirty-two or three was running as nimbly as he might through a foot of snow.

"My tutor; damn the idiot."
"Tutor? Looks more like a drill dergeant to me."

Master Herne smiled and the teeth were white and quite even. Moving closer to me he spoke quietly.

"Shouldn't we meet perhaps this afternoon? To talk of course . . ."

"Naturally, just to talk . . . " we both began to laugh, being unable to continue as the tutor was approaching.

"The summer-house you passed; at four," Herne whispered close to my face as he turned towards the house. It was then I discovered he was no godling dropped in my path. His breath stank. It was a smell I remembered from the back room of Vic's butcher's shop when meat had been left accidentally over the August Bank Holiday. Yet this imperfection was nothing—I've discovered worse since: disloyalty, pretence; a dozen greater flaws. Anyway I was certain Aunt Finlayson would have some buttermints or cashews. Herne's breath could not mar the fantasy I was concocting; only the thought of Waterloo that night and France next day could do that. Mr. Warren, the tutor, seemed for so thickly built a man both nervous and apologetic. We walked to the house together, he constantly enquiring if Herne felt he had a headache coming on. Me, I'd seldom seen any young man as ripe with health. True, he stumbled a little—but that was knowingly—so that he might brush my shoulder or clasp my hand with what seemed a desperate tightness.

Aunt Finlayson was in the hall to meet us. With a disapproving sniff, to indicate that my uniform didn't licence me to be free and easy with The Family, she took me to the servants' hall where lunch was about to be dished up.

Though the valet had gone with the Colonel and the Secretary with her Ladyship, we were still a dozen sitting down to roast chicken, two kinds of potatoes, sprouts and parsnips with home brewed beer to wash it down.

"Make the most of that young man," cook said, "the last decent meal you'll be getting for many a day."

"Just like home," (well, that was what she'd hoped I'd say, wasn't it?), "everything from the garden?"

"Gittings does his best but of course he's down to one boy now."

"The chicken home-reared too?" I asked.

It was Aunt Finlayson who answered after running her tongue along her top lip.

"We gave up rearing fowls some time ago. Too much trouble."

"That's one way of putting it," Curtis the chauffeur was swivelling his beer glass and didn't look up.

"He looks like young Eddie," the parlour maid Jennie spoke for the first time.

"My nephew," Aunt Finlayson sniffed, "does not look in the least like Eddie. He favours our side of the family and we—do I have to thrape it down your throat?—are Highlanders. Eddie was a Londoner and had a cockney face."

"Jennie means he looks like Eddie did at that age, Mrs. Finlayson. Not what he looks like now."

"Oh, Curtis, how could you?" Jennie was tearing at a handkerchief.

"I'm lost," I said, jerking a drop more cream onto the pudding, "who's Eddie?"

Aunt Finlayson pre-empted any other answer.

"Eddie was an assistant gardener here. He still does such work elsewhere I believe. The West Country I think."

"Tell him the truth Mrs. Finlayson. Eddie works behind hospital walls and not on visiting days neither."

"That will do, Curtis." My aunt nodded at me. "If you've finished your trifle, we'll take our coffee in my sitting room."

It had been interesting to have met the staff I'd so long imagined but as suddenly as they'd taken substance, they receded in importance as we talked in my aunt's quiet, orderly room. It was not likely I'd see any of them again for, if the War lasted, Aunt Finlayson would have reached retirement and moved to the cottage she'd bought near Oban. More imminent was the West Front but, overshadowing all, my need to slip away to meet Herne in the summer-house. It was already twenty to four. Having complimented my aunt on the lunch, I told her that I'd found it a little rich and would be glad of a handful of peppermints and a half hour to walk it off by looking round the grounds. As I expected, she didn't object, for I knew she wished to doze over a novel before tea. She only cautioned, "Now do be back before dark or you could lose your way. We've forty acres remember."

Of course he was waiting. I needn't have been apprehensive as I trudged through the snow that had begun to fall once more. The summer-house itself was dry and Herne had brought a hip-flask of brandy. We laughed and chatted and his eyes danced with the pleasure of being with me again. Now, I'd always taken the lead in any physical encounters; curiosity rather than pride, really. On this occasion, though, I found myself being explored and held in a grip so fierce that I could only guess at the loneliness and abstinence that triggered it. He would scarcely allow me to press my lips against his neck or run my fingers under his overcoat to warm them against his back.

"Why not take off your gloves? You're hot as a furnace," I murmured.

"Leave things as they are," his thumb was edging along the inside of my thigh, "my hands aren't pretty. An accident: could have happened to anyone, they tell me."

What with the cramped conditions, winter clothing and both of us over-willing to please I knew this was not going to be the most memorable hour for either of us to look back on. Slipping another mint into Herne's mouth so that I would not need to stop my breath as he kissed me, I tried to tell him so. What could have been more delightful than his reply?

"I telephoned through to the station. You're not going to get back to London tonight, you know. The snow's thick from Richmond to Wandsworth and the trains finished ten minutes ago."

"And you didn't tell me?"

"You wanted me to?"

"So, what happens now, Herne?"

"I avoid taking the sleeping muck they force on me from time to time and you slip along to my room in the North Wing. It's the end door; say midnight?"

"Only if you'll promise to take off your gloves. It doesn't matter, you know, when . . ."

He paused in lighting a cigarette. "If that wasn't just words. That it doesn't matter to you . . ."

"I meant it," I said and kissed the point of his left ear, noticing that there, too, a light down was spreading and he'd have to be barbered carefully in middle age. As we went our separate ways by the gate to what he called the Regency Garden, I could see little of his features in the thickening darkness. Only his eyes were luminous as he said with a desolate urgency *"You will come?"*

Having played the charade of telephoning the station a second time, I found Aunt Finlayson pleased enough with the idea of some company over a supper tray in her sitting room. Reading each evening while the secretary was away had become irksome to her and I proved an agreeable partner for her at draughts and dominoes since she beat me four times out of five, putting my clumsy faults down to a preoccupation with getting back to my regiment. It would have been the best part of eleven o'clock when we walked through the corridors to a small bedroom that had been made up for me.

"I'll remember this when I'm in France Aunt Finlayson."

I'd paused by a window and was looking at the park, silent under the snow and lit by full moon. "I wouldn't welcome a night like this with the Germans only a hundred yards off."

"It's the kind of night that encourages intruders," Aunt Finlayson was tired and was determined to steer me to my room. "We find it best to lock our doors here. I think you should do the same. It's good stout pine. Sleep well now. There'll be tea and shaving water at seven."

I turned the key, waited until my aunt's purposeful steps had receded, then softly unlocked the door once more.

I'd borrowed bootblack and brushes from Curtis and some Brasso from Jennie so I set to work smartening up my kit for the next twenty minutes. No matter what the weather in the morning, a South Hertfordshire man had to look his neatest. With boots set out under the chair on which I'd hung my tunic, I burnished my capbadge, then washed in the ewer and basin before putting on the pyjamas and flannel dressing gown Curtis had rustled up. They weren't a flattering fit for I was stocky rather than tall but I turned back the cuffs and licked my hair into shape with a dash of cold water on my comb. Perhaps in the lighting of Herne's room, a couple of pimples by my nose wouldn't be noticed and, when the light was out—which couldn't be soon enough for me, a slight blemish would be unimportant.

Midnight, Herne had said. It was nearly seven minutes to when I checked the time by my father's turnip watch, the old faithful gunmetal I'd taken with me and which I still have. No more than a minute later, while I was practising with a cigarette in the hope that I'd not be sick if offered one, the noise began.

A dog? If a dog then one much larger than the spaniels I'd seen Jennie feeding earlier and certainly not my aunt's comic terrier. The sound, more forceful and more frequent by the moment, came from the grounds. I went to the curtains and, easing one aside, looked out into the full moonlight crackling on settled snow. At first I detected no movement. Then there were two men stumbling, hurrying as best they might across the frozen acres. One I recognised as Mr. Warren, the burly tutor, for I'd noticed his ungainly strides earlier. Could the second be Herne himself? It was difficult to be exact for both were half-obscured by shapeless black bundles they were carrying. Sacks? No; they were nets—stout mesh that could ensnare whatever interloper it was that must very soon wake not only the household but half the locals in cottages along the road.

And then, lolloping between the beech trees away from the two pursuers, I saw it stirring up the snow in sprays as it outdistanced the runners. Since one was almost certainly Herne there was little reason to creep to his room until it had been captured. Where the beast had come from I couldn't guess but if this was not its first appearance (and the ready nets were evidence of that) no wonder they no longer kept livestock at Cheriton.

Twenty yards ahead of its hunters, the creature headed for the house itself, bursting the elegant gate of the Regency Garden like matchwood. Two storeys above I watched as it leapt again. I saw only what could have been paws, what might have been fur; heard a crash and supposed that whatever it was must have gashed itself on the windows of the Morning Room. At last I saw the faces of the two men. One, as I thought, was Warren; the other, Curtis. This meant poor Herne, waiting in his room on the other side of the house, could be sitting by an unlocked door and risking attack from some creature that had run amok.

Already I felt a protectiveness towards him. I wasn't sure that it would be welcome for I'd heard from Aunt Finlayson that the Colonel deliberately treated his son as an invalid who was never allowed to travel or take part in outdoor pursuits, much to the open disgust of the Countess. This, however, was no normal occasion. I moved swiftly to the door. It was then that I heard the first scrabbling and panting from the far end of the corridor. A fine thing that a soldier about to protect King and country had nothing but bare hands to defend either his own relative or the friend he would soon love from an attack by some predator. Yet what else could I have done but use what strength I had to tug a mahogany chest against my doorframe? As well I did so. For some purpose no rational being could fathom, the thing was at my door. Whose scent could be here but my own or the cool lavender of Aunt Finlayson?

Outside, but further back, I could distinguish the voices of Curtis and Warren.

"Soft now; approach softly man."

65

What would they do: shoot it or net it?
"Ready Curtis?" I heard.
"Ready."
"Then . . . now. Tighter at that end Curtis; tighter."
"Careful Mr. Warren. Your hand; now look what's happened to your hand."
"Nothing at all Curtis. The gloves took the worst of it . . . gentle with the net now. Throw the chicken. Throw it man."

And then there was no sound but a slobbering whimper until a roar—maybe as the nets were tightened—startled me again.

"That chicken's no good and you know it. Saw for yourself in the park this morning what's really wanted."

This morning? And my aunt had let me wander in the afternoon? Had it been loose from a cage somewhere in the grounds all day? Maybe the Countess had a sinister taste in pets.

"But that's not Eddie's old room, Curtis."
"That's as may be. I remember what Jennie said."

A moment later, Curtis again, but further off. "That hand'll need iodine you know." The whimpering and the panting faded. Ten minutes later I walked nervously to Herne's room. At least I knew he must be safe.

For a long time no one answered though I must have tapped a dozen times. It was Warren who opened the door, wearing only pyjamas. For the first time in my life I was jealous. How did a mere tutor have access to my friend's room at that hour and so informally dressed? He appeared to be waiting for an explanation. I knew that I was owed one and stood my ground.

"I suppose the noise disturbed you," he said finally. "One of the mastiffs got loose."

"Strange mastiffs you have round here. Not the only thing that's strange either . . ."

"I don't get your drift young man . . ."
"I'd come to see how Herne is . . ."
"Master Herne is sound asleep. Never knew a thing about it. Thank you for your enquiry though."

I was not going to get past that closing door and I was furious.
"No doubt you doped him again tonight?" I lashed out.

"Maybe; maybe not. I don't think the habits of The Family are anything to you, are they? Sleep well, Mr. Hodges. Or rather, goodbye. I doubt if I'll see you again."

He was wrong there.

Next morning, Aunt Finlayson was nowhere to be seen until, as I was about to go to her room to wish her goodbye, she came downstairs dressed for the shops, although it was barely half-past eight.

"I shall walk you to the station," she announced.

We were half-way along the drive before she paused in what was, for her, idle chatter that I began to think deliberate.

"Aunt Finlayson," I seized the moment, "what was going on at midnight?"

"Decent working folk were in their beds asleep, as I hope you were."

"It's not easy to sleep with some kind of creature being hunted under your window." Aunt Finlayson stopped. We had reached the rhododendrons and she rounded on me.

"I said you favoured our side of the family but I was wrong. Your father was a man given to romancing. All that travel alone on the seven seas had no doubt addled his brain. A creature being hunted? We have none at Cheriton that I'm aware. No snow has fallen since last night. Where are the marks of any creature in the snow? Or have those gardeners conspired to fill them in?"

It was true. No marks.

"Now wait a moment Aunt Finlayson . . ."

"I will not. I've no wish to stand here freezing while I listen to some foolish nightmare."

"Look. There were two men chasing something. Here. See for yourself: four sets of prints . . . or three and something that could be, well, paws."

"Probably a dog bounding after the postman. Now let's forget this nonsense or you'll be later than you already are."

Something glinting in the sunlight under the summer-house steps attracted me. I was over, had picked up three objects and was back by Aunt Finlayson in a trice. My brain had begun to whirl.

"Where is Mr. Warren this morning?" I asked, hoping my aunt would chatter again and that I would gain time to sort the questions I really wished to put.

"Giving a lesson to Master Herne I would imagine."

"I think you're wrong Aunt Finlayson." By this time we were turning into the London Road near the station. I had spotted Herne's tutor come out of a chemist. We chatted with him and then I said viciously, "I suppose you've been fetching some more dope for Herne. He chucked the last lot under the summer-house, you know. Would you like the bottle? And he dropped his glove there as well."

I gave him Herne's right glove and the bottle with heavy tar-like remnants of Tincture of Cannabis. He took both in his left hand. I saluted and with a meaningless smile he thanked me. Catching him off-guard I put out my hand. Automatically he pulled his bandaged right hand from his pocket.

"Sorry," I said, "last night's mastiff?"

As we hurried onto the platform, my aunt caught me by the arm.

"You know," she said, "don't you?"

"What I know adds up to less than nothing," I replied. Tutors who look like bruisers; an assistant gardener who disappeared and something that might have been a mastiff or maybe didn't exist at all."

"Tell me, did you like Master Herne?"

"Very much."

"So did Eddie the gardener. I called them David and Jonathan. Curtis called them something coarser but then Curtis is a coarsegrained creature."

67

"And then?"

"Jennie set her cap at Eddie and she's a forward lassie."

"But what's all this to do with Herne and Eddie being wherever he is?"

"You're a foolish boy but then your mother would marry a Sassernach. Eddie was badly injured and Warren is, well, a keeper."

"A keeper?"

"Just so. Here's your train now. Come back to us. But not here." I waved until the bridge obscured her and then sat bewildered, hurt and, yes, frightened. I needed a cigarette. Instead of the Woodbine packet, my fingers closed on Herne's left glove. I smoothed out the cream velour wondering if I might ever see him again and then put it in my tunic pocket with the turnip watch. It must have been all of two years later in an Army Field Hospital that I actually tried on that glove, recalling Herne and Cheriton. When I withdrew my hand there were half a dozen strong black hairs—not my own—adhering to my wrist.

"Mr. Hodges. I do declare, Mr. Hodges, you've been having forty winks. Come along now, the coach is ready by the summer-house."

As the guide strolled with me I asked what had become of the family. It had, she explained, died out during the Great War. The Countess accidentally shot her son one winter's evening. The Colonel then became a recluse and died of a heart attack on Armistice Night. The daughter never married.

As we reached the coach I suggested, "That accident with the gun. Would it have been in February perhaps, at full moon?"

"Now I know you've been in the area before," laughed the guide, "that's the kind of story scatty Jennie at the sweet shop invents. Lot of old nonsense."

Three Friends

by Jerry Rosco

For Glenway Wescott

AT THE BEAUBIEN métro station in East Montréal, Lucien Mason and his wife, Jacquelyn, waited without much patience for a train to take them home. Lucien, twenty-eight, was as restless as a child. Dressed in denim, he paced back and forth, his curly hair nearly hiding the green eyes as he looked down. Jacquelyn, dressed casually but well, tried to admire the graceful sloping white walls of the station, but what she really wanted was the comfort of their little flat and some tea. Sunday visits to her mother always ended like this.

Moving swiftly, nearly silently on its rubber wheels, a blue-and-white métro train swept into the station. The couple boarded a half-filled car and sat together. The train doors closed.

Three youngsters sitting next to Lucien and Jacquelyn were whispering and laughing. They were all fifteen or sixteen: two girls dressed like fashionable ladies of the 1920's and a boy with long blond hair and round gray eyes. When the boy looked up, his face shone radiantly beautiful, and, as he pursed his lips to begin a joke, it was easy to see the carefully applied white lipstick.

At the Berri station, the two girls kissed the blond boy with the lipstick and hurried off together. The doors slid closed. The boy removed his jacket and stretched his attractive form, clad in skin-tight clothing. Once he glanced at Lucien, briefly. Then he looked again, longer. Lucien was well aware of the energy he felt only a few feet away, but he avoided meeting the other's eyes. Then he saw the leather belt. It was an old Indian belt, hand painted, with a silver buckle. Years ago it had belonged to him.

The large gray eyes met his look directly. Lucien hesitated, but he knew his station was approaching. "Excuse me," he said, leaning forward. Jacquelyn looked at her husband.

"*Oui,*" the boy said, a little surprised but not shy.

"By any chance, are you a friend of Philip Perrot?" Lucien asked. The youngster's face brightened. "I live with Philip. We are good friends. You know him?"

"Yes, I gave him that belt long ago."

69

The boy looked down, and then up, his face filled with surprise. "You are Lucien," he said, extending his hand. "I am Serge Gaudreault. Philip speaks much of you. You are his better friend, eh?"

Lucien smiled, but his eyes dropped to the worn leather belt. "We are old friends but we don't see each other. Do you know Paul Moret?"

"*Oui,* Paul," the boy said. "He is a good friend with Philip."

"Yes," said Lucien, "Philip and Paul and I are good friends."

The métro train came to his stop, and Lucien was struck by the thought that within five or ten minutes this boy would be making himself comfortable at Philip's apartment—a place Lucien would never visit.

"Say hello to Philip for me," he said. The boy nodded and smiled at the couple as they moved out onto the platform. The train doors closed.

The evening had turned cool. Lucien and Jacquelyn walked home in silence.

Something was moving in the air on the quiet April night; some force, like all forces, was rushing to a conclusion and a dissolution. Something—something inevitable—was silently winding its web around the lives of several people and binding them to each other forever.

At Philip's apartment, Paul Moret waited alone in the living room while his friend showered. Paul, a muscular but gentle young man, looked carefully around the small room. As usual, he noticed the many photos, some of them recent, of the boys Philip knew. Paul smiled and shook his head. Although attractive himself, he'd never had Philip's luck in love. At twenty-eight, he felt old in some ways, while Philip, the same age, moved comfortably in a very young crowd.

"Want to go to a party tonight?" Philip asked as he walked into the room. He was wrapped in a long bath towel, his wet dark hair hanging straight to his shoulders.

Paul looked up at the slim, strong body he knew well and was tempted to pull Philip close to him. But he didn't. "Come on, Philip," he said, "you know I get up early for work."

"Sure," Philip said, bringing a hand to Paul's shoulder. "Whenever I'm on unemployment insurance I forget that other people work. But maybe we can see a movie together later in the week, eh?"

"Oh, for sure," said Paul, smiling now, "we don't see each other enough these days."

Just then the door opened and Serge walked in. "Âllo, Paul," the boy said, as he walked straight up to Philip and took his lover by the hand. "Philip, just now I see your friend, Lucien, on the métro. You and Paul always speak about him. He was with a nice woman. He remembers the belt I am wearing."

Philip, surprised, looked down at the Indian belt. Serge saw something strange in Philip's eyes.

"Did you like him, Serge?" Paul asked.

"Oh yes. He has such green eyes, like jewels," Serge answered. Then, in a soft voice to Philip, *"Tu vas bien?"*

Philip smiled and gave the boy a gentle push. "Yes, yes, I'm okay. Why don't you get ready for tonight? We're going to a party, remember?" Serge frowned and remained for a long moment before turning toward the bedroom door. Over his shoulder he said, "So. He is well and he tells you âllo."

Philip sat down beside Paul. "He's a funny kid," he said, "jealous of you, even jealous of Lucien who I haven't seen in a year."

"Well, maybe he's just curious. He's only known you five months."

"Six months," Philip corrected, looking toward the bedroom where Serge was making a little too much noise opening and closing drawers. "Tell me, Paul, how often do you see Lucien? What's he like these days?"

"He's the same as ever," Paul said. And he felt a stirring of the same old emotions that had overwhelmed the three friends years before. "He's maybe a little quieter these days. He's happy with Jacquelyn, he still works at that bar on Mount Royal Street, and I go there every few weeks. Do you want to see him?"

Philip shook his head. "No, I don't want to see him. I mean . . . I just make him uncomfortable. Now I think I should get dressed and dry my hair." As he reached for a pair of jeans, Philip dropped his bath towel to the floor, and the sight of his body, hard, flawless, broke something deep in Paul.

Paul stood up. "I'll be going now. Maybe I'll call tomorrow night and we can go to a movie?"

"Sure, call me," Philip said. He was busy dressing now, thinking of the night and the party ahead. Paul was about to leave the apartment when he noticed a photograph he'd never seen before. It was hanging in a frame near the door.

It was a photo of a blond youth of unnerving beauty; he was leaning against some large rocks on a shoreline. In the background, some people could be seen, seated on the shore and facing the ocean, but the boy had his back to the others as he looked, unsmiling, directly into the camera. He wore tight faded jeans and a T-shirt that revealed his shoulders and arms and well-developed chest.

"That photo," Paul asked, "who is the boy on the beach?" Philip laughed and slapped his friend's shoulder. "That one," he said, "is a god."

Paul nodded. "I believe it. Goodbye, Philip, I'll see you soon." And they kissed goodbye.

Less than an hour later, Paul was home, lying in bed and thinking of Philip. He thought of Philip's perfect body, and then his hand moved down his own body. Although he exercised often and was in good shape, Paul could feel just a bit of softness around his stomach. Imperfection.

Paul thought of the boy, the god, in the photograph. And he thought of how Philip's gods had taken his friend away, to a land of permanent youth, of necessary perfection, to a place where loneliness and age and death were not real destinies, but only moments of incomprehensible terror in the night, moments that would dissolve into forgetful sleep or into the warm embrace and lips of a young, firm-bellied, long-haired god.

Thinking of this, Paul fell asleep.

It was near dawn when Lucien Mason woke with a start. He looked around and saw only the dim, still room, and Jacquelyn sleeping beside him. Lucien was tense and uncomfortable and wondered if he were ill. Then he remembered the boy on the métro, and his thoughts turned to Philip.

Soundless pictures, like bits of old film, flashed through his memory. The three friends were seated around a table at La Grange, the all-night disco. A joint passed from Philip to Lucien to Paul. When the joint was finished, another was lit. Beautiful French boys, dressed in their best clothes, danced with young girls. Lucien would watch the dancers, fascinated. The boys were street boys mostly, hard as nails, and with a cool beauty which made their fancy clothes seem very correct. They were like an extraordinary society of regal beings. The girls knew it and were a part of it, but gave away nothing with the swift glances of their beautiful eyes. Lucien would always notice the time of night, or early morning, when many of the boys would begin to dance with each other.

Lucien recalled no conversation in particular, but he remembered the eyes of his friends: Paul's eyes, sad, unsure, alone; and Philip's eyes, like iron. And Lucien remembered a certain night alone with Philip, a failure, and Philip's half-smile as he lit a cigarette, his eyes for once showing regret. Philip had gambled with their perfect friendship, and destroyed it. They both knew it. The gamble, Lucien understood, had been worth the risk.

Lucien sat up in bed, wide awake. He looked at Jacquelyn, sleeping silently beside him. If it had worked, he thought, that would be Philip there.

In the shadows of the room, he saw the warm form beside him become Philip's body, the long beautiful hair, Philip's hair; the loosely curled soft hand lightly touching him became Philip's strong hand. He sighed heavily. If it had been that way, it would be okay, but he knew he was happy with Jacquelyn. And he knew he was lucky, because with her he could enjoy his love and never hide it from his family, his boss, his landlord, and all other interested and concerned people. Philip and Paul could not say the same.

Philip had lost several good jobs because he was just not discreet. Paul was more level-headed and kept his print-shop job, but he was being used by his boss. And they're still young, Lucien thought. What would happen when they were older? Paul is isolated now, and lonely. And Philip surrounds himself with teenagers and never thinks of the future. And yet . . .

Lucien stood up and walked to the window. He ignored the rows of old wood-framed houses on St. Timothé Street and looked up at the blue-gray sky of dawn. Strangely, the full moon was still visible. He could hear the wind blowing, an occasional car in the distance, and the pleasant first stirrings of the radiators in the flat. He had seen Philip very little in the last five years, and not at all in the last year. And yet, he thought, practically whispering the words aloud, I still love him as much as ever.

Day broke rapidly over the city, but with the usual strange stillness and gentleness of very early morning. Some cars were already moving east on St. Catherine Street and east and west on Dorchester—not the last of nighttime traffic but cars beginning the work day. Buses moved slowly along in the morning chill. Paul Moret waited for a bus to bring him to work. In the east, young people who had danced all night were now crowding into small coffee shops for breakfast. It was almost like any other morning.

It was hours before Paul was fully awake. On the back of his work overalls, the faded words "Chomedy Printery" were labeled. Above the cigarette pocket the word "manager" was stitched in red letters. Paul felt his job at the print shop had reached a dead end and he knew he would quit sooner or later. But through sheer routine the situation dragged on. At the moment he was showing a new boy how to stack and tie newspapers.

The boy, his long hair protected from the machinery by a knotted scarf, stood back and very earnestly watched the instruction. Paul skillfully handled the tabloid papers as they rolled one upon another off the press. Quick-counting them into stacks of approximately fifty, he showed the boy how to tie the papers quickly, before too many accumulated at the end of the run. After Paul tied three stacks, the new boy tried it, did it well, and looked up with a smile. Paul clapped him on the shoulder and walked away, looking back once at the agile youngster bending down at his work beneath the pounding iron machinery.

It was late afternoon when Paul's boss called him away from the printing press. The man—fifty years old, short, heavy, and grim—looked very angry. "There's someone in my office to see you," he said. He looked away from Paul and began to walk off.

A cold feeling, cold like an unknown guilt, came over Paul. He walked slowly to the small office at the end of the floor. When he turned into the room, there was Serge, sitting by the cluttered desk. He was dressed in tight garish clothes, discothèque clothes, but when he looked up his face and blond hair were wild, his eyes full of tears.

"Serge," Paul said in complete surprise, "what's happened to you? Do you need help?"

"Paul, it's terrible," the boy cried. "I come to tell you but I can't believe it's true. It's Philip." Paul looked at the boy's distress and heard the words, and felt years of his life, layer upon layer of his soul, collapse like a building turned to sand. "It's Philip," Serge cried, "he's dead, my Philip."

Everything moved away sharply in a rush of emotion, and Paul reached for the desktop to steady himself. Then he felt himself coming back, back to the dirty room where he stood above the frightened boy. Serge looked at him in

73

a strange way, as if he understood what he had just done with his words. Paul sank to his knees and put his arms around the child. They held each other close; it was the only thing to do because they had both loved the same person.

"I will die without him."

Paul heard the words and it took a full moment for him to realize the boy had spoken. "He did all for me," Serge said softly, "now I can't go back to his apartment, and I want to die. He thought I was a little boy, a crazy boy, and he was right, but to me he was all the world."

Paul sat back on the floor and looked up at Serge. He couldn't speak but he wanted to know what had happened.

"We were at a party last night," the boy whispered. "Very late, near the morning, he took a bad fall in front of the house of the party. Some others found him and would hold me in the house, but I push to the door and see everything." And the boy saw it again and put his hands over his face.

Paul stood up and pulled Serge to his feet. "Go down to the street and wait for me. I'll change my clothes and we'll take a taxi to my place and I'll . . . " He froze for a moment as a deeper level of realization rushed over him like a wave. "I'll take care of everything," he said.

The boy left and Paul went to a nearby room and changed into his street clothes. Before he could leave the room, his boss walked in. The man was showing the same anger as before.

"Paul," he said, looking at him in a temper, "I told you once before, do what you want with your life, I don't judge you, but please keep your little faggot friends away from the job. If a client was here and saw a kid like that, dressed like that, and I think with makeup, and crying about . . . what? A lovers fight!" He said in a fury, and then suddenly fell silent. He saw Paul's look. The young man looked past him and was putting on his coat.

"I'm finished," Paul said in a controlled voice. "Please mail me my paycheck." He tried to walk away but the man grabbed him. He knew his young manager and knew he was serious.

"Paul, what are you saying? Are you crazy? You've been here five years. Don't quit a good job . . . over nothing."

"It's not that. It's time, it's time to go." Paul looked at his boss and the man looked hurt and surprised.

"Kid," he said, "I won't let you quit. I said 'faggot' but I meant nothing by it. You know me, you know I meant nothing. I'm a crude man, my wife and kids always tell me that. And I was only in a bad mood because we're so busy on Mondays. I'm sorry you're having trouble with your friend, that boy. It's just, you know, business is business."

Paul walked past the man, then stopped and spoke without looking back. "The kid was bringing me very bad news. It's something . . . I don't know what I'll do. But I think I'm finished here and not because of anything you said. You're a good man, I know it better than anyone. I'll call you next week." He left the room and walked down to the street.

Outside, Paul was surprised to find it was raining heavily; Serge, with no protection at all, was standing perfectly still, waiting, and he was totally drenched. "Why didn't you wait inside?" Paul shouted above the noise of the downpour and the Sherbrooke Street traffic. The boy looked at him in confusion, dazed. Paul stood near the curb trying to find a taxi. Within minutes he was as soaking wet as the boy. Finally they got a cab. "St. Denis and Duluth," Paul said. The taxi started and stopped short. The ignition gave the driver some trouble, then the car started again, and stopped. Finally they were moving in the heavy traffic, the rain beating down steadily. At the corner of Peel, some teenage boys, shouting in French and laughing crazily, ran zig-zag through the maze of slowly moving cars. Paul looked at Serge and thought the boy needed sleep desperately. As the taxi approached St. Denis and was about to make a left turn, a small mail truck stopped short in front of them and they struck with a violent jolt. Serge hit his head on the front seat but was not hurt. Their driver was out in the rain, shouting at the mail driver.

At last, they were in Paul's apartment. Serge sat on the living-room sofa and began to remove his wet clothes. Paul brought him a heavy blanket and a blue-and-white capsule. "Take this," he said, "it's a Tuinal. You must sleep."

"But I am afraid to sleep, to dream of last night."

"No, you will not dream with that."

Serge took the capsule, finished undressing, and wrapped himself in the blanket. He watched Paul sink onto the bed in the adjoining room. There was a long silence.

"Paul," Serge called.

"Yes?" Paul answered, just barely audible. Both of them were speaking from the great distance of shock and loss.

"You were lovers one time with Philip?"

"Yes." The silence came again, but there was nothing else to say. Serge stretched out full on the sofa, pulling the blanket up to his chin. The drumming rain outside was hypnotic. Only last night the weather had been so different, cool but almost like spring. It had been the most beautiful night of his young life—and the dawn was the most terrible. But before that terror, the party had been beautifully unreal, like poster art.

They had arrived at the house in LaSalle in a taxi, Philip, Serge, and another boy Serge's age. The two youngsters walked on either side of Philip as they approached the old house. Music blared from the upstairs rooms, and the sound of voices and laughter. Very high stone slab steps led to the doorway. They climbed the steep stairway. A glass broke somewhere overhead.

When they reached the upper rooms, people were saying hello to Philip from all sides. Serge felt a flush of excitement. He looked at Philip, whose powerful blue eyes and long hair gave him the look of a celebrity . . . his usual look.

Each odd-shaped room revealed another handful of interesting young people. In one room, people were dancing. A tall handsome youth, said to be Hawaiian, danced passionately with a girl, his long black hair flying spectacularly—and his sharp black eyes glancing clearly in the direction of Philip.

It was a party with no formality or center. Everyone drank wine. Serge and the other boy followed Philip on through the remaining upper rooms, even through a dark room where lean nude bodies were coiled in silent rapture. Finally, a large skylight opened to a blue starlit sky. They climbed up and found half a dozen others scattered along the gently sloping roof. The full moon above was brilliant.

They lay on their backs, passing the wine bottle around. "How is my bébé-Serge tonight?" Philip had asked at one point, leaning forward, a little drunk, but gentle, somehow lyrical in his movement and his voice. Serge remembered looking up into that strong yet soft face, which at that moment seemed full of love. "I am well with you, Philip," he said, sitting up. His eyes were closed as the warm kiss brushed his lips, soft but intoxicating, short but eternal. Serge lay back on the cool roof, and when he opened his eyes he saw hundred of stars and a moon that glowed bright and full. All of the unhappiness of his young life had been worth it, he thought, just for the experience of this one perfect moment.

A tall youth moved across the roof and sat near Philip. They laughed and spoke rapidly in English, too fast for Serge to follow. So he looked at the sky, at the clusters of stars, and dreamed of other parties, and hotel terraces, and exotic vacations, all with Philip.

He noticed a silence and when he looked up Philip was sitting alone, holding the wine bottle, staring at something in the emptiness, and his look was sad, beautiful and solitary. From Serge's perspective, there was nothing behind Philip as he sat there alone, nothing but the blue-black sky and a galaxy of stars.

Now, as the Tuinal pulled Serge down to the threshold of a deep sleep, his body relaxing despite everything, he fought off the horror of death, tears streaming down his face, and concentrated only on that one image, that poster art, of his one and only love, fixed forever in that brilliant pose, immortal against the perfect sky.

Paul listened, dry-eyed and emotionless, to the gentle crying of the youngster in the next room. Finally, the tears gave way to soft steady breathing. Only then did Paul begin to sense fully what had happened. If Philip was dead— the conscious thought stabbed him like a knife—then there was no one, no one who truly knew him.

He understood there were things to be done. Philip's parents lived in the suburbs, and, though the police had surely informed them and everything was handled, he was sure no friends of Philip had gone to them—and he was considered a friend of the family.

He changed into dry clothing and prepared to leave, pausing for a moment to look down at Serge, who slept in drug-induced peace, his red swollen eyes closed at last to brutal consciousness. Paul thought: maybe the kid really loved him. I wasn't the only one who loved him.

Looking at the sleeping boy, Paul pulled back the blanket and saw him in all his beauty. The coiled young body, white, velvety, soft and perfect, moved him nearly to tears. For he saw what Philip had seen, much more than physical beauty: tenderness, sweetness, a precious and gentle flower which must at all costs be protected from the world. Paul covered the boy and left, locking the apartment door behind him.

In the twilight, the long ride on a nearly empty bus was not a bad thing for Paul. The soft darkness, the lights in the distance that appeared and disappeared, the simultaneous movement and stillness, all of it seemed so much like the vague reality of life. He did not think this but he felt it.

He rested his head against the window, looking at the ordinary approach of night on a day when time should have stopped, his hands resting uselessly at his sides, and, at last, the tears falling silently. The thought struck him that the best part of his life was over. And he knew Philip, if he were there in ghost and body and knew of that thought, would shout at him in disgust and disappointment until Paul remembered that, indeed, there is always more to life . . . even more than love between two people.

The bus left Paul standing alone on a quiet and dark suburban road. Walking toward the wood-framed house, he remembered many happy visits to his friend's family. Now, Philip's only sister was married and living in Toronto. And Philip's younger brother was living downtown, a musician in a rock band. So the parents were alone and Paul, approaching the well-lit house, was glad he had come. It was Mrs. Perrot who answered the door.

"Paul, I thought you would be here," she said, almost to herself. The small woman, now in her mid-fifties, looked at him with the sad gratitude of all mothers who grow older wishing for many things and asking for nothing. She took both his hands in hers.

They sat together in the living room. The house was completely quiet. "It's impossible," she said. "That's what I keep thinking. But slowly I realize that I have lost him." The look in her eyes pained him more than anything he had experienced that day. He looked down and listened to the words.

"He was the special one of my children," she said. "Always I believed Philip could do anything he wanted to do. His father wanted him to be . . . to be a little more practical, but I never judged him. I always knew that he would make us proud."

Parents' talk; half of it true, half of it wishes and regrets—Paul was familiar with it.

Philip's father was sitting at a desk in his small library when Paul walked in alone. The gentle man nodded somberly and looked down. "I'm sorry," Paul said, awkwardly, "he was my best friend. I knew how good he was. It was a crazy accident . . ."

"That's what life is, Paul," Mr. Perrot said, looking up at him. "It's always crazy accidents that decide everything." There was a long moment of silence.

The man obviously wanted to be alone. Finally, he said, "I'm sorry for you, Paul. I saw you boys grow up together. I know it must be very difficult for you. Sometimes love . . . " He stopped himself, then looked up again. "Look after your own health. Try to be happy."

When Paul was saying goodbye to Mrs. Perrot, the front door opened and Marc, Philip's younger brother, walked in. He wore a leather jacket and jeans. His long hair was wild and matted. His face, a somewhat coarser duplicate of Philip's face, haunted Paul on the trip back to the city. And the terrible and true words of Mr. Perrot's advice: "Try to be happy."

A cold wind was moving through the region and snow, totally unforeseen by the weather experts, was falling. It was surely the last snow of the season, but it was falling like a December storm. In less than twenty-four hours, there had been a calm night with a full moon, then an overcast day of heavy rain, then a night of sudden cold and snow.

Paul watched the storm through the bus window. The weather did not surprise him, nor could anything surprise him. Despite his emotions, he tried to see things clearly.

If I could wake up from this, he thought, and go back to yesterday, I would be no closer to Philip than I was. He would be with Serge, or whoever he chose, but he would not choose me. Maybe that isn't important. But today I am more alone than ever.

And the voice of Philip whispered in his ear, "Like everyone else, alone."

And Marc Perrot, with his common manner and hard eyes, was the closest link to the genes that had been Philip. Paul shook his head. It was no worse to think of Philip's body, now, dead, cold. The bus moved slowly through the snow, which was now sticking, into the city.

Miles away, in LaSalle, snow already covered the concrete landing beneath the stone staircase. The crazy accident was history—vague history because no one saw it. No one watched Philip's last moment as he sat on the thin railing, with one leg hooked over the side, his foot touching the outer edge of the top step. And in the warm glow of the wine, in the safety of others' admiration, there was no place for those annoying thoughts, those glimpses of loneliness and age and death that come at night. There was only Philip, his mind blank, his intoxicated body rocking from side to side as he waited for his friends. With no enemies in the world, with a good conscience and very few regrets, he was boyishly happy. Even when his foot missed the outer edge of the step and his body surged outward, and even when his other leg—reflexes slowed by alcohol—just missed hooking onto the thin railing, even then there was only surprise, not fear. And that unlucky step into darkness ended in a bright flash of final consciousness.

Philip, the vision of male beauty, with lean body and shining black hair and strong blue eyes full of kindness, with a dozen lovers who would never forget him, there all alone in the night, stepping outward, down through darkness, into light.

Lucien Mason looked up from the bar where he worked, down past the six customers who sat on stools watching television and sipping beer. He looked at the front door opening and saw Jacquelyn coming in from the snow, and he knew something was wrong.

The young woman walked the length of the bar, unconsciously brushing the snow from her coat as she approached her husband. Lucien leaned across the bar and took her hand. Her eyes were sad and he knew it was bad news.

"Can you close the bar early?" she asked. Lucien nodded "yes" and waited for the words. "It's Philip," she said, and from under her coat she took the early edition of the morning *Gazette*. "I read it here. It said, 'Philip Perrot, twenty-eight, of Montreal.' It said he died in a fall early this morning at a house in LaSalle. Can we find out if this is your Philip?"

Lucien leaned heavily on the bar. There was a sensation of sudden calm and tranquility, yet he heard the blood pounding in his ears. His eyes found Jacquelyn, and in her wide, sorrowful eyes he saw his only refuge, his only home, his only companion through the loneliness of his life. And he saw that Philip was dead.

"Can we telephone Paul?" she asked. "Would he know?"

Lucien leaned heavily on his elbows on the bar. "It was Philip," he said. "I woke up at dawn this morning. It must have happened then. I woke up and I was thinking about him. But we should call Paul. I'll close up and we'll go home and call him."

"Oh, Lucien," Jacquelyn said, looking into his liquid green eyes, "I never knew Philip, I never really knew him, and you and he were best friends, weren't you?"

"Yeah, we were," Lucien whispered. His face blanched. Most of his weight was pressing down on the hard wooden bartop. He realized they were speaking in the past tense, and that a great part of his life had been sliced away and was gone forever.

The web was closing, nearly complete. An inch of snow covered the ground, covered the concrete landing in LaSalle. But the force of Philip's life was drawing other lives together, closing the wounds of neglect and pride, softening the great regret of human carelessness.

The outside lights of the bar were off as Paul walked up to the building through the thick snow. The door was locked and, through the glass, he saw Jacquelyn sitting alone. She saw him and came to the door.

In the silence and warmth of the darkened barroom, Paul saw that the bad news had preceded him.

"I just told Lucien," Jacquelyn said. She looked at Paul for a long moment and saw exactly what he was seeing in her; both terrible sadness and wonderful strength. They'd never had the opportunity to become true friends, but there had always been a silent understanding and affection between them. In the warmth of her understanding now, Paul felt his resolve uncoil, and the greatest wound of his life showed itself in his large brown eyes. "Paul," Jacquelyn whispered, and they held each other close.

"Where is he?" Paul asked.

"He's in the back yard. He'll be here in a minute." Paul walked the length of the narrow bar. Through the back door he could see Lucien out in the yard, carrying a can of trash to the sidewalk. As Lucien walked slowly back across the yard, he slipped in the snow and fell to one knee. Slowly he got up and walked to the door. When he stepped inside and saw Paul, he was struck speechless, as if his friend had appeared there by magic. Finally, he said, "It was him?" Paul nodded, and their eyes could not meet in that moment.

They sat together at the bar with Jacquelyn, sipping drinks and looking at the morning *Gazette*. When Jacquelyn realized the two friends couldn't speak freely, she stood up.

"I'll sweep the place, Lucien. You boys take your time."

Paul smiled as Jacquelyn walked away, and Lucien said, "You see? I haven't been unlucky in everything."

"That's for sure," Paul said, and he thought of his own loneliness. And of the boy sleeping in his flat.

"Look," Lucien said suddenly, "I don't know what I feel. I mean, I hadn't seen him for a whole year. And we stopped being close years ago. I know we still cared about one another, but it was spoiled and we couldn't fix it."

"You would have fixed it some day," Paul said, "because Philip really cared, he really missed you."

"Missed me," Lucien said, in surprise. "But who was he? What made him influence us, and everybody, so much . . . all these years."

"You loved him," Paul said, unemotionally, "and so did I. He had everything. No one knew him better than us. Sometimes, I thought he lived at too fast a pace, but I was just jealous of his energy."

"I should have stayed close with him," Lucien said. "We should have tried to stay close friends. After Jacquelyn . . . "

"Listen," Paul said, "I know how Philip felt. He couldn't have been happy with a polite friendship. Don't you see?"

"Yeah, sure," Lucien said, the green eyes flashing. "Sex. I thought about that a lot. When you're older, maybe then you can afford to be dignified about things. But while you're still young, sex gets in the way of everything. Still, I wish . . . "

"Forget it," Paul said. "Forget what you wish. We can't change anything." They finished their drinks and began to walk to the front of the bar to join Jacquelyn.

Pain stabbed deeper into Lucien, a pain he knew would never completely go way. It was the kind of pain that, over years, one comes to cherish.

"You're coming with us, aren't you?" Lucien asked his friend. "I borrowed a car tonight. I can get it through this snow."

"Stop at my place first," Paul said, "I want to get that boy, Serge, the one you met yesterday on the métro. This whole thing has left him in bad shape."

As he drove through the snow to Paul's flat, Lucien thought of Serge, and in his heart he felt the meeting on the metro had been a signal to him, part of a movement of forces that could not be stopped. He ached now for his lost friend, Philip, and he felt awed by the power and sweep of life. Serge, the pretty youngster on the métro who had looked deeply into Lucien's eyes even before Lucien had noticed his old belt on the boy . . . Serge had come to him like a messenger from Philip. With a child's eyes and silken blond hair, wearing funeral white lipstick, Serge had brought him a final farewell that otherwise he would have been denied. It was equally fitting, a part of the mystery, that he should see the boy again tonight.

Paul entered his flat alone and saw Serge, still fast asleep, with his blanket kicked to the end of the sofa. He knelt beside the boy and allowed himself the simple physical pleasure of lowering his head to kiss the taut warm stomach of the adolescent, the sweet fragrance of the young body like the ritual incense of an ancient sacrament.

"Philip," the boy whispered, not quite awake, *"J'ai sommeil."* When Serge opened his eyes and saw Paul, he sat up quickly, looked around the room, then looked down, biting his lip, unconcerned with his nakedness, and fell back onto the pillow. "Paul," he said, speaking quietly in the stillness of the dark apartment, "you have the same touch of Philip, very gentle. It is good, a strong man who is gentle."

Paul held Serge close for a moment. "Come now," he said, "we must go with two good friends of Philip, the people you saw on the métro." Serge did not question this and dressed quickly in silence.

Outside, in the car, Jacquelyn and Lucien turned to welcome Serge as he and Paul climbed into the back seat. No one spoke of Philip, but each of the four people knew there was nowhere else to be on this night, nowhere but in this slowly moving car, with these other people, in the middle of an April snowstorm.

It was cool in the small apartment when they arrived, and Lucien began a fire in his coal-burning stove. They sat on floor pillows near the stove and Jacquelyn brought out a large bottle of Québec red wine and glasses. For several minutes a comfortable silence lingered. Finally, Lucien began to speak quietly with Paul, of many things in their past, and of some things in their future. Jacquelyn noticed Serge trying desperately to follow the rapid English conversation of the young men, as if in their words he would find some important secret he hadn't known. Instinctively, she took Serge by the hand and in French asked him where he'd lived before Montréal. As they talked about northern Québec, the boy's eyes brightened and he spoke freely while holding her hand firmly in his. Seeing this and understanding his wife, Lucien reached

81

out for Jacquelyn's free hand. The comfortable silence returned, accented by the crackling noises of the hot stove. Then Lucien stretched his other hand slowly toward Paul. Embarrassed, Paul took it. But instantly he realized how badly he'd needed exactly that contact. Feeling a sudden joy, feeling the close presence of the others, Paul looked up into the eyes of his best and truest friend, Lucien. He turned and saw Jacquelyn smiling at him, and saw Serge watching him intently, anxiously. Then, as if afraid to hesitate for even a moment, Serge suddenly leaned forward and slipped his free hand into Paul's hand, the fingers closing tight around it.

Hunter

by Felice Picano

IT WAS SUNSET when Ben Apres drove up to the hanging shingle that read "Sagoponauk Rock Writers Colony," and, on a smaller, added-on shingle, "Visitors see Dr. Ormond." An oddly Autumnal sunset, despite the early summer date and no hint of dropping temperature, as Ben stepped out of the ten-year-old Volvo that hadn't given him a bit of its usual temperament on the long trip. He urinated on a clump of poison ivy until it was shiny wet, surveying what appeared to be yet another rolling succession of green humped New England hills.

The muted colors of the sunset fitted Ben's own fatigued calm following weeks of torment, his final uncertain decision to come, and his more recent anxieties since the turn off the main road that he'd never find the place, that he'd driven past it several times already, the directions had seemed so sketchy.

He found himself gaping at the sky as though it would tell him something essential, or as though he'd never see one like it again. Then he made out some houses nestled in a ravine. The colony. He'd made it!

Dr. Ormond was easy to find. The paved road that dipped down into the colony ended at his front door in a shallow oval parking lot, radiating dirt roads in several directions. Two cars with out-of-state-plates were parked and a locally licensed beat-up Baby-blue pickup.

The active, middle-aged man who stepped out of the house chomping an apple, introduced himself, then looked vaguely upset when Ben introduced himself and asked where he would be staying.

There appeared to be a mixup, Dr. Ormond said. Another guest—and here Ormond threw the apple down—and went on to mention a woman writer of some repute—had unexpectedly accepted the colony's earlier invitations, thought by them to have been forgotten. She had taken the last available studio. They hadn't been certain Ben was coming this season either. Victor Giove hadn't heard from Ben in weeks. Of course, Victor hadn't heard from

Joan Sampson either, and she'd come too, though naturally, they were all delighted she was here.

Ormond motioned behind him vaguely. Ben saw a white clapboard, pitched roof house standing alone on a patch of grassy land. He supposed that was her studio, the one he was to have lived in.

Before he could ask, a plump middle-aged woman, her apron fluttering, her hair in disarray, was waving to them from the doorway. She'd already telephoned Victor, she called out. He was on his way. Mrs. Ormond, Ben guessed.

He leaned against the Volvo. Darkness was quietly dropping into the ravine. One or two lights were turned on in the Ormonds' house, other lights appeared suddenly in more distant studios. Ben wanted to wake up tomorrow morning in this enchanted glade, to spend sunny and rainy days here, long afternoons, crisp mornings, steamy nights. He would not allow the mixup to affect his decision. After all the inner turmoil, he was glad he'd come. He wasn't leaving.

Above all, he was grateful to Victor Giove, who was jogging toward them now, accompanied by a large, taffy-colored Irish Hound, the two racing, skirting the big oak, circling Ben and Dr. Ormond, the dog barking then nuzzling Ben's hand for a caress, Giove hardly out of breath, glad to see Ben. He took Ben's hand, clasped his shoulder, smiled, was as openly welcoming as Ormond hadn't been.

Victor was tan already; his curly dark head already sparkled with sunreddened hair; he looked healthier and more virile than he'd ever looked in the city, an advertisement for country living with his handsome, open-featured face, his generous, beautifully muscled body that loose clothing like the old t-shirt and corduroys he was wearing couldn't disguise. Ben felt Victor's warmth charge into his own body as they touched, and he knew that all things were possible this summer, even the impossible, even Victor.

"There's no place for Ben to stay here," Dr. Ormond protested once they'd gotten inside the Ormonds' living room.

"What about the little cottage," Victor said. "That's empty."

"What little cottage?"

"By the pond. I passed it today. It's all closed up. You don't need a full studio, do you Ben? Of course, he doesn't. He'd love the little cottage."

"It's a fifteen minute walk from here," Ormond said, unpersuaded.

Ben suspected he'd be crazy about the little cottage.

"He's young," Victor said. "It's not far for him."

"But it isn't ready for him."

"Sure it is. You helped clean it up yourself. Remember? It can't have gotten more than a little musty in the meanwhile. Besides, he can't go all the way back now, can he?"

Ben told them he'd already sublet his apartment in the city. He had nowhere else to go.

"You see!" Victor said. "Come on, Ben, dinner's ready. I'll take you to the little cottage after."

"Victor!" Ormond said, in a strange tone of voice. "That cottage was Hunter's."

"It belongs to the colony."

"You know what I mean."

"Ben's here," Giove said firmly. "Hunter isn't."

"No. I guess you're right."

"Then it's settled."

Four of them ate dinner. Joan Sampson was to have joined them but she called to cancel, saying she had work to do.

Ben did know they had no such thing as community dining at the colony, didn't he, Frances Ormond asked. Everyone took care of themselves. Except of course, everyone dined with whomever they wanted to. She hoped that Ben would feel as welcome at her table as Dr. Giove was. It was impossible for Ben to not like the transplanted urban woman who'd evidently found peace at Sagoponauk Rock. Like Victor, she radiated health and happiness. Ben would later discover that was a rare quality at the colony. Others had brought their sufferings and neuroses, unable or unwilling to let them go. They argued around kitchen tables just as badly as they had in Manhattan bars. They outraged and scandalized each other in country bedrooms with infidelities and treacheries as though they still lived in West Side apartment complexes. Over the following week, Ben sized up the colony members quickly. Only Mrs. Ormond was judged to be sound.

And Victor, of course. Victor, who was the reason Ben had come to Sagoponauk Rock, and the reason he had almost not come. Even after Ben had sublet his apartment. Even after Ben had turned off the exit from the New England Thruway and had driven north for what seemed hours.

After dinner, Victor got into the Volvo's driver's seat and drove through the dark, rutted road to the little cottage. Ben held an extra kerosene can Frances Ormond had given him, unsure whether the electricity was turned on.

It was, they discovered, after a long, silent ride through the deep darkness of the country, passing what would later become landmarks to Ben on his night walks and night drives: the community house, the first two studios, then Victor's, the apple orchard, then the fork past the pond.

The cottage was L-shaped: a large, bare bedroom separated by a small bathroom and cavernous storage closet from a good sized study area opening onto a small one-wall kitchen with a long dining counter.

Victor built a fire to help clear out the unseasonable chill. Ben went through the kitchen cabinets and found a bottle half full of Fundador. They sipped the brandy, talking about the program they'd tentatively set up the past April at school, which Ben as an apprentice writer would follow at the colony. He was only to show Victor a piece of writing when he was satisfied with it, or unable to find satisfaction in it. Some of the others at the colony never shared their work with each other. Victor and Joan had agreed to meet regularly to read to each other. Ben could join them.

Although it was only a three and a half month stay, Ben had decided he would write day and night. Not only the few short stories Victor asked for, but a novel too, *the* novel, the one he'd planned, the one he believed he'd been born to write. Free here of most distractions, he felt certain he'd get much of it done before the last school year rolled around again. He already loved the cottage.

Only the bedroom, after a second look, didn't seem as cozy as the rest of the house. Ben thought the bedroom's coldness was due to its appearance: low ceilings, uncarpeted dull wood floor, only a few pieces of furniture: hardly inviting. Perhaps a single nights' sleep would warm it up. The double bed—higher and wider than the one he was used to, was firm yet comfortable when he tried it out.

Victor had gone into the bathroom. He found Ben stretched out on the big high bed and stopped, lingering on the threshold.

For a long minute they looked at each other. Ben, his hands under his head for a pillow, felt suddenly exposed, then seductively positioned, inviting. Giove seemed suddenly bereft of his usual composure, uncertain, fragile, even frightened. Neither of them moved. Ben could feel the tension of the possible and the impossible filling the room like a thick mist.

"It's getting late," Victor said, his voice subdued, his hands suddenly gesturing as though controlled by someone else. "I'll come by in the morning to show you around the colony."

Ben was embarrassed now too, quickly sat up and got off the bed to see the older man out. In an attempt to cover over the shame he felt he asked, "Who had this cottage before me?"

"Stephen Hunter, the poet," Giove said, looking out into darkness.

"You're kidding. I didn't know he stayed here at the colony."

"Oh, everyone important comes to Sagoponauk sooner or later."

Ben was about to say something about how happy he was that the cottage had a literary past, but Giove said good-bye and was gone.

Ben settled into the dank chill of the sheets they'd found in the big closet and thought of that moment in the bedroom, of Victor's suddenly coming upon him, his hesitation, his distracted gestures, the quiet tone of his voice and his sudden decision to leave. If he had remained another minute, come into the bedroom, come closer to Ben, the impossible would have been possible, in this very room.

Ben climaxed with a sharpness he hadn't experienced masturbating in years, not since he was an adolescent. Wiping his abdomen with a handtowel, he wondered whether it was the fresh country air or seeing Victor Giove again after so long.

Victor didn't come by in the morning to show Ben around. Ben didn't see him until dinner time. But that was only the beginning of Victor's fluctuations of intense consideration and total aloofness that finally formed itself into an inescapable pattern.

That first morning, Ben didn't care. The bedroom faced east and he awoke to a sunny spendor of nearby trees and bright clear sunlight flooding every inch of what seemed to be a really handsome, though sparsely furnished room.

After a breakfast of bread and honey provided by Mrs. Ormond the night before, Ben wandered around the colony. He was still too awed to approach any studios closely, believing the other colony members would be intensely concentrating on their writing, and thus not to be disturbed. But he had enough to look at: the pond, surprisingly large, still and lovely, quite close to his cottage; the apple orchard stretching miles; the lively stream that formed a tiny marsh at the pond; the large old trees, many he'd never seen before; the young saplings everywhere; the fruit and berry bushes in demure blossom; the wild flowers surrounding the house; the cottage itself, beautifully crafted of fine woods, so that built-in tables, drawers, and cabinetry were integrated perfectly by color and grain, all of a piece.

He skirted the colony, later on, driving up to and along the two-laned highway, following Frances Ormond's instructions, locating in one direction a truckstop all-night diner, a gas station and another five or six miles, the tiny hamlet of Sagoponauk—where he purchased a backseat full of groceries and supplies. Driving in the other direction, past the colony, Ben found another gas station and an old clapboard roadhouse, containing a saloon and an Italian restaurant.

The peace that had settled on him momentarily the dusk before, returned when he drove back to the colony, and arrived to see the little cottage—highest of the houses on the property—aglow with fuschias and oranges, its western windows reflecting a brilliant summer sunset.

Victor apologized when he saw Ben. Besides doing some writing that day, he said he'd fixed a propane gas line to Joan Sampson's oven and hot water heater, and had helped Mrs. Ormond pick early apples for saucing.

Ben was embarrassed by the apology. He could spend all day with Victor. That was why he had come to the colony. But now that he was here, he could not justify deserving Giove's attention. Victor wasn't merely gorgeously unself-conscious—he was altruistic, giving his time and energy to anyone who needed it. Obviously there were others in the colony who needed it as much as Ben.

So Ben contented himself. Especially after the first few weeks, when he began to realize the impossible love between them could only occur suddenly, impulsively, unforgettably, like any other miracle.

87

Victor's comings and goings appeared to fit some obscure plan. Ben wouldn't see him for days, only to come upon him mowing a shaggy patch of lawn, or wrapping heavy black tape around a split waterpipe of one of the studios. Then Victor would come by the little cottage early one afternoon, spend all day, remain for a hastily concocted dinner, talk about people and writing and books until midnight. Only to disappear for days. Only to reappear again as suddenly, stretched out on the yellow plastic lawnchair at midday as Ben returned home from a walk, or suddenly diving past Ben's surprised face into the clear water of the pond and swimming to the other shore. His appearances were unpredictable. The hours he spent with Ben so full of talk, of intense attention that Ben would be charmed into persuading himself that Giove was merely being careful, getting to know Ben better, making sure of him before he would suddenly turn to Ben, put his arms around him, and . . .

That was when Ben would feel frustrated all over again, full of lust, and he would have to go into the bedroom, to lie down, to picture how it would be, sometimes masturbating two or three times after Victor had been with him, feeling his fantasies becoming so real that the impossible *had* to happen.

Once, Victor came by after dinner when Ben was writing, Giove lay down quietly on the sofa, began to read a magazine, and fell asleep. When Ben realized that, he couldn't concentrate. Even sleeping, Victor was too disturbing. Ben wandered around the cottage, trying to wake the older man by the noise he made. He even tried to fall asleep himself, but it was an absurd attempt—the bedroom felt as cold, as uninviting as the first night he'd spent there.

He finally decided to wake Victor: he was so tall, he had to sleep bent up; he'd awaken with cramps and pains. Ben didn't say it to himself, but he suspected that once they were in bed together, Giove would relent.

Victor stretched, got up, looked once at the bedroom hallway as though trying to make up his mind whether to stay, then said he wouldn't hear of it.

It was hours before Ben could fall asleep, even after he'd taken a mild sedative.

He had purposely not touched himself during those tormenting hours of unrest. During the night, however, half-awakened, he felt heat emanating from his genitals, couldn't fight it away, and worked groggily but efficiently to bring himself to orgasm. Dazed, exhausted, he sank back into slumber.

The following afternoon, Victor was at the pond again when Ben arrived for his daily swim. With him, sitting on the tiny dark sand beach, wearing a huge sunhat, was a chaperone, Joan Sampson. Ben remained with them only long enough to be polite.

After that day, Victor and Joan were always together, Victor seldom alone.

Even without her interference, Ben thought she was the least sympathetic person he'd met in the colony. She epitomized all he disliked in the others, their utter sophistication and real provinciality, their brusqueness, their bad manners, their absorption with themselves and lack of interest in anyone else except as reflections of themselves. Her frail child's underdeveloped body and the expensively casual clothing she wore, her bird-like unpretty face and unfocussed blue eyes that seemed to look only with disdain, her arrogance, her instant judgments and devastating condemnations of matters she couldn't possibly know, her artificial laugh, her arch gestures and awkward mannerisms—she might have been a wind-up toy. Next to her, large, naturally graceful, athletically handsome Victor, his Victor, looked bumbling. Together, they were grotesque.

Ben made certain he wouldn't see them together. He pleaded work when they asked him to join them for dinner, didn't show up for readings of their work, never went where they were likely to be.

The impossible, he began to see, was impossible. He had to forget Victor, to forget him, and above all to stop fantasizing about him.

When the cold showers and extra work he made for himself around the cottage no longer served to keep his mind off Victor Giove, Ben began to run miles every day along the two-lane road, to swim hours at a time in another, larger pond he'd discovered a short drive away. When he realized these methods were no longer working Ben got into the Volvo late one night and drove to the all-night truckstop diner.

Two cars—one he recognized as belonging to the owner—and a large red Semi, were parked in the gravel lot. Ben pulled up close to the truck, hidden from both the diner and the road and waited. When the truck driver finally came out of the diner, Ben rolled down his car window and asked for a light for his cigarette.

The trucker was close to middle-aged and heavyset, but he had kind brown eyes and an engaging grin. He lighted Ben's cigarette. When he asked if Ben weren't a little young to be doing this sort of thing, Ben shrugged, then leaned back in the carseat with a loud sigh. A second later, the trucker's lower torso filled the car window frame, the worn denims were unzipped, not another word said. Ben sucked him off and came without touching himself.

The following night, Ben stopped at the roadhouse and struck up a conversation with a travelling salesman who had a suitcase full of encyclopaedias. After a few drinks, Ben was able to convince the man he wanted something other than books. The salesman was younger than the trucker, thinner, better looking, just as obliging. They drove separately away from the roadhouse, met a mile further at a turn off, and made love in the backseat of the salesman's car for over an hour.

Ben drove out late every night. One time he picked up a longhaired hitchhiker who offered him grass. They smoked and Ben drove twenty-five miles before he got up the courage to ask if he could blow the kid. Sure, the hitchhiker said, unzipping, I was wondering when you were going to ask.

Several times he repeated his first night's success at the diner. He also discovered the Esso station outside of Sagoponauk had a removable plank at exactly the right height between the two booths in the mens' room. High school

89

boys came there after unsuccessful weekend night petting sessions with their girls and local older men furtively used his services at various odd hours. Ben became bolder, picking up strangers leaving the roadhouse. He was often misunderstood, sometimes threatened. The bartender, a married partner in the place, offered to guide likely men Ben's way in return for occasional favors. A week later he took his first payment sodomizing Ben on a shiny leather sofa in an office after the roadhouse had closed.

During all of these experiences, Ben never felt less frustrated, less craving of sex, or less in love with Victor Giove. But he told himself that whatever else he was doing, at least it was better than fantasizing about Victor and masturbating. That seemed to help.

Although he had gone to sleep very late, and was even a little drunk when he'd finally gotten back to the cottage, Ben awakened instantly, fully, as soon as he thought he heard the footpads in the darkened room. Fully alert, tensed, he kept his eyes closed, pretending to be asleep. Whoever had stopped at the foot of the bed was looking down at Ben.

Despite his terror, Ben didn't panic. Then, oddly, he felt a wave of intense lust passing through his body. Odd, since the young man he'd spent two hours with on a blanket inside a clearing they'd driven to had been both passionate and solicitous of Ben's pleasure: so that Ben had felt both mollified and physically exhausted when they'd parted with a long, lingering kiss at their cars again. Despite that, Ben now felt a biting, itching erection, a pressing need to masturbate as though he hadn't had sex in a month.

The fear returned. Ben almost shivered. He pretended to be disturbed in his sleep, mumbling loudly, rolling onto one side before waking up.

During his exertions, whoever had been at the foot of his bed left the room. Ben felt alone again. He listened for noises in the other rooms, waited a long time hearing nothing, then got out of bed, and crept first into the corridor, then into the rest of the cottage. The doors were all locked, the rooms empty. Puzzled, wondering if it were a dream, Ben went back to sleep.

Several nights later, he again awakened sensing someone at the foot of his bed. Once more he felt a scalding, sweeping lust over his lower limbs, the need to touch himself. Then fear reasserted itself, and he was cold again. While he was sleepily trying to get out of bed, whoever it was got away. He was certain it wasn't a dream this time.

Ben thought about the matter for the next two days and determined to ask Frances Ormond who else had a set of keys to the little cottage. Walking to the Ormonds' house, he came upon Victor Giove, surprisingly alone, sunning on a blanket spread over the grass behind his A-Frame studio. Victor was clad only in a pair of red, worn swimtrunks.

Ben moved on with a wave, but Giove hailed him over so insistently that Ben reluctantly joined him, and even took off his shirt to get some sun.

He was "pale as February," Victor told him, and would burn unless he put on some suntan oil. When Ben began to splash it on, the older man said he was doing it all wrong: he would show him how. As Ben lay on his stomach, he expected to feel the large strong applicating hands transformed into messengers of caresses. They weren't. They were brisk, efficient. They spread the lotion evenly: nothing more.

Giove didn't seem to have noticed that Ben had been avoiding him. Their conversation was the usual: what Victor was writing, what Ben was doing, what was happening among the others at the colony.

Ben stayed for almost an hour—his disturbance at their near-nude closeness had vanished. When he got up and put on his shirt Victor said: "You ought to get more sun. And rest more. How are you sleeping? You look sort of done in to me."

Ben was so stunned he couldn't answer. Why would Victor say that to him —unless it was Victor himself who was visiting him every night?

When Ben finally did say he was sleeping well, Giove seemed skeptical, then added, "Well, you know best," When he rolled on his stomach, his wide shoulders, his long, muscled back, two solid buttocks stretching the bright red nylon of his swimtrunks, his thighs and legs—honeybrown and flecked with sun-bleached hairs—all jumped out at Ben. He wanted to fall down there and kiss and lick every inch of that body for hours on end. The black curly ringlets of Giove's hair shone like white gold in the sun. Shoving his itching hands into his trouser pockets, Ben managed to mumble good-bye before tearing himself away from the spot.

He was imagining things, Ben told himself, walking away. Victor had only asked how Ben was sleeping because he'd probably heard Ben driving past his studio late every night for the past three weeks and was concerned.

Frances Ormond confirmed that she had hear Ben's Volvo at two and three in the morning at least a dozen times. She was far less subtle about it.

"That's the way Stephen Hunter began his terrible descent," she said, "staying out late, getting drunk in roadhouses, coming home late. Summer after summer. Night after night toward the end."

Ben thought it was none of her business, but defended himself by pointing out that he had written the two required stories and had already begun his novel. Late hours helped him work, he said.

She pursed her lips as though to counterattack, but changed the subject, feeding him coffee and freshly baked berry pie instead.

She told Ben no one else had keys to the little cottage. None were needed; the locks didn't work; anyone could get in if they wanted. Stephen Hunter had once told her he'd had enough of locks in the city. He wouldn't have functioning ones out here. It was his undoing, she added, because it enabled his murderer to get at him so easily.

Without much prodding, she narrated the grisly tale of three summer's past. The young vagabond had been captured in a saloon a few towns away. He'd confessed and was imprisoned. At first he made some foolish claim about Stephen owing him money and refusing to pay, about them being friends for years. Under pressure, his story changed into one of revenge. Stephen had molested him, he said. It wasn't convincing, even to the unsophisticated local sheriff.

Back at the little cottage, Ben discovered she was right—all the doors could be opened, the locks just flapped on their hinges. Ought he have them repaired? Yes. But whoever was visiting him at night did nothing but look at him. Was that reason enough to change something Stephen Hunter had done? Ben would never bring anyone back to the colony. He congratulated himself he never had. And he still couldn't get Victor Giove's words earlier that day out of his mind. He was almost certain it was Victor.

So he didn't repair the locks. And the next time he was awakened in the middle of the night and sensed the figure at the foot of the bed, Ben felt only a few seconds of the usual fear. The figure remained motionless. It seemed to be the right size for Giove. Then Ben began to feel the intense warm itch sweeping from the tips of his hair to the soles of his feet.

Slowly pushing down the light blanket, Ben let the dark figure warm him with its gaze, then began touching himself on his legs and groin. He thought he heard a sharpened intake of breath from his visitor, and Ben let go, slowly, luxuriously caressing and stroking himself, thinking of Victor at the foot of the bed watching him, wanting him, not daring to touch him. His climax that night was shared: he was certain of it.

When he opened his eyes, the room was empty.

He was visited every night for several weeks. Every night Ben awakened, sought out the outline of the figure against the lighter darkness of the room and succumbed to fantasies and sex.

During the day he often told himself he ought to be sure it was Victor and not someone else. But who else could it be? He searched the eyes of the other colony members he saw, looking for any signs of guilty, secretive interest. He found none. Then he would come upon Victor, racing around the lawns with the big Irish Hound, or sitting reading in a hammock strung outside of Joan's studio, and, though they seldom exchanged more than a few words, every word, every phrase seemed so couched with meanings relevant to their shared nights, Ben was convinced it was Giove.

Didn't everything point to it? Victor's insistence Ben remain at the colony that first night? His friendliness? His increased reticence with Ben since the night visits had begun? He seldom spoke to Ben of Joan, or of their work—as though it had only been an excuse. Ben came to believe their new silence—when they met at the local grocery store, or out on walks—was more eloquent than words. It spelled content.

Ben would be a fool to spoil it. The impossible had become the possible. Not in the open way he'd at first naively imagined, but tacit, secretive, and for that reason somehow more passionate than he'd ever fantasized. Victor must still have hurdles of attitudes, ingrained prejudices to jump before he could admit what he was wanting, feeling. Ben would give him time. Who knew what the next step would be in their growing closeness—so long as Ben didn't force it.

Ben had been visited that night as usual, all his lust and wakefulness drawn from him, as it always was, replaced by deep, calm, dreamy sleep.

People were marching down a small town street. Batons twirled, trumpets blared, signs and crepe-covered floats sailed past. Children bounced eagerly behind. The drum passed by very close, going bam bam BAM! bam bam BAM! again and again, sounding lovely and rich and mellow at first, then ominous, then emergent.

Ben awakened to someone hammering on his front door. He thrust open the bedroom window to the cool mountain summer morning. It wasn't quite dawn.

"Ben! What do you know about drugs?" It was Eugene Ormond, evidently recently awakened. If he didn't look so panic-stricken, Ben would have laughed.

"Joan Sampson's taken a pile of them. We're sure they're some kind of sleeping pills."

"What did they look like?" Ben asked.

"We found one that fell on the floor." Dr. Ormond showed Ben the red and blue shiny capsule—Tuinals.

Ben dressed and ran out to Ormond's pickup idling in front of the cottage.

"She's got to vomit them up, I suppose," Ben said as they drove toward her studio. "Then black coffee, to keep her stimulated."

"Frances thought the same. I hope she's all right."

"Where's Victor?" Ben asked. "He would have known."

They pulled alongside the studio. Ormond looked at Ben oddly, then said, "Didn't you know? He's back in New York. Has been for three days. That's what all this is about."

Before Ben could register the news, Dr. Ormond had stopped the truck and was urging him to come inside.

Joan was audibly vomiting. Frances, as audibly, was cursing about the stupidity of trying to kill yourself over a man, for Chrissakes, even one like Victor. There was a final spasm of vomiting, quiet, then Frances Ormond half dragged the small woman out of the bathroom and spotting Ben, asked him to help her walk Miss Sampson around a bit while Eugene made coffee, doubly strong coffee.

Their charge was light, but weak, her arms were useless, her head kept lolling against Ben's shoulder, words and saliva dribbled out of her mouth.

They wheeled her around for another five minutes. Another fifteen minutes were spent feeding her the coffee and ensuring she didn't vomit that up too. Then more walking around.

Joan was visibly recovered by the time the phone rang. She still looked awful and had allowed Ben to bring her into the bedroom where she was noisily sobbing, but at least she was safe.

"Get that, will you Ben?" Mrs. Ormond asked, looking up from where she was cleaning the bathroom tile floor.

Ben lifted the receiver and said hello. There was a confused mumbling from the other side. Then: "Joan. Is that you?" Victor Giove, perplexed.

Ben looked away from the phone, unable to say anything for a minute. Holding his hand over the phone, he barely murmured, "It's Victor." Saying the name was more difficult than almost anything he could remember in his life.

"Of course it's Victor!" Frances Ormond said, and came to take the call.

"You see!" Joan sobbed, standing at the threshold of the room. "He's seeing her again. He was with her all last night. He couldn't stay away from her. That's why he went back."

Frances Ormond hushed her. Ben moved away from them, feeling as though he were on the set of a movie where everyone was playing a known role and only he didn't know the scenario. He couldn't believe that Victor was in New York; yet there he was calling long distance in response to a call Mrs. Ormond had put through.

Ben walked slowly back to the little cottage. He felt dazed by the morning's events, but not so distracted he didn't notice it had rained the night before: the dirt around the cottage was still damp though drying fast. Two sets of footprints led to the tire tracks of the pickup. No other marks of someone walking around were visible.

That night he drank some brandy which kept him awake longer and made his sleep lighter than usual. When he was awakened during the night by the urgent panting breath at the foot of his bed, he immediately turned to the bed table and turned on the lamp.

The room was empty.

Energized by a need to know, Ben leapt out of bed and ran out into the other rooms. He even looked outside. When he returned to the bedroom a few minutes later, he thought he saw a wisp of smoke curling into the lower edges of the large storage closet. The closet was empty, but the morning chill caught up with him there, and he began to shiver so badly he had to get in bed and pull up the covers, waiting for sunlight.

"Stephen Hunter was homosexual, wasn't he?"

Frances Ormond looked across the distressed oak parquet of the old table at Ben.

"I guess they still don't talk much about those matters in college do they?" she asked, instead of answering him.

"The vagabond who murdered him was a hustler, wasn't he?"

"You seem to know all the answers. Why ask?"

"In the bedroom?"

"Stephen tried to get away," she said, "In the closet."

Ben wasn't surprised to hear it, only vaguely chilled to know his line of reasoning had been so on target.

"And Victor and Stephen were friends, weren't they?"

"Not by then, they weren't. They had been close friends. That summer they had a falling out."

"Because Victor wouldn't sleep with him?"

"You do have all the answers, don't you? Yes, Victor looked up to Stephen as though he were a god, but he couldn't bring himself to love him that way. Generous as Victor is with himself—I sometimes think he's too generous—people want more than he can give."

"And that's when Stephen began picking up hustlers?"

"No he'd done that long before he met Victor. You've read the sequence called "Broken Bones," haven't you?"

"Years ago," Ben admitted. He'd never thought it was about hustlers.

Frances got up from the table and went to another room. She returned with a copy of Hunter's *Collected Poems.* Ben found the page and reread the first few poems in the sequence. He was shaken by the harsh, beautiful images of lust and fear.

"And this is why you said you thought I was heading in the same direction?" Ben asked her.

"I don't care what you do. Just be careful."

"I've never brought anyone back to the cottage."

"Borrow the book," she pleaded. "Read him again, Ben. He has a great deal to tell you. All great poets do. But I think he has a special message for you."

Like every literature student of his generation, Ben had read several of Stephen Hunter's poems in class, and had even memorized one—a sonnet: "August, and the scent of tragic leafburn." Aside from that one, however, Ben had always thought Hunter overrated. He had preferred the more formal poets, Stevens and Auden and Aiken, to what he termed the wild men, Dylan Thomas, Lowell, and especially Stephen Hunter. Not that his opinion made any difference. Hunter was in every anthology, his work written about, eulogized, discussed, reinterpreted.

Ben rediscovered him, reading through the poems in two days, rereading them, then selecting out single poems and analyzing them.

Hunter's famous *Odes to an Unruined Statue* were suddenly opened to Ben as though they had been written in a language he could never understand until now. Victor was the beautiful man/object, the unattainable; Hunter, the critical observer and adoring fantasist. The *Window Elegies,* that dozen intensely wrought series of dense metaphors and precise, yet oddly angled images were illuminated as though a light had been switched on in a basement room. Their visionary style and metaphysical message were all held together by carefully delineated details of different windows through which the poet had seen a loved one. The description in the second elegy was clearly that of Victor's A-Frame studio here at the colony, the window Hunter had looked through night after night, spying on Victor.

Ben didn't go near the large closet, which he never used anyway. Nor did he sleep in the bedroom.

He felt safe on the living room sofa, even though it was cramped. And, whether it was because of his intense new fear, or whether there was a natural boundary to the presence, Ben was not awakened once by his nocturnal visitor while he slept there.

The locks were repaired, of course, just as a precaution. And he began to haunt his previous places of fast, usually anonymous sex, returning home late at night and sleeping deeply. When he didn't go out, he would stay awake at night, working, and sleep during the day. Everything he did seemed tinged by an undercurrent of excitement, as though anticipation were slowly building, but toward what end he couldn't even begin to say.

Giove returned to the colony. Ben sometimes came upon him swimming at the pond. Although Joan was no longer with him, and the older man waved Ben over to join him, Ben would plead an excuse and quickly leave. The one time Ben and he were thrown together, for dinner at the Ormonds', they found they had nothing to say to each other.

What Ben had thought to be a mutual secret content, he now saw otherwise. Victor was perceptive enough to understand what Ben wanted from him; he was trying to avoid having the same kind of problem he'd had with Stephen Hunter.

Ben knew that evening he'd fallen out of love with Victor. The golden aura that used to light the other man's steps through the tall grass, the sparkle that used to dapple his dark curls as he lay in the sun were gone. His eyes seemed tired, his face lined, his laughter constrained.

Ben knew why too. No man he could ever deem desirable would have been fool enough to not give so simple a matter as his body to a once in a lifetime met genius like Stephen Hunter.

It was August when Ben moved back into the bedroom. "August, and the scent of tragic leafburn," he reminded himself, when he awakened once more out of a deep sleep. He knew instantly that the presence at the foot of his bed was Stephen Hunter.

His body was beginning to tingle warm under the blanket cover he had protectively pulled up in that instant of realization. But Ben still shivered. The air about him stirred in cool eddies unlike any air he'd ever known. He heard what seemed to be fragments of whispered lines from poems, pleas, demands, obscenities. Stephen knew Ben, knew who he was, what he wanted, what he'd given up. Ben's teeth began to chatter. All he had to do was to reach over to the lamp table and put on the light, and he'd be alone, well, out of harm's reach. But if he did that, Stephen might never come back to him. Ben wasn't sure he wanted that either.

He suddenly thought of Victor Giove. Large, muscled, beautiful generous Victor. He thought of Victor's smile, the bulge of his crotch in those tan worn corduroys, the roundness of his buttocks in those scarlet swimtrunks, his rippling chest, his furrowed back, those ringlets of black curls, his Florentine profile.

The room became warm and still. So warm. Ben had to push the blanket away from him, letting the heat seethe around his body.

Keeping his eyes closed, Ben thought of Victor walking, running, swimming. Then someone else pushed Victor out of the picture and came into focus: a broad-shouldered, tall, thick-bodied man with intelligent deep-set eyes of indeterminate color, a craggy face, long straight honeycolored hair, straggly moustache and beard, the face, the body, the very photograph from the frontispiece of the *Collected Poems*.

Stephen Hunter was a great poet. A genius. A man who'd felt as deeply, as spontaneously as an oil geyser. He'd flown higher than a parachute jumper on mere thought. He'd filled himself with wisdom and suffering equal to any philosopher, any monarch. Compared to him, Victor was an oversized primate.

Ben relaxed, seeing without sight, the figure moving in front of him, as though undressing, feeling the figure reach out and slowly caress Ben, the multicolored eyes gleaming softly, the mouth working to form wonderfully original words of manlove lewdness. The raking gaze swept over Ben's body like electric fire. Only such a genius could provoke, could produce such utter pleasure, Ben thought as he gave in.

He was only slightly jolted when Stephen Hunter accepted. The sudden touch was of large warm hands pressing upon his spread thighs, the brush of warm skin on either side of his loins, like a soft large cat. But the tongue that invisibly licked before engulfing him was that of a man, the long bony nose and unkempt facial hair, when Ben reached down to gingerly touch them, those of Hunter's photo image; and Ben knew he had finally found what he'd come to Sagoponauk Rock Colony for, and why that first sunset had been filled with implications he could not at first decipher.

By the end of the summer Ben was a complete recluse. He had not been seen by anyone in the colony in weeks when most of the members went back to their teaching posts around the country. Joan Sampson and the Ormonds —the last to leave, in mid-September—tried to find him, but gave up after a series of attempts.

Both the Ormonds and Victor Giove used the house on a long late October weekend. The little cottage was empty, lived-in, although increasingly messy, dusty, ill-cared for. Victor felt guilty about the boy, and waited for hours one afternoon, then searched the area until sunset made it impossible. He left notes that were never answered and were never found on subsequent visits.

On his Thanksgiving break, Victor again drove up to the colony, this time to close off the water pipes against the winter and to make certain all of the houses were locked. He once more drove to the little cottage, hoping to find Ben and to talk him out of his foolish decision to remain isolated. He didn't find the boy; but walking away from the little cottage, he gasped when he noticed the roof of Ben's Volvo sticking up out of one edge of the pond.

Although the pond was dragged by State and local police for two days no body was ever found.

Victor relayed the sad, ambiguous news to Frances Ormond, who contacted Ben's family in Eastern Long Island. Neither of them heard from his relatives again.

The last two days of the Christmas holidays, Frances Ormond drove up to the colony by herself. She found several studios broken into: cans of tinned food opened, eaten, discarded. She cleaned up, repaired the windows and doors with local help, gathered all the remaining canned foods in the studios, bought more at the grocery store and dropped them off in a large cardboard box near the little cottage. She never told anyone she did this. Secretly, she was proud and envious that Ben had gone and done what she'd always wanted to do—live here all year.

It turned out to be an extremely fierce New England Winter. Storms raged weeks at a time. All but main highways were blocked by high snow drifts, and after, by ice layers most of which lasted until late March. Livestock froze in heated barns. Old people were stranded and died. Children and stragglers from stalled cars were lost in blizzards for months. Many local farmers closed up their houses and went south. Others remained indoors, barely surviving.

Even though they managed to get into the colony by early March, the snow plows couldn't get anywhere near the little cottage.

Easter brought on the first thaw. Victor drove up to the colony, bitterly hoping he would find the boy, and that he would finally listen to reason.

The door to the little cottage was still iced over and had to be kicked hard to open.

Inside, the main rooms were icily cold. Fires had been built, tin cans charred over the fire. Kerosene liters and sterno cans littered the living room floor. But Victor couldn't tell how long they'd lain there, a day or a month. It did seem as though the boy had gotten through the winter. That was a relief. He'd probably suffered so much he'd return with Victor to the city without much urging. Victor sat down to wait.

Although it was still cold, something else seemed to be missing from the cottage that Victor couldn't at first define: a disturbance he'd almost subconsciously felt every time he'd been here since they'd discovered Stephen Hunter's corpse in the storage closet.

When it finally was too cold to stay seated, Victor got up to leave the cottage. He wrote a note to Ben saying he would be at his studio; Ben could find him there. He was about to walk outside when he realized the bedroom door was closed.

Could the boy be hiding there?

Victor opened the bedroom door and remained quite still for a very long time.

The nude emaciated body of Ben Apres was stretched out as though in utter ecstasy on the bed. His skin was ashen, pale blue with frost, perfectly preserved down to the few frozen drops of semen that had splattered his gaunt abdomen and hung off the tip of his erection.

Victor understood why he no longer sensed the supercharged presence. The insatiable Stephen Hunter had finally found someone worthy of his love.

The Servant Problem
by Richard Hall

MEADE GAZED DOWN at the floor with distaste. Alan, his therapist, was already there, sitting cross-legged, holding up the goddamn pillow. Meade knew that pillow. It was brown corduroy, with a zipper along one edge. Meade had punched it, caressed it, consoled it and once, in a fit of childish fury, bitten it. Alan had been especially pleased with the biting episode. He had nodded afterward, his handsome face creased with approval, and remarked, "Well, *that* got the anger out."

What Alan didn't know, and what Meade hadn't gotten up the nerve to tell him, was that the anger always built up again the next day. Just as bad as before. Worse. However, he didn't want Alan to think the therapy wasn't working. So at each session, when Alan murmured, "All right, let's work on the floor," Meade had slid unhappily downward, concealing his distaste, repressing his doubts about the whole procedure, and mangled the pillow according to instructions.

But today, his distaste was greater than ever. He had had a particularly bad time at the office, though that was nothing new. He had also had an unsatisfactory session with the trick sent over by his call-service last night. And to top it off, he had just quarrelled with two of his best friends. Not a quarrel, really. They had simply begun to criticize him at dinner—maliciously, unfairly. He had listened to their slanders, his heart thumping and his forehead sweating, and found he was unable to defend himself. It was too shocking. A true betrayal, like Caesar with Brutus. At last, choking down his rage, he had flung down his napkin and walked out of Sonny's apartment. He had even walked all the way home—forty blocks from the upper East Side to lower Fifth Avenue, aware that his angina might flare up at any moment, to say nothing of the risk of muggers.

Alan was squatting on the floor, holding up the pillow. Waiting. Meade had the sudden impression that Alan was a trainer and he himself a broken-down fighter, doomed to punch the brown bag in a hopeless match forever.

He slid slowly down the floor.

"Now," Alan half-closed his eyes, glimmering at him (a trick Meade found especially irritating). "Let's try to work on some of our anger again." Alan wiggled the pillow. "This is someone you hate."

"My assistant. That sneak."

"What's her name?"

"Sandra. She's trying to get my job. I think she's giving Morty blow jobs on the side."

Alan nodded. He had heard the passion and was pleased. "Go on, I want to hear you get angry."

Meade fished around in his insides, looking for some anger. Although he had been furious with Sandra today, he couldn't quite find it now. The anger seemed to have evaporated coming downtown on the subway.

"Goddam you," he said. He glared at the pillow. It was quite frayed.

"I can't hear you."

"Trying to go over my head! Comptroller . . . don't make me laugh, you can hardly add two and two!"

"I still can't hear you."

Of course, words weren't enough. Alan expected him to do something. That was the point of gestalt therapy. You didn't lie around moaning and groaning about mommy and daddy. You had to act things out in the now.

Meade drove his fist into the pillow. It was foam rubber and sprang right back. "I'll kill you!"

"Listen to yourself. You're still calm. Your voice is absolutely even."

Oh God, he'd forgotten to raise his voice this time. He was so busy thinking about punching the pillow he had neglected his voice levels.

He raised his arm, ready to repeat the action, when suddenly the pillow, without his willing it, changed into the face of Sonny DeSaix and he was at the dinner-party where they had attacked him so unfairly.

"You lousy rotten sonuvabitch!" he roared at Sonny, smashing him in the middle of his Roman-senator nose. "Go fuck yourself!" His surroundings faded as a storm of anger invaded him. At the same time his skin prickled and he knew his face was purpling up, the pits and scars deepening into bloody crescents. That meant his blood pressure was rising, a bad sign, but he couldn't help it. He had to lash back. "That's the last time you'll see me at your house!"

He grabbed the pillow and proceeded to strangle it. It felt amazingly good. Then he lifted it and banged it against the floor. That was what Sonny deserved. Sonny and Bart both. Who the fuck did they think they were?

"You are the most selfish person I've ever met," Sonny had said to him with the cold venom of an adder. *Selfish!* When it was he, Meade, who kept the crowd together! Gave the parties, bought the tickets, arranged the bridge games. Cooked the big meals at Christmas and Thanksgiving. And they called him selfish!

Suddenly he heard Bart chiming in, his voice high and whiny. "I can't stand your gossiping. You are so destructive. Everybody's afraid to tell you a thing. You know what we call you? *Central!*"

His blood ran cold at the nickname, even now. If he passed on information, it was never with malice. People wanted to hear news about other people. They confided in him because they expected him to pass it on. Central!

Suddenly the vision faded and he was aware of a knife-like pain at the back of his head. "I have a headache," he announced.

However, Alan seemed to approve of headaches. "Do you want me to give you a massage?" he asked.

Meade looked at Alan warily. He didn't really know. He was exhausted. Suddenly he wished that he were talking to Elvira instead of to Alan. Elvira was his maid, a young woman with cinnamon skin and a cool, unfathomable manner. She had been born in Trinidad. She came on Wednesdays. He hadn't really begun to recover from the awful dinner-party until he had spent the morning with Elvira. He couldn't discuss Sonny and Bart in detail with her, of course, but that wasn't necessary. Elvira cured simply by being in his apartment. Dusting. Cleaning. Ironing. Singing as she worked. After three hours with Elvira he was calm again. How strange it was. He had sometimes thought that Elvira, who barely knew how to read and write, had done more for him than all his therapists combined.

He re-focused on Alan, who seemed to be moving toward him. He let Alan gentle him backwards until he lay full-length on his stomach. It was not really a comfortable position but he tried to make the best of it. Massage seemed to be an important part of gestalt too.

Alan was almost lying on top of him. Meade wished he wouldn't do that. He could hardly get his breath. Still, it felt good in a way. He could feel Alan's hard chest, curved like a shield, pressing against his kidneys. Then he sensed the outline of Alan's genitals against the back of his thighs. Alan was really quite humpy. He occasionally worked as a surrogate at one of the sex-therapy clinics. Suddenly Meade imagined that they were doing this in the nude. He wouldn't like Alan on top of his backside, of course. He would much prefer to have Alan under him. Or, even better, on his knees in front of him.

Alan's fingers dug into the hard, resistant patches of his neck and shoulders. His breath was loud and intimate in Meade's ears. At last, Meade went limp. He was really drained. At the same time, the screen of his mind went blank.

"Why don't we talk?" Alan's voice came from some distance away. Meade looked up groggily. Alan had moved to his easy chair. The massage was over.

It took him awhile to pull himself off the floor, almost as if he had been pasted to it like a decal. His flesh felt leaden, paralyzed by gravity. But he was less tired now, amazingly, and his headache was gone. Alan was smiling broadly. "That wasn't all about Sandra," he said.

Meade nodded. "No, it was somebody else." He explained about the trouble with Sonny and Bart, noting for the hundredth time the inadequacy of explanations. However, he couldn't bring himself to tell Alan about Central. The pain was still too great.

"Do you think their criticisms were fair?"

Meade shook his head. "No." He explained about his cooking, his hospitality. Alan glimmered at him and Meade could tell he was skeptical. He had a sudden image of Alan, Sonny and Bart, all lined up against him and the heat began to mount to his cheeks again. Then he recalled Dexter Troop, his previous therapist. Dexter had never been skeptical. He had gone to Dexter because of an ad in the *Village Voice*. Dexter offered to rearrange energy patterns and unblock chakras. This, Meade discovered, involved mostly hot towels. "Just a moment," Dexter would say at moments of stress, "let's get a hot towel on that." Meade had finally stopped seeing Dexter because he realized the man had nothing to offer except some techniques picked up in the violent ward at Islip. Still, Dexter had never been skeptical.

"Could it be that you're introjecting again?"

That was one of Alan's favorite words. He thought everybody introjected a lot. "I don't think so. They were really very nasty. I didn't imagine it."

He tried to keep the sulk out of his voice with only partial success. Why didn't Alan support him, instead of criticizing him? Looking at Alan now, so trim and smug in his armchair, it occurred to Meade that Alan probably didn't require much comfort himself. The hard life for Alan. Alan had been recommended to him by a writer friend noted for an almost unearthly self-discipline. The writer could turn out a novel in six weeks and a short story in six hours. After a few months with Alan, the writer was down to four weeks for a novel and an hour for a short story.

"Nobody likes me," said Meade.

Alan looked at him balefully. "That's pure shit and you know it."

Meade glared back. What did Alan know about the need for comfort? For love? What did Alan know about something as simple as eating, for example? Last year Meade had gone to a food therapist. This man, who had a fancy office on Park Avenue, used suggestion and hypnosis to get his patients to stop over-eating. This had helped Meade, but the fee was $60 an hour and he couldn't really afford it. His weight had soared as soon as he stopped going.

"I want you to say that again and really hear what you're saying. 'Nobody likes me.' "

Alan was infuriating. They were all infuriating, really. All except Elvira. At the thought of Elvira, his anger receded slightly. If only she were coming tomorrow instead of next Wednesday! If only he could afford to have her around three days a week instead of one! He had told Alan about Elvira, but he hadn't understood. Of course not. Such relationships were entirely outside of the range of Alan's experience.

Alan was eying the floor and Meade jerked his head back. He knew what Alan was thinking. More bullshit with the pillow. The silence alarmed him. Meade took a deep breath.

103

"You're right. It isn't true that nobody likes me. There is somebody." Alan, he noted, looked interested. "His name is Peter. Peter Pride." He paused, then added, "I don't think that's his real name. He uses it . . . um, professionally."

Alan, of course, didn't approve of hustlers. Alan had a lover named Vinny —they had been together for nine years. Although they were no longer monogamous, Alan had informed him that each was the other's "primary person." This was said during their first interview, before treatment began. In gestalt therapy you got to know something about your counselor's private life. Meade liked this openness, but at the same time had gotten the impression that Alan was bragging. Nine years with the same lover. It all reminded him of the Freudian analyst he had gone to fifteen years earlier, when he was still in his twenties. The Freudian kept a color photo of his wife and children on his desk. The gender was different nowadays, but the orthodoxy seemed to be the same.

"Yes, Peter Pride. I met him . . . well . . . the usual way. But he isn't like the other boys. He wants to be an actor. I'm going to help him. I've got contacts."

Alan was beginning to look disapproving. Meade hurried on.

"He's been over three . . . four . . . times. Spent the night. I didn't sleep at all, just hugged him all night long."

His frame heaved at the memory. It was true. Each time, Peter had arrived about eleven o'clock. They had stripped quickly and begun to make feverish love. Peter was 24, a native of West Germany. He had none of the American hang-ups about status and sex. He would do anything. Afterwards he slung his long-limbed body, the color of clover honey, onto the bed and, when Meade got out of the shower, entwined his legs around Meade's like a boa. After that, Peter would drop off to sleep while Meade stayed awake, secretly running his fingers up and down Peter's flawless skin. It was a sensation he could never get enough of. He would lie in the dark, steeping himself in the splendors of that silky integument, refining the world down to the one absorbing sensation in his fingers as the hours ticked by and he fought off sleep. Each morning after a night with Peter, he had felt marvelously refreshed, as if he had spent the hours under a waterfall of milk. His own body seemed remade, his damaged skin made whole, by the perfection of Peter.

He always gave Peter a little extra something in the morning, over and above the regular fee.

"What would happen if you met someone and didn't pay him?"

He'd been steeling himself for this question. "I'd be delighted. I just can't get the people I like without paying."

"Have you tried?"

He thought about his trips to the bars, the baths, the waterfront. Oh, there had been offers. He wasn't all that unattractive, in spite of his extra weight and grey hair. But there hadn't been anyone like Peter. "Sure I've tried," he replied.

"Are you sure it's Peter's looks that appeal to you? Maybe you like to pay." He'd heard that one before too. He didn't even bother to answer. It was ridiculous.

"I'm having a fantasy I'd like to share with you," Alan said. Meade settled back, casting a sidelong glance at the clock. Just another ten minutes, thank God.

"My fantasy involves you and someone your own age who doesn't look like a movie star . . ."

As Alan unreeled his images, Meade turned his mind aside. Absurd to think he could get interested in someone his own age. Besides, other men in their forties were mostly after youngsters. As Alan droned on, his eyes glimmering, Meade embarked on a fantasy of his own. It involved both Peter Pride and Elvira. He had summoned up a charming menage for the three of them. Something bucolic—the Berkshires, perhaps—but with all the latest conveniences, including a Cuisinart. Elvira would work all day at housekeeping chores while he and Peter skinny-dipped in a clear mountain stream. After that he would ask Peter to suck him off while Elvira stood around offering rum-and-lime concoctions from her native island.

"What do you think of that?"

He blinked rapidly. He hadn't heard a word Alan had said. "I think it's . . . unrealistic," he said thoughtfully. "Totally unrealistic."

Alan looked miffed and the image of Elvira, Peter and himself slipped back into Meade's mind. He had left out the best part. At the end of each day, they would have a treasure hunt. He would hide jeweled easter eggs under shrubs and rocks so that they would have the pleasure of discovering them. After each trove was found, they would run to him to express their gratitude. He would pretend it was nothing, even though the eggs had cost him a thousand dollars each.

"I'm afraid you're the unrealistic one, Meade. That's why you get so little satisfaction out of life." Alan searched his face. "What are you thinking about now?" he demanded.

Overcoming his reluctance, Meade told him about the cottage in the Berkshires. He went from that to the easter egg hunt, becoming more excited as he went along. He could feel Alan's eyes boring into him, but he refused to be intimidated. Alan's spartan life didn't qualify him to judge needs like his own. Alan had no true understanding of people who required extra love and support. A dull anger boomed in his chest, quite different from the violence he had felt toward Sonny and Bart a while ago. This anger seemed directed not only at Alan but at someone larger and less well-defined—perhaps at his grandmother, who had stroked his cheek when he was adolescent, predicting that his acne would disappear and that he would grow up to be a handsome man; perhaps at his father, who had given him inordinate amounts of attention after a big win at gambling, but had been morose and withdrawn the rest of the time; perhaps at his boy-cousins, lumpy with muscles, who had run in and out of his childhood scoring touchdowns and homeruns without half-trying. Could therapy undo memories like these? Did he even want it to?

"Is it possible that all the people in this cottage that you fantasize are really your servants? That you can only trust people who are totally dependent on you?"

What did that mean exactly? Did it have any meaning at all? Oh yes, rolled up somewhere in those words, a red dot at the center like a pimento in an olive, was a meaning of some sort. But it had nothing to do with him, with Meade Carandelle, who had spent more than four decades looking for enough truth to get him through each day.

"We have to work on this some more. Your servant problem."

"My servant problem!" The words burst out of him with surprising force. "It isn't my problem at all . . . it's more like yours!"

Alan smiled in a superior way and Meade knew he hadn't explained, hadn't done justice to the richness of his thought. And then a bright space opened up directly in front of him and in it he discerned therapists as far ahead as he could see, an avenue of bearded sphinxes past which he would be carried like a mummy to his tomb, unless he could understand deeply and truly the nature of his attachments. And he saw that in a sense Alan was right—the servant problem *was* his problem, but not in the way that Alan thought.

"I do not believe," he paused and shuddered at the energy that flew along his tongue, "that love is all give and take. One way is enough." He paused and a brief tremor shook him again. "*Either* way is enough."

Was that what he wanted to say? Was that it exactly? He thought about Elvira and Peter, seeing them exactly as they were—self-centered, greedy, manipulative. But he had always known that about them, known it to the deepest level of his self.

Alan was glimmering at him again. "It's important not to rationalize the inability to have meaningful . . . " Meade didn't hear the rest of the sentence. It didn't matter—he'd been hearing that sentence in various forms for most of his life.

Yes, they were self-centered. Takers. Users. But did it matter? Really?

"Love is not a two-way street." The words seemed to push out of his mouth with a life of their own. "You don't have to reciprocate. I mean," he corrected himself, "*they* don't have to."

Alan was off and running now with a description of his nine years with Vinny. They had shared many things, but the most beautiful thing they had shared was sharing itself. Meade had the sudden image of their life together as an apple pie which had been cut exactly in half.

"But that's not what I want."

Alan stopped his recital and tilted his head, looking at him as a bird might look at a worm. "Of course you do. You just can't let yourself believe in it."

"As far as I'm concerned, one night with Peter is worth nine years with Vinny!"

"Will you feel that way next week? When Peter's gone and you're all by yourself? You're always complaining about being lonely."

It was true. Some nights the loneliness in his bedroom enveloped him like a shroud. He could hardly breathe. He struggled against the memory, trying to regain the sense of new vistas, new hope, he had had just a few minutes ago. But it was hard. Alan's studio, the shag rug, the hateful brown pillow, all seemed to close down on him. He could see nothing ahead but more sessions like this one.

And then, suddenly, he heard a voice. It was soft and lilting, with an accent he recognized as West Indian. "Run for de doctor," it crooned, "tell him to come as quick as he can." He turned sharply, holding his breath. Was it coming from the next apartment?

Alan stood up. "I'm afraid our time is up."

Meade remained seated as Alan shifted impatiently. "It was a good session, Meade, we'll have to work on this some more."

At last Meade hoisted himself up, trying not to wobble. Would the voice sound again? Would there be further communication? "Yeah," he mumbled, "it was a good session."

At the door he half-turned. The room was quiet. Alan's hand was on the lock. And then, ever so faintly, he heard the voice again: "Mama don't want no peas and rice and coconut oil." He winced at the sudden pain in his chest. The voice belonged to Elvira.

"Are you okay? You want to sit down for a minute?" Alan's hand was on his arm, but he shook his head and brushed it away. If he was going to have an angina attack he would rather have it outside.

"I'm okay." With a last nod, he shuffled into the hall, holding the wall for support. He knew Alan was watching but he didn't look back.

He walked slowly down Fifth Avenue, taking long rest stops. The pain in his chest had subsided to a dull ache. He kept his hand pressed there while he thought about the voice. Had he been hallucinating? Had Elvira been singing calypso songs in his head? It was bizarre—just the sort of thing he hated. On the other hand, the walls in that building were paper-thin. Perhaps a phonograph had been playing in the next apartment and the voice had reminded him of Elvira's.

But even as he explained away the sound, he felt disappointed. If it hadn't been Elvira, then there had been nothing special about the session with Alan. It had been a failure, like all the others. He suddenly felt bleak. Nothing in his life had changed. Nothing would ever change. Looking around the streets now, at the New Yorkers with their sour faces and grey skins, he saw that tomorrow would bring all the usual troubles. It would be another rotten day. His heart gave another painful tug but this time he didn't stop to rest. That wouldn't help either. And it didn't matter. There was nothing ahead but endless sessions with Alan or with someone else just like him.

A stranger in a leather jacket was sitting on the front stoop of his house. He was tall and well made, with a broad smiling face under tawny hair. It was Peter Pride. Peter was waiting for him!

"Hello, Meade," Peter said cheerily. He pronounced it **Meet**. "I came to see how you are." Peter laughed at that, a dumb happy laugh, and Meade knew that Peter probably had no place else to spend the night. Still, that didn't keep his pulse from jumping nor a mindless joy from racing through him.

"Well come in," he said.

Peter towered over him as he unlocked the downstairs door, then the apartment door. As he fiddled with the key, Meade was deliciously aware of Peter's presence, of the smell of leather and Aramis, of the promise of adventure to come. Inside, before turning on the light, he grabbed Peter and hugged him tightly. The young man's body seemed a splendid thing, a feast of the flesh from which he had been absent too long. He registered the depth of Peter's chest, the slimness of his waist, the weight of his thighs, as his own face flushed and his blood pressure mounted another notch. But he didn't worry about that. He was free of care, free of the past, at least for now.

He propelled Peter into the bedroom and they began to undress. As Peter took off his shirt, Meade had the impression that nothing was real or true outside this room, outside the drama of their disrobing. And then, as Peter stepped from his briefs, his body blazing like a sun, something unclenched in Meade's chest and he saw quite clearly that only silly people could fail to understand that a loving servant was worth his weight in gold. That, in fact, love was not something you had to earn through good behavior or self-denial, rather like a parole from jail, but something you needed only the courage to ask for. And that it was not love that had failed him in the past, but merely the courage to ask for it. He had stood around stupidly, waiting, although the doors to the feast had always been open.

They lay down on the bed and he spent a long time running his fingers across Peter's chest, which was a smooth coverlet of shining moire silk, Peter kept his eyes closed while this was going on, his lips tilted in a blissful smile. Peter loved the attention, Meade knew, loved being worshipped. And Meade saw Peter's happiness as his own, Peter's participation as unlimited, despite the fact that Peter did nothing but lie very still, smiling.

And then, echoing very faintly in the bedroom, he heard a familiar voice. It was smooth and silky, rather like Peter's skin, and it lapped around him gently. "When my money run out I'd have no regret," it crooned, "I'll buy some of everything that money can get."

"You said it, Elvira," Meade giggled to himself. Then he began to lick Peter all over, rather like an ice-cream cone, deliciously oblivious to what his therapist —or any therapist—would care to say about the nature of his need.

Some of These Days

by James Purdy

WHAT MY LANDLORD'S friends said about me was in a way the gospel truth, that is he was good to me, and I was mean and ungrateful to him. All the two years I was in jail, nonetheless, I thought only of him, and I was filled with regret for the things I had done against him. I wanted him back. I didn't exactly wish to go back to live with him now, mind you, I had been too mean to him for that, but I wanted him for a friend again. After I got out of jail I would need friendship, for I didn't need to hold up even one hand to count my friends on, the only one I could even name was him. I didn't want anything to do with him physically again, I had kind of grown out of that somehow even more while in jail, and wished to try to make it with women again, but I did require my landlord's love and affection, for love was, as everybody was always saying, his special gift and talent.

He was at the time I lived with him a rather well-known singer, and he also composed songs, but even when I got into my bad trouble, he was beginning to go downhill, and not to be so in fashion. We often quarreled over his not succeeding way back then. Once I hit him when he told me how much he loved me, and knocked out one of his front teeth. But that was only after he had also criticized me for not keeping the apartment tidy and clean and doing the dishes, and I threatened him with an old gun I kept. Of course I felt awful bad about his losing this front tooth when he needed good teeth for singing. I asked his forgiveness. We made up and I let him kiss me and hold me tight just for this one time.

I remember his white face and sad eyes at my trial for breaking and entering and possession of a dangerous weapon, and at the last his tears when the judge sentenced me. My landlord could cry and not be ashamed of crying, and so you didn't mind him shedding tears somehow. At first, then, he wrote me, for as the only person who could list himself as nearest of kin or closest tie, he was allowed by the authorities to communicate with me, and I also received little gifts from him from time to time. And then all upon a sudden the presents stopped, and shortly after that, the letters too, and then there was no word of any kind, just nothing. I realized then that I had this strong feeling for him

109

which I had never had for anybody before, for my people had been dead from the time almost I was a toddler, and so they are shadowy and dim, whilst he is bright and clear. That is, you see, I had to admit to myself in jail (and I choked on my admission), but I had hit bottom, and could say a lot of things now to myself, I guess I was in love with him. I had really only loved women I had always told myself, and I did not love this man so much physically, in fact he sort of made me sick to my stomach to think of him that way, though he was a good-looker with his neat black straight hair, and his robin's-egg blue eyes, and cheery smile . . . And so there in my cell I had to confess what did I have for him if it was not love, and yet I had treated him meaner than anybody I had ever knowed in my life, and once come close to killing him. Thinking about him all the time now, for who else was there to think about, I found I got to talking to myself more and more like an old geezer of advanced years, and in place of calling on anybody else or any higher power, since he was the only one I had ever met in my twenty years of life who said he cared, I would find myself saying like in church, *My landlord,* though that term for him was just a joke for the both of us, for all he had was this one-room flat with two beds, and my bed was the little one, no more than a cot, and I never made enough to pay him no rent for it, he just said he would trust me. So there in my cell, especially at night, I would say *My landlord,* and finally, for my chest begin to trouble me about this time and I was short of breath often, I would just manage to get out *My lord.* That's what I would call him for short. When I got out, the first thing I made up my mind to do was find him, and I was going to put all my efforts behind the search.

And when there was no mail now at all, I would think over all the kind and good things he done for me, and the thought would come to me which was blacker than any punishment they had given me here in the big house that I had not paid him back for his good deeds. When I got out I would make it up to him. He had took me in off the street, as people say, and had tried to make a man of me, or at least a somebody out of me, and I had paid him back all in bad coin, first by threatening to kill him, and then by going bad and getting sent to jail . . . But when I got out, I said, I will find him if I have to walk from one ocean shore to the other.

And so it did come about that way, for once out, that is all I did or found it in my heart to do, find the one who had tried to set me straight, find the one who had done for me, and shared and all.

One night after I got out of jail, I had got dead drunk and stopped a guy on Twelfth Street, and spoke, *Have you seen my lord?* This man motioned to me to follow him into a dark little theater, which later I was to know all too well as one of the porno theaters, he paid for me, and brought me to a dim corner in the back, and then the same old thing started up again, he beginning to undo my clothes, and lower his head, and I jumped up and pushed him and ran out of the movie, but then stopped and looked back and waited there as it begin to give me an idea.

Now a terrible thing had happened to me in jail. I was beat on the head by another prisoner, and I lost some of the use of my right eye, so that I am always straining by pushing my neck around as if to try to see better, and when the convict hit me that day and I was unconscious for several weeks and they despaired of my life, later on when I come to myself at last, I could remember everything that had ever happened in my whole twenty years of life except my landlord's name, and I couldn't think of it if I was to be alive. That is why I have been in the kind of difficulty I have been in. It is the hardest thing in the world to hunt for somebody if you don't know his name.

I finally though got the idea to go back to the big building where he and I had lived together, but the building seemed to be under new management, with new super, new tenants, new everybody. Nobody anyhow remembered any singer, they said, nor any composer, and then after a time, it must have been though six months from the day I returned to New York, I realized that I had gone maybe to a building that just looked like the old building my landlord and I have lived in, and so I tore like a blue streak straightaway to this "correct" building to find out if any such person as him was living there, but as I walked around through the halls looking, I become somewhat confused all over again if this was the place either, for I had wanted so bad to find the old building where he and I had lived, I had maybe been overconfident of this one also being the correct place, and so as I walked the halls looking and peering about I become puzzled and unsure all over again, and after a few more turns, I give up and left.

That was a awesome fall, and then winter coming on and all, and no word from him, no trace, and then I remembered a thing from the day that man had beckoned me to come follow him into that theater, and I remembered something, I remembered that on account of my landlord being a gay or queer man, one of his few pleasures when he got an extra dollar was going to the porno movies in 3rd Avenue. My remembering this was like a light from heaven, if you can think of heaven throwing light on such a thing, for suddenly I knowed for sure that if I went to the porno movie I would find him.

The only drawback for me was these movies was somewhat expensive by now, for since I been in jail prices have surely marched upwards, and I have very little to keep me even in necessities. This was the beginning of me seriously begging, and sometimes I would be holding out my hand on the street for three-fourths of a day before I got me enough to pay my way into the porno theater. I would put down my three bucks, and enter the turnstile, and then inside wait until my eyes got used to the dark, which because of my prison illness took nearly all of ten minutes, and then I would go up to each aisle looking for my landlord. There was not a face I didn't examine carefully . . . My interest in the spectators earned me several bawlings-out from the manager of the theater, who took me for somebody out to proposition the customers, but I paid him no mind . . . But his fussing with me gave me an idea, too, for I am attractive to men, both young and old, me being not yet twenty-one, and so I began what was to become regular practice, letting the audience take any liberty they was in a mind to with me in the hopes that through this contact they would divulge the whereabouts of my landlord.

But here again my problem would surface, for I could not recall the very name of the person who was most dear to me, yes that was the real sore spot. But as the men in the movie theater took their liberties with me, which after a time I got sort of almost to enjoy, even though I could barely see their faces, only see enough to know they was not my landlord, I would then, I say, describe him in full to them, and I will give them this much credit, they kind of listened to me as they went about getting their kicks from me, they would bend an ear to my asking for this information, but in the end they never heard of him nor any other singer, and never knowed a man who wrote down notes for a living.

But strange as it might seem to anybody who will ever see these sheets of paper, this came to be my only connection with the world, my only life—sitting in the porno theater. Since my only purpose was to find him and from him find my own way back, this was the only thoroughfare there was open for me to reach him. And yet I did not like it, though at the same time even disliking it as much as I did, it give me some little feeling of a resemblance to warmth and kindness as the unknown men touched me with their invisible faces and extracted from me all I had to offer, such as it was. And then when they had finished me, I would ask them if they knew my landlord (or as I whispered to myself, my lord). But none ever did.

Winter had come in earnest, was raw in the air. The last of the leaves in the park had long blown out to sea, and yet it was not to be thought of giving up the search and going to a warmer place. I would go on here until I had found him or I would know the reason why, yes, I must find him, and not give up. (I tried to keep the phrase *My lord* only for myself, for once or twice when it had slipped out to a stranger, it give him a start, and so I watched what I said from there on out.)

And then I was getting down to the last of the little money I had come out of jail with, and oh the porno theaters was so dear, the admission was hiked another dollar just out of the blue, and the leads I got in that old dark hole was so few and far between. Toward the end one man sort of perked up when I mentioned my landlord the singer, and said he thought he might have known such a fellow, but with no name to go on, he too soon give up, and said he guessed he didn't know after all.

And so I was stumped. Was I to go on patronizing the porno theater, I would have to give up food, for my panhandling did not bring in enough for both grub and movies, and yet there was something about bein' in that house, getting the warmth and attention from the stray men that meant more to me than food and drink. So I began to go without eating in earnest so as to keep up my regular attendance at the films. That was maybe, looking back on it now, a bad mistake, but what is one bad mistake in a lifetime of them.

As I did not eat now but only give my favors to the men in the porno, I grew pretty unsteady on my feet. After a while I could barely drag to the theater. Yet it was the only place I wanted to be, especially in view of its being now full winter. But my worst fears was now realized, for I could not longer afford even the cheap lodging place I had been staying at, and all I had in the world was what was on my back, and the little in my pockets, so I had come at last to this, and yet I did not think about my plight so much as about him, for as I got weaker and weaker he seemed to stand over me as large as the figures of the film actors that raced across the screen, and at which I almost never looked, come to think of it. No, I never watched what went on on the screen itself. I watched the audience, for it was the living that would be able to give me the word.

"Oh come to me, come back and set me right!" I would whisper hoping someone out of the audience might rise and tell me they knew where he was.

Then at last, but of course slow gradual-like, I no longer left the theater. I was too weak to go out, anyhow had no lodging now to call mine, knew if I got as far as a step beyond the entrance door of the theater, I would never get back inside to its warmth, and me still dressed in my summer clothes.

Then after a long drowsy time, days, weeks, who knows? my worse than worst fears was realized, for one—shall I say day?—for where I was now there was no day or night, and the theater never closed its doors—one time, then, I say, they *come* for me, they had been studying my condition, they told me later and they come to take me away. I begged them with all the strength I had left not to do so, that I could still walk, that I would be gone and bother nobody again.

When did you last sit down to a bite to eat? A man spoke this direct into my ear, a man by whose kind of voice I knew did not belong to the porno world, but come from some outside authority.

I have lost all tract of time, I replied, closing my eyes.

All right buddy, the man kept saying, and *Now, bud,* and then as I fought and kicked, they held me and put the strait jacket on me, though didn't they see I was too weak and dispirited to hurt one cruddy man jack of them.

Then as they was taking me finally away, for the first time in months, I raised my voice, as if to the whole city, and called, and shouted, and explained: *"Tell him if he comes, how long I have waited and searched, that I have been hunting for him, and I cannot remember his name. I was hit in prison by another convict and the injury was small, but it destroyed my one needed memory, which is his name. That is all that is wrong with me. If you would cure me of this one little defect, I will never bother any of you again, never bother society again. I will go back to work and make a man of myself, but I have first to thank this former landlord for all he done for me."*

He is hovering between life and death.

I repeated aloud the word *hovering* after the man who had pronounced this sentence somewhere in the vicinity of where I was lying in a bed that smelled strong of carbolic acid.

And as I said the word *hovering*, I knew his name. I raised up. Yes, my landlord's name had come back to me . . . It had come back after all the wreck and ruin of these weeks and years.

But then one sorrow would follow upon another, as I believe my mother used to say, though that is so long ago I can't believe I had a mother, for when they saw that I was conscious and in my right mind, they come to me and begun asking questions, especially *What was my name*. I stared at them then with the greatest puzzlement and sadness, for though I had fished up his name from so far down, I could no more remember my own name now when they asked me for it than I could have got out of my strait jacket and run a race, and I was holding on to the just-found landlord's name, with the greatest difficulty, for it, too, was beginning to slip from my tongue and go disappear where it had been lost before.

As I hesitated, they begun to persecute me with their kindness, telling me how they would help me in my plight, but first of all they must have my name, and since they needed a name so bad, and was so insistent, and I could see their kindness beginning to go, and the cruelty I had known in jail coming fresh to mind, I said "I am Sidney Fuller," giving them you see my landlord's name.

"And your age, Sidney?"
"Twenty, come next June."
"And how did you earn your living."
"I have been without work now for some months."
"What kind of work do you do?"
"Hard labor."
"When were you last employed?"
"In prison."

There was a silence, and the papers was moved about, then:
"Do you have a church or faith?"

I waited quite a while, repeating his name, and remembering I could not remember my own, and then said, "I am of the same faith as my landlord."

There was an even longer silence then, like the questioner had been cut down by his own inquiry, anyhow they did not interrogate me any more after that, they went away, and left me by myself.

After a long time, certainly days, maybe weeks, they announced the doctor was coming.

He set down on a sort of ice-cream chair beside me, and took off his glasses and wiped them. I barely saw his face.

"Sidney," he began after it sounded like he had started to say something else first, and then changed his mind. "Sidney, I have some very serious news to impart to you, and I want you to try to be brave. It is hard for me to say what I am going to say. I will tell you what we have discovered. I want you, though, first, to swallow this tablet, and we will wait together for a few minutes, and then I will tell you."

I had swallowed the tablet it seemed a long time ago, and then all of a sudden I looked down at myself, and I saw I was not in the strait jacket, my arms was free.

"Was I bad, doctor?" I said, and he seemed to be glad I had broke the ice, I guess.

"I believe, Sidney, that you know in part what I am going to say to you," he started up again. He was a dark man, I saw now, with thick eyebrows, and strange, I thought, that for a doctor he seemed to have no wrinkles, his face was smooth as a sheet.

"We have done all we could to save you, you must believe us," he was going on as I struggled to hear his words through the growing drowsiness given me by the tablet. "You have a sickness, Sidney, for which unfortunately there is today no cure . . ."

He said more, but I do not remember what, and was glad when he left, no, amend that, I was sad I guess when he left. Still, it didn't matter one way or another if anybody stayed or lit out.

But after a while, when I was a little less drowsy, a new man come in, with some white papers under his arm.

"You told us earlier when you were first admitted," he was saying, "that your immediate family is all dead . . . Is there nobody to whom you wish to leave any word at all . . . ? If there is such a person, we would appreciate your writing the name and address on each of these four sheets of paper, and add any instructions which you care to detail."

At that moment, I remembered my own name, as easily as if it had been written on the paper before me, and the sounds of it placed in my mouth and on my tongue, and since I could not give my landlord's name again and as the someone to whom I could bequeath my all, I give the inquirer with the paper my own real name:

James De Salles

"And his address?" the inquirer said.

I shook my head.

"Very well, then, Sidney," he said, rising from the same chair the doctor had sat in. He looked at me some time, then kind of sighed, and folded the sheaf of papers.

"Wait," I said to him then, "just a minute . . . Could you get me writing paper, and pen and ink to boot . . . "

"Paper, yes . . . We have only ball-point pens, though . . . "

So then he brought the paper and the ball-point, and I have written this down, asking another patient here from time to time how to say this, or spell that, but now showing him what I am about, and it is queer indeed isn't it, that I can only bequeath these papers to myself, for God only knows who would read them later, and it has come to me very clear in my sleep that my landlord

115

is dead also, so there is no point in my telling my attendants that I have lied to them, that I am really James De Salles, and that my lord is or was Sidney Fuller.

But after I done wrote it all down, I was quiet in my mind and heart, and so with some effort I wrote my own name on the only thing I have to leave, and which they took from me a few moments ago with great puzzlement, for neither the person was known to them, and the address of course could not be given, and they only received it from me, I suppose, to make me feel I was being tended to.

Under the Hollywood Sign

by Tom Reamy

They are here, they are beautiful and cold, we look
at them and don't see them . . . and they wait,
for what apocalypse?

I CAN'T PINPOINT the exact moment I noticed him. I suppose I had been subliminally aware of him for some time, though he was just standing there with the rest of the crowd. Anyway, I had other things on my mind: a Pinto and a Buick were wrapped around each other like lettuce leaves. The paramedics had two of them out, wrapped in plastic sheets waiting for the meat wagon, and were cutting out a third with a torch. He appeared to be in the Buick, but you couldn't really tell.

My partner Carnehan and I were holding back the crowd of gawkers. A couple of bike cops in their gestapo uniforms were keeping the traffic moving on Cahuenga, not letting any of them stop and get out. But there were still twenty or twenty-five of them standing there—eyes bright, noses crinkled, mouths disapproving.

All except him.

That's one of the reasons I noticed him in particular. He wasn't wearing that horrified, fascinated expression they all seem to have. He might have been watching anything—or nothing. His face was smooth and placid. I think that's the first time I ever saw a face totally without expression. It wasn't dull or blank or lifeless. No, there was vitality there. It just simply wasn't doing anything at the moment.

And he was . . . Don't get the wrong idea—my crotch doesn't get tight at the sight of an attractive young man. But there's only one word to describe him—beautiful!

I've seen my share of pretty boys—the ones that flutter and the ones that don't. It seems the prettier they are, the more trouble they get into. But he wasn't that *kind* of beautiful.

Even though the word is used these days to describe practically everything, it was the only one that fitted. I thought at first he was very young: nineteen, twenty, not more than twenty-one. But then I got the impression he was much older, though I don't know why, because he still looked twenty. He was about five-ten, a hundred and sixty-seventy pounds—one of those bodies the hero of the book always has but that you never see in real life.

His hair was red, or it might have just been the light from the flashers. There were no peculiarities of feature; just a neutral perfection. I've heard it said that perfect beauty is dull, that it takes an imperfection to make a face interesting. Whoever said it had never seen this kid.

He was standing with his hands in his pockets, watching the guys with the torch, neither interested nor uninterested. I guess I was staring at him, because his head turned and he looked directly at me.

I could smell the rusty odor of the antifreeze dribbling from the busted radiators and the sharp ozone of the acetylene and the always remembered smell of blood. A coyote began yipping somewhere in the darkness.

Then a couple of kids got too close and I had to hustle them out of the way. When I looked back, he was no longer there.

They finally got the third one out of the Buick. When they pulled him out I could see the wet brown stain all over the seat of his pants where his bowels had relaxed in death. The ambulance picked up all three of them and the wrecker hauled off the two cars still merged as one. Part of the mess was dragging on the street and I could hear the scraping for a long time. The bike cops did a few flashy turns and roared away. The crowd started to wander off, and Carnehan and I began sweeping the broken glass from the pavement.

But there was only one thing I could think of: I couldn't remember the color of his eyes.

Nothing much happened the rest of the night. We cruised the Boulevard a few times, but there wasn't anything going on. A few hustlers still lounged around the Gold Cup and the Egyptian, never giving up hope. There was no point in hassling them—they'd just say they were waiting for a bus, and we couldn't prove they weren't. It was a pretty scruffy-looking bunch this late in the morning. The presentable ones had scored a long time ago. You could probably get most of these with an offer of breakfast.

Carnehan reached behind the seat and pulled an apple from the paper sack he always kept back there. He took a bite that sounded like a rifle shot and then offered me one. "No, thanks."

"An apple a day keeps the doctor away." He grinned and took another bite.

"You're keeping the entire AMA at bay."

He laughed; partly chewed apple dribbled down his chin. He wiped it off with the back of his hand. I kept my eyes on the street. "Why don't you eat soft apples? They're quiet."

"I like hard ones."

We stopped a car with only one taillight and gave the guy a warning ticket.

Then the sun was coming up. It was hitting the tops of the Hollywood Hills and illuminating the Hollywood sign. It looked decent from this far away. You couldn't tell it was made of rotting timbers and sagging sheet metal clanging in the wind. From here you couldn't see the obscenities scrawled on it.

We went back to the station, reported, and then into the locker room. The rest of the graveyard shift were wandering in, showering, and changing out of their uniforms. Cunningham has the locker next to mine. He had been on the Pansy Patrol and was wearing a shirt unbuttoned to the waist, no underwear, and pants so tight you could count every hair on his ass.

Wharton, one of the police psychiatrists, was leaning against the lockers talking to him. Doc was on his favorite theme again. He was telling Cunningham why he, Cunningham, was so successful on the Pansy Patrol. The fags recognized a kindred spirit; the fags always knew one of their own kind; if Cunningham would only stop fooling himself, just stop deluding himself that he was straight, just know himself, just start living a conscious life, he would be a happier, more fulfilled person.

I had been on the Pansy Patrol with Cunningham a few times and had seen him operate. I wasn't completely sure Doc was wrong. Cunningham was peeling off the tight pants and I watched in fascination, although I'd seen it before, as the sizable bulge in his crotch stayed with the pants.

Poor Cunningham.

He was standing there naked with a slight smile on his face, putting the pants neatly on a hanger, listening to Doc's clarinet voice. He looked a lot like the cop on "Adam-12," whatever his name is, the kid. The boys had even called him "Adam-12" for a while until they got tired of it. I couldn't keep from comparing him to the guy I had seen at the wreck, but Cunningham didn't compare at all. He was just a good-looking kid with a slim muscular body, and not much equipment. But it didn't seem to bother him. He always grinned and said it wasn't size that counted, it was technique.

I took off my own pants and looked at myself. I wasn't as young or as good-looking as Cunningham, but I did all right on the Pansy Patrol. I was bulkier and more heavily muscled and hairier; I guess I appealed to the rough trade crowd. I was never very comfortable without underwear, and thank God I didn't have to wear padding.

Wharton finished his catalogue of Cunningham's emotional failings. Cunningham looked at me and winked. "I don't really know anything about, Doc, but maybe the reason I'm not interested in sex with another man is because I'm just *not interested* in sex with another man."

Doc's lips got a little tight and his face was slightly flushed. I knew Cunningham had been reading Kingsley Amis again and had probably maneuvered Doc into the whole conversation—and Doc was eminently maneuverable. I'd heard most of it before, so I got a towel and started for the showers. Cunningham followed me and Warton followed him.

"You're right, Cunningham, you don't know anything about it!"

I turned on the water and began soaping. Cunningham got next to me and Doc stood at the door, still talking. Cunningham looked at me and grinned and said loudly, "Sorry, Doc, I can't hear you with the water running!"

There were about ten other guys in the shower, grinning at each other. Cunningham leaned toward me. "Hey, Rankin, you notice how Doc always manages to look in the showers?"

I shrugged.

"According to him everyone is either a fag or a closet queen."

"What about himself?" I asked.

He rolled his eyes and laughed. "Getting him to talk about himself is like catching fairies in a saucepan."

Carnehan came in, pitching an apple core into the wastebasket. I could see why he had never been on the Pansy Patrol. Then . . . I don't know why I thought of it, but the thought crossed my mind. I wondered what the guy at the wreck looked like naked.

I left the station and got into my five-year-old Dart. It looked like a nice day. There was enough wind from the ocean to clear away the smog. Of course, the wind was packing it into the San Gabriel Valley, but that was their problem, not mine. I went straight home and went to bed.

I was scrambling some eggs and watching *The Price is Right* when the phone rang. They were doing the one where the screaming dame has to zero in on the prices of two objects within thirty seconds. When she names a price, the MC says "Higher" or "Lower." This keeps up until she guesses the price. You can get it in ten guesses maximum. She started at a hundred on a color TV and worked up ten dollars at a time.

"Hundred and ten!"

"Higher!"

"Hundred and twenty!"

"Higher!"

"Hundred and thirty!"

"Higher!"

She got to three-seventy before her time ran out. Dumb dame!

It was Carnehan on the phone. "Hey, Lou, Margaret wants you to come over for dinner tonight."

"Hell, Carnehan. I wish you'd said something this morning. I've already made other plans." You stupid jerk! Don't you ever wonder why your wife is always inviting me to dinner?

"Got a heavy date, Lou?"

"Something like that. Some other time, Carnehan." No other time, Carnehan. Margaret's a pretty good-looking dame for her age, but not good enough to take chances with. You didn't even notice how her hand stayed under the table all through dinner last time.

"Margaret says how about Wednesday?"

"I'll have to let you know later." And you never even had a suspicion about what goes on after you fall asleep in front of the TV, Carnehan. If you ever found out . . .

"Okay, Lou. I'll remind you Tuesday night."

"You do that." And I'll have a good excuse ready. Not that I give a good goddamn if you do find out, but you could make a stink at the department. I don't want to lose my job, Carnehan. I like being a cop.

" 'Bye, Lou. See you later."

" 'Bye, Carnehan." I hung up the phone in time to see a granny-lady have an orgasm over winning a dune buggy.

I usually eat dinner about eight o'clock at David's. I know it's a fag hangout but the food's good and, since I let it be known I was a cop, the service is even better. I spotted him as I was leaving about nine. He went into the gay bar next to David's. It was called Goliath's, of course. I only glimpsed him from behind but I was sure of the red hair and body. Wouldn't you know he'd be a queer!

I paid my dollar and a quarter cover charge and went through the black curtains after him. I don't know what I was planning to do, but I hadn't been able to get him out of my mind. I stood for a moment, waiting for my eyes to adjust to the gloom and my ears to the plaster-cracking music. There were three small stages with naked boys dancing on them, wiggling their little round butts for all they were worth. There were also five screens showing movies of naked boys doing everything it's physically possible for naked boys to do and a few things I would have thought impossible before I joined the force.

Then there were the customers. A few were at the bar and a few were scattered around but most of them were packed like Vienna sausages against one wall. There was plenty of room and no need for the press of bodies—no need but one, and the busy hands told what that was. A few watched the movies but mostly they watched each other. One of the dancers was waving around a hardon and was getting some attention but not much. A couple of dykes at the bar watched him. I guess this is the only chance they have to see one.

I spotted the back of the red head in the middle of the mass, so I waded in. There's no way to move through something like that. No one can move out of your way; they're just as trapped as you are. You just wait and move with the current because the pack is in constant eddy as they move from one body to the next, trying to touch everything.

It was no more than thirty seconds before I felt feathery touches on my ass. I thought about my wallet, but I knew that wasn't what they were after. I pushed away the first hand that closed on my crotch and saw a pout of disappointment flicker across a face in front of mine. I put my wallet in my shirt pocket anyway.

After five minutes and fifty gropes, I finally reached the redhead but he was turned the other way. I was pressed against him and could feel his hard body. By pushing with determination, I managed to get to the side of him. He was standing face to face with another guy. Both of them had their eyes closed and their mouths slightly open, occasionally coming together in a lazy kiss. Their hands were out of sight but I could feel the movement.

It wasn't him.

This was one of the pretty ones. I might even have said beautiful if I hadn't seen the other one. But, like Cunningham, he was ordinary in comparison. He opened his eyes and saw me watching him and he smiled dreamily. I felt a hand massaging my crotch but I couldn't tell for sure if it was him. I was so disappointed I didn't push it away. Then my zipper went down and fingers expertly scooped everything out. The press was so tight I couldn't even get my arms down, much less move away. Whoever was working on me was very good and I couldn't help getting it up.

Jesus Christ!

I had a wild urge to take out my badge and shove it in every face in sight. I enjoyed my mental image of the panic it would create. But I didn't do it. I forced my arms down, pushed the clutching hands away, closed my pants, and got the hell out of there.

When I went into the locker room about eleven thirty, Carnehan already had his uniform on, sitting there reading a copy of the *Advocate* and eating an apple. He looked up when I rattled my locker.

"Hey, Lou! You missed a great dinner."

"It couldn't be helped, Carnehan."

"Don't forget about Wednesday."

"I won't."

I took off my shirt and remembered my wallet was still in the pocket. I put it on the shelf and took off my pants. I grabbed a towel and headed for the shower. I felt clammy. I must have sweated off a pound in that damn bar. Those groping bodies can generate a lot of heat.

Carnehan laughed out loud. He came toward me waving the newspaper. "Hey, Lou! Did you see this cartoon in the *Advocate*?"

"Why in hell would I be reading the *Advocate*?"

"Look, there's these two cops standing before a judge with a handcuffed fag and a hooker. One of the cops is saying, 'But Your Honor, you can get *hurt* chasing robbers and murderers.' Isn't that a scream?"

"Ha ha," I said and went on to the showers. He started rushing around the room showing it to everyone else.

I was almost finished when Cunningham came in. He turned on the water and stood under it leaning against the wall with his eyes closed and a sappy grin on his face.

"You look like the cat that swallowed the aviary," I said.

He sighed. "I am *exhausted*!"

"Let me guess from what."

"I met the most fan*ta*stic girl! A waitress at the Hamburger Hamlet on the Strip. I'm gonna give it two weeks and, if I'm *still alive*, I'm gonna propose." He rubbed his hand between his legs. "I tell you, Rankin, I didn't know I had it in me. Boy, I'd like to see Wharton try to convince *her* I'm a repressed homosexual."

I laughed dutifully. He began soaping and glanced down at me.

"You look a little shriveled up yourself. Have a big night?" He grinned goodnaturedly, wanting to share his sexual excitement.

"Yeah. Some women are just as happy with size as they are with technique." He looked a little wistful for a moment, then the grin returned. "Shit! If I had your size and my technique, I'd quit the force, put an ad in the *Free Press,* and open a screwing service!"

And I wondered about *him* again. With that face and that body, did he worry about size and technique? How did women react to him? Were they intimidated by his beauty? Was he as beautiful in bed?

I saw him going into the Vogue Record Shop on the Boulevard. This time there was no mistake. I told Carnehan to park the car and meet me at the entrance. When I went through the turnstiles, I saw him leaning against the end of the counter. I walked into the book department and watched him from behind a rack of paperbacks.

He had his back to me and it took me a moment to figure out what he was doing. The cashier was playing the *Symphonie Fantastique*—it was the passage where the two shepherds are calling to each other on their flutes and, at the end, one doesn't answer—and he was standing there listening to the music. Then he turned slightly and I could see his face.

I could feel the skin crawling on the back of my neck.

It wasn't the same one!

It was all there: the red hair, the magnificent body, the neutral beauty of the bland face. But the features were different. He had to be the other one's brother, they were so alike.

The lights in the store were very bright. No one else was in the place but the cashier and she had her nose in a paperback volume of Toynbee. His clothes were clean and neatly pressed but they were old and hadn't cost much when they were new. His hair was neat and not very long. His face was so smooth I doubted that he shaved. And his eyes were gray—just as beautiful and as neutral as the rest of him.

Finally the record ended and he left. I glanced at the book I had been holding. The cover was a photograph of Burt Reynolds standing with his back to the camera looking over his shoulder. He was wearing nothing but a football jersey, with his bare ass hanging out. I closed the book, put it back on the rack, and for some reason thought of Betty Grable.

The cashier never even looked up when he went out. Carnehan, standing on the sidewalk looking confused, never glanced at him as he walked by. The girl was watching me. She smiled but her eyes were guarded.

"Did you know the man who just went out?" I asked, trying to sound casual.

She glanced out the door, but he had turned left toward Las Palmas. She looked back at me. "I don't think so, officer. Did he do something?"

"No. I just thought I'd seen him before. Maybe in the movies or on television."

123

She shrugged. "Movie stars come in here all the time. Joanne Worley was in yesterday. Wendell Burton comes in every once in a while."

"Thanks." I left before she could give me a complete catalogue of the celebrities she'd seen. She raised her voice as I went out the door.

"Chad Everett was in a couple of weeks ago but I was off that day."

I looked down the Boulevard but didn't see him. I told Carnehan to wait for me and went after him. At Las Palmas I looked in every direction but there was no sign of him. The hustlers standing around the Gold Cup pretended to ignore me, but a couple of drag queens gave me defiant looks.

There was another bad one that night on the off-ramp at Western. Four cars were scattered half a block. There were seven dead and two others who probably wouldn't see morning. And there were two of *them* in the crowd. Two different ones.

I motioned Carnehan over.

"Yeah, Lou?"

"Carnehan. See those two guys over there, the ones with red hair?"

He looked confused. "Where?"

"You see the black dame in the yellow dress? The one with pigtails all over her head that make her look like an upside-down johnny brush?"

He snickered. "Sure."

"One of them is standing right beside her. On her left. You see him?"

Slowly: "Yeah."

"What does he look like?"

He looked up at me. "What d'ya mean?"

"No! Keep looking at him!" He looked back. "You still see him?"

"Yeah."

"Describe him to me."

He thought for a moment. "Don't forget. Tomorrow's Wednesday. Margaret's expecting you for dinner."

"*Carnehan!* Concetrate on the redheaded guy. Don't think about anything else. What does he look like?"

"I don't know. He's just a guy."

"How old is he?"

"It's hard to tell. The light's not too good."

"Is he under thirty?"

He considered. "Yeah."

"Under twenty-five?"

"Yeah. Yeah, I'd say so."

"Under twenty?"

He was silent for a moment. Good old Carnehan. His little pea brain was doing its best. "Maybe . . . but probably not."

"What about his face?"

"What about it?"
"Is it an ugly face?"
"No."
"Is it a handsome face?"
"Yeah, I guess so."
"How handsome?"
"Golly, Lou."
"Very handsome?"
"Yeah."
"Better-looking than Cunningham?"
"Yeah." His voice suddenly got excited. "Hey, Lou, is that a movie star or something?"

We went through the whole thing again with the other one. Carnehan finally saw them the same way I did, but he couldn't remember the one at the record shop. Later I asked him if he remembered the two good-looking redheaded guys.

"Sure. How could you forget somebody who looks like that? Especially when there's two of 'em. Hey, you suppose they're twins?"

"Are they still there?"

"Naw. They musta left," he said, looking right at them. "Don't forget about dinner Wednesday night."

Then they both turned and looked at me with their expressionless eyes. Or were they expressionless? I thought I saw recognition and speculation, but I wasn't sure. Carnehan was right. The light *was* bad.

They kept us hopping the rest of the night. We'd barely get through with one before we were sent to another.

An old hotel on Vermont burned to the ground. Half the department was there, keeping the curious out from underfoot, rerouting traffic. My eyes were burning and watery from the smoke, but it didn't keep me from seeing them.

I counted seven. Seven beautiful redheaded young men with perfect bodies.

I leaned against my locker in pure exhaustion, wondering if I should take a shower. I was grimy from smoke and dust but I was so tired I only wanted to go to bed. Cunningham came in, looking as beat as I felt.

He looked at me and sighed, shaking his head.

"What are you doing in uniform?" I asked, not really caring. "You off the Pansy Patrol?"

He started undressing. "Yeah. They called us in about three. What got into people last night, anyway? Seems like everybody was trying to get themselves killed."

The same thought had crossed my mind, but not seriously. I had other things to think about.

Margaret called herself the next afternoon to remind me about dinner. But I'd already laid out my plan of action.

125

"I'm sorry, Margaret. I was just about to call you. I'm leaving for Texas in about two hours. My father is very ill and I've taken a leave of absence from the department."

"Oh, Lou, I'm so sorry. Is there anything I can do?"

"No, thank you, Margaret. Everything's taken care of."

"At least let me drive you to the airport."

"I'm not flying. I'll need my car when I get there."

"How long will you be gone?"

"I don't know. My father isn't expected to live . . ." I let my voice break a little. "Say so long to Carnehan for me."

"Of course, Lou. You're sure there's nothing I can do?"

"No. Nothing. Good-bye, Margaret."

" 'Bye, Lou, dear."

Well, it wasn't *all* a lie. My father had taken three months to die seventeen years ago when I was in high school, but nobody out here knew that. The Lieutenant hadn't much liked the idea of giving me an indefinite leave of absence, but what could he do? I packed enough supplies in the Dart to last two people six weeks, paid my landlady two months in advance, drove up La Brea to the Boulevard, and put my car in the underground garage near Graumann's Chinese. I walked down to the Vogue and caught a double feature.

It was dark when I came out. I could hear sirens in several directions. I got in the car and drove to David's for something to eat. All I had to do was get in one place and wait, no driving around, no taking extra chances of being seen.

I had almost finished eating when I heard the sirens. I didn't pay much attention because there would be plenty of time and plenty of sirens, if tonight was anything like last night. When I came out of the restaurant there were little bunches of people standing on the corners looking south down La Brea. I walked over and saw a crowd around the Gordon, standing in that tense way they do when somebody's had it. This was going to be a lot easier than I'd thought.

I crossed over Melrose past the camera store, and eased my way through the press of bodies. The colored neon of the marquee made the blood look black. The guy was under a blanket, flat on his back on the sidewalk, one brown hand poking out from under the edge. The hand had blood on it and a spot had soaked through the blanket. More of it was smeared around on the concrete.

One of the cops talking to a couple of people was named Henderson. I only knew him vaguely, so he probably wouldn't know I was supposed to be on my way to Texas. I began sorting through a number of excuses for my delay just in case.

He saw me and waved. The patrol car was behind him at the curb, the flashers turning hypnotically, but losing out to the bright marquee. A young Chicano sat in the back seat looking dazed and surly. He wiped at his mouth with the back of his hand and I saw the glint of cuffs. A girl was hunched in the front seat weeping.

Henderson finished with his witnesses and started toward me. "Hello, Rankin. Don't you get enough of this on duty?"

"Just passing by. What happened?"

He groaned and shook his head. "Couple of kids in a knife fight over a señorita. Wonder if she was worth it."

"The way she's carrying on, the wrong one musta lost."

"Yeah." Another siren approached. "Here's the ambulance. See you around, Rankin." He walked away, being very official, moving the onlookers back another inch.

I looked over the crowd and saw him almost immediately. He was about twelve feet from me, his eyes on the blanket. As usual no one was paying him the slightest attention. I edged toward him as they put the body in the ambulance. The crowd began drifting away but I kept my eyes on that beautiful boy. I wasn't sure if I had seen him before, they all looked so much alike.

He turned and walked north on La Brea. I followed him across Melrose. A few people were still milling around the intersection, but I couldn't let him get too far away from my car.

I overtook him, touched his arm, and said, "Excuse me." I had my badge in my hand when he turned with a startled look.

My face was only a foot from his. I saw the clear, healthy skin and the bewildered gray eyes that looked at me with recognition. All the artists for the last thousand years have been trying to paint that face on angels, but their poor fumbling attempts never came close. It was only for an instant but I had to look away or be overwhelmed.

The traffic on La Brea moved by us silently, like a movie with the sound turned off. But, oddly enough, I could hear the hum and click of the traffic lights as they changed. I realized I was still stupidly holding my badge in my hand, and put it away. I forced myself to look at him again.

"Will you please come down to the station with me . . . " My voice cracked. Come on, Rankin, get hold of yourself! "It's purely a routine matter."

"What do you want?"

It was only four words, but I realized I'd never heard one of them speak. How can you describe music to a deaf person? Any actor in the world would trade his prick for that voice. My own words stopped and we looked at each other. Get your shit together! You're acting like some poor fairy who's just been propositioned by Robert Redford.

"I can make . . . make this official if you refuse to cooperate."

His shoulders sagged slightly. He nodded.

He followed me to the Dart without protest. I had been a little worried because I wasn't in uniform and wasn't in a squad car, but he didn't seem to notice. I had my revolver handy when I handcuffed him to the door handle, but he sat slumped in the seat looking at nothing.

I took the Hollywood Freeway to the Pasadena Freeway. I was going down Colorado Boulevard when he said, "Why are you doing this to me?"

127

I glanced at him but he was still looking at nothing. I almost turned the car around. I wish I had, but I didn't.

He didn't say anything else as I got on the Foothill Freeway and headed east through the San Gabriel Valley. It was almost dawn when I pulled off the pavement winding up Mt. Baldy. I opened the gate to the gravel road down the canyon. I drove through and put on the padlock I had brought with me. I drove up the canyon a couple of miles until the road ended at a cabin. It belonged to a director friend of mine who was on location in Jamaica and would be for several more months. He'd let me use it before. Besides, what he didn't know wouldn't hurt him.

I had to break a window to get in, but that could be fixed. I'd brought a pane of glass and a cutter. I turned on the electricity at the meter box and took him in. I took the chain I had brought, handcuffed one end to his ankle and the other end around the commode. Now he could use the bathroom and the bed, but the chain wasn't long enough to reach the bedroom door or the window. He didn't complain through any of this. He acted as if he didn't even know I was there.

I unloaded the car, put on a pot of coffee, scrambled some eggs, and tried to get him to eat something but he wouldn't. I finished eating, unpacked my clothes, took a shower in the other bathroom and went to sleep in the other bedroom.

He still wouldn't eat when I woke up. I took another shower and shaved. I moved a chair just out of the limit of the chain—he hadn't given me any trouble but I wasn't taking chances—and sat down to watch him.

He was still sitting on the side of the bed, where he'd been when I put on the chain, his magnificent body relaxed and his beautiful face calm. His cheeks were as smooth as ever. I knew for sure he didn't have to shave. His hands were folded in his lap and his eyes seemed to be on them. For two hours he didn't move except for gentle breathing. I didn't realize so much time had passed until the room began to get dark.

I turned on the lights and went to him, holding out my hand. "Give me your wallet." He acted as if he hadn't heard me. "Give me your wallet," I said again, louder.

He looked up at me then, puzzlement in his eyes. "I don't have one."

"Stand up," I said. He hesitated for a moment, then stood. I went over him quickly. He was telling the truth. He had no wallet; nothing but empty pockets.

I returned to my chair and sat, watching him. He stood where I had left him, stood as calmly as he had sat. "How many of you are there?" I said. He didn't seem to hear. "Look, we might as well get a few things straight. You're gonna tell me everything I want to know. We can do it easy or we can do it hard. It's up to you."

He stood for a moment in the same position, then looked at me. "I don't know." His voice still made the hair on my arms stand up.

"You must have some idea. A hundred? A thousand? Ten thousand? A million?" He shook his head. Maybe he wasn't going to let it be easy after all. I let it go; there was plenty of time. "I can fix you something to eat if you want. I'm not trying to starve you to death. Aren't you hungry?"

He said nothing.

"Look! It won't do any good to go on a hunger strike. Not one damn bit of good!" No response. I used my buddy voice. "You can have anything you want. Just name it."

He looked at me quickly. "I want to leave."

I laughed. "Anything but that."

He looked back at his hands. "I would like to bathe."

"Sure. Go ahead."

He moved his foot; the chain rattled. I dug the key out of my pocket and pitched it to him. "Unlock the cuff and throw the key back." I picked up the revolver. He unlocked the chain and tossed me the key. He started for the bathroom.

"Wait!" My heart was beating too hard. "Undress in here and leave the clothes." My mouth was dry and I swallowed. He took off his shirt and hung it on the back of a chair. He took off the shoes and socks and the pants and jockey shorts. His back was toward me but it wasn't modesty. He just happened to be standing that way. Michelangelo, you bumbling incompetent! If you could see this, you'd take a hammer to all those misshapen pieces of rock you spent so much time on.

He took a step toward the bathroom. I made a croaking sound in my throat. I tried again.

"Stop!" He stopped. "Turn around." He turned. I felt the blood singing in my ears. I don't know how long I looked at him. He stood unselfconsciously, totally unconcerned by my staring or his own nakedness. There wasn't a blemish on him. Light reddish-gold hair was scattered on his arms, legs, and chest. You could hardly see it until it caught the light. There was a darker, thicker patch of pubic hair, and he was uncircumcised. He wasn't as large as me, or as small as Cunningham. Either way would have been wrong, out of proportion, a staggering flaw. My own that I'd always been so proud of—it seemed now gross and mutilated. I felt the pressure of it and realized I had a hardon.

The gun was pointing at him. What would he look like with a bullet there? Nothing between those perfect thighs but blood. Would he writhe screaming? Would that inhumanly placid face show human agony? "Get out of here," I said.

While he showered, I put the clothes in a grocery sack and stuck them in the closet of my bedroom. When he came out of the bathroom, he looked at the empty chair, then at me.

"You won't need them. Put the cuff back on." He sat in the chair, snapped the cuff around his ankle. I could take it only for an hour. I got my bathrobe

129

and tossed it to him. He put it on but only because I told him to. It didn't seem to matter to him one way or the other.

I wondered if he had ever smiled. What would those perfect lips look like with a big happy grin on them? I could feel goosebumps popping out on my arms.

For three weeks I watched him do nothing. He sat in the chair and sometimes lay on the bed, but I never saw him sleep. I watched him and asked him questions, but the only things I learned for sure were: he didn't eat or use the toilet. He ignored me except when I forced him to answer a question. And the answers were usually meaningless.

Some days neither of us said a word. I would just watch his face and never tire of it, the way you never tire of looking at a perfect piece of art. Then, suddenly, it would be night again. He bathed every day, but I never let him remove the robe until he was in the bathroom. I didn't want to go through that again.

Sometimes I would force him to speak—not because I expected to learn anything, but because I wanted to hear his voice again. I was trying to find out what he did when he wasn't sirenchasing. I said something inane like: "Why aren't you in the movies? You wouldn't even need talent; with your looks you could make a fortune. The movies or television would eat you up."

He turned his head toward me. "My looks?"

"Don't you know how beautiful you are?"

"I'm ugly." His fantastic voice colored the words with subtle shades of despair. "Everything is ugly."

I studied him closely. I think he believed what he said. "Don't you want to be rich? Don't you want the luxuries of life?"

"There's no point."

"Why not?"

"We're here such a short time. There's no point in gathering possessions. There's no point in anything. And there's not enough time."

"Not enough time?"

He had drifted off in a reverie. "A very short time—but it seems like forever." Impatience, hope, futility, expectation, anticipation; the voice showed it all.

"But how do you pass the time? What do you do?"

I think he sighed. "We wait." he said. "We wait."

"What are you waiting for?" I yelled in exasperation. He didn't answer. I knew better than to continue with a frontal attack. I backed up and started in at a different angle. "You said, '*We* wait.' Are the others like you?"

"Yes."

A thought occurred to me. "Do they know you're here?"

"Yes."

"Why don't they try to rescue you?"

"They're afraid."
"Afraid? Of me?"
"Yes."
"Why?"
"You're dangerous."
"Dangerous?"
"Yes. They would do anything to prevent premature interruption of the cycle."
I started to ask what the hell he was talking about, but I knew it wouldn't do any good. "How am I dangerous?"
"You can see us."
"Do you know why I can see you?"
"No."
"Am I the only one?"
"The only one we know of now."
"Now?"
"It's happened before."
I changed directions again. "Are you afraid of me?"
"Yes."
"Why? I haven't hurt you."
"There is danger that you will interrupt the cycle."
"Why did you come with me so passively?"
"I couldn't believe you would do this to me." Again subtle shadings of accusation, hopelessness, and sadness in the beautiful voice. He turned his head to look at me. For an instant, the barest instant, I felt like a real son of a bitch. Then he looked away. He sat on the side of the bed, my bathrobe too big for him, the chain snaking into the bathroom.

Don't get the idea that he had become an unexpected chatterbox. That conversation is a distillation of three weeks' questions and silences.

About a week later, I went during the night to check on him. I hadn't been sleeping very well. My mind was full of wild, impossible speculations. I won't go into them but they consisted of men from Mars and other equally incredible flights of fancy. I started to put on my bathrobe but remembered he was wearing it. I tiptoed down the hall stark naked hoping to catch him doing something—doing *anything*.

The door to his room was always left open. I looked in cautiously. I couldn't see him anywhere. I started toward the bathroom, then saw him against the wall. I turned on the light. He was pressed against the outside wall of the room, my bathrobe crumpled at his feet. His arms were outstretched to bring as much of him against the wall as possible. He didn't seem to notice me, but then, he never did. I went to him and saw his face, the side of it flat against the wall. It was no longer expressionless. It was filled with the most overpowering hopelessness I had ever seen. I felt my throat constrict.

"What's wrong?" I whispered.

He didn't answer for a moment—not because he was ignoring me as he usually did, but because he was preoccupied. Then he said, very softly, in a voice caressed by a cold, bleak wind: "The small creatures in the forest; their deaths are so tiny and insignificant. There's hardly any life energy at all."

Then he really was aware of me. I saw him retreat until the eyes and face were neutral. I bellowed and slapped him as hard as I could. I remembered them standing around the wrecks. He fell to his knees, the crimson print of my hand on his face. I pulled him up by his armpits and looked into his empty face.

"Stop hiding from me!" I screamed and slapped him again. He slumped against me and my arms were around him holding him up. Our naked bodies were together, exciting me. The blood rushed to my groin and my erection was painful. He was there, in the eyes, not completely, but there. I put my mouth over his. He neither drew away nor responded but his bruised lips were sweet and I didn't want to stop.

I had been looking at his placid face for a month. I knew he was capable of emotion if he would let it show. He hadn't uttered a sound or responded in any way to physical blows. He had to have a breaking point somewhere. I pushed him onto the bed on his stomach. The chain rattled. I rammed into him, trying to hurt him. He was tight, very tight. It must have been painful, but he didn't cry out or even moan. It had been a long time since the last time —a month—too long. It only took a dozen strokes, my pelvis pounding against the flawless flesh of his buttocks, before I came. I shouldn't have waited so long. It burned.

I lay on him for a moment, then reached and pulled his face around. It was vacant. I withdrew, still hard. I pulled him into a sitting position facing me. That beautiful face. That beautiful, bland, bruised face. I put my hands on either side of it.

"Don't hide from me. It doesn't do any good. I can see you. I can see you!" He swam to the surface and looked at me. "Did you enjoy it? Did you even feel it?"

"Yes."

"Did it feel good? Did it hurt?"

"Yes."

"Why didn't you groan? Why didn't you scream? Why didn't you beg me to stop? Why don't you get mad? Why don't you curse me? What's inside you?" I put my hand on his breast and felt the hard nipple against my palm. "Do you have a heart? I can feel something in there. Is it a heart? What would I find if I got a knife and slit you open? Do you have sexual feelings at all?" I grabbed his penis and squeezed. It was soft but firm. "Has it ever been hard? You don't piss with it. What do you use it for?"

I put his hand on my tingling erection. He didn't pull it away. It just lay there. "That's what it's for. That's how a human uses it!" He started going away again. I slapped him. "Stay with me. Stay with me every second." I pushed him on his back. The chain clattered on the floor. I hooked his knees over my shoulders, watching his eyes the whole time. He tried to go away a few times but I slapped him back. I took a very long, slow time and I enjoyed the hell out of it.

The next morning I drove down the mountain to the village and phoned the Department. With direct dialing you can't tell where a long-distance call is coming from. My father was worse and not expected to live much longer. Yeah, too bad. I shouldn't be away much longer. Good-bye.

I started going to him every night. I hadn't meant to but I couldn't sleep without him. He didn't go away anymore and I didn't have to slap him. The bruises on his face faded finally. He was there all right but that was all. I never succeeded in bringing emotion to his face.

Finally I began sleeping in the same bed with him, touching him all night, feeling his hard nipples under the palms of my hands.

He woke me one morning, moaning. The window was gray with light and I could see his mouth moving. I touched his face. It was hot and dry. He spoke and the music in his voice was muted. "Why have you done this to me? I never harmed you. I've never harmed anyone. All we ever want is to survive until the birth."

"What's wrong with you?"

"It's time. The end of the cycle. The birth."

"Isn't that what you've been waiting for?"

"I'm not strong enough. I haven't collected enough life energy."

"I'll let you go. I'll take you back to L.A."

"It's to late. Too late."

He never said anything again. I watched him for three days. His fever got worse and the life went from his vibrant flesh. His skin flaked away in gray scales. He was struggling with all his might against something. I don't know what. But in the end he failed. His moans were so piteous that I had to put my hands over my ears. But I couldn't take my eyes off the disintegration of that magnificent creature.

And that's all he was, wasn't he? A creature. Something not human. It wasn't my fault that, by some fluke, I could see them. I didn't know this would happen. He never told me.

On the second day a hump began forming on his back. He was curling more and more into a fetal position as the hump forced him over. He began bleeding at the mouth. I put the shower curtain under him. When I rolled him over, my hands got covered with something like ashes.

On the third day he began to quieten and I knew it was almost over. He hadn't moved in several hours except for ragged breathing. There was a sharp cracking sound, like Carnehan biting into a new apple, only louder. The now ugly body trembled violently for a few moments, and then nothing. He lay facing me, his eyes open, the color of clay.

The breathing stopped.

It was finished.

I got out of the chair and walked around to the other side of the bed. The hump on his back had split and something white was sticking out. I reached down and pulled on it. It was a wing, a large, white wing covered with feathers. No, not feathers. Soft, white, silky hair.

There was a second wing but it was twisted and not properly developed. I pulled away all of the body and exposed what was inside it.

I cleaned up the cabin so no one would know it had been occupied. I packed everything back in the Dart. I buried them both in the woods, the body of the dead winged thing, and the husk that had held it. I drove back to Hollywood. It seemed as if I passed a wreck every half mile. I went into my apartment without noticing the apple cores in the yard. I unlocked the door, went straight to the toilet, and vomited.

I was splashing cold water on my face when I heard her.

"Lou? Is that you?" She walked in wearing a slip, her eyes red from sleep, and her hair sticking out on one side where she'd been lying on it.

"Margaret! What the hell are you doing here?"

"Oh, Lou!" She pressed against me. "It's been *awful!* Alfred found out about us!"

My head was spinning. "Who the shit is Alfred?"

She looked puzzled. "My husband!"

Jesus Christ! I'd forgotten Carnehan's first name. She was right. It was awful. "What'd he do? Do they know at the Department?"

"He hit me!" She began to blubber on my shoulder. "I was afraid. I've been hiding here for three *days!* He keeps pounding on the door but I stay quiet. He doesn't know for sure I'm here."

"How did he find out?"

"I don't *know!* He came home from work three days ago, screaming at me and hitting me. Oh, Lou. I was so frightened." She kissed me and her breath was bad. *His* breath had had no odor at all. "Come to bed with me, Lou. It's been so long." she whined.

I felt her doughy flesh through the thin slip. But it was woman flesh and I had to forget about him. I led her to the bed and began undressing. I was sticky. I hadn't bathed or shaved since he started . . . Stop it!

She pulled the slip over her head, unhooked her bra, and peeled down her pantyhose. Her tits were beginning to sag, her thighs were puffy, and there was a small roll of fat around her waist. Her skin looked muddy, not clear like . . . Stop it!

She walked toward me, smiling coyly. I wish I had been able to see . . . Stop it!

I pushed her roughly onto the bed and she squealed. Margaret liked it rough. I was about to make her very happy. She gasped deep in her throat every time my pelvis slammed against her flabby flesh. It was good—but . . . Stop it!

I lay on my back, half asleep. Margaret lay on top of me, licking my nipples and trying to coax it back up again. It hadn't lasted long enough for her, but she was wasting her time and she was heavy. I closed my eyes, trying to stay awake. I felt her hair on my face. There was a noise and her head hit mine. Her breath rushed out in one stale puff and I felt something dripping on my cheek.

I focused my eyes. Carnehan was standing over us, his nightstick raised. I couldn't move Margaret's dead weight. "Carnehan! Don't!" I yelled. The stick came down. I remembered I hadn't locked the door.

When I came out of it, it was dark. I was in a moving car. My head hurt and the car sounded as if it were driving in the bottom of a well. I could feel dried blood in my left eye; maybe mine or maybe Margaret's. I tried to wipe it away but my hands wouldn't move. I heard the clink of handcuffs and felt the door handle. My head was leaning against the glass. It felt cool. I opened my eyes and saw brush going past and a sea of lights spread out below. I could see a dozen fires burning. We must be somewhere in the Hollywood Hills.

I turned my head and looked at Carnehan driving the car. He stared straight ahead. "Carnehan, what do you think you're doing?" The words didn't come out as forcefully as I had intended. He ignored me. "Carnehan, Margaret doesn't mean anything to me." That was the wrong thing to say. Think straight! "She's not worth it, Carnehan. I'm not worth it. Neither of us is worth destroying yourself!"

He wasn't listening. "You can't hope to get away with this." Of course he didn't. "Why don't you just write it off as a mistake?"

The car had been bouncing around for a while. We must not have been on a main road. I couldn't raise myself high enough to see ahead. After a bit Carnehan stopped the car and got out. He opened the back door on my side and began dragging out Margaret's naked body. She must have been already dead, the way she flopped around like a rubber dummy. He dragged her a few feet from the car and rolled her down a hill. I could hear her crackling the brush, then silence.

Carnehan opened my door and the handcuffs pulled me out. I felt sharp rocks digging into my butt and realized I was naked too. He pulled out his revolver.

"Carnehan! Don't be a fool!"

He shot me in the stomach. Good old Carnehan. He remembered what we'd been taught: always aim for the gut.

He unlocked the handcuffs and pulled me to the edge. All I had to do was overpower him and get away, but I decided to wait because I was very tired. I rolled down the hill like a sack of potatoes. I didn't feel the prickly pears and sharp brush. The pain in my belly was too fierce. I hit something hard and I think my shoulder broke.

I was lying on my back, my head leaning against whatever I'd hit, looking back up the hill. The car drove away. Carnehan, you bungler! I'm not dead! You wasted it all!

The sound of the car died away. It was very quiet, just crickets and the faroff rumble of traffic. You couldn't get away from that sound anywhere in Los Angeles County. A slight wind was blowing, making some loose sheet metal creak and groan somewhere near by.

I couldn't just lie here. I was bound to die if I didn't get help. I tried to move and looked up. An immense "Y" loomed over me. I was under the Hollywood sign. I couldn't see Margaret anywhere. Let me rest a moment more and get my breath back. Damn fuckin' Carnehan. Are you gonna be surprised when they haul you in and I'm there to point the finger. I looked down at my stomach. A mistake. But it doesn't hurt so much anymore. I must be in shock. I've heard that happens.

I can see my prick. It looks wrinkled and shrunken, even smaller than Cunningham's. This is a hell of a time to be thinking about pricks! My shoulder hurts worse than my gut. I can feel blood on the ground under my back. I've rested long enough.

What's that noise? Sounded like a twig cracking somewhere in the darkness. What if it's a coyote? I wonder if it will attack me. Probably not. Do coyotes react to the smell of blood the way sharks do?

Footsteps. Not a coyote. People. More than one. I'm saved! Up yours, Carnehan!

There are four of them: four redheaded young men who don't look a day over twenty. Four perfect faces that I used to think were overwhelmingly beautiful—until I saw the face of that dead winged thing. But I did see it. And I had to cover it because the beauty was too painful to look at.

Four magnificent bodies that only a few days ago would have sent the blood rushing to my penis—if I hadn't seen the pale body of the winged creature, all the more beautiful because it was sexless. A body I knew would have gleamed had it been alive.

Now these four faces seem drab and plain and the four bodies might belong to trolls.

But the eyes! They stand around me, watching me with eyes I still think beautiful because the winged creature's eyes were closed in death.

Those four pairs of beautiful, bland eyes look at me the same way Carnehan looks at an apple he's been saving for a special occasion.

Ask a Marine

by Daniel Luckenbill

"I, too, am a victim of posters"
Genet, *Querelle*

GOING INTO the bus station, I passed a sailor and a Marine, both in uniform. I used to think these boys outside were the ones who might be picked up. I had tried striking up conversations, but usually they were waiting for relatives or a wife. Boys who were passing time between buses and maybe had a long stopover stayed inside. They played the pinball machine or listened to the jukebox, or had a coke at the counter.

San Bernardino was one of the first areas of Los Angeles to be sighted by migrant Okies and has remained a haven for people who like horses and small towns. Country-Western songs were playing on the jukebox. A man with a draft-beer husky voice was singing about wide-open spaces, even as San Bernardino was leveling its downtown to build another shopping center. I listened to the song for a while, trying to believe in its innocent dream.

A boy in the lobby attracted me. He wasn't particularly handsome. He was short with a plain butch face and clothes which were old and dirty and clung to his thin frame. His plain black shoes were scuffed, but they were service shoes of some sort. They were not the black mirrors they would be, polished for inspection, sitting under some bunk in a barracks somewhere, but there was still a hint of that spitshine he'd had to give them. He stood in the corner by the pay phones and was looking back and forth from the two entrances to the station. If he was waiting for a family or a girlfriend, there was no hint of anticipation in his expression. And there wasn't the boredom of just waiting for a bus. There was some kind of apprehension in his features.

When he went to the john, I followed him. An old lady in rhinestone-rimmed glasses looked up from her knitting to ask me the time. I hadn't followed anyone yet that afternoon, so I passed by the shoeshine man near the door of the john without my usual nervousness. The boy was standing at the urinals. I left two between him and myself. I could see his cock. It wasn't big, but the combination of his youth, his body fresh out of uniform, and his lost and worried expression was enough to turn me on. He stood shaking his cock, and I lingered, but another boy came in.

He spoke to the first: "Got to be going pretty soon, man."

"Yeah, but the tickets are no damned good."

I was more attracted by the second boy, who wasn't showing anything. He cupped his hands around his cock so that all I could see was the flow of piss streaming onto the cold porcelain. He glanced up at me, then left quickly, not even going through the motions of running water over his hands. The first boy stood at a basin, soaping his hands, scrubbing them, rinsing them—all the time looking up into the mirror. After drying, he took a comb from his back pocket and ran it through his short hair, involuntarily, as servicemen do, remembering its former length. My hair was just as short as his, but I carried a comb for times like this when it was convenient to have some excuse for lingering at the john.

Never being very good at openings, I was usually shy about starting conversations. I saw the boy had finished and was about to leave, was going to say nothing himself. Bluntness scared a boy away for good or paid off.

I spoke up. "You look like you could use a bit of money."

"Hey, yeah, spare some? My buddy and me, we're trying to get to Las Vegas."

"Well, yes, I could spare some—for a favor."

"What kind of favor? What do you—?" He broke off, as he saw me staring at his crotch. "Hey, no, I don't go for that stuff." He pushed at the john door quickly and left.

I decided to leave the station, thinking the boy might get together with the other and cause some sort of trouble. The Marine in uniform was still outside. He stood with his duffel bag and suitcase and a paper sack full of gift-wrapped packages piled about him, next to a recruiting poster in a standing metal frame. The boy was sexy, he did some justice to his counterpart on the poster, a painting of an idealized boy. Clean-cut, square-jawed, blue-eyed.

Did boys who grew up to look like this one on the poster just naturally join the Marines? It was impossible to know if the artist had found one of these perfect few and copied him, or created a composite, according to his idea of manhood and Marines. Did a boy with just one of these features—this serviceman standing here now with his straight brow and deep-set eyes—stand and stare at the poster and decide to join up, take on along with the uniform the other qualities of that face?

The slogan on the poster was: ASK A MARINE. The idea was, if you want to know what it's like to be a man among men, ask a Marine. All I could think of was what an old queen had said at a party: you know the old saying, honey, I never met a Marine who wouldn't turn over. I wasn't quite sure why this excited me so much. If there was any turning over to be done, I would want to do that. But the sentence tantalized me, made me think every time I saw a cute marine I could have him if I really tried.

I walked around the block. The midday summer sun centered my thoughts. I remembered pictures in a magazine I'd looked at when I was on pass from my Army training in Oklahoma. Two straight boys, cute and naked. The photographer had shown them from every angle imaginable. There were cocks seen from the side, seen straight-on, seen almost from underneath as you would if you were sucking.

Legs spread, bent at the knee so you could see the full shapes of the balls and the downswinging curve of the crack of the ass. This was one boy. The other was turned over. The torso shrunk with the perspective of the camera, thrusting the ass and backs of the thighs at you, legs spread.

In most of the pictures the boys had their arms around one another, were smiling like they were having a good time and enjoying their nakedness as much as the photographer. I looked at the pictures until I had ached with wanting to be there, to touch them. Not sex so much, even, as just seeing the two boys naked, and having a real presence to decorate my fantasies, so like the photographer's.

Desperate now, I went back to the station and straight to the john to see what might be there. I washed my hands slowly, still hoping something might turn up, gave a start when I saw the boy again—his face reflected in the mirror. I wanted to leave, but the boy spoke this time.

"You still give me some cash?"

"Sure, but for a favor . . ."

"Yeah, yeah, I understand. I need the money."

"I'm just here visiting my family, I don't have an apartment or anything. I'm in the service myself. I guess we—"

"Hey, how'd you know I was in the service?"

"Your shoes. And your short hair."

"I forget sometimes about the shoes. And the hair, I guess that really gives it away, huh?"

"We can go to a motel, I guess there's one close by. I'll check in, find out where the room is and come back and tell you. You sure you want to do this, sure you'll be here when I get back?"

"Sure, I can use the money." He paused. "My name's Don."

He was there when I got back. But so was his friend, the one he was talking to in the john.

"This is my buddy, Elden," he said. "Mind if he comes along?"

Elden was certainly the cuter of the two. I put a Marine uniform on him, and, yes, he looked almost like the boy on the recruiting poster. But I had visions of the two ganging up on me, knocking me out the minute we got into the motel room. Those thoughts were quickly displaced by the idea of seeing the two boys naked together. It would be like in the magazines. Two boys lounging with their arms about one another, or wrestling on the floor.

"Well, I'm not sure—"

"It's okay, he knows the score."

"It's all right. I need money just the same as Don does."

They looked at one another. They spoke with lowered voices, calculating something. Elden asked Don: "How much time we got?"

"I don't know, you're the one that looked at the schedules, not me."

"I don't remember."

"Don't remember? You said you were going to take care of everything, for me not to worry."

"I remember they run pretty often. Settle down, don't worry about it." Don was quiet, seemed reassured. Elden turned to me. "How much you gonna give us?"

"We hadn't talked about that."

"We're trying to get to Las Vegas," Elden said.

"That's what Don told me. Sounds like a nice place for a leave."

"Leave, shit. We're AWOL."

"Elden, don't—"

"He ain't gonna say nothing. We're AWOL. MP's caught us hitchhiking on our way to Las Vegas. They got so much to do, they just gave us tickets back to Pendleton, told us we'd get it twice as bad if we didn't show up. But there's no way you're gonna get us back there. We figured with the money you give us we can get a couple Greyhound tickets. Tried cashing these in, but no go."

"How much are the tickets?"

"Eleven bucks," Elden answered. "Eleven each."

"I guess I can manage that."

"That's all we need, just enough money to get us on a bus and out of here."

"Look, my room number is twenty-seven," I said, "you can come up the back stairs and I'll let you in."

The room was no different from any other motel room. There were two double beds, a chest beside each with a lamp. A chair and a bureau with a mirror were the rest of the furniture, all finished with a plastic mar-proof surfacing, burnt here and there by cigarettes fallen from ashtrays where they were left to burn out. The colors in the room were bland, except for orange bedspreads—which would come off at night—and a touch of orange in the pictures, to carry out the scheme. A low-volume muzak came from a speaker in the wall —music totally anaesthetic in its sounds. There was everything you needed for one night and no longer.

Someone must come occasionally to change the towels and the glasses wrapped in paper and the paper band over the john. It was no wonder wild and violent things happened in motels. You would have to have wild sex to make you believe you were still alive. If you came here with any sort of desperation, this would be the place to convince you to end it all. A criminal could easily be convinced that nothing existed outside this room and would fear no consequences. The world was just as empty and packaged. Then I thought of seeing Elden and Don naked. That would add the life. I had my shirt off and shoes off when they got there. Elden looked around, obviously pleased. He flopped on one of the beds. "Not bad," he said. "Real nice. We ain't slept in a bed for five days."

"Sleeping wasn't exactly what I had in mind," I said.

"Oh, yeah, sure . . . " He sat up, flashed a smile at me.

His face was relaxed, soft. The tension from being in the station and not knowing how he would get out of there had left his face. He looked even younger. About seventeen. Marines usually joined young. They still believed things like joining the service and becoming a man, seeing the world and becoming a hero. The recruiting posters were probably not far off. Some sort of study would have been made, I supposed. A staff of psychologists behind the drawing of the picture and the writing of the captions—they would know what would appeal to these boys. Elden and Don seemed to have seen through it all quickly enough. It all seemed so calculating and cold, using these boys like this, preying upon their insecurities and dreams of glory to get them to join up and be killed.

Elden was enjoying lying on the bed and I thought he might fall asleep. He did look tired. Don looked completely exhausted. He still stood by the door, as if not ready to come into the room and face up to what he'd let himself in for.

"Hot in here," Elden said, "I think I'll take off my shirt, too." He looked directly at me to see what effect this would have, so I decided not to let anything show. Elden's chest was covered with soft teenage hair, light brown, not dark or wiry at all. Shaped from the conditioning exercises of boot camp, he was not overly muscular, but pleasingly proportioned. "I sure do feel dirty." Again he smiled and looked directly into my eyes. "Think I'll take a shower first." He got up, began unbuckling his pants as he moved toward the bathroom. I heard the spray of the shower being turned on, the buckle hit the tile floor.

Don said nothing, just sat down on the chair near the door. Elden's dazzling perfect good looks had overshadowed him when they were together, but now I found myself more drawn to him. His eyes were large and seemed even larger with the shaved head forcing concentration on the features of the face itself. He didn't have the good luck Elden had with the exercises in training. His body thin to begin with, the exercises and bullying had honed him down even more—had made him wiry, his expression wary.

"Why don't you take off your clothes and get into bed?" I was rather amazed at how blunt I was being. But then I was paying for it. There was no sense in not getting what I wanted.

He knew this was what he was here for, but he wasn't going to do anything on his own as Elden would. He responded, though, to my order. He quickly slipped his naked body between the sheets of the other bed.

"Let me look at you."

He lowered the sheets to where black hair curled and twisted.

"Hey, Don," Elden yelled from the shower, "this is great, real hot water and not ten guys around, grabbin' ass."

I moved to the bed where Don lay on his back, legs together and arms at his side, as if folding himself up and trying to disappear. I pressed my face into his crotch hair, sweaty from the days on the road. He didn't move, so I put my hand under the smooth hairless ass, turned him onto his side so I could suck better. The cock was small but bone-hard. I sucked desperately—trying to get it to the point where it would release itself, soften, relax again. My mouth didn't seem to be doing the job, but I kept at it.

The sound of the water stopped and Elden stood at the door to the room, dripping wet, a towel covering him as he started drying. He turned on the TV to a baseball game, then moved toward the bed.

"Hey, Don, those Pirates of yours ain't doing so well."

He stood in front of me. He dropped his towel. His cock wasn't large, but was nested beautifully in dark hair, so much darker than the hair covering his chest and flat stomach, his full legs. I stopped trying to make Don come.

"Do you like to be blown?" I asked Elden.

"Yeah, I guess so. Sure."

My lips encircled the cock already raising itself. Elden remained standing as I sat up on the edge of the bed. My hands played with the soft hair on Elden's body as my mouth moved quickly on the cock just the right size for sucking—not choking—large. I moved my mouth and lips around it, up and down on it. Elden stood still, not pumping and not breathing hard. I pressed the double softness of the ass cheeks—the full softness of the flesh, the light softness of the covering hair—and moved my mouth even more. Still, Elden did not move. Then I felt his body stiffen, lean into me as if losing balance. Come shot into my mouth. After the first spurt I felt the hips move back and forth frantically, trying to make it last. Quick, jerky pumps then it was over. I took my mouth from the cock, swallowed, and lay back on the bed.

Elden's body relaxed into the contours of the bed. He was all softness and contentment. "Don, Clemente's got a hit. Run, maybe ... "

I snuggled up to the teddy-bear softness of Elden's body. "You're very sexy. I liked blowing you."

"Yeah, it was all right." Elden looked straight at the TV and was scratching his balls and tugging at his dick.

"Have you ever had a blowjob before?"

"Yeah, once. My buddy's father, he—Hey, Don, homerun."

"Guess that'll show you what team's got it," Don said, "what team don't."

"What was that about your buddy's father?"

"Oh, yeah, well once, one afternoon, I was going over to see John and he wasn't there, just his old man. The old lady was gone and the old man was drinkin' beer, just watching TV—"

"Elden, we gotta find out when that bus leaves."

"Pretty soon," Elden answered. He moved his body flat against me. He was getting another hard-on. I played with that with one hand, then ran my hand up and down the soft furry body, moved my other hand on Don's smooth skin.

He was not aroused at all. I thought I didn't like hairy bodies. I didn't like the way they looked in pictures, but I was enjoying Elden. It was nice to have Don's smooth body at the same time.

Even with my caresses, Don didn't get hard again, so I concentrated on Elden, went down again on the hard-on. "Do you think you can come again?"

"Yeah, maybe. Sure."

I worked fast and this time Elden worked with me, jutting up as my mouth went down, pulling in the opposite direction as my mouth slid to the head of his cock. I felt the bed shaking, Don was getting up and going to the other bed, Elden shot.

"That's pretty good," I complimented him. "Coming twice in such a short time."

"Guess it works." Proud of his accomplishment, he smiled at me.

"You're not so big, but very sexy."

Elden was still grinning. "That's what my girl says. Small, but it does the damage."

"Damage?"

"Got her pregnant before I joined up. But it's all right. She got married to my buddy."

"Your buddy John?"

"Yeah, how about that? I dunno if he knew about the kid when he married her. Guess he knows now. Been about five months."

"Sounds like a rotten trick to me."

"Hell, he won't care. We're buddies."

"You're sure all of this is turning out all right?"

"Sure. That's where me and Don are going. John's got a ranch in Nevada. I used to work there for his Dad. Nice there, wide open spaces and all." He paused, letting this sink into his mind. His eyes seemed to open wider when thinking of the long vistas. He was playing with his cock again. "You ever been to a rodeo?" he asked me.

"No."

"I hadn't neither, not till last year. I'm from Kansas and I met John there and he said come on out west here. It's the greatest thing, a rodeo. Damn baseball and stuff, you can have it. Rodeo's something else." Elden didn't or couldn't define what that something was, but I found myself thinking about it. Getting into Elden's thoughts and looking out of his eyes, trying to decide what dreams were satisfied by going to the rodeo.

"Yeah, I want to live on a ranch and all. So nice there, wide open spaces. Nobody to bother you. Do what you want. Outdoors where there's no people. Out in the sun. Goddam, look at this here body now—white as the sheet. Except for the neck and all."

He sat up, moving away from my touch. He bent his legs, put his head on his knees. "Yep, that's where we're going. Don can work there too. Always need an extra hand."

"But you're AWOL. The MP's will catch you again."

"Naw, they never check on the buses. We can get to Las Vegas and then change clothes again. Get into something clean, get rid of these shoes. Don can work there with me and my buddy. No more of this Marine bullshit."

"It sounds very good, if you don't think you will get caught."

"Goddamit, we ain't gonna get caught." His body tensed again, after the relaxation of the shower, after the sex and forgetting and dreaming. His hands knotted into fists, his legs drew up tighter. He jumped up from the bed. "This was a fuck-up this time. We didn't have no money so we were hitchhiking. Out there on the side of the road with our short hair and these damn black shoes and all, we got picked up by the state cops. We was almost to Las Vegas and they picked us up and we didn't have no passes, so they called the MP's on us. Well, they won't catch us again."

He paced the length of the room twice. "I've got to shave. Maybe take another shower. Better we look, better off we are. Don't want to look suspicious."

Don sat on the edge of my bed. "Elden, don't you think we'd better call about the time?"

"Have him do that. I'm gonna shave." He went into the bathroom.

I felt Don's body turning, touching mine. "I think I can come," he said, "like Elden."

I touched his stretched-out legs, pinched the muscles into his bones. "You must have had a shitty time in boot camp to go AWOL so soon."

"Shitty? Ain't the half of it. Fuckin' miserable the whole time. I'm short."

"What does that have to do with it?"

"In boot camp, they always find the shortest guy in the barracks and he's what they call the house mouse. Gets stuck with all kinds of crap. Hey, house mouse, do this, Hey, house mouse, get me this, I need this."

Don moved his body as I moved my hands over it. He moved with the caresses, then moved against them to get more pleasure. He savored them, the contact.

"Elden was the only one who treated me decent. He sorta had to go along with the rest, but he stuck up for me most of the time. Don't never want to go back there."

"But don't you think you'll get caught? You can't hide forever." I pulled down his shorts, but he brushed my hand away and took them off himself.

"Elden's got it all figured out. Says nobody ever goes where this ranch is. He's got it all figured out and he's pretty smart."

I touched him between the legs, reached under his balls. "Turn over," I said. He responded, as he had to all of my previous commands. His legs were spread apart like the boy's in the magazine. I grasped the two ass cheeks, lifted them toward me so that Don was on his knees and I could move my face to his rear. I kissed the white skin, bit it gently, licked at it. Then moved my tongue to the tight hole, thrust it in hard. He moved his ass even closer to my face, ground it around my flicking tongue.

"You think Elden is still busy in there?" he asked.

"Sounds like it."

"The water's running, huh?"

"Yes."

He put his hand on my dick, guided it to where my tongue had been. "Maybe you'd like this," he said.

I looked at him from the angle of the photographer. His ass was spread open wider than any I had ever seen in photographs. He was offering himself and I thought of taking. In the picture, the boy's torso was foreshortened. Don's, as I moved closer, spread out. I moved my hands from his narrow hips to the narrow waist, to the small of his back and up the vee of his sides to his shoulders. They were curved down into the bed, his face was nearly buried in the pillow. The goddam house mouse. I didn't fuck him. I pumped my dick with my hand and spilled my come onto the cheeks of his ass.

"Was that OK?" he asked.

"Yes, yes, thank you."

He got up. There was a splotch of come on the sheet beneath him.

"Let me call about the bus," I said.

"I'm going to wash up."

He didn't take long. He came back out of the bathroom and went to his pile of dirty clothes and began slowly putting them back on.

"The bus for Las Vegas leaves at eight," I said. "It's only six-thirty. I'll leave and you two can stay here until time for the bus. I've got to go home. My mother's expecting me."

"We can stay here and watch some TV, I guess. Don't think we'd better go back to the bus station." He stopped putting on his clothes.

I went to the bathroom. Elden was standing at the mirror, still shaving, going back and forth over his face, making sure he didn't miss a spot. I put my arms around his soft body, wanting somehow to reassure him. There were so many odds against him.

"Hey, watch it, I don't want to cut myself."

"I'm sorry. I just wanted to touch you one more time. I've got to go."

He put down the razor and pressed his body full against me. He reached down and scratched his balls, pulled at his dick. It worked all right. He smiled. They were going to Las Vegas.

I left Elden in the bathroom with himself and the razor and the mirror and his comb. I got dressed. Don still had on only his jockey shorts and socks, was sitting on the edge of the bed, waiting to be told what to do next.

Marines are completely crazy, I thought. When my Army unit had relieved a company of marines at Khe Sanh, that company moved out on foot to take a hill they considered important. The Army moved by helicopter and would have landed on top of the hill, but no, the Marines were hoofing it. And through a valley, where, in the mountains on either side of it, there were known entrenched NVA artillery positions. The point men knew they stood very little chance of getting to that hill, but someone was telling them to go and they went. Marines were always wanting to take some hill or other. Then having to abandon it.

I took out all the money in my wallet. "I've got twenty-nine dollars. I'll need a buck or two for the cab home. This will get your tickets, with a bit left over."

"We could use some extra. Maybe get a hamburger."

Elden came out of the bathroom, still naked. "You leaving now?"

"Yes, I've got to get home."

"He gave us twenty-seven dollars."

"No shit!"

Don showed him the money. Elden took it and counted it. Then, exultant, he gave Don a punch in the shoulder. Not expecting it, Don fell back onto the bed and Elden jumped after him, bouncing up and down. I watched their two chests meet. Elden's hairy chest pressed into Don's thin white body as Elden gave him an exuberant bear hug. Don shied away.

I unlocked the door, opened it slightly. Elden sat up. His eyes dimmed, looking ahead, not looking back. I could see the anxiety in them; the impossibility, the longing for something, the tasting of it seemed too much for him: he looked ahead from Kansas plains and now back across California desert like a pioneer with a dream crazy as his. It would be better if they could set sail, enter that swirl which would spin them away from time into quiet.

Then he saw the room, his reflection in the mirror, his body, mine, and his eyes seemed to reel, seemed whirling, as if they had caught up with that crazy song spinning around and out of the jukebox at the bus station.

"I've got to go."

"Hey, man, you're all right," Elden said. "Thanks a lot." His face again showed the confident smile. He hugged Don again out of sheer joy and this time the embrace was returned and Don was smiling, too.

When I opened the door, even the dull sunset light from the east flashed onto the mirror, obscuring them. I closed the door a little to block the glare, look at them one more time. From a distance details were blurred and in the mirror Elden and Don seemed flat, like in photographs.

Meet Me in St. Louis Louie

by William S. Burroughs

AUDREY CARSONS at sixteen was in many ways older than his years. He already possessed the writer's self-knowledge and self-disgust, and the God-guilt all writers feel in creation. In other ways he was younger than sixteen. He was sadly lacking in social graces and worldly experience. He could not dance, play games, or make light conversation. He was painfully shy, his knowledge of sex culled from *Coming of Age in Samoa* and a book entitled *Sex and Marriage*. His face was scarred with festering spiritual wounds, and there was no youth in it. At the same time he was compulsively infantile. The combination was not pleasing when compounded with sick self-disgust, fear, and impotent rage. He had the look of a desperate and thoroughly unsuccessful black magician caught out with cards raining from his sleeve. There was a horrible unknown odor about him of a frozen mummy thawing out in a fetid swamp.

"You are a walking corpse," Mrs. Greenfield told him indirectly through a friend who she knew would repeat her verdict. It was a way she had. Years later when he heard she had died, Audrey got his back. It's a way writers have.

"It isn't every corpse that can walk."

"He looks like a sheep-killing dog," snapped Colonel Greenfield, a fine old whitey with a clipped grey mustache.

Audrey got his back there too, when he heard about the colonel's death from a massive hemorrhage.

"I *am* a sheep-killing dog."

The mills of a writer grind slowly but they grind exceeding fine. He felt himself locked up somewhere in a dingy attic, watching helplessly while shopkeepers shoved his change back at him without a thank you. Bartenders took one look at that face and said:

"We don't want your type in here."

These slights cut his raw wounds like rock salt. He felt that nobody wanted his type anywhere. He read *Adventure* magazine and dreamed of himself in sun helmet and khakis, a Webley at his belt, his faithful Zulu servant at his side. These dreams were banal and childish even for his years, consisting mostly of gunfights at which he excelled. Since adventure was a virtual impossibility in a midwestern matriarchy, these were paper-thin dreams, 19th century nostalgia. What he hoped for most of all was to escape from his tainted flesh through some heroic act.

He was the only scholarship boy at an exclusive school known as the Poindexter Academy. Audrey read *Adventure Stories* and *Short Stories* and saw himself as the Major, a gentleman adventurer and IDB (Illegal Diamond Buyer) ... in a good cause, that is. He read *Amazing Stories* and saw himself as the first man to land on the moon and drew diagrams of rocket ships. He decided to be a writer and make his own Majors and Zulu Jims and Snowy Joes and Carl Cranberrys. His first literary composition, "The Autobiography of a Wolf," was inspired by a book called *The Biography of a Grizzly Bear*... Feeling the snow under his feet; his blazing eyes; his fangs; and licking the blood off the face of his wolf mate Jerry. Audrey was a little vague about the sexes, and saw no reason why he couldn't take Jerry, a red-haired wolf, as his mate. Later he took on another mate, a delicate albino wolf with blue eyes who froze to death in a blizzard. Whitey had always been a delicate wolf. When Jerry dies of consumption, spitting blood into the snow, Audrey is so weakened by grief that he is attacked and eaten by the grizzly bear as a punishment for plagiarism.

His family were in very modest circumstances. It humiliated him to attend classes in his patched blue suit—shabby patches, not the splendid leather things on the elbows of a worn Brooks Brother jacket. He was invited to some of the parties, and some of the mothers tried to put him at ease. "That nice quiet Carsons boy," said Mrs. Kindheart. Her kindness was of course the kiss of death, under the cold eyes of Mrs. Worldly.

The hero of his stories was a young aristocrat lounging disdainfully at the wheel of his Stutz Bearcat, exercising a *droit de seigneur* over provincial debutantes of St. Louis. As it turned out he had underworld connections, was perhaps involved in illegal diamond buying, white slavery or the opium traffic. At the opening of the Academy in mid-September, such a hero did indeed appear. Aloof and mysterious, where he came from nobody knew. Audrey thought of him as the man Flamonde in the poem by Edward Arlington Robinson:

The man Flamonde from God knows where
With firm address and foreign air

There were rumors of Tangier, Paris, London, New York, a school in Switzerland where the boys took drugs. His name was John Hamlin and he lived with relatives in a huge marble house in Portland Place. He drove a magnificent Duesenberg. Audrey wrote: "Clearly he has come a long way. Travel-stained and even the stains unfamiliar, cuff links of a strange dull metal that seems to *absorb* light, large green eyes well apart, his red hair touched with gold, a straight nose, a beautiful cupid's bow mouth ... " He scratched out "beautiful"—too fruity he thought—and substituted "perfect." And the new boy took a liking to Audrey, while he turned aside invitations from sons of the rich.

"They bore me," he told Audrey, who flushed with pleasure. He was flattered and flustered by Hamlin's attention. He would come home blushing to remember the agonized stammerings and attempts to be clever that didn't quite come off, convinced that Hamlin must despise him. But Hamlin remained friendly in his detached way. And Audrey continued to peck away at his typewriter, amending his lame conversation with the New Boy until it sparkled with epigrams.

It was Tuesday afternoon, October 23, 1928—a clear bright day, leaves falling. October's bright blue weather. Audrey walked up Pershing Avenue to the corner of Walton. He was thinking about a story he was writing with John Hamlin as the hero. It was a ghost story about a mysterious encounter in Harbor Beach where his family spent the summers.

"I could never find the cottage again. But once I described the boy to my father, who said yes, there had been a John Hamlin among the summer people, but he was killed in an auto accident outside St. Louis."

Right at his elbow the calm voice: "Hello Audrey. Like to take a ride?" And there was Hamlin at the wheel of his Duesenberg. He opened the door without waiting for an answer. Audrey got in. Hamlin shifted gears and the Dusenberg shot forward, slamming the door. Right turn on Taylor—the trees and red brick of the Catholic school flashed by and Audrey glimpsed the gold dome of the cathedral glittering in cold sunlight. Right on Lindell Boulevard heading west, houses and trees a blur of red and green and yellow as the Dusenberg gather speed. Skinner . . . city limits. The streets were oddly empty.

Hamlin was silent, his eyes fixed on the road. Outside Clayton he pressed the accelerator to the floor. The car seemed to leave the ground in a swirl of dead leaves. Audrey must have dozed. The car was moving slowly over a dirt road, but what he saw bore no resemblance to the Missouri countryside. It looked flat and dusty and there were people by the side of the road dressed in white robes. Suddenly six young boys naked except for colored jock straps barred . . .

⸻⸻⸻⸻⸻⸻⸻⸻ MEET ME AT THE FAIR

. . . the way. The leader was carrying a Mauser pistol clipped onto a rifle stock. Audrey recognized this weapon from the Stoeger catalogue, *The Shooter's Bible,* which he read religiously, studying each weapon and deciding which ones he wanted to carry when he became a gentleman adventurer. He knew the calibre of this gun, nine millimeter, but not the same cartridge as the Luger. He knew that the wooden stock also served as a holster; that the magazine, which was not in the handle but in front of the handle, also served as a hand hold to steady the weapon; that the magazine held nine cartridges. The leader stepped to the side of the car. Hamlin spoke briefly in a language unknown to Audrey and the leader nodded.

149

"We leave the car here," John said.

Audrey got out. They were on the edge of what looked like a vast fair—booths and lights as far as Audrey could see in a sepia twilight. He decided that the nonchalant thing was to ask no questions. He followed John through the square where a number of acts were in progress, each surrounded by a circle of onlookers. He glimpsed these acts out of the corner of his eye, for John was walking rapidly as if he had an appointment to keep.

"For I have promises to keep and miles to go before I sleep," Audrey recited inanely to himself.

In one circle two boys were practising Jiu Jitsu. Audrey had once ordered a book on jiu jitsu through a mail order firm in Wisconsin. He found the instructions and diagrams quite incomprehensible . . . 'Seize your opponent by his right sleeve with your left hand and pull sharply downwards while your right hand secures his left lapel. At the same time move your left foot quickly behind his right heel. Straighten your body with a twist to the right. He will be thrown heavily to the ground.' As he watched, one of the boys fell backward with a foot in the other's stomach. He straightened his leg, every muscle outlined like marble in the dying sun, and the boy sailed over the heads of the onlookers and lit on his feet like a cat.

Other acts were enigmatic. In one circle boys were dressing and undressing at prestidiginal speed. He passed a circle where a strange woolly monkey was attacking a dummy with a knife while the trainer stood behind him giving inaudible signals. There were no noisy children about, and no families. The people he passed were dressed in colored jock straps, leather jock straps, knee length shorts, and Arab robes. Most of them seemed to be adolescent, with a sprinkling of older people. A white-haired man passed in a fiacre. Around the square were lodging houses, cafes, Turkish baths and boardwalks. He caught a whiff of the sea. Streets and alleys opened off the square. Boys lounged in doorways.

As he walked along, Audrey glimpsed scenes that sent the blood singing in his ears and pounding to his crotch. Why, some of the boys were *out of control* (Audrey's term for erection) and *doing things together*. He could feel the pull in his groin. John had turned into a weed-grown cobblestone street—blue twilight and trees ahead—this looked like St. Louis again. Here comes the old lamplighter. Ah here we are. Red brick house on the corner. The lawn was weed-grown and there were leaves on the cracked sidewalk. John opened a side door under a portico.

"My father's house. Enter."

Dark stairs to the top floor. John opened a door and turned on the light. It was an attic room with a double brass bed, a washstand, a copper lustre basin and pitcher. Audrey saw some sepia prints on the wall that seemed to represent the fair they had just walked through. There was a bookcase with leatherbound giltedged books. John took off his jacket, tie and shirt, poured water into the basin, and washed his face and neck. He dried himself with a blue

towel, sat down on the edge of the bed and took off his shoes and socks.
He lay down on the bed with his knees up and pillows behind his head, selected an orange from a basket of fruit on the night table. He peeled the orange and the smell of oranges filled the room. He ate the orange, spilling juice on his naked chest. Audrey was washing with his shirt on, the collar turned back.

"Toss me that wash rag, Audrey."

John wiped the orange juice off his chest and licked his fingers. He lit a cigarette and looked at Audrey through the smoke.

"I want to see you stripped, Audrey."

Cold in the stomach untying his shoes shoes falling to the floor pants folded on the chair. He stood up.

"Take off your shorts too."

They caught in a way that made him uncomfortable fell to his ankles he kicked them onto a chair his nakedness John's hand rubbing lubricant and the silver sparks went off behind his eyes. His head exploded in pictures. It seemed that he had lived in this room for a long time a ceiling crossed by car lights from the street and the opening and closing of doors these stairs . . .

"You know both of us use the copper lustre basin in the attic room now Johnny's back."

Drifting sand, fish smells and dead eyes in doorways, shabby quarters of a forgotten city. I was beginning to remember the pawn shops, guns and brass knucks in a window, chili parlors, cheap rooming houses, a cold wind from the sea. Dead eyes seemed to be looking at some distant beginning to remember the boy, an old skating rink . . . any minute now . . . Who said Atlantic City? . . . wire rusty around jagged holes . . . Van's Surgery . . . writing croaker . . . Globe Hotel . . . Great Atlantic Accident . . . name address hotel quite right? . . . a number . . . police line ahead frisking seven boys against a wall. Too late to turn back, they'd seen us. And then I saw the photographers, more photographers than a routine frisk would draw. I eased a film grenade into my hand. A cop stepped toward us. I pushed the plunger down and brought my hands up, tossing the grenade into the air. A black explosion blotted out the set and we were running down a dark street toward the barrier. Behind us the city went up in chunks.

GREAT ATLANTIC ACCIDENT . . . READ ALL ABOUT IT.

We ran on and burst out of a black silver mist into late afternoon sunlight on a suburban street, cracked pavements, sharp smell of weeds.

"Roller skate boys very close now." The Dib touched pillars and posts as he walked. He pointed to a stucco building that occupied half a block. "There, in old skating rink."

The rink was boarded up and looked deserted from the outside. The Dib knocked on a side door, which opened silently on oiled hinges. In the doorway stood a tall blond youth in a blue jock strap. He carried a machine pistol under one arm. He looked at me with metallic grey eyes.

"Come in," he said and stepped aside.

I looked around for the Dib. He had disappeared. "He's gone."

"*Naturlich.* It is his work."

In the middle of the rink some boys in blue jock straps were skating. Sunlight poured through a broken skylight of wired glass. The wire was rusty around jagged holes, made I would guess by grenades or mortars. Mattresses here and there, boys sat naked smoking hashish and drinking tea, a work bench along one wall where boys were sharpening knives, oiling skates, repairing bicycles, a long bicycle rack by the work bench. On a mat four boys were practicing judo and karate. Others threw knives into a target. Scene from a silent film. No laughing no shouting no horse play. Boys turned to look at me as I passed, faces unsmiling, eyes cool and watchful. All movements were purposeful and controlled. No boy was fidgeting or standing aimlessly around. The boy with the pistol took me to what had been the office of the rink. It was fitted out as a ward room, maps on the wall, pins in the maps.

"Do you have any ammunition?" he asked me.

I put a box of fifty shells on the table.

"We must distribute these. We have five .38 police revolvers here." He handed me five shells.

He stepped to the door and spoke in the language. A thin dark boy, face spattered with adolescent pimples, came over from the work bench. He was naked except for a blue jock strap. He motioned for me to follow. Dusty window boarded up, boys at a table peeling potatoes and cutting meat. He slid behind a counter where the skates had once been issued to noisy teenage patrons. He measured me with his eyes and dumped some clothes on the counter—sweat shirts, blue jeans, blue jock straps, socks. He passed me a bowie knife 18 inches long with a worn black belt and sheath. I hefted the knife in my hands. The handle was a knuckle duster that ended in a brass knob. It was a beautifully balanced fighting instrument honed to razor sharpness.

"Just take any locker empty and change," he told me.

I stashed my clothes in a locker and changed into blue jeans and sweat shirt.

"You want to be measured for skates and crash helmet and bucklers."

The cobbler was an old man in a dusty room, tools and leather laid out on a long table. He looked at me from eyes faded as pale sky. Unhurried and old, he measured my feet, head and forearms. The boy leaned against the door jamb watching. The cobbler completed his measurements and nodded.

"Bath?" the boy asked. Walking behind him I spotted a pimple where his naked buttocks rubbed together and another on the left cheek. He felt my eyes, stopped and turned to look at me over his shoulder. I touched the pimples with my finger tips, caressing his buttocks. He moved slightly and rubbed his jock strap dusty windows boarded up wooden benches smell of sweat and mouldy jock straps several boys changing. The boy sat down on a bench and pulled his jock strap down, tossing it into a locker. He had a half erection. He looked down as his cock got stiff.

"You strip."

I pulled off my clothes. He looked at me with unsmiling appraisal. "You fuck me this time," he decided.

He led the way through a green door. A shower room with white tile floor had been fitted out as a haman. A youth had just poured a bucket of water over himself. He turned with an erection, shook water from his eyes, measuring me with his thin brown body. He reached out a slow foot and brought it down my calf and said something to the dark boy. Three youths sat on a bench comparing erections. The boy filled a bucket, poured half of it over me and the rest on himself. We passed a piece of carbolic soap back and forth. One of the youths tossed us a towel and we dried our bodies. There was a tube of KY on a shelf. I picked it up. The boy leaned forward holding his cheeks apart. I touched his pimples then rubbed the lubricant on his ass and up inside the ring squeezing my finger hitched hands around his hips and pulled him towards me feeling the spasmodic milking movements as I slid it in and out the electric warmth of his quivering body. The other youths stood around us watching silently and at the climax let out a little sigh from parted lips. We walked out naked into the rink.

It was late afternoon and the sides of the rink were in shadow. Some of the boys were cooking and making tea. Others were engaged in group sexual exercises. A circle of boys sat on the karate mat looking at each other's genitals in silent concentration. Now one of the boys was getting stiff. He walked to the center of the circle, turned around three times and sat down hugging his knees. He looked from one face to the other. His eyes locked with one boy and a current passed between them. There was a click as if a picture had been taken. The boy in the center of the circle opened his legs and lay back with his head on a leather cushion. A drop of lubricant squeezed out the end of his phallus as he arched his body and squirmed. The boy selected kneeled in front of the other studying his genitals. He pressed the tip open and looked at it through a lens of lubricant. He twisted the tight nuts gently with precise fingers as if he were tuning up a piece of machinery, handling the phallus as a precision instrument, running a slow finger up and down the shaft, rubbing lubricant along the divide line, feeling for sensitive spots in the tip. The circle of boys sat silent, lips parted, watching faces there calmed to razor sharpness. The boy who was being masturbated rocked back hugging knees against his chest. Quivering in an ecstasy of exposure his body blurred out of focus. He lay there unconscious. Two boys carried him to a mattress and covered his body with a blue blanket. Another boy took his place in the center of the circle.

I was tired and hungry. Some boys motioned me to sit down, handed me a plate of stew and a wedge of dark Arab bread. After eating I found a mattress and fell asleep. When I woke up the rink was full of yellow grey light. A boy was leaning on his elbow looking at me. It was the boy who had touched me

153

with his foot in the bath. Our eyes met. There was a click in my head a melting of the stomach on hands and knees a band squeezing my head tighter tighter taste of metal in the mouth. I was looking down from the ceiling then out through the broken skylight turning figure eights in the morning sky.

There are about thirty boys here of all races and nationalities: Negroes, Chinese, Mexicans, Arabs, Danes, Swedes, Americans, English. That is, they are evidently derived from racial and national stock corresponding to Negroes, Mexicans, Danes, Americans et cetera. However, these boys are a new breed.

After a breakfast of bread and tea, six boys put on jock straps, crash helmets and skates and buckled on their knives in preparation for a reconnaisance patrol. The blond boy with the machine pistol will accompany them as patrol leader. Others are busy at the work benches, sharpening knives, oiling skates, fixing bicycles, improvising weapons. One weapon works on the crossbow principle with strong rubber bands instead of a bow. Lead slugs are fed in from a magazine on top of the weapon and drop into a slot when the gun in cocked by pulling the bands back. The rifle models are amazingly accurate up to twenty yards and the slugs embed themselves in soft wood. A murderous bolo is made by attaching lead weights to each end of a bicycle chain. The boys practice continually with these devices.

The pimple boy approaches with a folder under his arm, wearing blue jeans. He looks like an American school boy except for the cool eyes alert and disengaged. He address me in a curiously unaccented English.

"I teach you picture language," he taps folder. "No good talk old language." He clears a space on the work bench and opens the folder. The written language is a simplified script obviously derived from the Egyptian. The pictures are then transliterated into verbal units. Any picture can be said in a number of ways according to the context. For five days, we study ten hours a day. My previous study of Egyptian hieroglyphs greatly facilitates my progress and I am now able to converse with some ease. Pictures rise out of the words. I am learning something of the history and customs of the wild boys. Once a year all the wild boys meet in one spot to compare weapons and fighting techniques and to indulge in communal orgies. This festival is known as Xolotl Time.

"Many different boy some almost like fish live all time in water since he begin."

I ask what he means by begin—since birth?

"Wild boy not born now. First he made from little piece one boy's ass grow new boy. Piece cut from boy after he get fucked. Boy like much get fucked give best piece. Grow new boy then boy give piece take new one back his tribe. Boy grow like this not like boy born no good cunt. Boy grow from piece change many different way. Some boy no talk make pictures in head. Boy make cry kill man over there there." He points across the rink. "Other got electricity in body. Boy live far south warm wet place very sweet very rotten inside. Dress up like woman kill many soldier." (These boys who are called "Bubus" secrete a substance from the rectum and genitals which leaves erogenous sores rotting flesh to the bone.) "You scratch feel good scratch more pretty soon scratch self away jump around in your bones. Some boy he glow in dark. You come near soon die. You come near little bit every day you all right. Very good for fuck. Him very hot inside. Other boy he look you come off in pants." And the dreaded "laughing boys": "You laugh too piss self laugh guts out." (The "laughing boys" also communicate fatal fits of sneezing, coughing and hiccuping.) "Other live blue place in mountains got little high blue note you hear that you need all time you hooked. Boy got poison teeth like snake. Lizard boy live on cliffs hand so strong crush bones." The boys with built-in weapons are known as biologics. Other of more or less normal physical attributes specialize in the use of some skill or weapon ... glider boys, knife throwers, bowmen, slingshot boys, blow-gun boys. "Got darts all different size some so small you think mosquito bites you then turn blue and die." One tribe specializes in musical weapons. "Got music so sweet man walk over cliff. Make sound knock down wall shake guts out."

"Many boy tribe come Xolotl Time all different every time more different. Not need take piece now. We make Zimbu boy. Make many Zimbu Xolotl Time." I ask when this festival occurs. "Different time place every year. I think this time in south on sea maybe not know for sure till two weeks before time all boy stop fuck jack off he get there hot like fire."

The spoken language has great flexibility and extraordinary vividness through immediate pictorial association. If you can't see it you can't say it. As to the origins of this language, the boy is vague. "Wild boys written long time ago in picture book. Book called 'breathing book.' One man come show us piece from book." The wild boys have no sense of time and date the beginning from 1969 when the first wild boy groups were formed.

I now have my skates, crash helmet, and leather bucklers for the forearms, all perfectly tailored like extensions of my body. The skate rollers can be locked and rubber caps adjusted for walking uphill. Tomorrow I will go on patrol. Patrols consist of six boys on skates and one boy on a bicycle. The bicycle boy is the patrol leader. This job rotates and leadership is informal. It is his job to coordinate the activities of the patrol and the information gathered. He carries a pistol and field glasses in addition to the standard bowie knife.

We set out at dawn through ruined suburbs, a crescent moon in the china blue morning sky. The patrol leader is a tall thin Negro boy, ears flat against his small head, a distant savannah in his eyes. The boys are skating in a line, hands on each other's shoulders. We come to an intersection of subdivision streets which forms a wide expanse of cracked weed-grown pavement. The leader rides ahead to the top of a steep hill on his bicycle and scans the surrounding country through field glasses. He comes back and says one word which means empty land to sky. A boy rubs his jock strap and with one accord the boys sit down pulling their jock straps down over their skates. They skate on slow circles touching each other's genitals and buttocks as they pass.

A boy skates up behind me, puts his hand on my shoulder and guides me to a broken wall. Three of us brace ourselves against the wall then we are twisting in circles spinning the moon and the sky throwing sperm across the cracked pavements.

In the late afternoon we pass a ruined building. US Consulate. On a windy hillside we sight a herd of goats. The goatherd waves and runs towards us, wind whipping his torn djellaba. Young actor is about thirteen. He tells us a truckload of American soldiers passed the Consulate this morning and asked him where the wild boys were hiding.

"Americans very bor bor. Give me cigarettes, chocolate, corned bif. Believe everything what I say."

He takes a stick and draws a map to show the false route he has given them. The leader studies the map, sketches it on a clip board, pointing and asking questions. Satisfied that the map is accurate, he hands the boy a piece of hashish and a switch knife. The boy snaps the knife open and cuts the air. "One day kill son bitch Merican."

I put my hand on the back of the boy's neck. He moves eagerly under my hands like a dog, squirms out of his djellaba and stands naked in the wind, pubic hairs blown flat against his groin. He arches his body as I jack him off . . . the wind spatters sperm across his lean brown stomach.

That night we decide on an ambush plan for the truck. Our undercover agents working as cooks, bus boys, waiters, bartenders have administered Bor Bor to the American troops. The effect of this drug, which is held in horror by the wild boys and only used as a weapon against our enemies, is to lull the user into a state of fuzzy well-being and benevolence, a warm good feeling that everything will come out all right for Americans.

"We like apple pie and we like each other, it's just as simple as that."

Jolting along in the truck . . . "Oh God, isn't mother a grand person? She's got all the good qualities . . . " Muttering squirming bursting into maudlin song:

"Your mother and mine . . . "

"With a heart that was willing to share . . . "

"Let me bang her twice a month and what could be fairer than that unless it's our old Colonel. When I die I want to be buried right in the same coffin with that fine old blue-eyed whitey—always putting his hands on our shoulders and calls us Son and weeps like a baby over the dead and wounded. He was an Eagle Scout at birth."

A truckload of tough soldiers, crooning, singing, weeping, muttering, smiling, squirming around like randy dogs under Massa's kind old hands. A Sea Org member of Scientology leaps up and screams out: "THANK YOU RON THANK YOU RON THANK YOU RON! . . . "

Another soldier throws his arms around the Jew from Brooklyn . . .
"You Jews is so warm and human!"

Another sobs out: "All the darkies is a-weepin' cause Masa's in the cold cold grave . . ." As he buries a good Darky and a dead dog . . .

"Cried like babies right in front of each other—'why be ashamed to show your heart son' said a wise old whisky priest and I sobbed in that good man's arms and the cop threw his great paws around both of us and we cried all over each other."

Mother and Old Glory, kindly priests, good cops, adorable prison wardens rocked in the arms of Bor Bor . . .

A thin sliver of moon in the blue black sky. The cold at night here grabs your flesh into goose pimples. We slung an iron telephone pole thirty feet long between chains, a line of boys on skates on both sides down a steep hill, the pole pulling us along faster and faster like a comet—hit the truck dead center and knocked it over spilling those Bor Bor heads on the cold cold ground. We swept around from both sides and cut them to Old Glory and back. Under a rough cross formed by the skewered truck we broke thin ice in a fountain and washed the blood off us. We now have a supply of firearms for the next operation.

The roller skate boys swerve down a wide palm-lined avenue into a screaming blizzard of machine gun bullets . . . humming boys, a vibration that sets the teeth on edge and rages through the brain like buzz saws . . . messages whistled through cold alleys, taken up by the barking of dogs, reach the remote communes in a few hours . . . he was coming down windy streets, white shorts slapping, mouth open, their hairs up at the first ripple whimper off putrid sweet legs throw back their heads and howl the winds ass hairs erectile— plant boys who know the weeds and vines, marijuana behind enemy lines, hay fever on the wind, water hyacinths snarl the boat propellor, marijuana sprouts by the barracks, thorns scratch the Colonel's boots, boys who can call the locusts and fleas, beautiful diseased Bubu boy stands by a black lagoon, fragile dream boys of shaded dawn wait by attic windows in a lost street of slate roofs and brick chimneys, shaman boys the young faces dark with death, a young red-haired soldier, his ears trembling, yelps, ejaculates strange streets dank school toilets a wind across the golf course naked semen spurting shy spirits in a world of shades boy touches a shoulder under the blankets gasping as the other holds his knees back his thin buttocks his rectum wet morning cobblestone rain in cobwebs the blue desert who exist can breathe there tenuous rose vines bodies cool backs his little teeth scream and help boys cuddle whimpering in sleep, a naked boy with his back to Audrey rubs against another, the boy turns and grins at Audrey.

Late afternoon light I could touch the sea wall the stone the vines I could see my body and the sand the face down there a thin pale back two boys laughing blue youth in their eyes sunny the house behind him bleakly clear I am the boy as a child and this is me lying naked on his underwear rubbing himself my room and me there he smiled to watch him do it jumped across a gleaming empty sky I could feel unknown hand orange in the shed long long how long it was the skies fall apart dust of the dead in his eyes into his eggs tighter tighter then I was spurting into a ruined courtyard a smell of oats.

Back in Mexico City, the man who was the boy's father tried to raise money to come back and dig some more in the ruins, but the Mexican authorities said he had no right to do this and took what he had found away from him and sent some Mexicans to the ruins. The man began taking morphine again and I spent most of my time in the streets to stay out of the house. I remember an American from Texas with prison shadows in his eyes talked to me in the park and I went back with him to his apartment.

It was some time after that that a man came to the club and selected me as his caddy. He was a youngish man, about thirty, with very pale grey eyes . . . fat, but I could see there were muscles under the fat, and I could see that he had something special he wanted from me as soon as we got out on the golf course. First he told me I shouldn't be hanging around in Mexico, that I belonged in America because I was an American and he could arrange this but first I would have to do something he wanted me to do in order to "square myself" as he put it. Then he told me that "the free world" as he called it was fighting for its life and I could help. There was a man they knew was working with the Commies and they wanted to get him. I'd already seen this man, he bought me a sandwich and an orange drink . . . now all I had to do was to get the man you know what I mean to start something with me and they would nail him and that would be it—after that I could go to America and live with a decent family and go to school, now how did that sound to me? I told him I was born in Mexico and didn't want to go to America, that my parents were here and I had to help them with the money I made. Then he grabbed me by the arms and I saw he had a snubnose .38 in a holster under his arm.

"All right look at me when you talk and stop lying. I know all about you. Your father is a junkie and your mother is a lush and you've been peddling your ass in the Alameda for the past year . . . "

I told him that I would do what he wanted and he showed me Mexicans wouldn't let him take me to America. Then he said he had news for me and he pulled out a piece of paper and held it up so I could see it was my Mexican birth certificate. Then he tore it up and looked at me and his face got all black and ugly. I was looking beyond him at the brush fires along the road.

"Listen you little pansy shit you want to go back to a reformatory? You want to get gang fucked till your asshole splits open? HUH? Well I can sign a court order and get you into a federal reformatory in Texas before you can fart . . . "

I told him that I would do what he wanted and he showed me a place by the pond.

"Right here where your boy friend cornholed you. That picture gets you out of parental custody . . ."

I had already decided what to do but I decided to argue or he would get suspicious—he was like that, could see people's minds—so I asked if I could stay in Mexico if I did what he wanted and he said I could if I wanted to and I knew he was lying or if I was allowed to stay he would want more such work from me but I pretended to believe him. It was set up for the day after tomorrow which would be Friday.

When I got back to the changing shed Johnny was there alone and I told him what had happened and the plan I had. As we walked out through the parking lot Johnny unscrewed the cap on the man's gas tank leaving it held by the very end of the screws so it would fly off on the first bump. We were sure to be suspected so we went to hide out with Tio Mate in Northern Mexico in a little town surrounded by opium growers. If anyone asked we were not there. We read about it in the papers the next day but the heat was not on right away as we had expected because somebody else had been there before us with an explosive device devised by the CIA itself to be attached to gas tanks. That of course sent them running after professionals or enemy agents within their ranks.

Charm

by Graham Jackson

for Ian

WHEN ALAN OPENED the door, Gregory was there, curly head haloed by the heat. Eyes smiling and keen, just as they had always been. Six months before, Christmas Eve, he had come to say goodbye for Gibraltar, only then the curls were damp with snow.

They didn't say anything, they looked at one another and grinned. Alan in jeans and a T-shirt, Gregory in a crumpled lilac shirt and white pants dirty at the knees, knapsack on his back.

They embraced.

The sun poured into the cool hall-way, fierce along Alan's arms where they clutched Gregory's back.

Alan purred. Gregory laughed his sweet, soft laugh.

"So."

"So. Here I am. Again."

"Ah."

"You're looking good."

"You haven't changed."

"No?"

"You're browner."

"It's peeling. Down my back."

"Let's see."

Laughter.

"Jus' the same. Dirty old man."

"Umm." Alan squeezed Gregory's buttocks.

"That feels nice."

"Good."

"So."

"So."

They stood at arms' length, eyes taking in everything greedily, the heat curling about the doorway in wisps like smoke. Alan closed the door and together, arm in arm, they bumped along the narrow hall into the kitchen where Gregory rummaged through the refrigerator for the ginger beer that was always there.

Alan opened the cans and put some biscuits on a plate.

They sat across the table from one another, a pine table cluttered with Alan's correspondance and papers, notes for essays, a political journal, and a copy of *The Shropshire Lad.* A clear glass bowl was filled with white locust flowers. Alan ate as though he had fasted for weeks; Gregory slowly, the biscuits ambrosia, the experience a sensual one.

Their eyes met and laughed. Gregory pointed at the roses, thick around the window. Alan nodded.

"Did you get my cards?" Gregory's foot sought Alan's.

"Yes."

"All of them?"

"Twenty-seven."

"Thirty-one."

"Well, that's the bloody post office for you. Someone filched the stamps probably. Bloody people."

"You get the cards from Tangiers?"

"I think so."

"You like the stamps?"

"I don't remember."

"You'd remember if you got them."

"Oh, the one with the Arab boys."

"They're in Berber costume."

"Nice."

Laughter. Alan watched while Gregory sipped his ginger beer from a tall glass.

"What's that around your neck?" A small gold charm glistened in the hollow of Gregory's throat.

"Symbol of Libra."

"Where'd you get it?"

"In Valetta."

"Oh."

"Actually I didn't get it."

Alan looked up from his empty can.

"One of the girls in the group bought it off an old lady in the market."

"She gave it to you?" Alan leaned back in the chair.

"It was the only sign the lady had."

"Funny." He took off his glasses and rubbed his eyes.

"I know. But it's real gold and she only wanted a little bit for it."

"You don't believe it's real gold . . . ?"

"Sure. It is."

Alan laughed, a snort.

"I'm the only Libra in TM. Isn't that weird?"

"Yah."

"Look." Gregory handed a little package in blue tissue across the table. Alan put his glasses back on and looked at the parcel as though he did not know what to do with it.

"It's for you."

Alan took it.

"It's not going to bite."

Alan unwrapped the tissue slowly, almost shyly. A charm on a gold chain fell into his palm. Like Gregory's, only different.

"It's the symbol for Cancer."

"Where did you get it?"

"After we left Malta, I kept an eye out for one for you. I got it in Capri. In a little gift shop. You don't think it will ruin your image?" He said it with a side smile. "You can tell everyone it's an anarchist symbol or something."

Alan turned it over in his palm.

"The guy who sold it to me wanted me to come and work for him."

Alan snorted again and lay out the charm full-length on the table.

"No. He was married and had two kids and everything."

"I don't know how you do it."

"Charm." Gregory leaned back in his seat and chuckled.

"Yah." Alan stood up abruptly. "Come on."

Gregory rose, eyes bright. "About time."

They went upstairs.

That night in the cool of the air-conditioned living room, Alan plugged in the electric fire and they drank tea flavoured with orange and cloves. The sign of Cancer gleamed on Alan's throat. Gregory pillowed his shirt behind his head and stretched out, humming quietly.

"Oh, I almost forgot." Gregory propped himself up on his elbow. "My uncle was telling me about a piece of land we might look into."

"Are you crazy? You know the price of land these days."

"It's cheap."

"Cheap!"

"Yah. He showed me a picture of the house and everything. Sixty thousand. That's cheap."

"Where is it?"

"Newmarket."

"Newmarket! I don't want a place way the hell and gone."

"It's just north of Toronto."

"How do we get into the city?"

"I've got the old car."

"That's good for another fifty miles, that thing."

"So I'll buy a new one."

"Yah." Alan poured another cup of tea and passed it to Gregory. "What happens when you're not around?"

"There's buses."

"Buses! Jesus, you know I hate buses."

"You should see the house though."

"You got the picture with you?"

"No, but it has everything we wanted. Ten rooms, not counting bathrooms, and a basement apartment. You could have a whole floor to yourself and never see anyone if you didn't want an' when I had friends from the group over, they could stay in the basement."

"As long as they stayed there. I can just see them looting through the refrigerator. We'll have to put locks on the cupboards."

Gregory laughed. "There's about an acre of land around the place, too."

"So you could have a garden."

"Yah." Gregory's eyes were wide.

Alan smiled. His hands caressed the cup. He smiled again.

"I want to grow herbs: mint and marjoram and vegetables, squash, turnip, beans, corn ... "

"You're going to need farmhands."

"You can supply them." Gregory prodded Alan with his foot, delighted.

"It's just a question of money."

"We'll get it."

"When?"

"Soon."

"How?"

"Your new book."

"No book on left-wing anarchists is going to net me sixty thousand profit."

"I'll get it."

"How?"

"I don't know. Mitch wanted me to do a record and Joan offered me a job at the CBC hosting this music programme. I could get enough for a down payment."

"I don't know."

"But it's what you wanted. We've talked about this for years."

"Six," he said, without meaning to.

"Now you're unsure."

"No. I want it. You know how much."

Alan reached out and they held one another.

"It's eleven. I'm tired. I think I'll go."

"O.K."

Gregory rose, put on his shirt. Alan watched him from the floor, the lean legs, the flat boy stomach, the hard round nipples, the long neck and glowing curls. Gregory would be twenty-six soon, he hardly looked it, except about the eyes sometimes when he was tired, like now ... Gregory smiled nervously.

"I'm going to Quebec."

"Oh." Alan stood up, shook his legs.

"They've got a new retreat up there."
"Oh." Alan looked at his hand on Gregory's shoulder.
"Up north."
"TM sounds like a healthy business. India, Peru, Gibraltar, Quebec. Maybe you should borrow some money from the guru for the house."
"He probably would do it."
Alan sniffed. "When?"
"When am I going?"
"Yah."
"Next Friday."
"For how long?"
"Till October. It gets pretty cold up there in October."
"Eat lots of herbs."
"Yah."
They embraced, briefly, hard.
"I'll see you tomorrow."
Alan went with him to the door. "Great."
The night was restless. Cats quarrelled. The cicada sawed in the elms and, in the distance, a subway tunnelled east. Gregory walked down the drive, the knapsack in his hand almost scraping the ground. Alan wanted to call out, "Stay, I'll be thirty next Friday," but he didn't.
Instead he shut the door, feeling the charm about his neck. He smiled to himself, unhooked the charm and wrapped it back in its blue tissue. Safe.

A week-Friday, Gregory took a train to Montreal and, from Montreal, a bus northbound.
Alan went on. Waiting. But not really waiting.

A Marriage of Convenience

by Peter Burton

AS THE LETTER was post-marked from Bath I knew it would be from James Howard. Since we first started to correspond, a little over three years ago, I have received a letter or postcard from him every three or four days. He writes about the most trifling things. The correspondence seems much more like a conversation, a dialogue, with points raised and discussed in some detail from one letter or postcard to another. I suspect that as Howard doesn't possess a telephone—he has an almost spinsterish dislike of any kind of domestic appliance—correspondence is a substitute for conversation.

Howard's constant barrage of letters and cards can be rather tedious; especially as I feel obliged to write some kind of reply almost upon receipt. I know that a silence of more than two or three days is likely to bring forth a whole series of rather cross postcards which demand explanations as to my lack of prompt reply. Usually Howard appends some irritated post-script in which he complains about the decline in good manners. He relates this decline in manners to the accelerated speed of our contemporary society. The point is taken; for a while future letters receive my immediate attention.

Although we have corresponded so regularly over these last few years, I have yet to meet Howard. I now feel it is unlikely that we shall ever meet—the contents of his latest letter intimate this. The letter—written in Howard's usual terse style—came as something of a surprise to me:

> *Dear Bob* (he wrote)
> *You may have heard that I am to be married in three weeks. The woman is pleasant enough—a comfortable widow of middle years. She has two young sons. I shall be leaving Bath—not without regrets, as I have known many happy years here—and moving in with my wife at her home in Bristol.*
> *As my future wife knows nothing about my homosexuality, it is obvious that my collection of books and periodicals on the subject must go. It wouldn't do for her to suspect anything—most especially as I shall be adopting the two lads.*

165

> *I am sending my collection of 'dubious' literature to you under separate cover and would appreciate your arranging the sale of the same through one of your bookdealing chums. A cheque would be appreciated in due course.*
> *I cannot impress upon you enough the need for absolute discretion in all future correspondence!*
> *All best wishes*
> *Howard*

Something about the letter seemed sinister. I am not sure that I can exactly pin-point the details which made me feel slightly uncomfortable; I suspect it was the generally furtive air about the whole letter. Somehow I could envisage the unsuspecting widow; picture the two sons. What age *were* these two boys anyway, I wondered. 'Young' is such a misleading word—and for someone of Howard's age, which I have always presumed to be around sixty, twenty could seem young. To me the expression 'young sons' rather suggested two boys about eleven or twelve, but then I am twenty years younger than Howard. Certainly, if the boys *are* pre-teen they will have nothing to fear from Howard —and maybe, anyway, his rather eccentric tastes will preclude these adoptive sons from his desires.

I suppose I should explain, fill in the few details I know about Howard. Details will give reason to my feeling of disquiet.

I have published two books and a considerable body of journalism yet, though I make a small living from my writing, I am not well known. I would not expect to see either of my books prominently displayed in any major bookshop, nor placed anywhere on the bestselling lists. But I am happy; that is the most important thing. And it was through my writing that I first encountered Howard.

A little over three years ago, I published my first book: *Golf: A Brief History*. The book hadn't sold sensationally, but it had sold enough copies to make a paperbacked reprint worthwhile. I was rather proud of my effort. James Howard is a golfing fanatic. He had read my book. His first letter to me was addressed care of my publisher. That first letter was friendly enough— a brief acknowledgement of the merits of my book with comments on several minor inaccuracies in the text. I duly replied, promising to correct the errors should there ever be a second edition of the book. As with most 'fan mail,' I expected my reply to be the end of the correspondence.

By return of post, I received another letter from James Howard. In this letter he raised points about the recent British Open tournament at St. Andrews. This time, I didn't reply immediately. A week passed; then I received a postcard from Howard in which he asked if I'd received his previous letter. I thought this rather odd. How was he to know that I wasn't away, or that I was extremely busy and unable to catch up with my mail? I began to form a mental picture of James Howard.

Bath, I have always remembered as a beautiful old spa, filled with good bookshops, pleasant pubs, and several excellent restaurants. But it has always seemed basically a town of old or elderly people; maybe even a place of retirement. Beckford, I remember, spent his last years there, after the sale of Fonthill. Howard, I suspected, must be a retired gentleman—perhaps ex-army or from the colonial service.

Thoughts of the army or the colonial service produced a mental impression of a rather squat, red-faced man, probably with a thick but neatly clipped moustache. I imagined him dressed in thick tweed suits, heavy walking shoes and, perhaps, carrying a stick for use on hikes around the surrounding Somerset countryside. Golf, I knew, was his game. I could also imagine him as a cricket enthusiast, maybe keen on fishing. I certainly didn't imagine him as one with any interest in literature. Nor in sex. At least, I tended to picture him fumbling drunkenly with local prostitutes in Aden or Bangkok or Cairo. In these last two suppositions I was wrong.

Two letters a week, from Howard, became a regularity. At first these letters discussed the current golfing tournaments; politics—remarkably he proved to be rather a socialist; current events about which we were both only as informed as our newspapers. In one letter Howard enquired about future writing projects. I was then preparing my second book, a novel about public school life and set just before the last war. This letter received the most astonishing reply; astonishing, at least, because it cut right across several of my preconceptions about James Howard. I will quote only a brief passage from it—*"I expect you will be writing about the exotic hothouse atmosphere which prevailed—probably still does prevail—in those places,"* he wrote. *"Assignations in Chapel, love-notes furtively passed in class, long summer days with happy afternoons spent behind the cricket pavillion with one's particular friend. Oh, I remember it all so well!"*

This wasn't at all the kind of thing I expected from the James Howard I had created in my mind's eye. My reply was discreet, though I suggested that the finished work would undoubtedly please Howard and bring back happy remembrances of things past.

It was after this letter that the correspondence became much more personal, more intimate. Golf, politics and world affairs were relegated to the more obscure reaches of our letters. Now our letters were taken up with discussion of the public school novel; from *Tom Brown's Schooldays* to the most recent examples of that absorbing blend of fiction and fantasy. From the public school novel we moved on to the exhilarating adventure yarn for boys, once so popular but now superseded by trashy thrillers and lurid volumes of sexual exploits. Howard even brought into this conversation by correspondence nov-

167

els of war and novels of science fiction. Throughout these books we were especially interested in observing the streak of homosexuality. It was in the discussion of some of the science fiction and war stories that I began to perceive —dimly at first—the nature of Howard's particular fascination; his particular *bent*.

Injury and affliction seemed to absorb Howard. He discussed it at length— and I noticed that there was always more of a fascination with some volume in which one of the characters had to go, as it were, under the surgeon's knife. This interest was most apparent when Howard was writing about war novels— I remember a detailed discussion about a novel by Martin Boyd. Howard had been positively entranced by a sequence in which the hero meets again a beautiful boy—half of whose face had been shot away in a First World War shell attack. Blindness was another recurring theme in Howard's letters. I distinctly remember a letter in which he wrote at length about blindness in fiction—citing one of Delany's science fiction stories as a classic example. And I remember a letter in which Howard talked about one of Burroughs' novels—*The Wild Boys*, I think—commenting that some of the boys were *"provided with interesting disabilities."*

It was apparent that Howard was fascinated by boys; with an exaggerated sense of literary values he claimed Michael Davidson's *The World, The Flesh and Myself* as one of the major works of autobiography in the twentieth century. This fascination with boys I could understand; it was an absorption I shared. But this interest in violence and the fruits of violence convinced me that Howard's interest was in more than just boys.

The clincher came in a letter in which Howard wrote about a youth he had met on a train journey between Bath and Bristol; was he, I wonder, on his way to meet his 'comfortable widow'?

The boy, it appeared, had been Howard's only companion in the carriage. Somehow they had begun a conversation—haltingly, I imagine, as I cannot picture Howard as the type of man who would easily make conversation with strangers. It was neither the conversation nor the boy's looks which had seemed to interest Howard. Towards the end of the letter, he had written: *"He had been in an accident at his place of work. He had lost the middle and index fingers from his left hand. I confess, I felt an almost overwhelming desire to take that incomplete hand in mine, raise it to my lips and kiss those pathetic stumps. I resisted. I suppose I shall not see the boy again."*

Howard, I decided, was fascinated by boys. But he was most strongly drawn towards *mutilated* boys.

The barrage of letters and cards which seemed to proclaim this obsession disquieted me. Mutilation, injury, amputation—it seemed markedly unhealthy. I was soon to find out how extreme was his interest in this peculiar field.

Very recently, whilst dining with two close friends, I happened to mention my strange correspondent and his equally bemusing obsession. One of the friends—a journalist for a tabloid newspaper—asked the name of my peculiar friend. I told him. He then asked where James Howard came from; I told him. I asked if he knew him.

"No," my friend replied, "but I do know of him. In fact, some years ago I wrote a story about him for my paper. I'm sure it must be the same fellow. There couldn't be two like him down in Bath."

The port was passed again; we lit cigars.

"What was your story?" asked our host.

"Gruesome," explained the journalist. "Kinky and gruesome. You see, this James Howard amputated his left arm. He hacked it off, just below the elbow, with a meat cleaver. And he very nearly died from loss of blood."

"But why?" I asked.

"As I remember it, Mr. James Howard said that he'd hacked off his arm in the interests of science!"

Howard's package of books and periodicals arrived. Through the good offices of a friend in the second-hand book trade, I had managed to sell the various volumes. Payment was not large but, I presumed, it would satisfy Howard. I typed out a letter congratulating him on his forthcoming marriage, asked one or two questions about the widow and her sons, enclosed the cheque and posted the letter.

This morning I received my last letter from James Howard.

Dear Bob (he writes)

Thank you for your good wishes and the cheque. The amount seemed rather small; are you sure that you filled the cheque out correctly?

You ask about the woman I am to marry—though I cannot think why you should be interested. I have already told you that she is a widow, of middle years, comfortably situated. Her husband was killed in a motoring accident six years ago—when the boys were eight and ten respectively. Though his wife was not in the car, the two boys were. They were both blinded and received dreadful injuries.

It is my intention to become a friend and helpmate to the boys—and, of course, to their mother.

I have been considering our correspondence in the light of my marriage and have decided that it might be a good thing if we ceased to write.

I will destroy all your letters and would appreciate your doing the same with mine.

I shall remember you with affection.
    etc. etc.

I shuddered as I finished reading the letter. Then I thought back over all I had learned about James Howard. Somehow it all seemed horribly sinister. Maybe I am just over-reacting.

169

But enclosed with the letter was a small black and white snapshot. Scrawled across the back, in Howard's bold and familiar handwriting were the words: *Jamie and Derek, my adopted sons.*

The photograph showed two boys of about fourteen and sixteen. Their blind eyes, beneath mops of fair hair, seemed to gaze towards the camera. Their faces showed hope and expectancy and a wonderful innocence. But I felt my heart lurch as I realised that in the horrible accident which had killed their father both boys had lost limbs.

The Last Piece of Trade in America

by John Mitzel

BY THAT TIME, all America had gone fluffy.

More than just a passing fad or fancy, effeminacy of the most outrageous sort had arrived, spread and stayed. Rooted in a successful political and ideolocical foundation, the merchandisers had made their logical move and completely transformed a once virile nation of taciturn, self-sacrificing pioneers and steel-tough workers into a giggling mass of disposable, squeezable and *cuddly* citizens.

To be elected "First Lady" was now regarded as the highest honor in the land. Accommodations for the new lifestyle were everywhere apparent: football players of both sexes wore larger helmets to hold their *coiffures* in place while on the gridiron—The Saturday Night Date was more important now than the game itself! The most disturbing industrial injuries were Broken Fingernails and Dry, Scaly Skin. The most serious public offense was Unwanted Body Hair. Police officers, army recruits and all other uniformed personnel were required to watch their diets and keep their torso measurements within a strict proportion. This they eagerly did with Smart Lunches of dressy lettuce, spam, cottage cheese and jello. The only major crimes the constabulary had to deal with were wig-shop heists and people being ugly in public. It was felonious Not To Try To Be Beautiful.

Material success alone was no longer the Big Dream of the populace. This was the age when Elegance and Good Taste were the capstones of The Great American Experience. Even tough contract bargaining between union leaders and management in the major tertiary industries—catering, swimming pool repair, interior decorating—were thoroughly polite and strictly followed the established rules of etiquette. Not only *could* everybody become a Society Lady, *everybody had!* The last pair of baggy white men's drawers had long since been hung in the Smithsonian's new Antique Couture Wing (a/k/a "Campy Clothes Collection").

And yet somewhere in the hinterlands of this frilly, fluffy culture, hidden away in some bleak mid-western state, Stanley "Butch" Markman was just about to quit his rural cabin where he'd many years before been left as a foundling and where he was raised by a craggy hermit straight out of an early misanthropic strain of American Literature. After the old man died (Stanley had wrapped him in a sheet and buried him aside the Old Oak Tree), Butch decided the big city was the place for his future, the place where a man could make a fair and honest wage with hard labor. His hair combed back and matted down with bacon fat, three days worth of face stubble, a dirty t-shirt, grubby coveralls and mudcaked boots, he put his thumb out as he paced the country road, watching the spiffy cars spin toward the metropolis.

It wasn't long before a creampuff, the driver that is, pulled over in his lavish, highly-personalized sedan, filled with a fashionable fragrance.

He leaned over to speak out the passenger's window:

"Going my way, baby?" asked the teased head. "Hop in! What's your name, cutie?"

"Butch."

"*Heaven!*" shrilled the silly billy. He swelled his eyes. "I can *certainly* see *why*. Have a cigarette and relax, toots."

The car raced down the highway, a metal and glass bubble filled with loud music and the strains of the familiar seduction of The Last Innocent to the ways at the end of Big City Living.

In town, Butch walked the streets for awhile. An idle and curious crowd, many with painted faces and hard voices, slowly grew in his wake and followed him. Brash, vulgar, short-lived, these harlequins of the streetcorners, even after they had had what they wanted from him, were probably the least calculating of the bunch Butch was to meet, ultimately too stupid to be deeply malevolent. And, after the first nights of revelry, drinking, doping, hanging-out and petty theft, the police vans descended—the vans had been painted by America's leading cop-art designers, each's pattern coordinated with its district's distinctive characteristic (theatres, antiques, leather goods, hi-tone dining, secure investments, etc.). All were pinched in the bust except Butch; he was left alone out of admiration for the novelty of his manliness.

This same manliness was to get him into the chic apartment of the last gentlemanly Metropolis bachelor—'30's "sophistication" being his hold-out against the new decadence of Fluff and Elegance. He took Butch in and, though Butch had not yet learned it, kept him separate enough, even if as caricature, to give him an Identity that could bolster fantasies. For this, others would be grateful.

"It's kind of you, sir, to do all this for me, but I want you to understand that I'm just happy when I can hang out in a bar and listen to the juke and strike up talk with the other guys."

"To begin with: there are no 'other guys' and haven't been for ten years. Trust me, and keep to your own number and you'll do all right."

"Huh?"

Through this connexion, Butch would walk into dance bars and cause a riot of desire; stud service fees reached unprecedented levels (or so it was said; no one had any memory of anything that had happened before yesterday).

One night, Butch came home in a svelte, open-necked, red nylon jumpsuit and a shell necklace. His keeper thwacked him good with a riding crop. "You are never to allow anyone to buy you or give you anything, do you understand? Once you get sucked into *that*, you'll turn out just like the rest of them, vile creatures."

"Aw, hell, I thought he was just trying to be nice to me."

"Kind, yes. Kind of subversive. What your pea-brain can't grasp is that they actually *hate* you deep down. That's why it'd satisfy them to make you a replica of *them* in a flash if they could. As good citizens, they must possess and destroy you. Why do you think they all became 'fluff' to begin with? They're like you, *dumb*, and they got caught up in a game the end of which they could not foresee. The results of which *you* see. So, ride 'em good, hillbilly. Don't listen to a word they say. There's nothing inside their bubbleheads but that incessant chatter of everything that is unimportant in life. Tomorrow, I want you to get your hair cut in the old fashioned military style."

The jumpsuit—as well as the soft sweaters, scarves, floppy hats and tiny jewels—that Butch had received went into the rubbish, and for one week he was obliged to keep to an itinerary which comprised only bus stations, greasy spoons, gin dives and pool halls. This was done to maintain his contact with his roots, such as they were, to make sure he stayed *plain* white trash and didn't catch the contagion of *haute elegance* of the uppitty trash. It was hoped that this punishment would become his pleasure.

Yet, even in these sleazy emporia he wasn't safe from the contagion. Small, *cute* conspiracies had formed to trick him into getting his nails trimmed and lacquered, his pants custom made, his hair tinted and styled. These were great temptations to one as easily conned as was Butch; in fact *he* thought many of his temptresses quite nice folks.

The time came, alas, when Butch had serviced every orifice in town which had sought the attention. Butch soon became somewhat passé for the trendy, garnering only the flattery of those few not indelibly fashion-conscious. Others would wait years for him to return again as a "new" item. In the most chi-chi circles, his making messes, passing out drunk, cutting up expensive fabrics with beer can lids was not only *not* funny or amusing anymore, it was not tolerated. Much fluff, of all sexes, simply barred him and treated him as though he didn't or even *shouldn't* exist.

Having been consumed, transformed from The Latest Thing to mere litter junking up the city, Butch became subject to harrassment from the very same fluffy fuzz who had earlier thought him The Most. A few times he was arrested for no reason and held overnight, during which he was introduced to the vicious side of fluff constabulary —*the humiliating things he was made to do!* Fluff decadence need not be as flabby as it appeared.

His use to his master diminished, and, with a gift of cash, Butch was sent packing. It was suggested he return when he could cut his own way.

Butch fell back onto working the streets, going with strange creatures who were visiting from all parts of the world, gabbing with sorry faces, living in the manner of an unconscious exile, the wretched fate of a discarded bauble in Fat City. Even after months of exposure to their culture, he was still amazed how much everybody looked alike. What people thought were other people *he* knew were grotesques: talking heads with powdered faces in sleek and unnaturally taut bodies (wrinkled by booze even so), clad in couturier-copies and having a fabulous time.

He turned more aggressive and met with indifference. He tried starting fistfights in public places and found absolutely no social support. After a particularly destructive brawl, Butch was hauled into a tastefully done-up Courtroom, found guilty of being A Big Nuisance, and was literally *slapped* on the wrist by the presiding judge and told to stop it. In its way, it was a devastating sentence.

Alone in his room one night he fell apart. He cried, snivelled, moaned. He tossed and turned. He heard accusing voices. By daybreak, a new resolution steeled him. He studied his face in the mirror, shaved more closely than usual, trimmed his sideburns. He ran his comb through his hair and dropped it into bangs on his forehead. Instead of tucking in his shirttails, he knotted them at his navel. Trouser legs rolled, loud striped socks, no shorts, Butch went out dancing. It was a straight line from that step into being just another shrill voice once yokel now elegant matching itself with the masses in all but the most minute matters, having fully learned fast what is actually written in small type at the base of that Lady in the harbor: If You Can't Be An Event, Play Safe.

The Guermantes Way
by George Whitmore

THE NIGHT BOOKER told me about his brother, he began by way of explaining why he'd dropped the wine glasses. He must not have heard me come in (I was barefoot) because when the screen door swung to with a clatter he dropped all six of them and broke every one on the kitchen floor.

As he swept up the broken glass, he explained how his brother used to surprise him all the time—by sneaking up behind him and smacking him across the back of the head, for instance.

Then, picking up the little splinters of glass with a wet paper towel, Booker told me how his brother used to put him between the mattress and the springs on the bed, then sit and bounce on top of him. He pulled other little tricks on Booker, too—like making him eat bugs, tripping him on the stairs, giving him a cherry belly, hanging him from the tree in the back yard like the old tire they used for a swing. His brother used to hold his head under the water in the swimming pool, pinch him until his arms were bruised black and blue, light kitchen matches and place them against the soles of his feet while he was sleeping.

Booker told me all this in a calm little voice while he wiped up the floor. His back was to me. The old gym shorts he always wore were rutched down in the back to reveal his jock and the beginnings of his tight, round little ass.

"What did your folks do?" I asked.

"Then sent him away to school when he stuck a jackknife in my foot playing mumbletypeg."

As Booker went about cooking dinner and I cut up the vegetables for salad, he told me all about his revenge fantasy. It was very elaborate. He wanted to kill his brother.

Specifically, he wanted to rent a car and drive down to Baton Rouge, park a few houses away from his brother's, creep up to the living room window—his brother and sister-in-law would be sitting inside, watching TV—and shoot his brother in the back of the head with a thirty-ought-six deer rifle.

The sister-in-law would be grateful. Booker would get back into his rented car and drive non-stop to New York. There he would drop the rifle into the Hudson at the 79th Street boat basin. He would go home and take a shower, then to bed, to enjoy the first uninterrupted (by nightmares, that is) sleep of his young life.

That's a brief resume of it. I'm leaving out all the bright little touches of humor. His very detailed scenario had quite a chilling effect on me, as I sat at the kitchen table slicing tomatoes, watching them bleed under the knife.

"Some fantasy," I said.

"Yeah," Booker said, sliding his Tuna Surprise onto the rack in the oven.

"Do you do that a lot?" I asked.

"What?"

"Fantasize."

"Oh, no. Never. Just about that." He turned around and leaned against the sink. His baby blue eyes were shining with pleasure. Then he sat down at the table. He must have realized I was looking at his crotch. Even with the jock, anyone could tell he had a hard-on.

This was the first inkling I ever had that Booker might not be quite what he appeared to be—an overgrown Boy Scout. As a matter of fact, he'd once confessed to my friend Carl that he (Booker) had been an *Eagle* scout, not exactly a badge of honor in our set. In many ways he still was.

That summer Booker and I were housemates in the Pines. I never would have thought of him as a housemate, our personal styles were so different. But Carl had said "never another Fire Island summer, never again, absolutely not," and it was Booker (cash in hand) or some creep I didn't know at all.

Booker was aptly named. (No, he wasn't black, though he did come from the South.) He was bookish. The summer we were housemates, he was reading through Proust for the third time. In French.

He would have been tempting, had it not been for that overall scoutish air about him and the fact that we'd already had sex once in the past—it wasn't bad, but it certainly wasn't memorable. I'm not heavy into leather, but I do like the role playing and I like the costumes. Booker didn't even warm up. Too bad, I remember thinking at the time. He was awfully cute (though I never would have used that word to his face)—about five-eight, blond-to-auburn haired, and seldom out of that old pair of gym shorts (that I ever saw).

Of course, I was a bit worried at the beginning of the summer. I'm a hedonist, to say the least. There are several very good reasons why I choose to spend my summers at the Pines. Reading is not one of them.

But Booker turned out to be the ideal housemate—always considerate and unobtrusive (unlike the animals I've wound up with past summers). For my part, I went out of my way to be sure I didn't offend what I assumed were his delicate sensibilities. I kept the heavy stuff out of the house. I didn't indulge, either, in any Monday (or Tuesday or Wednesday or Thursday) morning quarterbacking about my exploits in the meat rack. And life with Booker—so tranquil, so organized, so downright bookish—seemed to add a special spur to my sex life in the bushes and elsewhere that summer.

Then Daniel entered the cozy little setup. Unobtainable Daniel. Daniel Daniel Daniel. Daniel was the weekday trick Booker met in the weight room at the Y one muggy day in June. Daniel was pumping iron and inflating hearts as well as his own very perfect, very beautiful lats and pecs.

Yes, Daniel would love to go out for a cup of coffee. Yes, Daniel adored Celine, too—in spite of Celine's politics. Yes, Daniel felt that Pound was a more difficult question. Yes, Daniel lived right up the street. No, Daniel was too tired today after his workout . . . And the next evening, after the ballet (getting the tickets had been one of those through-the-eye-of-the-needle ordeals) Daniel was a little headachy . . . And that next week, and the next, and the next—until I was ready to go back into the city and rape Daniel myself, just from hearing about it.

At last, in the middle of July, Troy fell.

"How was it?" I asked, literally salivating from the news.

"Very nice," Booker said.

We were lying on the beach. Booker's well-oiled chest rose and fell to the rhythm of the surf. Just perceptably. My own heart was pounding. "Is that all?" I nearly shouted at him. "Is that all you can say? 'Very nice'?"

"Well, what do you want me to say?"

"You finally land this hot number all of New York has wet pants over and all you can say is 'very nice'?"

Booker's eyes flickered open, briefly. His face was still expressionless. "Well, it was. Very nice."

I got up, pulled off my trunks, ran down the beach and took a running dive into the first big wave that came in.

"Has he showed up there?" It was Booker on the phone from the Botel.

"No," I said. "Why don't you just come back to the house? You've been down there waiting for him since six."

"I hope he's all right."

"He'll probably call. He probably got held up. He doesn't need you to meet him at the ferry. He knows the way." I hung up.

It was getting on my nerves. Booker and Daniel. Another weekend of bitching and kvetching I didn't need. This was true love?

Booker came home. It was his night, so he began cooking the dinner he'd bought for Daniel—flank steak, summer squash, salad—for the two of us.

Daniel arrived, characteristically, during dinner. I was almost relieved to have someone—even Daniel—break the sulky silence over the dinner table.

As soon as he heard Daniel's footsteps on the stairs, Booker ran outside to meet him on the deck. They went into their little dance outside in the dark. I couldn't help but hear:

177

"I said I was leaving the *city* at six, not taking the six o'clock ferry," said Daniel. "Oh," said Booker, "I had the distinct impression you said the ferry." "Well, I didn't." "Well, I waited." "It's just that I was disappointed. I was looking forward to seeing you on the dock." "Well, I was disappointed, too. I waited for two hours." "You drunk?" "No," said Booker, mightily offended. "Do I look drunk?" "Will you help me with these?" "Poor baby. Are you all right?" "That nice man, that James, helped me. It was a good thing he spotted me." "I *waited*," Booker said. This was followed by low muttering.

Daniel came in, leaning on a cane. Booker was behind him, with the bags—Daniel did not travel light, even for a weekend on the Island.

"What's that for?" I asked, pointing to the cane.

"I had a little accident," Daniel said, mysteriously.

"He pulled his back at the gym," Booker said, hustling the bags into his room.

"Don't say that," Daniel said. "It sounds so crass." He sat down.

Booker fretted and fussed over him, got him a cushion, cut up his meat, worried over him, apologized again for missing the ferry, hovered over him. The cane kept falling onto the floor with a loud crack and Booker kept retrieving it and propping it up again.

"Where does it hurt?" I asked after dinner.

Daniel stood up (with no apparent difficulty), dropped his chinos, pulled up his T-shirt in the back, pointed to the location on his spine. He gave me a full rundown on the injury, his doctor's diagnosis, the drugs he was taking, the prognosis for recovery—all with his chinos hanging down around his knees.

Daniel was as big and as beautiful as all Booker's lovers had been—curly-headed, dark, mustachioed, with dark smooth Arabian-looking skin—but not as dumb as any of the others by half. He knew the effect he was having on me. And on Booker.

"More coffee?" Booker asked.

I went off to see some friends, then out to dance at the Sandpiper, then into the bushes about four in the morning. Some guy asked me to piss on him, so I did, and he thanked me. "I've been looking for a number to do that for the past hour and a half," he said. "You're welcome," I said. All in a night's work.

When I got back home it was getting light out. Booker was up, reading. His greeting was rather curt. I took it that the evening hadn't gone well. When I'd left, he was trying to make Daniel comfortable out on the deck in a lawn chair, with little success.

The next day Daniel insisted on walking down to the beach. I looked up from my blanket just in time to see them creeping down the steps and onto the sand. Daniel's big arm was around Booker's shoulders and Booker was staggering under the weight. I could see Daniel's mouth moving in a mask of (feigned, I was beginning to suspect) pain. He gestured here and there with the cane, picking out a spot for them to put their beach sheet down. They didn't see me, which was just fine with me. I napped a bit and when I got up to go back to the house I saw them walking down the beach towards the Grove, Booker still bent under Daniel's arm.

I ate out that night.

When I came back to nap and change for dancing, Booker was reading aloud to Daniel out of *The Guermantes Way*. Daniel was sitting on the couch, with his legs propped up on a cushion on the coffee table, sipping at a big cool glass of Perrier with a lime wedge in it. All was peaceful. Proust, read in Booker's prep school French, wafted into the bedroom and put me to sleep. As Proust always will, no matter which language.

I ran into Mickey Ryan at the Ice Palace and we ended up together for what was left of the night. It was your standardized ritual scene. Mickey has this harness you put him in, and after you shave him of his week's growth of body hair he likes you to be his seventh grade Spanish teacher and fuck him.

Booker was out on the back deck when I came home.

"Don't go in there," he said.

"O.K.," I said. I was blissed out on qualudes and I'm very docile after a scene like the one with Mickey anyway. I sat down on the railing. "Why not?" It occurred to me to ask.

"You're not going to like it." Booker was shivering in the early morning air. He was wearing nothing but the gym shorts.

"Why am I not going to like it?" I was a little less blissed out now.

Then I noticed the bruises.

"How'd you get those?"

There were big red welts on his shoulders. I leaned over and looked at his back. There were a couple of big marks over his kidneys, too.

"Is that fucker still here?" I hissed.

"No."

"What the fuck did he do to you?"

Booker shrugged.

I went inside. He was right, I didn't like it. A couple of straight-backed chairs lay smashed in the center of the floor. The table with my stereo and tape deck had been overturned. There was broken glass everywhere. A round, surprisingly symetrical hole had been bashed out of the window next to the front door. The cane was hooked into the hole it had evidently made in the glass, and hung down outside over the front deck, like a cock at half mast.

"I'll take this out of that fucker's ass," I shouted.

"I'll pay for it," Booker said. He was standing just inside the kitchen door.

"Look out," I said. "You'll get your feet all cut up." But he'd done that already and his feet were bleeding. "Go outside and sit down," I said.

I got a cooking pot and filled it with warm water, my boots crunching in the broken glass, and took the pot and a dish towel out onto the deck. I squatted down at the bottom of the steps and washed Booker's feet. First I pulled out a couple of splinters of glass.

"I'll kill that fucker," I said. And meant it. "Where is he?"

"I don't know."

I ran the wet dish towel over the soles of Booker's feet. He was feeling no pain.

"I couldn't stand it anymore," Booker said tonelessly.

"I can understand that," I said, looking up at him.

He raised an eyebrow.

"He's a spoiled, petulant asshole," I said.

"You *don't* understand," Booker said. "I started it."

"If you mean you should have known from the beginning..."

"No. I mean I started it. I hit him with the cane."

I sat back on my heels.

Booker explained. It had started over the pronunciation of Guermantes. Daniel said it was one way, Booker said it was another. Daniel insisted it wasn't, Booker said he (Booker) should know. It escalated, of course, with each one dropping it (mock concessions) and the other picking it up again. "He was ruining Proust for me," Booker said simply. Daniel then asked for more Perrier. Booker got up to get it. Daniel shifted on the couch. The cane fell to the floor. Booker went to pick up the cane. "Oh, leave it there, for God's sake," Daniel said. Booker picked it up. And then, for some reason (without thinking at all what that might have been) Booker swung it and cracked Daniel right across the face. Just like that. It opened up a nice, tidy little cut on Daniel's cheek bone. The cut began to bleed. Booker looked at the cut. Astonishment was written across Daniel's face. Then, Booker realized he (Booker) was smiling. Daniel realized it, too. Daniel put his hand up to the cut, looked at the blood on his fingers, then back at Booker, who was standing there, still smiling. Booker handed the cane to Daniel. The rest, as Booker said, belatedly trying to make a stab at humor, was history.

He was smiling now, too.

"Booker," I said, "You are one fucked up dude."

"I guess I am." His smile broadened, but a tear popped out of the corner of his eye.

I got up and planted one foot on the middle step, leaned down and put my arms under him, picked him up and carried him into the house. He was lighter than I'd remembered.

I put him in the shower, took off my own clothes, and got in with him. I washed his bruises and washed the night's dancing and sex off myself. Then I got out, dried off, dried him off, put alcohol on his wounds—he didn't even wince—picked him up again and carried him into my bedroom.

I put him on the bed and got in next to him. I pulled the sheet up over us. I put my arm around him. He snuggled up against me. I could feel him against my thigh. He'd been getting turned on in the shower. He'd been hard by the time I finished drying him off.

"Tomorrow, Booker," I said, "or rather today—we're going to go down to the Grove and buy you a little black leather vest, and I think chaps, too. And some little studded leather wrist cuffs. And a cycle cap, for sure. I have everything else here. For starters, you're going to tie me up"—my cock was rising pleasurably—"and put tit clamps on me. And a blindfold, of course. Just your standardized ritual scene. And then you're going to be my seventh grade Spanish teacher and fuck me. How does that sound?"

He was sleeping.

Virility

by Daniel Curzon

1: Attraction

JOEY SHOULDN'T HAVE been attracted to Jeff, for if someone had asked him what his "type" was, he certainly wouldn't have described Jeff. He would've said something about "Latin types," about having to get to know the "whole person." Joey wouldn't have mentioned a word about liking a hairy body, even if the hairs were honey-hued. Nor would he have said a word about wanting to look into cavernous black eyes, like those of a cougar lurking deep within a cave. No, Joey would have said he appreciated leaner men, not burly ones like Jeff, ones with small noses, not with aggressive hunks of flesh on their faces. In Jeff's case, Joey would even have joked that the face was "well-hung," meaning the remark as a put-down. He wouldn't have, theoretically, even listed being "well-hung"—in the crotch, that is—as an important asset. That was for size queens, who of course were preposterous in their interest in raw beef.

Yet when Joey first saw Jeff at the All Ranks Swimming Pool, he got an erection that didn't die down all the while Jeff and the other pilots were practicing rescue techniques in the water. Joey had intended to take an early-morning swim before reporting to work at the Dispensary, where he gave blood tests and immunizations most of the day, but the pool was being used. The trainee pilots were jumping off the diving board in their flight suits and boots and life-preservers, looking bulky, covered with buckles and straps. One after the other they walked to the edge of the diving board and jumped off, then swam under a huge white net arranged so that it just touched the surface of the water filled with dead bugs, and clambered into the big life raft at the other end. Joey, in fact, edged his way up to the wire fence, getting as close as he could, watching the burly man, who was giving orders to his men, the only one who didn't have on full equipment like the others, dressed, up to his waist only, in his greenish-grey flight suit, its arms tied in a knot around his middle. Evidently he was in charge of the training, squatting at the side of the pool, scooping a handful of water on the head of one of the younger pilots who was having trouble getting his buckles untangled from the net. "Sutter, you'd drown if this were the South China Sea!" the burly man yelled angrily. There was an air of playfulness about the men, since they realized they were training in the Ubon Swimming Pool instead of in an ocean. So the leader's voice was authoritative, mocking, and Sutter, splashing about in the chlorinated bugs, tried hard to get his buckles and straps in order and finally managed to swim underneath the long net and crawl up into the life raft with the first two pilots. Overhead, a barrage of noise from three Phantom jets shook the whole base. "You're next, Fullerton!" the burly man commanded, waving directions through the rumbling noise.

Joey put his fingers into the x-shaped wires of the fence and kept his eyes on the man in charge, although he was merely standing beside the diving board now, his bare arms folded over his thick, bare chest. One of his hands went up and brushed a fly away from his cheek, and Joey noticed that the cheeks were scarred a bit, pitted with what must have been acne ten or twelve years before. Now the scars were masked by the suntan and by the gold-grey moustache over the stalwart mouth giving instructions to the next trainee. "No! No! NO!" the leader shouted at Fullerton. "You trying to cost the Air Force *money?* You'd sink before a plane could find you, you dumbbell! Come here!" Fullerton had to paddle over to the burly man, who knelt on one wet knee at the edge of the pool and gave private directions while the other six trainee pilots waited, glad they hadn't been singled out for a reprimand. As he was gesturing, the burly man casually reached down between his legs and scratched the crotch of his flight suit, giving it a pull as if his flesh were troubling him. Joey clutched hard at the wire fence and felt his insides buzz, then pinch. To his amazement, he found that he wanted to go over and kneel down on both knees, before the burly, half-naked man.

The training went on for more than an hour longer; Joey stayed at the fence, even though he knew he was late for work and Dr. Brunner would scold him again. But he couldn't take his eyes off the thick-chested man, whom he heard one of the trainees call Jeff. The man hadn't even glanced over toward him, and yet Joey wanted to . . . wanted to run up and lick the greenish-grey flight suit, to feel the several zippers cold on his tongue. *No! Jesus Christ! What's the matter with me!* Joey reprimanded himself. *Like a dirty book! How stupid!*

Tingling, he forced his hand down from the fence, forced his eyes away from the burly man; yet when he looked up again the man was staring at him, with just a hint of a smirk on the lips, reaching up to scratch at a flat nipple, running his wide hands through the chest hairs, giving an order to the trainees to get out of the pool, telling them that if this was the best they could do, they'd better give up wanting to be pilots. Sheepishly, teasing one another, the trainees climbed out of the life raft and went into the shed behind the pool, where they could change out of their wet clothes. "Again tomorrow at 0-8 hundred!" he shouted to the group as it disappeared. "Sharp! And let's try to snap it up tomorrow, okay!"

The man himself began to untie the white net from the sides of the swimming pool, his physique like a Portuguese fisherman's, Joey thought, except that no Portuguese would have that ripened hair, that head of stark, almost smoky hair. He came over to Joey's side of the pool and began to fold the net by pulling one end up over the other. Joey knew that he should leave, because he no longer had an excuse to be watching. The three or four passersby who'd stopped to watch the training had gone away long before. Yet he lingered.

"You interested in being a pilot?" the burly man suddenly asked him.

Joey became flustered—and yet excited because the man had spoken first. "No, guess not," was all he said.

"You seem pretty interested," the man replied. Did he mean something more? Was there an invitation in the dead-black eyes hovering in those deep sockets?

Joey squinted, pushing on the wire fence in agitation. The sun was just beginning to attack, as it did day after day in Thailand. "Oh, I was just intrigued by the rescue manuevers," he responded at last, feeling slight, almost skinny in the presence of the other man, although he knew that he was strong enough.

"We'll think you're a guerilla spy," the other man teased, not quite grinning.

"No, I just work in the Dispensary," Joey answered. *What's wrong with me! Giving him my address like that! Why don't I just say outright that I want to sleep with him! It's a wonder I didn't tell him my bay in my hootch!*

"Been here long?"

"Two months. In the Air Force six months." Joey felt his throat fill with dry air. He wondered if the trainer could tell that he was aroused. He adjusted his shirttails so that they covered his swimsuit. "How about yourself?"

"Just three days. Came down from Nahkon Phanom."

"TDY?"

"No, PCS." He smiled. "So perhaps I'll be seeing you again?"

"Could be." Joey smiled back, fiddling with the top button of his orange shirt, rubbing his tennis shoe along the shrivelled-up grass at the bottom of the fence. Why hadn't he gone to the gym with Sherman during these two months, the way Sherman had urged; he could've developed some muscles by this time, with a chest like the one on the man beside the pool, who was lifting the folded net and hugging the air bubbles out of it.

His muscles ripple, Joey thought. *They actually ripple.*

"Gets lonely around the base, I suppose?" the burly man asked. "Hey, sorry, by the way, my name's Jeff Strover." He came close to the fence.

"I'm just an airman," Joey said, unable to stop himself.

"I'm tolerant!" Jeff laughed. He stuck two fingers through the fence, offering to shake.

"Joey Wedgewood."

"Hi!"

When his own fingers touched those from the other side, Joey felt as if he'd been splashed with scalding water.

"Your wife here with you?" Jeff asked, not letting go of Joey's fingers as soon as he should have.

"No, I'm not married."

"Too young, huh? Or are you a free spirit?" Jeff insinuated.

"You might say that," Joey was quivering inside, close to being dizzy. *Was* the man making an overture, or was he imagining it? "Is *your* wife here?"

"No, she's back in Florida."

Joey's heart shrank. So he had a wife; that was a bad sign, although of course he'd met married men who liked other men for sex.

"So you work in the Dispensary, huh?" Jeff inquired, because the conversation had stagnated. "Do you spend all day sticking sharp things into people?" The teeth revealed themselves, spaced teeth, but clean ones; they didn't show under the gold-grey moustache unless he tilted his head back.

Joey felt saturated with longing. *I've been without sex too long,* he told himself. *Though I can't remember feeling this way about anybody before.* The increasing heat of the morning seemed to infiltrate his body and mingle into a lust that caked within him like . . . like hot mud. He felt his words slipping out against his will, despite all his usual efforts to be cautious because of the military's rules against homosexuals. "I only stick them in sometimes. Not all day."

Jeff let his hand drop to the vicinity of his crotch, where it dangled nonchalantly. "I'd like a job like that myself. Sticking things in people, I mean." He looked directly into Joey's eyes.

Did he really mean what it sounded like? Should Joey seize the chance? What if it was all a misunderstanding! What if he said something and then the burly man beat the shit out of him?

"You go into town much—Ubon I mean?" Jeff asked.

"No, not usually. I had some shirts made." He touched his orange shirt.

"No *teelock?* No special massage?"

"Not my style, I'm afraid," Joey answered. He found his hand on his curly dishwater-brown hair, stroking it out of nervousness.

"No?" Jeff paused, sizing up Joey. After a long second, he said, "Well, how would you like to suck me off sometime then?"

Had he heard right? Joey couldn't even lift his eyes from the ground. Had the man *really* said that? What was he supposed to say? It was a trap—of course. A trap. Joey said nothing.

The pilot didn't seem embarrassed. If he'd miscalculated about the other's sexual interest, he looked prepared to break into a loud guffaw, passing it all off as a big put-on. "Didn't I see you cruising the Recreation Center last night?" Jeff asked.

"Did you? I didn't see you."

"Either you were cruising or you had the runs so bad you ought to see one of those doctors over in your Dispensary!" He touched the thigh on the inside of the leg, leaving his broad hand there on purpose.

"What's *that* mean?" Joey asked, feeling himself leaking into his swimsuit.

"You must've gone into the john half a dozen times. I was playing poker near the ping pong tables."

"I thought I was more discreet than that."

"Not to the trained eye," Jeff smirked. "How about it?"

"I'm supposed to be at work already."

"Come into the bathhouse, where my trainees are changing."

"In *there*?" Joey looked incredulous.

"The cubicles are around the corner. They can't see." Jeff struck a pose, with his legs spread; there was a bulge in the crotch of the flight suit. "I'm horny as hell!"

Joey raised his eyes to the man's face. "Are you making fun of me?"

"I'm serious! Come on!"

"But the . . . "

"Please." He touched the inside of his thigh.

"I'm afraid."

"It'll be okay. Come on!"

"No . . . not now," Joey said, his heart spinning.

"It'll be okay!"

Joey stepped back, unsure of the expression on the man's face. Was he mocking him? Was he really serious? "I've got to . . . leave now."

The pilot's lips closed into a thin line. "How about later then?"

Joey turned away and mumbled, "Yeah, maybe later . . . "

"Okay, I'll be looking forward to your mouth then, fella." He smiled.

Above them several jets screamed as if they were falling out of the sky.

2: Repulsion

Joey went out on the rickety porch of his hootch to see what all the commotion was about. Several of the men, barefoot, in shorts, shirtless, were dumping pails of water on the Thai maid, who was laughing shrilly, showing her two gold teeth. She lifted the plastic juice container she'd filled, and flung the cold water at one of the airmen, who stumbled backwards and received the water full on the side of the head. He too laughed uproariously, and started to chase the maid, who ran around the corner of the hootch.

Joey remembered. It was a Thai holiday of some sort. The water was supposed to represent a blessing. But the holiday had turned into a day of splashing and dousing everyone in sight, amid giggles and stumblings and breathiness from running. Across the drainage ditch he could see a naked-chested young man in glasses waiting on the second floor of another barracks to dump a pail of water on the next person who walked out of the building.

He wanted to go back inside and finish the book he was reading, but the horseplay was too disturbing, and his roommate, Guiterrez, was snoring more loudly than usual, after an all-night drunk in town. So Joey walked toward the chow hall, thinking he might have a late breakfast, although he wasn't hungry.

He had no appetite since coming to Thailand; he'd lost twenty pounds, making him one hundred and thirty-six, not enough for his height. He felt bored and homesick, but realized that he would've been reading on a Saturday morning back in Denver too, and his homesickness had no focus to it; he didn't miss his mother and father as much as he thought he should. As for his younger sister, Jane, a letter every six months said all that they had to say to each other. What had possessed him to refuse to go to college, to sign up for the Air Force! Had it been to show them he had a will of his own, that he didn't need them, none of them? It all seemed so pointless now.

When Joey got to the center of the base, where the five main roads angled off like a star, he paused. He could go to the BX, he supposed, although he'd looked at the camera and stereo equipment umpteen times already. Or he could see if they had any batteries in yet; he'd been without his radio for three weeks now. Or he could go bowling. Bowling at ten in the morning. Bowling at midnight. Why did the goddamn military provide so many bowling alleys—every single base he'd ever heard about had one—and hobby shops and barber shops and jewelry shops and chapels! And yet it refused to acknowledge the other passions—the passions of the unmarried—that men might have. Of course the military didn't even admit the "perverted passions"; it only recognized "the bowling instinct." Joey looked over at the Soft Ice Cream truck parked by the Recreation Center. Should he have a root beer float for breakfast? Or a Seven-up float for variety? That's what a change of pace meant in Ubon, home of the Wolf Pack, a Seven-up float instead of a root beer. Home of the Wolf Pack!

Or he could walk through the billiard-playing chicanos and blacks in the Recreation Center and sit in the latrine and stare at the old messages scribbled on the wall, maybe whittle more at the opening between the stalls that he'd started. He'd scratched a pinhole during the first month, but then had quit for a while, since there was never anybody on the other side anyway. Well, hardly anybody. Just the big-bellied Master Sergeant with the bad breath and, a couple of weeks after him, the civilian with the red bangs—probably dyed bangs at that—who'd stuck his slimy red phallus under the partition for five seconds and then disappeared, and never returned. *Yes, what should it be today—and for the next ten months?* Joey asked himself.

Somebody with dried shaving lather on his face ran up to the Soft Ice Cream truck and sprayed some water on the listless Thai girl who worked inside. She didn't giggle, but some gooey strawberry syrup flew out the window and spattered on the pants of the man with lather on his face.

Joey felt disgusted with all of them, and slightly envious. Nobody had even tried to splash him. He wouldn't have minded, not in his faded Levi's and denim shirt with the sleeves torn off. He loitered, almost expectantly, at the crossroads for someone to come up and annoint him with the cheerful holiday water.

Suddenly he heard a dog squeal. Down Thunderbolt Road a passing pick-up truck full of GI's was pursuing one of the shorthaired, mange-spotted Thai dogs that skulked around the base. Half a dozen fully grown men were standing up in the rear of the truck, aiming their water pistols at the terrified female, which ran back and forth several times, its paps swinging loosely, before it finally escaped across some gravel and into a deserted field. Joey hated them, their cruelty, wondering what could make men want to inflict pain on a dog, on anything, even in "fun."

He heard a bicycle pedal up behind him, and, when he looked around, he saw Jeff, the pilot from the pool, grinning at him.

"How goes it?" Jeff said, all conviviality.

"Can't complain," Joey lied automatically.

Jeff looked more tanned than he had three days before; he was wearing his captain's pale blue shirt and dark slacks, the two silver bars on the cap gleaming. *So he's a captain. He'll make major before he's thirty. I bet. He's the kind the Armed Forces want—armed force in every muscle!*

"Where you been hiding yourself? Haven't seen you since—" Jeff drew a line in the air with the flat of his hand.

Joey's spirit rose. "I looked for you."

"Where? Over at the pool?"

Joey nodded.

"Haven't been back. We cancelled the training here. Something else came up." He gripped the handlebars of the bicycle. "Though I must say I've been thinking about our little plan!"

Joey felt his knees give a little. "If that's a compliment, thanks."

"I caught too much sun yesterday, behind my trailer." Jeff touched his reddened neck.

"I haven't been doing much of anything." Why didn't he tell him about the book he was reading, about vampire legends. Maybe Jeff was somebody he could talk to seriously. "Did—"

"We had a mission over to Laos," Jeff interrupted. "But don't tell anybody I said so. Officially we're not there."

Joey scratched at his elbow, uncomfortable. He could feel himself getting aroused again. The man's eyes were dark, without fear, even maleficent. Joey realized, in a panic, that he wanted to go down on Jeff right there in front of everybody.

He changed the subject, or, rather, picked up Jeff's. "Do you fly to Laos often?"

"Can't reveal the secrets of war," Jeff snickered. "Even if this isn't really wartime."

"Oh, it's just a peacetime war?" Joey asked sarcastically.

"Well, I'm collecting flight pay!" Jeff said merrily.

"Do you drop bombs?" Joey asked directly, imagining Jeff sitting in a cockpit flying over a village in Laos or Cambodia, pulling some levers or ordering the gunner to do so. Napalm bombs or Smart bombs or just ordinary bombs would begin to hail themselves on whatever was below: animals, birds, crops, people eating rice, hunkering down in the shade of pineapple trees, not very special or intelligent people, but human beings nevertheless. "*Do* you?" Joey wanted to know.

"That's my job!" Jeff said forthrightly. "Why?"

"Don't you ever have scruples?"

"I love to fly. Just love it!"

"Do you like dropping bombs?"

"Do you work on the flight line? Do you load bombs on planes?" Jeff retaliated, perturbed.

"No. Remember, I told you I work in the Dispensary?"

"That's right! I forgot!" Jeff bounced on the bicycle seat. "Yeah, I drop bombs. You might say it's for a living. You patch people up in the Dispensary. You might say I provide you *your* job!" He didn't blink away from this audacity.

"Not exactly. Not the same people get treated. In fact, the only burns I've treated here were from smoking in bed."

"Are you a pacifist or something?"

"Not precisely—after all, I am in the Air Force."

"You seem pretty worried about the bombing."

There was something in Jeff's strength that made it difficult for Joey to talk freely, although he did with other enlisted men, even earning the nickname "Karl Marx," although he wasn't a Marxist. But he forced himself. "Don't you worry about the bombing—ever?"

Jeff made the bike's wheels rotate as he rolled to and fro in the red sand at the edge of the sidewalk. "Not a whole hell of a lot. I fly planes for the Air Force—that's what they pay me for."

"There are other jobs."

"Not so many. Besides, I like this one."

"Did you fly in Vietnam?" Joey watched a blue dragonfly dart up close to the spokes of Jeff's bicycle, then flit away.

"A little. I was mostly training pilots back in the States. Just three missions in Nam."

"And did you kill anybody?"

"I can't say." Jeff shrugged. "I tried."

Joey felt pale, undernourished, almost shy, though he was furious too. "Don't you care?"

"Listen, they were trying to kill *our* guys too. Don't get all soft-hearted-weepy about a bunch of slope animals!"

"They were men and women and children!" Joey raised his voice. Two sergeants in sloppy fatigues looked over at him as they headed down Mig Alley. "They dug holes and put our guys in them and then pumped exhaust fumes from trucks down on them until they suffocated to death. They tortured them with sharp bamboo sticks and knives, so don't tell me!"

Joey tried to look unflinchingly into Jeff's eyes, but had to settle for a flickering glance. "Do you have a collection of *ears?*"

"No, I don't have a collection of *ears!*"

"There aren't any ears left when you get finished with your 'job,' is that it?"

Jeff's face tightened. "Don't be so damned self-righteous! Just because you never had to make a decision, Airman First Class, about whether you were going to get into a plane and kill somebody!"

"I wouldn't be able to do it!"

"Are you proud of yourself for that?" Jeff stood up, holding the bicycle with his thighs. "Are you proud of the fact that you couldn't do a man's job?"

"I wouldn't be proud of myself for doing what you call a *man's* job—that's for sure!"

"Sometimes the only solution for a problem is strength—and men to use it."

"Bullshit!"

"I'm not surprised. Look at yourself! No chest, a girl's waist. Even your hair curls over your ears! That's how I picked you out even before I noticed you cruising the Rec Center. There's even something feminine about your features; they're too round in the jaw, or something. You're soft!"

"Nobody asked for your beautician's analysis, thank you!"

Jeff threw up both hands. "See what I mean—the way you just answered back. It's fruity."

"We're getting off the subject. I'm sorry if I'm 'fruity' to you!" He shoved one hand into his back pocket clumsily.

"Don't lose your cool, kid."

"I don't like to be insulted. Even if you are an officer, we're talking privately now. And you may discover that your 'fruity' friend—excuse me, acquaintance—is really a 'citrus fruit,' full of citric acid."

Jeff shook his head a fraction. "That's just what I'm talking about!"

"Well, frankly, I don't give a shit! My fruity is every bit as good as your butch act!" Joey squirmed inside, knowing that Jeff was *not* pretending to be masculine.

"I like *men,* that's all," Jeff said, spreading both big hands. "Men who act like men."

So do I! Joey cursed himself. *So do I! Why do I want you to hold me in your arms right this minute? I want you to pin my arms to my sides and fall full length on top of me, rutting on top of me!* "I think your job for the Air Force is despicable!" he heard himself saying.

"I'm not ashamed of what I do!"

"Well, I am! I don't think we can discuss the subject anymore!"

"Why don't you get out of the service if it upsets you so much?"

"I wish I could!"

"Turn yourself in!"

"I don't relish martyrdom."

"So let's leave it at that! I'm not that hard up."

"Neither am I!"

"Hey, hey," Jeff manuevered, "this conversation is getting heavy." He grinned, pushing the front wheel against Joey's kneecap. "I was hoping we might get together again." He pushed the bike again. "What d'you say, huh?" "Go bomb some peasant and fuck his corpse!" Joey spat. He started to stride away toward the library. Then he heard Jeff calling something. When he turned around, he was bombarded with a stream from a water pistol that Jeff had kept hidden in his rear pocket.

"Up yours, sissy!" he said loudly, and fired another round of humiliating water, soaking Joey's collar and ears, the beads dropping off into the dust like shells.

3: Attraction

He stopped Joey near the Officer's Club by deliberately crossing over as Joey started into the Outdoor Snack Bar. "Sorry about the other day, kid." He held out his hand. "Forgive me?" At first Joey refused, but finally took the heavy brown mitt, half expecting it to crush his hand, but Jeff's merely covered, firmly but pleasurably, his small-fingered white one.

"What's there to forgive? You shoot whoever you want to." Joey took a step toward the Snack Bar. "See you around."

But Jeff wouldn't let him go. "Why don't you come into the O Club with me? Want to?" Jeff was wearing his flight suit today, something bulky jammed into a pocket on the leg.

"I'm not supposed to go in there."

"Come as my guest." Jeff leaned closer. "Or would you like me to *come* as your guest?" He smiled dirtily, as if they'd grown intimate.

"I thought our fly-boys were taught to be wholesome—you know, cleancut, straight-arrow types."

Jeff took up the teasing tone. "Are we? Who told you that? I don't consider sex unwholesome. Do you?"

"I don't get enough of it to judge. Any more."

"I know what you mean! I used to like it any way at all—orally, anally, maybe even nasally. Over here, though, I've hardly had any!"

Joey felt vaguely stung. "So you want me to come to the O Club with you, have a couple of drinks, then give you a blow job in the men's room. Is that your plan—the mission?"

Jeff deflected the animosity. "It's up to *you!* We might make it a little more mutual than that."

Joey felt his resistance give; he grew raw and yearning somewhere beneath his skin, just below the stomach. "I'm not allowed in the Officers' Club."

"You can at least come in for one drink at the bar. Or is your dance card all filled up for tonight?"

"What were you planning to do?" Joey nodded at the white stucco Club, which was decorated with palm and banana trees in front.

"Supposed to meet some guys from my unit for chow tonight about nineteen hundred hours, but we could have a drink together, maybe make some plans." Jeff smoothed his moustache. In the setting sunlight the acne scars made him look sinister. What was there in that chest—or was it the chin, the lips?—that compelled him to stay, Joey wondered. What made people attracted to others? How did it all work?

"I don't really think we have too much in common," Joey said, hating his words as he spoke them, his body coveting Jeff's.

"You might be surprised?" Jeff persisted. "The guy who shares the other half of the trailer with me has gone TDY to Korat; I was thinking of having you over for . . . whatever."

"You were?" Joey sensed his body taking over from his will. He hated officers, NCO's—from the hard-ass lifers to the Air Force Academy pretty boys—hated all of them, and was counting every day until he could get out of the fucking Air Force! Joining was the worst decision he'd ever made in his life ... . and yet he wanted to be held in Jeff's efficient arms. Yes, to be screwed by him. The image passed in and out of his brain like a flare, but it registered. Yes, he wanted Jeff to screw him . . . right now . . . here on the ground in front of the Club, on a picnic table in the Snack Bar . . . anywhere at all . . .

Joey cleared his throat, stepping aside to let some sergeants with six-packs of beer pass by.

"How about it?" Jeff pressed.

Joey thought about Sherman, his only friend on the base, Sherman who was waiting for him at the tennis court, or who would be in fifteen minutes. He should keep the appointment, play some night tennis, although it would mean a court littered with insects, dead and wriggling moths and rice bugs, crushing them underfoot, having a Pepsi afterwards with Sherman, who was balding at twenty-four, who knew less about everything than Joey did at nineteen, a balding, talkative mini-intellectual who had read a few books—this was his best "friend." How awful! The things people had to put up with to have a "friend" in the military! Yes, he ought to keep the appointment. "How much do drinks cost in the Club?" he heard himself asking.

"No sweat!" Jeff smiled, leading the way up the steps to the entrance.

Inside it was dim, cool. To their left the Reno Room was boisterous with gamblers. Further along toward the rear some pilots in flight suits were exchanging dollars for Baht; a few others were paying their dinner bills. All of a sudden a loud whoop rang out of the main bar to their right as Jeff pushed open the swinging doors and signalled for Joey to join him. Jeff waved at four pilots sitting at a table, drinking. "Hey, Strover!" one of them yelled, waving his bourbon and soda.

"Later!" Jeff said easily, ushering Joey to a private table. "Sit down. Make yourself to home."

Joey sat down, feeling unsettled.

Down at the other end of the long curved bar three pilots noisly began moving chairs out of the way, making a path on the floor. They started hollering at their companions, who ran over and dropped the ice from their drinks on the wooden floor. Soon a dozen or more were throwing their ice cubes on the cleared path and stamping on them, crushing them. The other customers, including a few wives, watched carefully, uncertain what they were up to.

Joey said in a superior tone, "They act like rowdy high school ball-players, don't they?"

"It's Happy Hour! Besides, they're celebrating. Spectre has been transferred out of here."

Joey felt smug, yet his insides tickled in discomfort as though worms were squirming in his belly. Somebody in the rambunctious group knocked something over with a crash.

"What d'you want to drink?" Jeff asked, raising his arm for the Thai waitress.

"Whatever you have."

"Two Scotch and waters," Jeff ordered when the girl approached.

"How you today, Jeff?" the waitress said. She placed her palm on his neck and massaged. "I no see you!" She was wearing short shorts, big-busted. "Where you go?"

"Had No. 1 date, Sumalee!" Jeff teased back, telling her nothing.

The waitress frowned, wrinkling up her powdered cat-face, her pouting lipsticked mouth. "You no like me?"

"Oh, sure!" Jeff patted her behind. "You No. 1 girl!" He put his arm around her hips and gave her a squeeze, looking ironically over at Joey. "Two Scotch and waters, okay?"

"Can do easy." She gave his neck another brief massage and then walked provocatively over to the bar in her thick-soled shoes.

Joey folded his thin arms in front of himself, not knowing what to do with them. "Quite the ladies' man, I see."

Jeff lit a cigarette and blew the smoke away from them; it was the same color as the tips of his hair. "I do all right. Smoke?"

"I don't smoke."

Jeff put the pack away in the zippered pocket in his sleeve.

Joey nodded at the waitress. "Does she smoke dick?"

"We haven't gotten that far."

"Don't get a disease!" Joey said, surprising himself. *Am I jealous?*

"Don't plan to." Jeff grinned. "Do *you* have any diseases?"

"Heartburn."

"That's not catching, is it?"

The pilots at the far end of the bar were getting louder, throwing more ice on the floor. One of them had gone behind the counter and dipped up a bucketful of crushed ice; he climbed back over and began sprinkling it in a straight line, making a runway. A tall pilot had gotten three bags of ice cubes from the kitchen and was spreading them too. The men started breaking up the ice cubes with their black boots.

"What are they up to?" Joey wondered.

"They're just having fun," Jeff replied. "Good evening, sir!" he called with exaggerated politeness to a colonel who walked by with a WAF major, on his way to the dining room. The colonel acknowledged him with an agreeable nod.

"Are you being transferred too?" Joey asked.

"Don't know yet."

Jeff held Joey in the grip of his eyes momentarily. "Miss me?"

Joey snorted. "I hardly know you!"

"You know me better than a lot of people."

"Why? Because you shot me with your water pistol? Because we've talked about having sex together?" He was oddly delighted when he saw Jeff look around to see if anyone had overheard. "Nervous?"

"Not really. I'm just not anxious to be kicked out of the Air Force, that's all! I've got seven years in."

Joey leaned forward confidentially. "Isn't it strange that you're such a combination of strength—and fear!"

"Who's afraid?"

"You are. You're the big, tough, butch pilot, and yet you're afraid of that colonel, afraid of your buddies finding out that you sleep with men."

"What are you, a psychologist?"

The waitress came over with the drinks on a tray, and Jeff paid her, overtipping her. She winked at him and tried to sit on his knee, but another table wanted service, and she sauntered off.

"So this is the O Club?" Joey said snidely.

Jeff slammed his cigarette into the ashtray. "You can leave any time!"

Joey's guts coiled. He didn't want to leave, he realized. His snideness was a disguise. "I wasn't planning to leave," he answered softly.

"Fine." Jeff sat back and sipped his drink. "Will you be free later?"

"Free for what?"

"Are you being coy? Free for fucking, what else!"

"Your place or mine?" Joey managed to joke, but he sensed that he was losing in the contest, if it *was* a contest between them.

"I'll meet you in front of the Rec Center, what d'you say? We'll go to my trailer. All right? I should be through by ten hundred hours."

"Yes, Master."

"For God's sake, no one's forcing you!"

The cigarette smoke in the barroom was beginning to irritate Joey's eyes. "Should I bring vaseline, or do you have engine grease?"

Jeff glared at him. "Are you sure it's not *you* that's afraid—what's with all these 'jokes'?"

"Pardon me. I'm out of my element, I guess." Joey's cheeks began to flush. He didn't fit here, and yet he wanted to stay. He took a paper napkin out of the dispenser and wiped his humming forehead.

"Can't you just be casual?" Jeff continued, lighting another cigarette.

"Why don't you learn to smoke?" He offered the package.

"No, thanks."

Joey put his knuckles on his own temple, trying to suppress the hectic beating; he was wet under the arms as well. He made himself look away from Jeff. What was happening to him? He closed his eyes hard. But he still wanted to reach across the table and unzip the flight suit, to . . .

"*Yahoo!*" one of the pilots bellowed. "*Yahooeee!*"

When he looked over, Joey saw two pilots lifting a third by his armpits and thighs, carrying him to the runway made of crushed ice, which extended halfway down the barroom now. They had gotten up some momentum and let him go, making him slide on his butt down the pathway between the tables and chairs and patrons. The slider whooped even more loudly as he came to the end of the ice and bumped into a bar stool that the tall pilot put there at the last second as a joke.

"Men'll be men!" Joey said, tasting his drink, which was too strong.

"They're simply having some fun. Don't be so *hard* on them."

Joey sniffed his drink. Jeff didn't understand the complications of his feelings, not at all. He wondered if Jeff was as direct, as unperturbable inside as he seemed on the outside. Could his wife back in Florida make him lose his impeccable calm?

Somebody knocked over a chair, and a Thai waitress screeched into a giggle, dropping her trayful of drinks. Two of the pilots started to chase her in order to slide her down the ice runway, but she ran away across the sunken Hurricane Room, next to the barroom, where bands and nude go-go dancers entertained later in the evening. One of the pilots staggered up to the runway and threw himself headlong onto the slippery strip, his arms outspread like wings.

Intruding into the mischief, a bass voice made an announcement over the loudspeaker: "Good evening, ladies and gentlemen. Tonight's Happy Hour Bingo will begin in fifteen minutes—at 18:30. Cards are now on sale at the cashier's cage or from your waitress. Tonight we will be playing for eighty-five dollars in sixty-four numbers. Remember, Happy Hour Bingo begins in fifteen minutes in the Hurricane Room." The voice stopped.

"Do you want to have dinner in the dining room here?" Jeff asked, drawing his forefinger through the warm ashes in the ashtray.

"I've already eaten."

"Do you want to play Bingo?"

Joey laughed, because he thought Jeff meant it as a jest. "*Bingo?*"

"They just started it about two weeks ago."

"You play *Bingo?*" Joey watched Jeff swallow a sip of his Scotch.

"I played once—Wednesday. Didn't win."

"You'd actually play Bingo?" Joey was incredulous. "Only women play Bingo. Or old men." He thought of his mother's Bingo evenings at the Oddfellows Hall. They were always filled with overweight, pretzel-eating types and tired old men, no doubt with weak prostates.

"My navigator won sixty-five dollars the other night."

"You mean they really play *Bingo* in here?" Joey swiveled his eyes around the Club, taking in the emblems of the squadrons displayed on the walls behind the counter. They were mostly skulls and devils and zigzag lightning bolts and murderous eagles with machine guns.

"You have something against Bingo as well as bombs?" Jeff teased.

"Strover'll do it!" some drunken pilot was saying to his companion, lumbering toward Jeff and Joey's table. "Come on, Strover! Get your ass up here! It's your turn to fly!" The two came up and grabbed Jeff's arms, propelling him toward the runway of crushed ice. Jeff protested, but he was only counterfeiting concern. He glanced back at Joey and said, "Only be a minute." He shrugged, effortlessly, casually. The ease of the man made Joey sick with envy.

The two drunken pilots carried Jeff off and skidded him gleefully on the ice path, scattered and melting now. Jeff didn't even lose his balance, and jumped up immediately at the end of the slide. In fact, he was so proficient the patrons in the bar applauded.

Making his way over to Joey, he shook the hands extended toward him from different stools and tables. "That was outstanding!" he said when he returned.

"Was it?"

"You ought to try it, Joey. It'd be good for you."

Joey looked up at the man standing beside him, his greenish-grey crotch near his face, his leg touching his, a hand on the backrest of the chair. It was all so controlled that nobody would ever suspect that it was sexual, only two buddies talking.

"Want anything else?" Jeff said slyly.

"Yes, I want you," Joey whispered, trembling. He gulped at his drink.

"Bingo cards?" the waitress inquired as she came near them.

"I'll take a couple!" Jeff said, reaching for his wallet, in the leg of his flight suit. He paid the girl and put one of the cards in front of Joey. "Perhaps you'll win eighty-five dollars."

Joey stared down at the Bingo card before him. It was pink. In the sunken Hurricane Room next to them some of the wives and other customers were taking their drinks to the tables near the stage. The grey-templed Bingo caller was adjusting his microphone.

"Would you rather go in there?" Jeff pointed. "So we can hear better?"

"Are you really going to play *Bingo?*" Joey began to shake, his heart numb. He looked up at Jeff's strong chest, the broad hands holding onto the pink Bingo card. He reached up and yanked it out of Jeff's grasp. "No! I don't want you to play *Bingo!*" Frantically he ripped the card into several pieces, then stood up. "Let's go now!" he said into Jeff's ear. *"Now.* Let's go right now! I want you right now!"

4: Repulsion

The MAC Passenger Terminal was crowded and sweltering. The air-conditioner had broken down during the morning. Joey sat trying to listen to the TV set in the corner, but something was wrong with the sound. A sports announcer was saying something garbled about the Lacrosse players that swooped ferocious balls at one another amid the electronic snow on the faulty TV. Joey got up and bent over the drinking fountain, pressing the pedal. A trickle barely came out of the nozzle.

Where is Jeff? He hasn't forgotten, has he? He so often forgets what I tell him. Even my birthday yesterday. Sometimes he doesn't pay attention when I'm talking. Has he forgotten that I promised to see him off? Is he embarrassed? Has he left already, because he doesn't want his flying buddies to know that a man, an airman at that, has come to the airport to say goodbye to him? Is he embarrassed by my love?

Joey was embarrassed by it himself, but he couldn't stop it. If anything, it seemed to be getting worse. He felt foolish following Jeff around the base, following him today to the airport at seven-thirty in the morning, desperate to say goodbye, to get a pat on the shoulder, maybe a furtive squeeze in the cramped latrine before Jeff flew down to Utapao for some rescue training in the Gulf of Siam. He would be gone at least a month, maybe two. Joey felt powerless with desire, at the same time full of a weightless emotion, like anger, that would not localize itself. Was this love? It was nonsensical, sickening, but it wouldn't wither, wouldn't leave him.

He went over to the warped doors near the In-Country Booking Desk, and stared out at the airplanes sitting on the airfield: squat C-130's and the C-41's. The sleek F-4's that Jeff and his pals were going to fly down to Utapao were further on, getting last minute checks from the ground crew. The airfield stretched as far as he could see, metal slabs fastened together up near the Terminal, asphalt pavement beyond that, blistered weeds in the open fields beyond that. Where was Jeff? Where *was* he?

An Air Policeman in uniform strolled into the Terminal with his German shepherd on a leash. Joey stared at the man and the dog with hostility. The dog would be used to smell people's luggage, looking for drugs, even marijuana. Joey had tried marijuana twice, hadn't like the effects, but something in him raged at the idea of the German shepherd sniffing through his luggage—the cry of discovery if the dog detected anything! Did they have a dog to sniff out "obscene material" as well? Joey looked at the sign that said NO WEAPONS, NO AMMUNITION, NO DRUGS, NO OBSCENE MATERIAL PERMITTED ON PLANES. Yes, did they have a Dobermann that could smell out pictures of men touching each other? Did the trainer sic the dog on the offender right then and there?

Where *was* Jeff? Joey heard a plane rumbling somewhere in the distance. Then he caught sight of it coming in for a landing. Its wheels hit the landing strip perfectly, not even a bounce. A couple of fork-lift cargo haulers rolled out of a hangar, heading toward it. Joey wondered how many airplanes the military had. Millions of dollars—even billions—had been spent on all this equipment. Billions! So that Jeff and his buddies could drop deadly, impersonal bombs on Vietnam, on the guerillas in obscure jungles. Billions of dollars, thousands of men practicing rescue maneuvers in the Gulf of Siam, in the South China Sea, swooping their murderous bomb-filled planes through Asian skies, learning to be admirable defenders of democracy. Was that what Jeff was—a defender of democracy, an upholder of justice and right? Or was he a killer? How *many* people had he killed already on secret missions? How many more would he kill, devastate from the coolness of these Asian skies, streaking down out of smoky clouds. Obscene Material was permitted on planes. What *was* obscene material if bombs weren't? No room for pictures of men embracing each other, because there had to be room for the obscene material, obscene *materiel,* that the professional killers needed for their professional killings.

Joey wanted to leave. He mustn't be late for work again. Dr. Brunner had warned him it would be more than a reprimand next time. Besides, Jeff wasn't coming back to the Passenger Terminal to say good-bye. He hadn't wanted Joey to come to the airport at all, and had made that quite clear. *You want me to come to your trailer, but you don't want me to embarrass you by showing up here to say goodbye.*

Abruptly Joey twisted around when he heard a group passing by the other set of doors on the far side of the Terminal. He caught a glimpse of Jeff, dressed in his flight gear, complete with helmet. Jeff saw Joey too, but didn't acknowlege him.

Joey shoved open one of the doors to leave, but hesitated. The group with Jeff in it had spotted the German shepherd and was playing with it, giving it a strap to yank on. In the tug-of-war, its iceberg-white teeth grasped the strap, and wouldn't let go until its trainer told it to.

He could see his own face reflected in the window of the door when he turned away from Jeff. He didn't like his own face; it was narrow; his eyes bulged unbecomingly. He wouldn't want to go to bed with himself, he realized.

Jeff and the others came into the Departure Lounge and sprawled in the plastic seats that were bolted to the floor. They were disgusted with some delay. Outside, the ground crew was checking the fuel system. Joey waited with his back turned, hoping Jeff would come over and say something, maybe apologize for forgetting his birthday, for standing him up at the cafeteria. Finally, Joey swung around, searching out Jeff's eyes. Jeff's arm went up in greeting, but it was all but indifferent.

Joey walked over to him any way, sitting down in the next seat. Jeff shifted, rocking back and forth in the cooped-out plastic seat. They were sitting side by side, saying nothing.

"I knew it wasn't a BUF!" one of the other pilots, a few rows behind them, growled to someone.

"Like hell you did!" the other person argued back. Joey didn't know what they were disagreeing about.

After five minutes, Joey turned his head toward Jeff. "Remember me?"

"Sure do. How's it going?"

"Terrible. How're things with you?"

"We're having trouble with the fuel intake."

"Is that all?"

"We should be taking off in a few minutes." Jeff scratched at his large nose. He seemed bulkier than usual because of his helmet and gear.

"Are you really going to Utapao to practice rescue maneuvers?"

"That's what I told you." Jeff looked away.

Joey didn't believe him. "Are you sure you're not flying over to Cambodia to . . . ?"

Jeff sat up from the slouch he'd gotten into. "Questions, always questions!"

"Are you?"

"Am I what?"

"Are you flying to Cambodia to bomb something?"

"Can't say?"

"You *are,* aren't you!"

"Shut up, will you!" Jeff said under his breath.

Joey wanted to throw up. "You don't mind doing it, only *saying* it."

"It's none of your business."

"It is *too* my business!" Joey felt something like tears behind his eyes; his nose burned cruelly.

"It's not your business, so drop it!" Jeff checked behind him to see if the others were eavesdropping.

"You're going to destroy people today, aren't you? You do it all the time, don't you, you and your pals!"

Jeff's voice was chilled, almost inaudible. "I'm doing what I believe in."

"So did Hitler!"

"Shit!"

Joey felt his lashes grow moist, the eyeballs itching. "*Why* do you do this? *Why?*"

"*Why* do you bug me about it?"

"I hate you, did you know that?" Joey could feel snot dribbling out of his nose, over his lips. "Why do I ache for you and hate you both? What's wrong with me?"

"Hey!" Jeff said through gritted teeth. "Hey, calm it down, will you!"

199

"Why do I *want* you and *hate* you—tell me that? I'm so ashamed . . . I'm so ashamed I love you."

"Then *stop* loving me!" Jeff coughed loudly to cover up his own words, standing up. "You think we can go now, Hazzard?" he asked somebody.

"I think I can stop loving you now," Joey said quietly, tasting the vile snot running into his mouth. "I can't love you . . . not with you doing what you're doing . . . I hate you . . . I hate you . . . " He drew his palms over his face, hiding his eyes; the snot and tears grew warm and slimy in the cradle of his hands.

"Hey, let's go, gang!" Jeff ordered, moving away. "It's probably ready!" He shooed his crew out of the doors toward the morning-lit runway, not looking back.

Joey sat there, trying to stifle his sobs, until the Reservations Sergeant noticed and came over and asked him what was the matter. "Just someone I love that I hate," he said, getting up to go to work. "But I'm free now. Free now."

5: Attraction

Joey knelt awkwardly on the scatter rug of the trailer in just his brief, with Jeff straddling his shoulders, starting to come. Joey felt the sour taste of the baptism spurting into him, and he sucked up close to the unzippered grey-green flight suit, making wet marks on the cloth, drinking in the dying spasms of Jeff's thrusting body. "You okay, kid?" Jeff worried, thinking that Joey was going to choke. "You really eat it up, don't you!"

"I'm so glad you're back, so glad, so glad! Next time you come, I want you to ride me like a dog, okay! Ride me like a dog with my head down and you fucking me like a dog humping a bitch in heat, okay?" he said, looking up at the pilot towering above him.

Another Time, Another Place

by Graham Jackson

TODAY IS SUNDAY. Fred has been working too hard again. There are signs of strain around his mouth. The doctor told him to take it easy; he'll be forty-five next week after all. (My God! I'll be forty-seven in April!) This afternoon we went to the park. It was sunny and warm and I thought maybe a walk and the smell of burning leaves might revive some of his old colour. Fred used to have a beautiful colour in his cheeks, but lately, he's been very pale. I get scared. It's not only the work that makes him pale; it's everything, the years; me, too, I guess.

The park has changed since we last took a stroll—how long? Two or three years ago, I guess it was. We live right across the street. Today we took our old route following the stream. In our day—it was 1953-54 when we bought our little house—the park attracted families with baby carriages, and painters. Today it was filled with kids—boys mostly—near the Japanese gardens. I was surprised: so many boys, and men, too—younger than us, though—stretched out sunning, playing tag, reading, just chatting. Just boys. No families at all. It was like stepping into a strange country. Boys smiling and two on the bank —their backs to us—holding hands. Not in our day. It was never like that. I looked at Fred. I guess my mouth was open. He smiled and shrugged.

"Let's sit down."

"The grass is probably wet."

"Sit on my sweater."

"It's you I'm worried about."

"Just for a bit." He smiled at me.

"Sure. I don't care." Sometimes his smile really irks me. "No. You keep the sweater. Let's sit over there."

"No. Here in the sun. We can watch the people."

"Watch—!"

"If you don't want . . . ?" He smiled again.

"Sure. I don't care," I said. I could have murdered him.

I met Fred in The Ballroom. It was the only place to go in those days. A beaded curtain separated the club from the store in front. It was a gift shop

201

during the day: imported colognes and ties and shoe-trees, not very swanky for all that—how could it be? Anyway this beaded curtain looked like something out of *Shanghai Express*. And there was one of those glass balls that spun above the dance floor—out of a hundred other movies. The Ballroom was only open Fridays and Saturdays but it was always packed; you could hardly move. And there were always one or two cops on duty and if any couple got too close to each other, they'd be on you in no time.

I was twenty-four when I first admitted everything to myself and decided I couldn't mess up some girl's life by marrying her and pretending. I'd been making the rounds for a year. I had sex with a lot of men; I couldn't call it making love because I didn't love any of them. Then I met Fred. One night I got a little high—drunk—before going to The Ballroom. The smoke and the heat really got to me and I spent the first hour or so retching in the john. I was so sick I thought I must have eaten something bad for supper and I was just trying to figure out what I'd had when this voice says, "You all right?" and I look up and this fellow is looking at me over the partition. Me on my knees and Fred looking down like he was buried up to his eyes in marble. You could only see his eyes and all of a sudden I started to laugh and he laughed and said, "Salmon steaks!" and we both howled till the tears came to our eyes. He told me he was getting down in case the coppers wondered what in hell was going on. He told me to get up and he'd meet me outside.

I cleaned myself up and chewed a few life-savers. By this time, I guess I was flushed. I went back out on the dance floor. He was standing just inside the door. He was six foot three inches tall—the most beautiful man I'd ever seen—with brown, curly hair and a big smile and thin—skinny as a beanpole. The colour in his cheeks was red; it was almost unreal. I fell in love right there. And so did he, I think. He was no dummy and he seemed really pleased when I told him I read a lot. Later we discovered our taste in books wasn't anywhere near the same. I like novels like *Jane Eyre* and Fred likes biographies of royalty and books about crazy ladies who lived in Burma with head-hunters, that sort of thing. Fred collected crazies; 'eccentrics,' he called them. He was always bringing home the weirdest people: dwarfs and carnival dancers and dotty women who kept cats and smelled of lavender all the time. "They're lonely," he used to say. But this came much later. We didn't live together for over a year after the night we met and danced. We went back to my place afterwards and I made real love for the first time. God, it was beautiful holding him close to me, listening to him breathe in the night. Fred says *he* always held *me*; 'how could anyone hold someone who was six foot three?' But I did; I remember. I cradled him almost, like the little boy he is. Those nights were heaven to me—what I'd always wanted. Then the excitement began to wear off a little and one morning when I was late to work because Fred and I had made love in the shower, I realized, maybe for the first time, what had happened and, all of a sudden, I was scared. What if anyone found out I was in love with another man? Because that's what it was! Love! How could anyone find out? But they might . . . When you're in love you're bound to betray it to someone and then . . . Job, family—your whole bleeding life—down the drain. I was scared and so, I found out later, was Fred. The same thing, the same questions.

Over the next year we almost broke it off ten or eleven times. We always came back together. The longest break lasted about three weeks. I almost turned into an alcoholic. No Ballroom—I was afraid of meeting Fred, only I wouldn't have because he was out walking the streets every night or crying on his sister's shoulder (a great lady, Anne!)—just me and the bottle. Well, that break was mended and all the ones after until, one night in bed—we were always in bed, as much as we could; it was the only place we felt safe together, the only place we could never hurt each other—Fred said if we ever broke off again, he'd shoot himself rather than walk the streets and as he didn't want to do that especially, we'd better get ourselves a flat and to hell with everything. (Fred could always give the most serious thing a funny twist just by the way he said it.) "If I'm going to die," he said, "I'd rather die at their hands." I went out the next day and rented a flat. A year or so later, we'd saved enough to buy our little house. But it hasn't been easy.

"What are you thinking about, Skeezix?"
"About when we met."
"The Ballroom." He was quiet for a minute; he smiled to himself. He looked at me almost sadly for a moment and then looked away along the bank where there were boys sun-bathing. He didn't say anything and I felt hurt. He fished around in his knapsack and offered me some peppermints.
"How long have you had those?"
"Twenty years."
"Hah, hah."
"A plum perhaps?" He held out a bright, purple plum.
"Where did you get that?"
"I snapped my fingers." He snapped his fingers. "And a boy appeared in cut-off jeans, rather like that one, bearing plums." I must have frowned or something, because, all of a sudden, Fred became very self-conscious and turned away.

I looked at the boy he had pointed out. He was about nineteen or twenty, with long, blond hair to the shoulders. He was naked to the waist, or hips would be better, skin-tight blue jeans cut off to just below his crotch. Everything bulged nicely. For a second I wanted to squeeze his bulge and kiss him. Then, ashamed of myself, I looked at Fred: still so thin and beautiful. The boy probably had his eye on Fred, cruising him. Anyone would; I would. Would he look back? I've put on a bit of weight, not too much, but I'm four inches shorter than Fred and every extra mouthful shows now. Still, most men my age look a hell of a lot worse than I do. The boy smiled at Fred and for half a second I expected Fred to hold out his arms to the boy, but he only blushed and smiled his big smile. That blush was the first colour I'd seen in Fred's cheeks for months.

Another boy came up behind the first and made as if he were goosing him. The first boy laughed and the two moved off a bit and lay side by side on the bank. The second boy, older and more butch than the first, pulled off his shirt and wrapped it around his head like a turban, all the while singing something that sounded very funny—or dirty—in a foreign language. He had a couple of medals and a crucifix around his neck and thick, black chest hair, so I figured he must have been Italian or Spanish. Fred said later he was sure the boy was singing in English because he heard the word 'love,' and that the breeze garbled the words, that was all. We couldn't hear what they were saying lying there in the sun but I was sure from the sound of their voices that they were discussing conquests. They probably had many. The older boy, especially, looked promiscuous, with his thick lips and brown, hard body. It was only later that I realized both were wearing the same ring on the fourth finger of the right hand.

Just like us almost. Our rings are a little different; the stones are different. We couldn't afford to do anything else, not in our day. We were forced to live by white lies. That's what's worn Fred down, I'm sure: all the white lies. You wonder if there will ever be a time when you don't have to tell white lies. But those rings were really something in our day. They caused a real scandal; our friends were either shocked or worried about us and, for a long time, some of them wouldn't even see us. We had few enough friends, too. That's what happened when you found a lover in those days. You were isolated; nobody wanted you around. Normal people, so-called, thought you were making fun of them or something, and queers—'gay' people, they call them now—didn't want you cluttering up the playing field. That's Fred's expression. That's what life was like: a game, a hunt; and you had to be single to participate. We wanted friends but nobody had any time for that; they were too busy scrambling from bed to bed trying out different makes. Our families were no comfort—except for Fred's sister, Anne. My parents became more distant over the years as they realized what Fred and I really were to one another. I haven't seen them in years though I still get a card at Christmas. Sometimes I think it's a good thing Fred's parents were dead before all this happened. A cold shoulder from them would have killed him, I'm sure: he worshipped the ground they walked on. So Fred and I spent most of our time alone. We'd go to movies and concerts—I love romantic piano music—and to the ballet—Fred likes ballet, especially the old classics like *Coppelia*. Sometimes we'd go to one of the bars but we always felt so out of place and no one would come over to our table, even people who used to know us. I'd end up drinking till I couldn't see and Fred would have to almost carry me to the car. We haven't been to the bars much lately, for the past few years anyway, maybe five even. I wonder what it's all like now.

I sat quiet for a minute, contentedly, while the sun grew hot along my arms. It was several seconds before I realized that Fred had been talking.

"You weren't listening."

"I'm sorry. I was thinking."

"Clatter, clatter. You can't hear anyone for that infernal clatter."

"I said I was sorry!" I didn't mean to be sharp; I never do. Fred looked down between his knees where his big hands patted the grass. "What were you saying?"

"Nothing. I was just babbling like a brook." He repeated the phrase two or three times and then I realized he was nervous or embarrassed. I looked around and caught sight of the two boys down the bank. They were close now and they were kissing. Not lightly, passionately! Out there in the sunlight. Almost naked and people walking above. I turned to Fred. He was scarlet. I tried to look offended or upset but I don't think I could have managed either. I was stunned. In the sunlight! Fred tried to smile. I was scared; I wanted to get up and run but Fred put his hand on my knee. I froze.

"They'll be all right. They'll be all right," he said. Over and over in his soothing voice. After a minute when I realized no one had set dogs on us I tried to smile too. Fred took his hand away and I rubbed my arms to warm my palms which were cold and clammy. We both looked at the boys, their tongues flicking now, like little snakes.

"Are you sure?" I wasn't even sure he'd heard me.

"The other day Sally asked me for dinner," he said. "She's the new girl I told you about. Young, about twenty, has her hair bobbed. The one you said I was falling in love with." He was speaking very slowly. "She asked me about my ring."

"Why?"

"She liked the stone, I guess."

"Nosy bitch!" I tried to sound sharp. Fred didn't bat an eye; he knew it for what it was. He was silent for a minute.

"I told her."

"What!"

"About us."

"What about us? For God's sake!" I wanted to hit him.

"That we'd been together for twenty years." I almost bit my tongue even though I knew it was coming.

"You did?" My voice was very low as though I might burst out in a rage.

"Yes." I looked along the bank. The boys were watching us, I thought.

"What did she say?"

"She'd like to meet you. I'm to bring you with me when I come to dinner."

"A freak show." I was so excited I was shaking.

"Not Sally. Her brother's gay."

"Gay!" I laughed then—or giggled (Fred says I giggle). We both laughed harder than we had in years. I wanted to kiss Fred. I think he knew that; he hugged me around the shoulders.

"Come on," he said. "Get up." We got up. I brushed my trousers. It sounds silly but I was embarrassed almost to look at Fred, I felt so happy. I looked at the boys. The younger boy smiled. His friend smiled and waved. I couldn't help it. I waved back. The sun was so warm. I turned to Fred. There was colour in his cheeks.

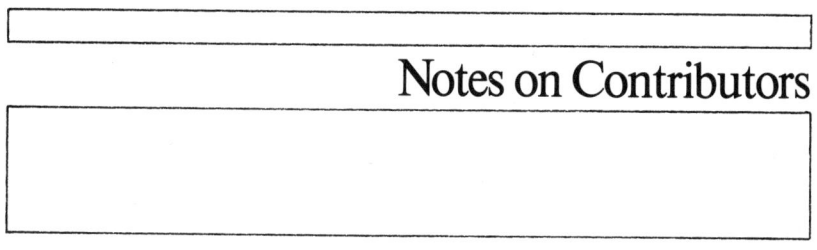

Notes on Contributors

William Burroughs has, since the U.S. appearance of his highly acclaimed novel *Naked Lunch* in 1959, been one of America's most innovative writers. His other books include *Junkie, The Soft Machine, Exterminator!* and *The Wild Boys*. "Meet me in St. Louis Louie" is excerpted from his novel *Port of Saints*, first published in a limited edition in England in 1973.

Peter Burton was born in London in 1945 and has been involved in the British gay press as a writer and publisher since the late '60's. His short stories and criticism have appeared in *Transatlantic Review, Gay News* and other periodicals and anthologies. He has pub- one book, *Rod Stewart: A Life on the Town*.

Daniel Curzon is the author of three novels, *Something You Do In the Dark, The Misadventures of Tim McPick* and *The Revolt of the Perverts*, and a collection of short stories, *Among the Carnivores*. He is a frequent contributor to the gay press. Several of his plays have been produced in San Francisco.

John Mitzel (or Mitzel, as he prefers, finding his given name useless) describes himself as a "pornographer by trade." He is the author of several books, including *Some Short Stories About Nasty People I Don't Like*, and a study of John Horne Burns. His forthcoming collection of essays and interviews is called *A Hasty Bunch*.

John Gilgun has published fiction in *New World Writing No. 16, Paragraph, Mississippi Review, Blueboy, Gay Literature* and other periodicals.

Richard Hall is the author of *The Butterscotch Prince*, a novel. He is contributing editor (books) for *The Advocate* and writes for a number of other publications. His play *Love Match* has been produced in New York and Minneapolis.

Graham Jackson is the author of two books of short stories, *Gardens* and *The Apothecary Jar*, and a collection of dance criticism, *Dance As Dance*. He has also seen several plays which have seen productions in New York and Toronto; the most recent is *Charlotte: A One-Woman Play About the Author of "Jane Eyre."*

Daniel Luckenbill has lived in Los Angeles since his discharge from the U.S. Army. He served as an Artillery lieutenant in Viet Nam. His stories have appeared in *Gay Literature* and *Gay Sunshine*.

Felice Picano was born in New York City. He has published four novels, *Smart As The Devil, Eyes, The Mesmerist* and *The Lure*, and a collection of poems, *The Deformity Lover*. His work has been translated into several languages. He is the publisher of the gay publishing house Seahorse Press.

James Purdy published his first book in England in 1957 and won acclaim from such literary figures as Edith Sitwell and John Cowper Powys. Since then his work has been translated into over thirty languages. Among his later novels are *The Nephew, Malcolm, Eustace Chisholm and the Works* and *Narrow Rooms*. His *Two Plays* was recently published by New London Press.

Tom Reamy, whose promising career ended with his untimely death in 1977, published a number of stories during his life, some in *Fantasy and Science Fiction* magazine. His novel, *Blind Voices*, was published posthumously, and a collection of his short fiction will appear soon.

Peter Robins has been contributing stories to gay publications since 1970 and is a founder member of Gay Authors Workshop in London. Most of the stories in his collection *Undo Your Raincoats and Laugh* are set in the Thames Valley where he was born.

Jerry Rosco is a New Yorker who has made many stays in Montreal. He has written for *The Village Voice, Christopher Street* and other publications, and is currently writing a collection of stories based in Montreal.

David Watmough was born in Cornwall and makes his home in Vancouber. He has been engaged for ten years in writing the fictional autobiography of Davey Bryant. So far this has covered three volumes, *Ashes for Easter, Love and the Waiting Game* and *No More Into the Garden*. A new volume, *Unruly Skeletons* is being published this year. He has also published a collection of plays.

Edmund White is the author of two novels, *Forgetting Elena* and *Nocturnes for the King of Naples,* and of *States of Desire: Travels in Gay America*. With Charles Silverstein he co-authored *The Joy of Gay Sex*.

George Whitmore is a poet, playwright and freelance writer. He has published a collection of poems, *Getting Gay In New York,* and, this year, *The Confessions of Danny Slocum*. Several of his plays have been produced in New York, most recently *The Rights*.

Ian Young is the author of several books of poetry, including *Double Exposure* and *Common-Or-Garden Gods*. He edited the gay poetry anthology *The Male Muse* and is the publisher of Catalyst books. He is a columnist for *The Body Politic* newspaper and a frequent contributor to the gay press.